One
Christmas
in Paris

Also by Mandy Baggot

One Christmas in Paris

Mandy Baggot

bookouture

Published by Bookouture

An imprint of StoryFire Ltd.
23 Sussex Road, Ickenham, UB10 8PN
United Kingdom

www.bookouture.com

ISBN: 978-1-78681-081-6
eBook ISBN: 978-1-78681-080-9

This book is a work of fiction. Names, characters, businesses,
organizations, places and events other than those clearly in the
public domain, are either the product of the author's imagination
or are used fictitiously. Any resemblance to actual persons, living or
dead, events or locales is entirely coincidental.

To Paris,
Beautiful. Vibrant. Strong.
Liberty. Equality. Fraternity.

ONE

Up-Do Hair, Kensington, London

Leo: *I'm sorry. Can we talk?*

Ava Devlin swiped the email hard to the left and watched it disappear from the screen of her iPhone. That's what you did with messages from liars and fakes who had whispered one thing into your ear, as they wrapped their arms around you, and did the complete opposite when your back was turned. She swallowed back a bitter feeling. She had always worried that Leo – successful, rich, good-looking in a Joey Essex kind of way – was maybe a little bit out of her league.

'Boss or boyfriend?'

The question came from Sissy, the hairdresser who was currently coating Ava's head in foils and a paste that felt as if it was doing nuclear things to Ava's scalp.

'Neither,' she answered, putting the phone on the counter under the mirror in front of her. A sigh left her. 'Not any more.' She needed to shake this off like Taylor Swift.

Giving her reflection a defiant look, she enlarged her green eyes, flared the nostrils of her button nose and set her lips into a deliberate pout she felt she had never quite been able to pull off. With her face positioned like she was a Z-list celeb doing a provocative selfie on Twitter, she knew she was done. With men. With love. With everything. Her ears picked up the dulcet tones of Cliff Richard suggesting mistletoe and wine, floating from the salon sound system. Her eyes then moved from her reflection to the string of tinsel and fir cones that surrounded the mirror. This rinky-dink Christmas crap could do one as well. Coming right up was a nation getting obsessed with food they never ate in the other eleven months – dates, walnuts, an entire board of European cheeses – and a whole two weeks of alterations to the television schedule – less *The Wright Stuff* and more *World's Strongest Man*. And now she was on her own with it.

'Well,' Sissy said, dabbing more goo on Ava's head, 'I always think Christmas is a good time to be young, free and single.' She giggled, drawing Ava's attention back to the effort Sissy was putting into her hair. 'All those parties... people loosening up with goodwill and...'

'Stella Artois?' Ava offered.

'You don't drink that, do you?' Sissy exclaimed as if Ava had announced she was partial to Polonium 210. 'I had a boyfriend once who was allergic to that. If he had more than four it made him really ill.'

'Sissy, that isn't an allergy, that's just getting drunk.'

'On lager?' Sissy quizzed. 'Doesn't it mix well with shots?'

Ava was caught between a laugh and a cry. She swallowed it down and focussed again on the mirror. Why was she here having these highlights put in? She'd booked the appointment when she'd had the work do to go to. Now, having caught Leo out with Cassandra, she wouldn't need *perfect* roots to go with the *perfect* dress he'd bought her. She didn't even like the dress. It was all red crushed velvet like something a magician's assistant might wear. Like something her mother might wear. But Leo had said she looked beautiful and she remembered how that had made her feel at the time. *All lies.*

'Stop,' Ava stated abruptly, sitting forward in her seat.

'Stop?' Sissy clarified. 'Stop what? Talking? Putting the colour on?'

'All of it,' Ava said. She put her fingers to the silver strips on her head and tugged.

'What are you doing? Don't touch them!' Sissy said, as if one wrong move was going to detonate an explosive device.

'I want them off... out...not in my hair!' Ava gripped one foil between her fingers, pulling.

'OK, OK, but not like that, you'll pull your hair out.'

'I want a new look.' Ava scooped up her hair in her palms, pulling it away from her face and angling her head to check out the look. Nothing would make her jawline less angular or her lips thinner. She sighed. 'Cut it off.' She wanted it to come out strong, decisive, but her voice broke a little at the end and when she looked back at Sissy, she saw pity growing in her hairdresser's eyes.

'Well... I have to finish the tinting first.' Sissy bit her lip.

Ava didn't want pity. 'Well, finish the tinting and then cut it off,' she repeated.

'Trim it, you mean,' Sissy said, her eyes in the mirror, looking back at Ava.

Ava shook her remaining silver-wrapped hair, making it rustle. 'No, Sissy, I don't want it trimmed. I want it cut off.' She pulled in a long, steady breath. 'I'm thinking short... but definitely more Bowie in his heyday than Jedward.'

'*That* short.' Sissy was almost choking on the words.

'You did say a change was good,' Ava answered. 'Change me.' She sat back until she could feel the pleather at her back. 'Make me completely unrecognisable even to my mother.' She closed her eyes. 'In fact, especially to my mother.'

With her eyes shut, she blocked out everything – Cliff Richard, the tinsel and fir cones, Leo. A different style was just what she needed. Something that was going to go with her new outlook on life. A haircut that was going to say, *You can look, but if you set one eyelash into my personal space, suggesting joy to the world, you will be taken down.* Nothing or nobody was going to touch her.

Ava's phone let out a bleep and she opened one eye, squinting at the screen. Why didn't Leo just give up? Why wasn't he suctioned to *Cassandra* like he had been for God knows how long? She was betting *Cassandra* had never had to use Clearasil.

Sissy leant forward, regarding the phone screen. 'It says it's from Debs.'

Cheered considerably, Ava reached for the phone, picking it up and reading the message.

> *I know I said not to bring anything, but I totes forgot to get something Christmassy. Can you get something Christmassy? To eat... like those crisps that are meant to taste like turkey and stuffing or roasted nuts and cranberry. And bring red wine, not white, because I got three bottles of white today. And if you've completely forgotten all about coming to mine tonight for neighbourly nibbles before I leave for Paris then this is your reminder. Debs xx*

Debs texted like she was writing a dissertation. There was no OMG, FFS or TMI with Ava's best friend. And Ava *had* forgotten about the 'neighbourly nibbles'. That was what having a break-up on your plate did to you – addled your brain and fried the important relationship circuits. Well, she was taking control now – elusive and aloof to anyone but her best friend – and the only frazzled motherboard was going to be the one with wires connected to men.

Ava looked into the mirror at Sissy. 'After you've cut it, Sissy, I want you to make me blonder,' she stated. 'And not the honey kind.' She smiled. 'The Miley Cyrus meltdown kind.'

TWO

Julien Fitoussi squinted as the shards of light from the crystal chandelier at the entrance to the ballroom pierced his retinas. He closed his eyes, floaters cascading like winter rain. He should have stayed at home. His compact, functional apartment overlooking the Seine. That view of the river changing and warping into anything he wanted it to be. In the summer the rippling water could be full of light and hope, now, in the winter it was the deep, dark pit of despair he needed it to be.

Opening his eyes, he adjusted the lapels of his jacket and moved his shoulders a little. Ruffling a dark head of hair he took in his surroundings. 'Christmas opulence' would be the title if this were an exhibition. All that glitters is... completely unnecessary. There were *two* Christmas trees here, not green but gold, covered in lights and bling that could have been borrowed from Busta Rhymes. A string quartet was playing carols at the far end of the function room and, all high on free drinks, the people from his father's world buzzed together like rich worker bees layering up the hive. Lauren would have hated it. He swallowed. *He* hated it.

'Ah! Here he is!'

His father's voice, followed by the man himself, broke into his space and Julien forced a smile as Gerard approached. The love he had for his father, not the world he did business in or the free drinks, was the only reason he had forced himself out of bed and into a tuxedo at seven p.m. on a Friday.

Gerard kissed him on each cheek in turn then whispered in his ear, 'You're late again.'

Julien gritted his teeth as a wave of emotion rolled through him. Anger mixed with guilt, swirling together like one of the expensive drinks his father's employees were currently sipping.

As Gerard stepped back, Julien saw his step-mother-to-be, Vivienne, and a large woman wearing a hat of fruit and octagon-shaped spectacles. He widened his smile at the ladies, moving forward. '*Bonsoir.*'

'*Bonsoir*, Julien,' Vivienne said, kissing him. 'This is Marcie, the lady I was telling you about... Marcie, this is my step-son, Julien.'

Julien arranged his face into an expression of understanding but he really had no idea who this woman was or when his step-mother-to-be had mentioned anything about a woman with half a pineapple, a guava and several satsumas on her head.

'From *Parisian Pathways* magazine,' his father hissed like an angry king cobra.

'Ah, of course,' Julien said, none the wiser. 'It is a pleasure to meet you.' He didn't mean it. She was now another irritation who had kept him from covering his head with the duvet and wishing the night away.

'I have seen some of your work, Monsieur Fitoussi,' the walking, talking greengrocery display said.

Vivienne was nodding her head up and down almost eagerly. He wasn't sure what he was supposed to say but he knew exactly what he was *going to* say.

'I am not working at the moment.'

That felt good. And, directing his eyes into the thick of the ballroom where guests were milling around a champagne fountain and a large waterfall of chocolate fondue, he could see his words hadn't prompted the world to stop turning. That felt even better.

'What he means is... he's taking some time out and... redirecting his focus... waiting for his new muse,' Vivienne jumped in.

If that statement hadn't been so utterly tragic he might have laughed. Was that what Vivienne thought? Was that what his father thought? He smiled at Marcie and her fruit bowl. 'What I mean is' – he plucked a glass of champagne from a passing waiter – 'I am not working at the moment.'

Marcie shook her head, pushing her octagon-shaped glasses up her nose. 'I understand,' the woman said. 'I have to say our thoughts have been with you all.' She looked directly at Julien then.

'Really?' Julien asked abruptly.

'Yes, it was such a tragic loss for everyone concerned. We all felt it.'

'Although it got only a tiny column in the newspaper.'

'Julien—' Vivienne started.

'You were injured, weren't you? Going in to rescue people.'

The heat invaded his cheeks instantaneously. He wanted to step away before he felt the urge to grab her and her citrus display and hurl them both into the fondue.

'Thank you, Marcie, but Julien, he was one of the lucky ones,' Gerard answered.

Julien snapped his head round to view his father. '*Lucky.*' The word almost didn't make it past his lips.

Gerard didn't engage, just continued to focus on Marcie, a pious look on his face. 'It has been a terrible time for all of us as a family.' Gerard picked an olive-festooned canapé from the tray of a passing waiter. 'Everyone is still bearing the loss.'

Everyone is still bearing the loss. Julien didn't believe what he was hearing. His sister Lauren, and twenty-five others, had been trapped in a burning apartment in the city centre just a year ago, and twelve of them never made it out again. Lauren and the others who had died in the fire hadn't made headline news. Did they not count? This woman dressed as a healthy-eating advert had no idea just how black things had been. Lauren was dead, she wasn't coming back and Julien's life had never felt so empty and pointless. And *that* was the real reason why he wasn't working at the moment.

'Her name was Lauren,' Julien said, staring at his father who was chewing up the canapé. 'You do remember your daughter, don't you?'

His eyes went to Vivienne and she gave him a sympathetic look. Not complete understanding maybe, but sympathy nonetheless.

'So, Marcie,' Vivienne started, taking a good grip on the woman with the five-a-day display. 'Why don't we go and speak to Jean-Paul? He's the actor I was telling you about. Up and coming. Gerard and I saw him last year in a production in London.'

Julien took a step into their path, ignoring all his future stepmother's warning signals and anxious looks at his father. He addressed the woman. 'So, you want me to take photos I assume. Smiling, happy people? Celebrities perhaps? Fodder for your magazine? Fantasy pictures to tell people everything is always wonderful in Paris?' He put his hands both sides of his mouth and shouted. 'All is well! We have great cafés and Gerard Depardieu, *non*?'

Suddenly his father's fingers were gripping his forearm and pulling him away from a retreating Vivienne and Marcie, the women shifting up the room in a glimmer of sequins and a sway of citrus. When he met Gerard's gaze there was pure white fury written in his father's expression.

'What the hell was that?' Gerard seethed. 'You are here to show support to the company. Vivienne thought it would also be a good opportunity for you to re-engage, get a new job.'

'Why would she think I want to do that?' Julien asked, folding his arms across his chest.

'Because you haven't fucking worked for over a year!'

'So fucking what?!' Julien fired the words at his father's face, anger and hurt spiralling through his body. He was breathing hard now, more pain and heartache reaching his chest than air for his lungs. He shook, his body trembling as Gerard simply plucked a handkerchief from the top pocket of his suit and wiped his face, as if Julien's words had tainted his skin.

'Go home, Julien. If you're going to be like this then I don't want you here,' Gerard stated coolly. 'Get yourself together.'

Julien bunched his hands into fists as the string quartet started to play 'Vive Le Vent'. Was there a time limit on grief? Was there a moment, perhaps one morning, when you woke up and suddenly everything was all right again?

He focussed on his father, shaking hands with a tuxedoed clone, reaching for another expensive tiny canapé.

'*Monsieur?*' a waiter asked, offering a tray of champagne glasses towards him.

Julien looked at the white alcohol fizzing in the tall, slim glasses. Bright effervescence bursting with every bubble that popped on its surface. It sparkled and shone. Just like his sister had.

He shook his head quickly at the waiter before making for the door.

Bursting out of the hotel, Julien hit the cold air of the centre of the fourth arrondissement and grounded himself on the pavement, willing his anger to subside. He closed his eyes and breathed in. The aroma of garlic, sizzling meats and tobacco hit his nose as he let himself get caught up in the street sounds – mopeds, laughter, dogs barking. Slowly he opened his eyes, adjusting to the dark, the only light coming from the wrought-iron lamps each side of the road. A café opposite – Deschamps – was bursting at the seams. Its clientele sat outside, in the French way. Now, in December, there were no floaty dresses or tailored shorts – all the customers were enveloped in winter coats and scarves, barricaded against the harsh wind that threatened snow, gloved hands gripping small cups of *café* or tumblers of beer.

Had Julien had his camera with him and if he hadn't still been grieving for his sister, he might have snapped a shot of this perfect portrayal of French winter life. Lauren had adored the café culture of their homeland. They'd meet up on a Friday night like this, after work, drink copious amounts of alcohol, just remembering to order food before the kitchen of their chosen brasserie closed for the evening. Over something with chicken or just a large portion of *pommes frites* and bread they had talked about their week. He smiled now. Lauren had always been so full of stories about the department store she worked in. A picky woman she had had to help dress for a wedding, or a badly behaved child she had pulled a face at when his mother wasn't looking. His sister had been a whirlwind in life. But, just like a whirlwind, she had spun fast and furious and then... was gone... leaving nothing but memories and her family's broken hearts.

The chill whipped under his tuxedo jacket and he waited for traffic to lessen before he stepped across the road towards the café. There was only one thing left to do to ease his way out of this night and into the morning. Get drunk.

THREE

Ava hated it. She looked like the love child of a toilet brush and Billy Idol. This wasn't Bowie in his heyday, this was simply hay – only blonder and shorter and just as smelly. But she hadn't admitted she hated it to Sissy. She had instead composed her face into what she thought was the look of a rock musician and had given the mirror the appropriate attitude. Then she'd handed over an extortionate amount of money and fled the salon, on a clock to get to Tesco before she was supposed to be at Debs'. Except Waitrose was much closer and time was of the essence. She only hoped, after forking out for her new hair, she could afford their nibbles.

Waitrose seemed to have 'luxury' Christmas crackers at the end of every aisle – prizes ranging from nail clippers and golf tees to a plastic moustache and a Chinese puzzle. Ava was having trouble finding anything she wanted. Festive crisps she was going to get last, firstly she needed to grab chocolate – milk chocolate, the biggest slab they had – and ensure any red wine she bought was over thirteen per cent.

She navigated a stand of 'luxury' mince pies and Christmas puddings. Everything was 'luxury' around here including the prices. She was going to have to start watching the pennies now she had told Leo they were over and he could keep his job as well. She'd never liked selling apartments even though she was good at it. It was always just meant to be a stopgap. The job she'd snapped up to distance herself from her mother's modelling agency and to try and head off her mother's intention to still push modelling gigs her way. She could almost hear her mother now, a rewind from the time before she got the apparently apocalyptic tattoo no manner of cover-up was going to fix: *It's Dubai, darling. A night in the Burj Al Arab. They wanted Tina but she's in LA. If you'd just do this incredible juice-fast diet all the girls are on, you'd be in perfect shape in two weeks – a month tops.*

And that was the heart of their relationship. Rhoda Devlin, former model, now a partner at an agency Ava had been signed up to as soon as she was old enough to smile, still trying to direct her life. Still wanting her to be the model daughter in every sense of the phrase. She couldn't wait for her mother to see what she'd done with her hair. Perhaps, at last, she would see that apart from a little work on the agency's social media accounts, she wanted no other involvement.

Her phone trilled and Ava dipped her hand into her black leather messenger bag and retrieved her phone.

Rhoda Rhinestone.

It was a petty nickname for her own mother but it did make her smile every time it flashed up. Flash was appropriate, her mother had always thought she was two sequins above everyone else. Ava read the text which had apparently come in an hour ago.

> *Brilliant news, darling! Wonderful opportunity for you on a beach in the Azores if you detox. I've booked us into a fantastic retreat in Goa. Yashtanga and spa treatments. I've emailed through the details…*

Ava's gaze broke away from the text as the email arrived in her inbox. The woman was unstoppable. She had no idea what Yashtanga meant and 'spa treatments' was code for mud, clingfilm-style body wraps and colon cleansing. Another beep and a second message arrived.

Leo could come with you. Sun, sand and smoked tofu should
smooth over relations.

Ava gritted her teeth, the words blurring as her eyes reacted to the horrible realisation that she hadn't been the only one Leo had been in contact with today. He had obviously spoken to her mother and she would lay bets that he hadn't mentioned the fact he was sleeping with the woman in charge of selling the penthouse suites.

'I just *want* to get to the biscuits for cheese.'

Ava received an elbow to her side and looked up at a large man dressed all in tweed, green Hunter boots on his feet, a flat cap on his head. He was in the centre of London looking like he'd just walked off the cover of *Angling Times* – and he had just shoved her because she was in his way.

'Do you mind?' Ava shot back, her body prickling from his ignorance and the messages from Rhoda Rhinestone.

'Do *you*?' the reply came. 'I'm *trying* to get to the biscuits.'

'Well now,' Ava began, hands on hips and standing her ground, 'I'm not moving an inch until you learn some bloody manners.'

'What did you say?' the man asked, squaring up to his full six feet.

Ava narrowed her eyes at him, angst about Leo, her mother, her horrible hay hair, bubbling dangerously under the surface. 'I said,' she started, 'if you don't learn some manners pretty bloody quickly I'm going to take down those *luxury* biscuits for cheese and shove them right up your—'

'Is there a problem here, madam?'

It was a youthful, happy, smiling, full of pre-Christmas cheer staff member with a badge that said 'Justin'.

'Yes!' Ava exclaimed. 'Yes, there is a problem! This... excuse for a gentleman, has forgotten his manners en route to the *lux-ury* biscuits for cheese.'

'This *lady*, although I use the term *very* loosely, has decided to verbally attack me for absolutely no reason whatsoever,' the man dressed in green responded.

'You!' Ava said, pointing a finger. '*You* think you can just swan in here with your gentry gait and your... and your snooty boots... I bet... I bet you've got a Land Rover parked outside you don't even need!'

'How dare you!'

'How dare I what?' Ava continued. 'Voice an opinion? Want a *please* or an *excuse me*? Manners are a requirement to shop here, aren't they, Justin?' She nodded at the shop worker, her blonde spikes barely moving an inch due to the amount of putty Sissy had rubbed in.

'Well, I...' Justin answered as a small crowd of shoppers began to congregate at the end of the aisle to watch the exchange.

'All I wanted,' the man yelled. 'Was my biscuits for cheese.'

'*Please*,' Ava interjected angrily.

'Oh for God's sake... *please*,' the man stated with an infuriated sigh.

Satisfied, Ava reached up to the shelf and pulled down the biscuit box, offering it out to the man. He grabbed it, whipping it from Ava's grasp and almost sending her off balance.

'For your information,' the man hissed as Ava straightened up, 'I have a Nissan Navara and, going by your hair, I'd say *you* were one of those loud-mouth lesbians who wishes she was a man.'

Now Ava was seething. She reached onto the shelf. The first thing that came to hand was a multipack of Ryvitas, followed by Carr's water biscuits and a rather weighty plastic orange box of Jacob's crackers. She threw them, one after the other, at the retreating gamekeeper-garbed man who was swearing and cussing but could do nothing but shield his head with his hands as Ava continued to attack.

Gluten-free breadsticks were for Cassandra – she probably ate them herself – the artisan kale chips were for Leo because he liked upmarket crap like that – they hit the man in the eye – and the final item to make its mark, before security took her by her arms, was rice crackers from Thailand.

'That was assault!' the man bellowed, cheeks as red as a fox-hunting jacket. 'I want her charged! You saw it! You all saw it!'

Ava tried to shake off the two security guards. 'Oh, go on back to your Nissan Navara and your lamping... or whatever else it is you're pretending to do in central London dressed like that!'

'Ava?'

Ava turned her bright blonde head in the direction of a voice she recognised all too well. Her mouth shut then and she closed her eyes. Now she was wishing for a police van. Being arrested would be far preferable to having a conversation about this with her mother.

FOUR

Julien raised his index finger at the barman indicating his need for a refill. He was three glasses of beer down, in the middle of the Friday party crowd, yet not part of their happy thriving mass. He was there but not there – an isolated island, unreachable, untouched by the rest of the planet.

'Merci,' he said to the barman as another beer glass was set down in front of him. He took a swig, the foam froth catching his top lip. Shifting slightly on his stool at the bar he turned to face the room. The sound of joyful chatter from the many customers rose over the background music playing from the café's speakers. Couples held hands, smoked, dined on mussels, crêpes and *gougères*, a group of young men in the corner played air violin in time to nothing in particular, and four women dressed in short frocks, thick tights and Ugg boots – designer shopping bags at their feet – laughed over a carafe of red wine. Hanging from each front window frame by a red-and-white checked ribbon were rustic rattan stars covered in a coating of glistening snow spray. Fir cones tied together with gold tape cascaded down between each window. Christmas was coming whether anyone wanted it to or not.

'Julien!'

Hearing his name, he turned. Coming his way was his best friend, the only friend he hadn't completely pushed aside. Didier. Julien waved a hand, not wanting the company but knowing it was inevitable.

'How are you, my friend?' Didier greeted above the hubbub of talk, leaning in to kiss Julien on each cheek then slapping him on the back.

'I'm good,' he lied, widening out a smile. 'Very good.'

Didier appraised him, his chocolate-coloured eyes bulging from his mocha skin as he seemed to analyse Julien's statement. He put his hands on his hips and tilted his head a little. 'Then why are you here alone?'

Julien realised his mistake now. Didier had left a message – make that several messages – on his voicemail about coming out with him tonight. He hadn't responded.

'It was... a thing... a business thing... with my father.' Julien pulled at the lapel of his tuxedo as if his dress explained every-thing.

Didier pulled up a stool and sat down. 'You could have called me back to tell me that.'

Julien blew out a breath. 'I wasn't sure I was going to go. I suppose I didn't really... in the end.'

'You are fighting with him again,' Didier stated, beckoning the bartender.

'No,' Julien said, shaking his head.

'Why do you always try to lie to me, Julien? Am I not your friend?'

'Of course,' he said quickly. 'OK, we may have had an ex-change but... not really a fight.' How did you describe yelling about your dead sister to your father, step-mother and a woman wearing a basket of fruit as couture?

'You should have said you would come out with me tonight,' Didier said, taking a packet of cigarettes from his pocket. He bit one out with his teeth then lit up.

Julien had no answer for that. He picked up his glass of beer and buried his mouth in the liquid.

'So, you will come out?' Didier continued.

'I am out,' Julien answered.

'Not here,' Didier said, blowing smoke in Julien's face. 'To a club. Dancing. More drinks until the morning comes.'

Didier's exuberance burst from every pore. He had always been that way, ever since they studied at college together. Bright, intellectually as well as creatively, he was the very epitome of someone who lived their life blowing in the breeze, making decisions on the throw of the dice.

Julien shook his head. 'Not tonight, I'm tired.'

Didier struck him with another look that suggested disbelief. 'Tired?' he asked. 'Tired because you have slept all day?'

'What?' He hadn't slept all day today. He had watched a couple of reruns of *Sous Le Soleil* and stared out his window as the gendarmes took away a singing man dressed as *Papa Noël.*

'You are fooling no one, Julien,' Didier said, his eyebrows meeting in the middle. 'When was the last time you picked up your camera?'

What was it with everyone? He'd spent years with a camera strung around his neck, living and breathing his art, not once had anyone said to him *Julien, when was the last time you put your camera down?*

'Is there a point to this, Didier?' he responded. 'If I answer will you stop asking me to come dancing?'

'Lauren would not want this,' Didier said.

A breath left Julien and floated into the air, mixing with the smoke and the scent of crème brûlée. 'At least you are not too scared to say her name.'

'What do you mean?' Didier asked, resting his cigarette in the ashtray on the bar.

Julien shook his head. 'My father... he likes to pretend she didn't even exist.'

'I am sure that is not true,' Didier insisted. 'I saw him... at the funeral... he could hardly stand.' He flicked the ash from the end of the cigarette before reinstalling it in his mouth. 'That is not the behaviour of a man who does not care.'

It was true. His father hadn't coped well with Lauren's service. Gerard was supposed to speak, tell the large congregation what a full life she had led in her twenty-five years. Instead he had clung on to Vivienne, burying his head in her shoulder, his face contorted with grief, leaving the words to be read by the priest.

'He has moved on now,' Julien stated, absentmindedly.

Didier smiled, smoke escaping from his thick lips. 'That is how the world works, Julien. We have to move on.' He stubbed out his cigarette. 'I know Lauren would not want to see you like this. Stopping life,' Didier continued. 'Not taking photographs.' He nudged Julien with his arm. 'She loved your photographs,' he said. 'And she definitely understood them more than me.'

Julien smiled then. Didier liked simple things – the Eiffel Tower at night, the Place de la Concorde, boats on the Seine. His friend had struggled with the more arty shots he liked to take – flowers in the hand of a small child looking up at her grandfather, two bicycles leaning against each other outside the Louvre. Those photographs had been at the centre of his last exhibition. He had received praise from critics and press alike, sold more prints than ever before and received a string of commissions. Now it all felt like a world away.

Julien looked around him. Smiling faces, animated chatter, the sound of an accordion drifting in from outside. His stomach contracted as two plates of *croque monsieur* were brought out by the waitress. He almost craved the soft, melted cheese and smoked ham. When was the last time he had felt hungry?

'You should take more photographs,' Didier stated, sipping his drink. 'Have another exhibition like before.'

Julien blew out a breath. 'It isn't as simple as that. I can't just go out and take some pictures, book a gallery and hope that people come.' He sighed. 'It takes planning... and... inspiration.'

And that was what he was lacking the most. Inspiration. Motivation for his job and pretty much the entire rest of his life.

'You could take photos of me,' Didier stated, wide-eyed, then posing as if he were a model.

'You want my new muse to be you,' Julien said.

'Why not?' Didier asked, hands on hips, still pouting. 'My mother says I have the look of Sébastien Foucan and he has been in a James Bond movie.'

Julien shook his head, trying not to laugh.

'You think I am not good enough for your camera?' Didier asked, sounding insulted.

'I think you would get bored or lose concentration as soon as you saw a beautiful girl or needed another grand crème.'

'I could be your practice, then,' Didier suggested. 'Tomorrow! We could go out, I could lay myself naked across the steps of the Sacré Coeur holding a kitten.'

'You do that and the gendarmes will take your freedom,' Julien replied.

'No kitten, then,' Didier said. 'But tomorrow. Let's go out, you can take some photos of the city and I will buy all the coffee.'

Julien sighed. 'I can't.'

'Julien...'

'I'm sorry, Didier.' He swallowed. 'I'm just not ready.'

FIVE

Kensington, London

'I don't know what you were thinking,' Rhoda breathed. 'If one of those security personnel decides to make a quick buck, you, throwing savoury snacks around, is going to go viral. And that isn't the sort of publicity the company needs.'

She wanted to say no one would recognise her as Rhoda Devlin's daughter and no one would care, but the best thing to do was say nothing. She kept her mouth clamped shut, teeth gripped together like an advert for Fixodent. She hadn't said one word since Rhoda had waded in with apologies and a fifty-pound note (who carried those in the real world?) before bundling her into her Audi. Silence was a tactic she had been employing since the Armageddon tattoo.

'And... you'd better give me the name of the salon that did *that* to your hair so we can start legal proceedings.'

Ava bit her teeth so hard the enamel started to ache. Why had her mother been in *that* Waitrose? Why had Leo had the absolute gall to text her? Couldn't everyone, for once, just leave her alone?

'Ava, are you listening to me?'

Flicking her eyes to the rear-view mirror, Ava caught her mother's eyes. It was only then she realised Rhoda had pushed her into the back seat. Not like a celebrity. Like a child.

She heard her mother inhale as if she were in the middle of a session of reiki. Her father had cited the abdominal breathing in the divorce proceedings and, even then, Ava had understood completely why that might be considered an irreconcilable difference.

'Don't worry, we can fix this. I know someone who can transform unspeakable hair disasters because, believe me, most top models have been there.'

It was time to talk. 'I'm not a top model, Mum, I never was.'

'No, but you could be, if you do all the things I've been telling you to do for years.' Rhoda sighed. 'I know you haven't been keeping to the diet I planned for you.'

Ava closed her eyes. The brown rice had almost made her long for anorexia and she was sure you could clean limescale off a toilet bowl with grapefruit.

'Ava, are you listening?' Rhoda bit.

She nodded.

'We can fix all this. Get you back on track, yes?' Rhoda suggested.

She just needed to stay quiet. Just utter suitably vague responses.

'The assignment in the Azores could be your big break,' Rhoda continued. 'But we need to get you perfect.'

Of course she did. Because she had never been good enough. Her ears weren't the right shape and her neckline sagged. She looked bloated if she ate breakfast before a shoot... the list was endless. And that's why she had started inventing injuries and accidents and blaming public transport on no-shows when she was still at school. And it had worked... to a degree. There were fewer offers, despite Rhoda still sending out her portfolio. And then, after tearing up Rhoda's diet plans and spending her wax and mani-pedi allowance on Wagamamas, they had stopped altogether. Ava was, for the moment, just the girl in charge of Twitter. But her mother, almost four years after Ava's last, grudging, catalogue shoot, showed no signs of giving up.

'You can drop me just here,' Ava said, looking at the window and not really knowing where she was.

'What? Don't be silly, Ava. I'm taking you back home.' Rhoda's eyes appeared in the rear-view mirror again. 'We need to get ready for India and the Azores.'

'Mum—'

'I have these marvellous little pills that really stop your cravings.'

Ava started to pull at the door handle, no concern for the fact they were cruising through London's festive streets. She wanted out of there, even if it meant pitching herself onto the tarmac underneath the strings of multi-coloured fairy lights and illuminated angels. It failed to open. 'Have you put the child lock on?'

'For goodness sake, Ava,' Rhoda exclaimed, pulling the Audi into the kerb.

Ava continued to try the door, yanking at the handle in desperation.

'Calm down,' Rhoda ordered, turning off the engine and shifting her body in her seat to look at Ava. 'You'll get blotchy and crease your forehead.'

'I don't care!' Ava wailed. 'Why would I care?!'

She wanted out of the car. The air was getting thin like she was 30,000 feet up in a Boeing with the window open. She gave the door another push.

'You're so like your father when you're like this,' Rhoda breathed.

Ava closed her eyes. Not that same old same old. When in doubt, blame the man who'd had the good sense to escape. She swallowed. That was cruel. The breakdown of her parents' marriage hadn't just been Rhoda's fault. Her father hadn't talked, or tried, just packed a bag and handed everything over. Rhoda was good at exhausting people. But, away from that stress now, her father was unblotchy with a forehead that wasn't creased.

He smiled a lot more and went to watch Tottenham every other week. He had a girlfriend called Myleene and they spent summers in the Philippines. She suspected any heavy breathing Myleene did involved something tantric she'd rather not think about in relation to her dad.

Anger diluting a little, Ava let out a sigh. 'Could you take me to Debs'?'

'Why?'

'Because that's where I'm meant to be. That's where I was going before the guy in tweed started being rude and I threw Ryvita's finest and... you came.'

'I don't like that girl,' Rhoda said with a sniff, pulling down the visor and checking her reflection in the vanity mirror.

'Why not?' Ava asked.

'She's so...' Rhoda started. 'So...'

Ava waited, sensing the type of thing that was going to come out of her mother's mouth.

'Ordinary,' Rhoda finished off.

Ava's hackles were back up, defensive on her best friend's behalf. She opened her mouth to say there was nothing wrong with ordinary, that ordinary was safe and cosy and comfortable. She closed it again when she realised what she had already been aware of for years. Her mother thought 'ordinary' was a mortal sin. Why be 'ordinary' when you could enhance everything with a potion from the Chinese herbal shop or chicken fillets in your bra.

'I know what you're doing, Ava,' Rhoda stated. 'And I want you to know it's OK. I understand.'

Did she? A flicker of hope danced in her insides.

'You were going for a short crop like Natalie Portman tried.'

Hope fell to the bottom of her stomach like an ungraceful Sugar Plum Fairy.

'The thing is, Ava, you don't have the cheekbones for that style,' Rhoda continued. 'And I think you know that... so really this was just a cry for help.'

Instinctively, Ava's fingers went to where her strawberry-blonde shoulder-length hair should be. A good ten inches higher up and they found the short crop of platinum. 'This isn't a cry for help.'

Rhoda breathed out. 'But you've lost Leo.'

Ava furrowed her brow, her mother's tone saying so much. *She* had lost Leo. Not Leo had lost *her*. And Leo wasn't a cute puppy who had wandered off into the woods and was roaming alone in Epping. Leo was a cheating arse who had lied to her. For months. She was better off without him. Even if it meant she would be single for Christmas... and possibly forever.

She shifted, unable to stay enclosed in the car any longer, bearing the brunt of her mother's pent-up wrath because Ava had never been the next Cindy Crawford. Leaping forward, she clawed her way over the gearstick and into the passenger seat.

'What are you doing?!' Rhoda yelped. 'You'll scratch the leather seats.'

And that comment said it all. Ava pulled the door handle and scrabbled out, a draft of icy wind freezing her newly shorn scalp. She'd get the Tube or hail the first for-hire cab, anything rather than sit here another minute more.

'Ava, get back in the car,' Rhoda called, seatbelt restricting her from leaning too far.

'No,' she replied.

'We are going to Goa. It's going to be nothing but chanting and mung beans. Your soul is going to be just as cleansed as your dermis, I promise.'

She didn't want her soul cleansed. The only thing she wanted to scrub away was this constant feeling of inadequacy. But the problem was, she had never been able to say no to her mother. She'd always had to look for another way out, or make something up. A sprained ankle or overdosing on Kettle chips and going up a dress size. And this time wasn't any different.

Ava pulled her coat closed, teeth chattering as the evening's dropping temperature touched every uncovered inch of her. 'I'll call you tomorrow,' she stated as softly as she could manage.

'What time?'

Ava swallowed, holding on to the door of the Audi as her mother's eyes, false eyelashes to rival Nicole Scherzinger, looked back, waiting for an answer.

'Schedule in eleven o' clock,' Ava responded. 'Goodbye, Mum.'

Without waiting for Rhoda to work up a response, she pushed the door hard and watched it slam shut, closing out her mother's opening and closing mouth and the rose-gold earrings circa pictures she'd seen of Grace Jones in the eighties. Then she about-faced and headed off towards the line of hanging snow-flake lights suspended from the railway bridge.

Cabs were hard to come by on a Friday night and Ava's cluttered bag wasn't giving up her Oyster card so, by the time she'd walked across the borough and made it to Debs' front door, she was colder than a character from *Fortitude*.

She knocked – hands red and swollen from the frosty air – and within a few moments the door was flung open, Debs appearing in a Christmas jumper and a skirt with flashing lights. The sweater pronounced 'No rein here, deer, just snow' with a motif of two glittered-up reindeers, hooves in the air, looking like they were about to perform something choreographed by Michael Flatley. The skirt was glowing on and off with a multitude of colours and, for a second, Ava was blinded.

'Ava!' Debs exclaimed, as if Ava was Father Christmas himself. 'Goodness, you didn't have to go to so much trouble with the wig! Is it meant to be Cruella De Vil or Elsa from *Frozen*?'

Before Ava could open her mouth to say anything, Debs had stepped forward and pulled her into a bear hug. Large plastic candy-cane earrings almost took out one of Ava's eyes. She closed them, relishing the scent of LUSH products and eau de Lambrini as Debs hugged hard.

'It's not a wig,' she whispered.

Debs let her go then, standing back and staring at her, eyes focussing on her scalp as if looking for the weave.

'It's not?' Debs said, voice still a little uncertain.

Ava shook what was left of her remaining hair. 'Leo *was* cheating on me,' she began, 'with the girl I told you about.' She sniffed. 'The one who looks like Ferne McCann. And' – she looked up at Debs – 'I went to Waitrose to get red wine and Christmassy crisps and I threw things at a really rude man and security came and then... my mother and...' With every word that passed her lips her breath was becoming shorter and shorter, each piece of rotten drama suddenly activating inside her. Her eyes began to smart with tears to the strains of Greg Lake's 'I Believe in Father Christmas' filtering out from the house. 'My mother wants to take me to Goa, then the Azores,' she continued. 'After she's fed me lentils, plastered me in Clinique and fitted me with a hair integration.'

'Don't say any more,' Debs ordered, gathering Ava up in a warm hug she'd delivered so many times before when the going got tough at home, school, or wherever and whenever Bitchy Richy Nicola in the year above had decided to verbally attack her. 'I know what we're going to do.'

Ava closed her eyes and took comfort in the gesture before releasing Debs. 'Pickle our livers in Kopparberg?' She pressed her index fingers to the escaping tears before they froze.

'Yes!' Debs answered enthusiastically. 'And wait until you taste the homemade damson wine Ethel brought round. She said she made it in 1988 and I totes believe her.'

Ava let a small laugh escape. 'Maybe it will make my hair grow back.'

'I like your hair,' Debs said, pulling Ava closer as she stepped into the house. 'It's very... European.'

'Is it?'

'Yes, and that's a good thing,' Debs continued, pulling Ava into the house and closing the door on the dark and the freezing air.

'It is?'

'Yes, because it's going to go beautifully in Paris,' Debs said, putting her arm around Ava's shoulders. 'First come and say hello to everyone and start marinating your internal organs.' She smiled. 'Then we'll get online and book you on my Eurostar. What you need is a change, Ava. France to be exact.' Debs waved a hand like she was depicting an artist's landscape. 'The Parisian air, the French food... the French men.'

'You need someone to help you with your latest article, don't you?' Ava guessed.

Debs' smile wobbled.

'Debs?'

'Is it that obvious?' she asked with a sigh and a light laugh.

'Just a bit.'

'I was going to ask you anyway. Before'– Debs stopped briefly – 'the TOWIE woman and the cosmopolitan hair.'

Ava smiled at her friend. 'In that case... have you got any Stella?'

SIX

Julien stood in front of the Saint-Jacques Tower as the snow began to settle on the pavement. It was the earliest he had made it out of his apartment in months. Not only was it still light, it was before lunch, and around him the city was in full swing. Buses, cars, sliding over the thin coating of snow on the roads, wipers swishing the flakes away from windscreens.

The last couple of days had passed without unusual occurrence. Didier had called. He hadn't answered. He had people-watched from his Juliette balcony, eaten from cans when his stomach protested and drank from bottles when his memories got overwhelming. But now, he was here, his camera around his neck, looking at one of the monuments he'd always admired. The monument in the photo he'd forgotten all about until he found it, loose at the bottom of a box of Lauren's things. There it had been last night, under her favourite cranberry-red, woollen beanie, the corner of it stuck inside a well-thumbed copy of a Jackie Collins novel. He'd pulled it out, his sister's vibrant smile like a punch to his gut. He'd stared at the picture until his eyes ached, hoping somewhere in the depths of him that looking would bring her closer again.

He tilted his head a little, eyes raising upwards with the gradient of the building. It was beautiful. A creamy white guardian standing over the street below, it's flamboyant Gothic design representative of the Parisian ways. Gargoyles gurned down along with the sculptures of saints and the four evangelists – lion, bull, eagle and man – on each corner of the tower. Julien tipped back his head, the camera to his eye and clicked.

The almost insignificant little noise his camera made caused a tightening of his core. It was the first time he had heard that noise in so long. That tiny sound used to be as present in his life as breathing. He lowered the camera and took a long, slow breath, his gaze going from the tower to the street around him. The city always carried on. Resilient, brave, caught up in living. He watched a line of school children walking along the pavement led at pace by their teacher. Cheeks red with cold, woollen hats on their heads, breath dancing in the air as they chatted with excitement. Fearless and innocent in a changing world.

Could that be a theme for him? Contrast? Like night versus day? Dark versus light? The old flamboyance of the Tour de Saint-Jacques compared to the modern Pompidou Centre only a few streets away? He wasn't sure how he felt about the Pompidou Centre with its steel supports and air ducts. It might make the inside uncluttered for the museum, but was its outside beautifully different or downright ugly?

Beauty. Now that could definitely be a theme. It was different things to different people. One person's view, appreciated by their eyes, held in their heart. It was certainly a better idea than capturing a naked Didier with a kitten. He smiled, a genuine reaction brought on by thoughts of his carefree friend prancing nude around the steps of a French church. And then it started, a rolling, unstoppable sensation that filled every inch of his insides. Laughter, uncontrollable laughter. A ray of winter sunshine hit his cheeks and suddenly it was like he had been reawakened. He was here. He was alive. He stretched out his hands, palms to the sky, letting the snowflakes fall onto his skin as his head tipped back. *Beauty. Resilience. Life.* It was still there. The little things. The smallest pleasures. He had his theme.

SEVEN

Debs' house, London

'So, are you sure you girls have got everything you need?'

It was Debs' mum, Sue, who had asked the question and Ava answered by holding up her passport. Sue had come round early with tins of treats for them to eat on the train – sandwiches, cakes and cheese straws. She was also in charge of feeding Debs' fish while they were away.

Sue laughed, her wavy blonde hair shaking in response. 'Clothes, Ava? Something to keep you warm?'

'I happen to know that your daughter has a fine selection of jumpers I can borrow if I get cold, and besides, I can't go home again just now.'

She had been avoiding her mother's phone calls for the past two days and sneaking about between dusk and dawn so there was no chance of her being kidnapped by Rhoda and put on the next plane to India.

'I really think you should call your mum, Ava. She'll be worried about you,' Sue said softly.

Ava looked up at Sue. Hair held off her face by a claw clip, make-up natural and at least three tones less orange than Rhoda's. She was wearing a pencil skirt and quite a funky animal-print blouse. Modern, tasteful, nothing designer, her smile warm and genuine. Debs' mum had virtually adopted Ava and she had been coming here for comfort and real food since senior school. There was no calorie counting in this house, just a never empty biscuit tin and pizza on Saturday nights. Here there had never been any expectations. Just an accepting welcome, an old comfy sofa and a listening ear if asked for.

'I'll call her from the train station,' Ava offered. She wouldn't. But she didn't want to make Sue party to this, and it would make her feel better. If she actually believed her.

'Promise me, Ava,' Sue added, eying her with suspicion.

There was no getting away from it now. She couldn't make a promise.

'I can't call her,' Ava stated. 'If I call her she'll make me go to India.'

'I'm sure she won't—' Sue began.

Debs entered the kitchen, pushing a wheelie case, a giant holdall on her back. 'She will, Mum. This is totes the best way. Ava needs to disappear.'

'Disappearing is perhaps a drastic way of putting it,' Ava said.

'Shall I call her?' Sue suggested. 'Maybe when you're in the tunnel, actually under the water—'

'No!' Ava and Debs said at once.

Sue looked a little taken aback and Ava moved then, putting an arm around her shoulder. 'I'm sorry,' she said, resting her head against Sue's. 'I know it's a lot to ask, but she can't know where I am until it's too late and Goa's not a goer.'

''Til Goa's a goner,' Debs suggested.

'But,' Sue started, 'if you tell her how you feel then…'

Ava sighed. 'My mum isn't into feels.' She smiled then, letting Sue go. 'And she would probably have a stroke if she knew what goodies you've given us for the journey.'

Debs put her hands to her mouth. 'I don't remember packing my Christmas-tree jumper with the talking elf.'

'What?!' Ava exclaimed. 'Go and get it!'

Debs about-turned and headed out into the hall, boot-clad feet thundering up the stairs.

Before Ava could turn her attention to anything else, Sue swept her up into a hug, squeezing tight and patting the space between her shoulder blades. The familiar scent of something by Impulse, not something uber-exotic or expensive, was comforting.

'Debs told me about Leo,' Sue said softly.

Ava swallowed. 'She did?'

'He doesn't deserve you,' Sue continued. 'And you don't deserve to be treated like that. You're a lovely, lovely girl and you're better off without him.'

'I—'

'Cheating on someone... going behind someone's back... taking your trust and throwing it away as if it doesn't mean a thing...'

The squeezing was getting tighter. 'I—'

'No one should have to go through that.' Sue sniffed and drew away quickly, turning towards the kitchen roll and tearing a piece off.

'He didn't even like Coldplay. I should have seen the signs,' Ava said.

She swallowed. She hadn't been sure Leo was 'the one', but having him signal their relationship meant so little by sleeping with a colleague who looked like Heidi Klum and gave office doughnuts a look of disdain every Friday really hurt. She hadn't been good enough. The memories of the times he'd held her and told her she was beautiful were all tarnished like cheap earrings.

'One Christmas-tree elf jumper,' Debs said, coming back in and holding up the item of clothing before squashing it into a gap in her suitcase.

'You're going to have a lovely time but don't forget to eat. I remember what Paris is like,' Sue said with a sigh. 'You two will be so overawed by the beautiful sights and the sounds of the accordion playing, the coffee, the—'

'Mini bar in our room,' Debs added with a grin.

'I know the last time I went there I didn't eat for twelve hours and felt a little bit giddy when I rode on one of those merry-go-rounds with the gurning horses.'

'Note to self... no gurning horses,' Ava stated.

'And keep your energy levels up for all that shopping,' Sue added.

It was the complete reverse of a pep talk from Rhoda. That would have been *don't eat before shopping so you can fit into a size zero.*

'Shopping!' Debs exclaimed. 'My totes favourite word.'

'Apart from "totes",' Ava teased.

'Come here,' Sue said, opening her arms to her daughter and almost inhaling Debs into her bosom. 'Now, listen to me, no worrying while you're away. Concentrate on your work. Everything is fine.'

'I know,' Debs answered.

Ava's interest was piqued. Debs hadn't indicated everything *wasn't* fine. Or perhaps she had been so caught up in her break-up with Leo and her break away from her mother she hadn't been taking enough notice.

'You too, Ava,' Sue said, opening her arms to release Debs and welcome Ava in. Ava stepped into the hug and closed her eyes. Who needed Leo when she had her best friend, her best friend's mum and Paris in her sights?

A loud blast of a car horn broke up the hugging and Ava forced a smile. 'I guess that will be the taxi.'

'Uber actually,' Debs answered. 'I'm trying to save money before we get to Paris and are at the mercy – that's with a "y" not a "ci" – of the Paris taxi drivers.'

'That's a good idea,' Sue said. 'I remember them too.' She smiled at the two women. 'Bon voyage!'

'More like bon appetit,' Ava said. 'The cheese straws are all for me, aren't they?'

'Come on, Ava,' Debs ordered, heading out of the kitchen towards the front door.

'Bye, Sue,' Ava said, waving a hand. 'Oh, just to say, if you fancy some of that purple wine in the fridge, I really wouldn't have more than one glass.'

EIGHT

Paris, France

'I've been thinking,' Debs started. 'You really shouldn't give up your job.'

Ava peeled her cheek off the taxi window and came to. The Eurostar trip had zapped her. Now she was crushed against the door of a Parisian cab next to Debs' giant suitcase, even bigger handbag and Debs herself.

'Which one?' Ava asked, her eyes going to the wintry scene through the glass. 'Because I'm thinking of telling my mum where she can stick her Twitter and Flickr.'

'Not that job,' Debs stated. 'The other one. Ending things with Leo doesn't mean you should give up everything.' Debs sniffed. 'You were totes amazing at that job. And why should you run away from it when it's Leo's fault? The... philanderer.'

Ava looked at her best friend. Debs liked to talk. In fact she *loved* to talk, but she had been decidedly quiet on the train. And every syllable of the word 'philanderer' had been sounded out.

'Is everything all right, Debs?' Ava asked.

'Of course,' she announced, shaking her hair off her shoulders and smiling. 'Just looking forward to spending some time with my best friend in one of the most beautiful cities in the world.' She breathed in noisily.

Ava supposed Debs had a point about the job. She had just thought it was easier. Throw in the towel, never have to see the guy again, move on and away from the awkward situation and avoid wanting to slap Cassandra the next time they brushed shoulders in the ladies' toilet. Plus, what else was there for her? Giving up flogging luxury apartments was a step closer to her mother's clutches and modelling aspirations.

'I'll need to think about the job,' she answered, her attention back to life outside. 'The very last thing I need right now is to have to move home.'

'What about your dad?' Debs suggested.

She shook her head. 'No, I couldn't do that either. I think Myleene is good for him and I like her but she's so...' The words *beautiful, great at cooking, slim, clever* were all there waiting to be picked. 'You know.'

She looked out of the window. The traffic was manic. Bumper to bumper, crawling at the pace of a tortoise through a dusting of white on the ground, each vehicle taking it in turns to beep their horn. It didn't achieve anything, nothing moved quicker, but it was the Paris way. She looked past the traffic, to the buildings each side of the street. Arches and decorative sconces, large brightly lit windows full of French chic, boutiques oozing style and expense, everything draped in a much classier festiveness than at home.

'Well, I think you should totes stop worrying about your mum,' Debs added. 'I can tell, you know. For a second the other night, after the third glass of Ethel's homebrew, you were considering going to Goa just so she would stop messaging you about it.'

'I wasn't considering it,' Ava insisted. She turned to her friend, ears adorned with flashing Christmas trees blinking on red and green, a Norwegian knit jumper on underneath her coat. 'Besides, I'm here, aren't I? With you, in Paris. Marked safe from Rhoda Rhinestone.' She paused. 'And you still haven't told me exactly what we're going to be doing.'

Debs smiled, her cheeks puffing up the way they always did, a dimple on each one. 'Ah,' she said. 'You're going to love it.'

'It isn't dressing up like a Dalmatian again, is it?'

Debs laughed, shaking her head. 'No.'

'Or getting people to try three different kinds of mustard.'

'I liked that task,' Debs said as if it were a challenge from *The Apprentice*.

'Promise me there are no costumes involved at all.'

'Well...'

Ava looked at her best friend, adorned in Christmas-themed tat, face rosy, eyes bright. They were in Paris. The city of light. Whatever Debs was going to make her do, it was better than wallowing in self-pity at home... or being forced onto a flight to a retreat then an assignment where she would be contorted into sexy poses wearing something skimpy she hated herself in.

Debs grinned. 'No costumes,' she said. 'I'm aiming to write two pieces. One's on Christmas shopping and the other is even more fun than that.'

'I'm interested to hear what you think is more fun than your ultimate hobby.'

'Dating and the rise of foreign hen weekends,' Debs said, eyes widening. 'You and I are going to visit all the top spots singles ladies go to for a piece I've provisionally entitled "Singles, Sex and the City".'

'Whoa!' Ava exclaimed. 'I hope that isn't for *People's Friend*.'

'It's for *Diversity*... hopefully.'

'Didn't they win *Britain's Got Talent*?'

'Not the dance troupe. It's a new magazine for twenty-something women like us. I've got a copy' – Debs delved into the giant bag on her knee – 'somewhere in here.'

'It's fine,' Ava said, looking back to the window. 'It's probably better I don't see it.' If she was honest the thought of behaving like a tribal hen-weekend goer wasn't filling her with joy. She wasn't sure she was up for the singles hot spots of Paris either. The tequila shots would be quite welcome. The men, well, she might want to punch them just for being the same gender as Leo.

'Ooo!'

The squeak of excitement had Ava turning back from the window as Debs pulled something out of her bag.

'I can't seem to find the magazine but I've found this!' Debs shook the piece of paper, a little scrunched up with the ragged holes at one side like it had been torn from a notepad. 'I was looking through some old school books the other day...'

'Like you do.'

Debs laughed. 'Memories!'

Ava looked at her, confused. 'That doesn't look like any sort of note you would have written. It's far too creased.'

'This one isn't mine,' Debs said, grinning. 'Mine is being pressed back to perfection in between the pages of a hardback copy of *Anne of Green Gables*.'

Ava shook her head. 'You're not still re-reading that, are you?'

Debs pulled her lips into a firm line. 'Until I find my own Gilbert Blythe, then, yes.'

Ava made a grab for the paper but missed and let out a grunt of frustration. 'Well, not that I'm really interested but... what is it?'

'This one is yours,' Debs stated.

'My what?'

'Your wish list.'

Ava sighed. 'I still have no idea what you're talking about.' She folded her arms across her chest in a bid to keep some warmth in. The taxi driver had opened his window and smoke from his cigarillo was swirling out of the three-inch gap as well as letting in all the freezing air.

'You must remember!' Debs unfurled the notepaper. 'You, me and Stacey Edwards. We lay out on the grass after our A-level geography exam and wrote these.' Debs sighed as if her mind was drifting back. 'We were high on the end of study and the knowledge there would be no more Mr Morton's B.O.'

Ava remembered the teacher with the body odour issues but not this... had Debs said 'wish list'?

Debs cleared her throat. 'Shall I read it out?'

Ava shrugged. 'I can't remember even writing it.'

'OK,' Debs began. 'Ava Devlin's Wish List.' She stifled a laugh with the hand that wasn't holding the paper. 'You've underlined the title twice, which means you were totes serious.'

'Or that you *made* me do it,' Ava suggested. 'You were always the queen of underlining... and bubble writing.'

'I still am,' Debs answered. 'But we are digressing.' She cleared her throat again. 'So, Ava Devlin's Wish List, underlined twice... Number one... get very drunk.' Debs stopped reading. 'Wow, I thought you might have actually taken this seriously.'

'Didn't you say I was eighteen?'

'Well, I didn't write that sort of thing on my list.'

'What did you write? 1. Marry Gilbert Blythe?' Ava straightened herself in the seat as the taxi driver swerved to avoid a cyclist. 'What's my number two? Killing my mother?'

Debs put her eyes back to the page. 'Number two... shave my hair off and dye my head green so I don't have to model any more.'

Ava touched the platinum strands still holding their spiky position. It wasn't completely shorn or green but it was definitely modelling repellent. She smiled at Debs. 'I'm quite liking my eighteen-year-old self.'

'Number three... oh I like this one... get a dog... oh that's sweet... oh.' Debs stopped.

'What? I like dogs.'

'Get a dog... to annoy my mother. I'll put it in her bed and never give it flea treatment.'

Ava grinned. 'That's still quite a good idea.'

Debs put the list down. 'This is sad,' she announced. 'All these things you've written down... they're all things you needed to do because you felt your life was horrible.' Debs sniffed.

'The half I lived with you and your mum was pretty cool.' She sighed. 'And like you said, I obviously didn't take the list thing seriously.' She nudged her friend's arm. 'I do Wish Number One quite a lot and it only ends up horrible first thing in the morning if I've really gone for it... like with Ethel's wine.'

'Well, I think you should make a new one,' Debs instructed.

'A new plan to frustrate my mother? I think the Waitrose incident and running away to Paris have probably done enough.'

'No, silly, a new wish list.'

She faced the window again. What was the point? Right now, travelling through a Parisian winter wonderland, she had no idea where her life was going. She didn't need a wish list to add to the confusion. Her mind went to Leo. When had he realised she wasn't pretty enough or funny enough? Maybe she should have appreciated him more. Perhaps it was her fault. Maybe she had done something to make him need Cassandra.

'So?' Debs said.

'What?'

'We need to get you a new wish list.' Debs pulled in a breath. 'One a little more mature.'

'What did you put on yours after marrying Gilbert Blythe?' Ava asked. 'Seeing the sunrise over Ayers Rock? Parachuting into the Grand Canyon?'

Debs shifted in her seat.

'You did, didn't you?'

'And I still haven't got to Australia. It's probably one of the only places I haven't written an article about.'

'Well, I don't need a wish list,' Ava stated.

'Come on, it doesn't have to be a road trip across America or skydiving. It can just be a list for Paris,' Debs suggested. 'Just something to stop you thinking about Leo.'

'I'm not thinking about Leo,' Ava snapped.

'Or your mother.'

'I wasn't thinking about her... but now I am.'

Debs passed the ancient notepaper across to her. 'Come on, it will be fun. A *Paris* wish list. I'll make one too.' Debs grinned. 'Number one, highly intoxicating cocktails like singles in the city.'

Ava screwed up her nose. 'Number two, line stomach with more than snails and frogs legs.'

Debs laughed. 'Do you remember the time we let the frogs loose in science class?'

Ava smiled. 'How were we supposed to know that Damian Cranbourne had an allergy to frogs? I mean, seriously, who has an allergy to frogs?'

'It wasn't just frogs though, was it? The poor thing was allergic to everything.'

'Eggs.'

'Which ruined the fun we used to have stinking out the coach on trips.'

'Stones.'

'He wasn't allergic to stones,' Ava remarked. 'No one can be allergic to stones.'

'He was, I swear!' Debs said laughing. 'And feathers.'

'Now you're making it up!'

'I'm totes not, honestly.'

'Damian Cranbourne,' Ava mused. 'I wonder where he is now.'

'Living in a house made of straw, not stroking birds or eating omelettes?' Debs suggested.

The taxi screeched to a halt, shooting Debs' suitcase forward and crushing Ava's Converse-clad feet.

'We are here,' the taxi driver announced. He gestured to the snowy outside, golden fairy lights twinkling from the trees at the edge of the pavement. Ava looked through the condensation of the window and read the sign. *Hotel Agincourt.* She really hoped there wasn't going to be any battling. She could do with a rest.

'I know what you're thinking,' Debs said, collecting her bags together.

'I hope there's no fifteenth-century weapons at the bar?'

'What?'

'Hotel Agincourt?'

'I know!' Debs said, grinning. 'A hotel with *gin* in its name! Shall we go and get one? We can make our wish lists!'

'Don't you have articles to write?'

'Oh, Ava, research is all important,' Debs responded with a giggle.

Ava offered the taxi driver a smile as Debs opened the cab door and stepped out. He thrust out his hand. 'Cinquante.'

She pressed a note into his hand. 'Merci buckets.'

NINE

Tuileries quarter

Julien blew out a breath that was visible in the air. The bright, clear, cold morning had given way to a snow storm that had the clouds darkening and flakes whirling around in a stiff wind. As he stood outside the brasserie in the Tuileries quarter, tiny snow crystals gathering on the shoulders of his coat, he looked in through the window, eyes skipping past the Christmas adornments to the people at the tables inside.

He had been surprised to get the text message from his stepmother this morning after what had happened a few nights ago. He could see her now, sat at the very back of the restaurant, toying with something on the front of her blouse, her long dark hair set on her shoulders as usual, her demeanour appearing a little tight. He liked Vivienne. She had been in his life for so long. It was time his father married her. His mother had left them without a second thought, just packed a bag one day and never came back... until Lauren's funeral. Then she had appeared, feigning grief and loss, when she had had no part of their lives since deciding to leave them. Julien bristled now, remembering his mother closing her arms around him, her tears wetting his jacket. He had stood stock still, shown no emotion, saying nothing. What was there to say? It was Vivienne who had rescued him. She had taken hold of him and made excuses about seeing other family members, leading him away from a reunion he hadn't needed that day. He hadn't seen his mother since.

Taking another breath he pushed open the door. A wave of heat and the smell of freshly baked bread and croissants hit his nose. As the bell chimed he saw Vivienne look up. She smiled and he began to weave his way between the tables towards her. As she rose from her seat he quickly waved her back down.

'You would like another coffee?' he asked, gesturing towards her cup.

'No, thank you,' she answered.

'Something to eat? They do good eclairs here,' Julien said, still hovering by the table and filling the space with words.

'No, Julien, thank you. Please, sit down.'

He watched her hands stray to a brooch on her blouse. He remembered it at once. It was a diamante cat, a red crystalline bow around its neck. He had been with Lauren when she had bought it for Vivienne at a Christmas market the year before last. Vivienne's sadly deceased bright white cat, Pepe, had been much loved and Lauren had said the brooch looked just like the animal. Julien swallowed back the memory and sank into the seat opposite her. As he did so, the camera, still around his neck, caught the edge of the wooden table.

'Your camera,' Vivienne said, her hands going to her mouth.

'Yes,' Julien replied, taking the strap from around his neck and placing the camera on the table.

'You are taking photos again?' Vivienne breathed.

He nodded. He didn't want to make a big deal out of it. Even though he knew it *was* a big deal, a huge thing just to have his hands on a camera again.

'That is so good,' Vivienne said, her eyes alive. 'So good.' She paused. 'After the party...'

Julien cleared his throat, looked into the candle on the table. 'I must apologise for that.' He looked up at her. 'I should not have said the things I said. I should have said a lot of other things that I did not say.' He paused. 'I was rude.'

Vivienne shook her head. 'No... I should not have tried to push things your way with Marcie. It's just—'

He watched her fingers tighten around the cup of coffee, losing herself in her thoughts.

'I am worried... about your father.'

His heart stepped up a gear. 'There is something wrong?'

She shook her head. 'I do not know. I only know that, despite how he is, so controlled in public, so blasé... Julien, I know it is not what you think, but he is still very much grieving for Lauren.'

Julien swallowed, the deep despair in his step-mother's tone biting him.

'He barely eats and he does not sleep.' She shifted in her seat. 'I thought he was coming out of it earlier this year but then we had the anniversary and...'

'But you are getting married soon,' Julien said, as if that were some sort of answer.

She nodded and he noticed her eyes were moist. 'I know.'

'And at the party, he was himself... with his business contacts... snarling at me.'

'It is nothing but a front and, he worries about you too,' Vivienne stated.

Julien shook his head. 'He hides from what happened to our family. Then, when he is forced to confront the fire, he calls me lucky.' He swallowed. 'I am not lucky because I lost my sister. And I failed to help save eleven other people.'

'Oh, Julien, why do you think he does that?' she asked, putting down her cup.

He shrugged.

'It is because he cannot bear to think of what he lost. Focussing on your survival and what you did for the others that night stops him from remembering...'

'Lauren,' Julien said. 'Her name was Lauren.'

Vivienne's fingers went to the cat on her blouse, the tips brushing over the stones, nodding slowly. 'I miss her too, Julien.'

He swallowed, Vivienne's words trying to seep under his skin. 'Why did you need to see me, Vivienne?'

She met his eyes. 'I have arranged the final suit fitting for the wedding.'

He looked back, confused.

'You can do this alone, of course, but... I thought it would be a good opportunity for you to talk with your father.'

Instantly he was on edge. 'I don't know. After last week...'

'We all say things in the heat of the moment, Julien. Sometimes our concerns get smothered by other things, no?'

'Like rage?' he suggested.

'Like refusing to work again?' she countered.

His eyes strayed to the camera on the table for a second before going back to her.

'Julien, I will postpone this wedding if I think your father is not going to fully be there.' She shook her head. 'Right now it is like his mind is locked and he can't move on and... I just don't know what to do.' A sob left her and she muffled the sound with a hand over her lips.

Julien reached across the table then, taking her other hand in his. 'I will go to the suit fitting,' he said, squeezing her fingers. 'I will try to talk to him.'

'You will?' Vivienne said, looking relieved.

'I will try but I cannot promise he will listen,' he said. 'And I do have one condition.'

'What?'

'I really do not want to take photos for *Parisian Pathways*.'

She smiled then and nodded her head. 'OK.'

'Good,' he replied. 'Then we have a deal.' He regarded a pair of plates being carried by a waitress. 'Eat a pain au chocolat with me?'

She nodded. 'Yes... but we must share. I have a wedding dress to fit into.'

TEN

Hotel Agincourt

4. Put on weight
5. Get drunk again
6. Make number 5 number 4
7. Climb the Eiffel Tower and kiss a random man at the top of it
8. Get surgery – the three Bs – boobs, bum and belly
9. Grow real eyebrows

Ava couldn't read any more. Her eighteen-year-old-self sounded unhinged. She took a long suck of the cocktail in front of her. She wasn't sure what it was but it contained a cherry and a glittery angel on a stick, a real holly leaf attached. She turned the paper over and looked at Debs.

Debs was hunched over a notepad, scribbling away, earrings still flashing, making satisfied noises as pen hit paper. Ava didn't even know where to begin. Her gaze went around the hotel bar. With its wide, black-and-gold Christmas tree in one corner, beautifully wrapped gifts stacked underneath like they were waiting for a child to unwrap them, and a roaring log fire beneath a marble mantelpiece, it was the perfect pre-Christmas scene. She settled herself back into the chair. She needed to relax. She was here in France with her best friend in a city she truly loved. She just needed to forget that the last time she came here was with Leo in the spring and he'd told her he loved her. *More lies.* She sat forward again, refocussed on Debs.

'What have you put?' Ava asked.

Debs pulled her paper towards her like she was protecting a government secret. 'I can't show you yet.' Debs' eyes went to the blank piece of paper and reindeer-shaped pen she'd given Ava. 'Why aren't you writing?'

Ava shrugged. 'I don't know what to write.'

'But, we're in *Paris*,' Debs emphasised. 'There must be things you want to do here.'

'I only knew I was coming here a few days ago. I suppose I just thought I'd do whatever you were doing.'

'And that's what needs to stop,' Debs said forcefully.

'What?'

'You not doing what you want to do.'

'I do what I want to do. I did this to my hair, remember?' Ava pulled at a lock of white to emphasise the point.

'But you did that because you were upset. And you took the job selling apartments just because your mother wanted you to audition for a tinned meatballs commercial and you needed an excuse.' Debs huffed. 'You shouldn't need an excuse. I know it's hard but you just need to tell her, once and for all, you're not interested.'

It was easy to say and Ava knew that's what she should be doing but it was a lot harder to put it into practice.

'That wasn't why I took the job,' she said quickly.

'No?' Debs looked unconvinced.

'No,' Ava said, a little overdramatically. 'I took the job because I've always wanted to sell luxury apartments.' Her mouth struggled to make the words sound anything close to sincere. 'You know what, if you want me to make a list, fine, I'll make a list.' Ava grabbed the reindeer pen and started to write.

'1. Get drunk?!' Debs exclaimed. 'No! Don't copy the other one!'

'Why not? Why do I have to have plans and dreams and know what direction I'm going in?' Ava asked. 'We're not all the same, you know. We don't all have to have a job we love, travelling to exciting cities and writing about them, with parents who love us, and a great house with neighbours who bring round homemade wine.'

The second she got to the end of the sentence, probably before, she realised she hadn't wanted to say any of those things and she sounded like a complete idiot.

What was worse was when she looked back over at Debs and saw her friend's bottom lip wobbling, tears ready to spill like a melting glacier.

A stab of guilt hit her square in the chest. Why was she taking all this out on Debs?

'Oh, God, I'm horrible,' Ava announced. 'Truly horrible.' She looked around for something to pass to Debs – serviettes, a beer mat. She settled on the map she had picked up at Gare Du Nord. 'Here, blow your nose on the Metro then tell me what's going on.'

Debs took the offering and dabbed at her nose with the shiny paper, shaking her abundance of hair. 'I can't.'

'You can't, what? Tell your absolute best friend in the world what's making you cry? I'm the one person you *can* tell.' Ava swallowed then whispered. 'You're not pregnant, are you?'

'No,' Debs replied, wiping her eyes on a photo of Versailles.

She was now so worried she really didn't want to ask the next question. 'You're not ill are you?'

'No,' Debs blubbered.

'Well, is it work?' Ava asked.

Debs moved her head in neither a nod nor a shake, but the expression on her face told a tale. Ava had only seen the look once before. When Debs' parents had split up. Sue and Jon had divorced less than a year after Ava's parents had split. For weeks back then there had been days and nights of boxes of Kleenex, comfort eating and almost stalkerish watching of every Johnny Depp film ever made – Debs had poured her heart out, Ava had poured the Diet Coke out, held her and told her everything was going to be all right... eventually. But until then they had each other and Ava had been through it and there was light at the end of the divorce tunnel.

'Debs, just tell me,' Ava begged.

'It's... Gary,' Debs finally sniffed out.

'Step-dad Gary?' Ava queried. 'The best step-dad in the world who always picks us up at two in the morning and brings kebabs? Taxi Dad?' Ava put her hands to her mouth. 'God, Debs, *he's* not ill is he?'

'No,' Debs sniffed. 'But he might be after this trip.'

Ava blinked. 'You'd better explain.'

'I think he's having an affair.'

The absolute shock of that statement had Ava tightening her hold on her glass. She shook her head straightaway. 'No... that's just mad. I mean, Gary is the best,' Ava said.

'I know.'

'He might work a lot, away sometimes granted, but he adores your mum.'

'I thought so.'

'Come on, Debs, he does,' Ava said. 'Remember their wedding? He swayed her around the dance floor to that awful, ancient Bryan Adams song. No one does that unless they're really in love.' Ava folded her arms across her chest. 'I don't believe it.'

'I don't want to believe it either but the things Mum said...'

'Tell me,' Ava said. 'Having just been involved with a cheater myself I think I might know the signs.'

Except she hadn't known or seen the signs. Any of them. She still didn't know if there had been any.

'It's the usual clichéd stuff,' Debs said, wiping her nose in the direction of Place de la Concorde. 'Whispered phone calls. No one there when Mum answers the home phone.'

'Well, that's not suspicious. I get calls like that all the time. It's usually one of those telesales people trying to find out the times of day I'm in.'

'He's Skyping.'

'And…'

'It's someone called Francine.'

'Maybe it's someone he works with,' Ava suggested.

'Yes,' Debs agreed. 'It is.'

'Yes it is, what?' Ava asked.

'She does work for his firm in one of the offices in France,' Debs admitted. 'The office in Paris.'

Ava sucked in a breath. 'Whoa, wait. You're not about to say something crazy are you?'

'I don't know?' Debs said. 'Am I?'

Ava took a suck of her cocktail. She knew how the idea of her step-dad having an affair would hurt Debs. Jon had had an affair with someone he worked with. If Gary was doing the same, putting Sue and Debs through something they had already lived through once, she was probably going to want to slash his tyres.

'I want to follow her,' Debs stated.

'What? Like private-I style? Mireille Enos in *The Catch*?'

'Gary is in France this week,' Debs added. 'He told Mum he's at the office in Toulouse but—'

'You think he's having sex with Francine in Paris.'

'I don't know!' Debs exclaimed. 'But it's like Dad all over again. Mum tells me not to worry but how can I not worry? She didn't tell me anything at first… she told Lindsay from Ladbrokes and Lindsay told me… and… I just want to get to the bottom of it.' She sighed. 'Whatever *it* is. Good or bad.'

Ava sat forward in her chair. 'Just a thought… but have you or your mum considered just asking Gary?'

Debs looked at her as if she had just said the world was in fact not a sphere but octagonal and the sea was actually blue Curacao.

'Oh, Ava, how can she ask him? After what happened with Dad… she's just terrified.' Debs pulled in a breath. 'She made me promise not to say anything to anyone and—'

'OK… you're right… I get it.' Ava sighed, mind working overtime.

Debs looked incredulous and shook her head.

'So, what *are* we going to do? Apart from trail this woman?'

'Oh, Ava, I really didn't invite you with me for this. I—' Debs began.

'Just you try and stop me helping,' Ava warned.

Debs sighed. 'She's got a mystery meeting scheduled in her diary for the day after tomorrow and… well… who's to say it isn't with Gary?'

'Or it could be a salon appointment,' Ava said, her fingers going to her hair. 'Or meeting someone… a friend… a colleague… not a married man.'

'It's not a hair appointment,' Debs said confidently. 'She writes that in pink and her hairdresser is called Delphine.'

She watched Debs swallow.

'You hacked her calendar, didn't you?' Ava said.

'Maybe… but I didn't mean to… I was trying to hack her email and who knows, if I had, I could have had my answer already and I wouldn't be thinking about what disguise to wear.'

'You promised me no dress-up!'

Debs gave her a watery smile. 'I just hope that I'm wrong about this. If Mum's been duped again then—'

Ava reached forward and took hold of Debs' hands. 'It won't be that. Gary…' She drew in a breath, stopping herself from launching into a speech about how everything was going to be all right. She really didn't know that, couldn't guarantee it. She smiled. 'Whatever happens, Debs, I'm here for you.' She let go of her friend's hands and picked up her glass, raising it in the air. 'To Agincourt.'

Debs picked up her glass. 'Agincourt.'

Ava took a large swig of her drink, put it down again and looked outside where the snow was battering against the window. She hoped the storm eased up a little overnight. Snow was nice when it was white and shiny and not six feet deep; it wasn't so nice when it burned your cheeks and was accompanied by a gale-force wind. Evil snow would also make it harder to appreciate the beauty of the city.

From the table her phone began to trill. Ava's eyes went to the screen. *Leo*.

ELEVEN

Outside Brasserie Du Bec, 8th Arrondissement

With his winter coat pulled up around his neck, Julien looked across the street at the brasserie just visible through the swirling snow. He could see Didier, the outline of his friend's chocolate-coloured shaved head, sat at a table by the misted-up front windows. His stomach took a dip. Picking up the camera was one thing, meeting his friend after months of declining invitations was another, but Didier had chosen a seat furthest from the fire exit.

The biting cold nipped every exposed inch of skin and he pressed his lips together, shielding them from the elements and deliberating some more. He sighed. What were the chances really? Of history repeating itself? Life was going on, *had* to go on.

And then he watched Didier turn his head towards the glass and before Julien could think about anything else, his friend was waving a hand excitedly. He waved back and took a step off the pavement into the road.

A cab beeped its horn as Julien weaved around it, making for the warm, welcoming glow of the brasserie. He was about to move forward into the entranceway when the revolving doors of the adjacent hotel spun in his sightline and someone barrelled out of it.

It was a woman, with bright blonde hair, cropped short and spiky. She was wearing a fitted denim blue coat that touched her knees, jeans and red Converse, a mobile phone was pressed against her ear.

'...why are you calling me? There's nothing I want to hear you say,' the woman said.

She was English and he really shouldn't be looking or listening to the conversation. But something was insisting he *did* listen and there was such a mix-up of emotions on her face he felt compelled to *keep* looking.

'Leo, listen to me,' the woman went on. 'All these words and apologies are pointless. It's over. You made that clear and now I'm making it *crystal* clear. I don't want you! And I don't need you! And now... well... now I have France!'

Julien watched her gaze go up the street towards one of the most famous landmarks in the city, the Arc de Triomphe, bathed in gold, lines of traffic just visible, colouring the night with red and white lights.

'And I have my best friend and… I don't have my mother and I have the possibility of possibilities... and... and... Camembert!'

Julien stifled a laugh, still watching.

'So I'm going to say goodbye now or perhaps, as I'm in France, I'll say à *bientôt*, no... because that means "see you again soon" and I really don't want to. So, I'll say *au revoir*... no, hang on, that's still not quite final enough.'

Julien watched her pull in a long slow breath, inhaling snowflakes and wind and not seeming to care.

'Right, I'm going to say *fin*. Just that. *Fin*. Because that's what this is, Leo, this is the end.'

His camera was up to his face before he'd even realised it. He snapped off a shot as the woman ended the call and he carried on clicking as she closed her eyes and lifted her face to the snow storm like the weight of the world had been removed from her. Her bright hair against the backdrop of the midnight blue sky, the streams of white bulbs spiralling around the trees, the expression of relief and release on her face was nothing short of magical. He held his breath and took another shot.

'Hey!'

He pulled the camera away from his face just in time to realise the woman was coming closer and the peaceful expression had been replaced by a furious one as she stomped through the snow towards him.

'What d'you think you're doing?'

'I... nothing...' Julien spluttered.

'Were you taking photos of me?'

Up close and despite the fact that she was shouting at him, the woman was very attractive. It was her eyes more than anything. Large, green, looking at him questioningly now.

'No,' he replied on instinct, then followed it up. 'Not exactly.'

'What's that supposed to mean? You either were or you weren't,' the woman snapped.

She reached out and grabbed hold of his camera, tugging it towards her and turning it around to view the screen. His neck strained as the strap tightened and he placed his hands over hers, tried to regain some control.

'*Arrêtez*,' he said.

'Yes,' the woman answered. 'I know what that means and it's what you should have done. You can't just take photographs of people.' She pulled the camera, the strap pinching his neck some more.

'Why not?' he replied, contorting his body to relieve some of the pressure around his neck.

'Because it's an invasion of privacy!'

'You are Madonna?' he answered, one hand still on top of hers as they battled for the camera.

'What?'

'I ask if you are a celebrity so I know how much money I can make for selling these photographs I may or may not have taken.'

'You can't do that!'

'Let go of my camera, s'il vous plaît.'

He wrestled the device from her grip and as he regained control she slipped, her Converse not gaining any traction on the snow-covered pavement, her body heading for the floor.

Instinctively he reached out, caught one of her arms and closed his body around her, buffeting her descent until she managed to get two feet flat on the ground. She was still twisted, halfway between standing and falling, him holding her weight, her eyes staring up at him.

For a fleeting moment he just looked, watched her blink long eyelashes, the short, platinum hair collecting snowflakes like tiny diamonds. She weighed practically nothing in his arms but he could feel the energy pouring from her, the pent-up emotion she had delivered to whoever had been on the telephone and, here in the street, to him, upset about his photography.

'You are OK?' he whispered as she straightened up, releasing herself from his arms.

'Why? What's it to you?'

'You are hurt?' he asked, worry nipping.

'No, I'm fine.'

'You are sure? I would hate to think...'

'Ava? Are you all right?'

Her name was Ava. He took a second to look at her, as if deciding whether the name suited her, then directed his gaze towards the woman who had spoken, coming out of the hotel doors. This woman was of similar age with a lot more hair and more appropriate footwear for the snow.

'Yes, I'm fine.' Ava glared at him. 'Apart from being pounced on by paparazzi.'

'What?!' the other woman exclaimed, hands going to her mouth.

'Please,' Julien said. 'I apologise.' He turned the camera, showing her the screen. 'I will remove the photographs.' He began to press the delete button. Had he taken six? More? He stopped when he had counted to five and powered it off again. 'There,' he said, looking to Ava. 'There is nothing more.'

'Are you from a magazine?' the other woman asked.

'I have not introduced myself.' Julien shot his hand forward towards Ava. 'My name is Julien Fitoussi and no, I do not work for a newspaper or magazine.'

'I'm Debs,' the woman announced, stepping forward and shaking the hand Ava had ignored. 'And this is Ava. Ava's actually been involved with photography.'

'You have?' Julien asked.

'No, I haven't,' Ava said, looking at Debs.

'No?' Julien asked.

Her body language was now defensive. She had folded her arms across her chest and taken a step back from him. Why was she so compelling? Why couldn't he take his eyes from her?

'Ava was a model,' Debs carried on.

'Debs!' Ava hissed.

Julien nodded. 'I can see why this would be the case.'

Ava raised one eyebrow. 'With my hair like this?'

He answered straightaway. 'I was not looking at your hair.' He quickly realised how that had sounded and cleared his throat. 'I only meant... when I was taking your photograph, I was trying to capture your energy not your appearance.'

'What sort of photographer does that?' she asked.

'One who does not take photos to sell anything but the photo itself.'

He carried on looking at Ava, watching his words sink into her consciousness. Every single thought running through her head was appearing on her face – confusion, frustration, annoyance, something softer.

'Julien!'

Suddenly there was Didier, a few yards away, jacketless, his thin light-blue shirt getting soaked by the snow. 'That is my friend, Didier.'

'We were just going to find somewhere to eat,' Debs informed. 'Could you recommend anywhere near here?'

'You would be very welcome to join with us if you would like.' He didn't know these women at all. Inviting strangers to join him for dinner wasn't something he had ever done before. It was Didier's style not his. What was he thinking? 'An apology for taking photos like the paparazzi,' he added.

'That would be lovely, wouldn't it, Ava? It's our first night here tonight,' Debs began.

'No,' Ava said quickly. 'We can't. Because I actually made a reservation at a restaurant near the Eiffel Tower.'

'You did?' Debs exclaimed.

Ava nodded. 'Yes, and we ought to get on the Metro over there or we'll be late.'

'Ah well, a restaurant near the Tour Eiffel, cannot be missed,' Julien said. He held his hand out again, this time to Debs. 'It was very nice to meet you.'

'You too,' Debs said, shaking his hand for the second time.

'À *bientôt*, Ava,' he said, holding his hand out to her. He waited for her to take it, her fingers cold in the warmth of his palm. 'Hopefully not *au revoir* or *fin*.'

He watched a knowing expression form on her features before he relinquished his grip and headed towards Didier.

TWELVE

Brasserie Du Bec

'Well,' Debs began, her eyes on the two men going into the brasserie, 'he was totes gorgeous, wasn't he?'

Ava looked through the light snowfall, watching Julien and Didier being shown to a table by a waitress. Boughs of Christmas foliage hung from the beams in the ceiling, it looked warm and less Arctic than the street they were standing on.

She turned back to Debs, shaking her head. 'No, he wasn't.' She breathed out, watching her carbon dioxide mix with the snowflakes. 'He was a photographer. Just like all the self-obsessed, fame-hungry photographers I've stood in front of for years wanting me to look this way and that way and touch my arse with my nose.'

Debs tilted her head a little. 'Can you do that?'

'No!' Ava exclaimed. Although her arse was a lot bigger now than it was when she last did an assignment. That was why her mother was suggesting a detox retreat, with nothing but watery juice and a tape measure to monitor progress.

Debs linked her arm through Ava's. 'So,' she began, beginning to walk. 'What's the name of this restaurant you've booked for us?'

Ava stopped moving. 'I haven't really booked anywhere,' she said. 'I just said that so we didn't have to spend the evening with some randoms. I mean, I know he said he was a photographer but he could as easily be a...'

'Nice person?' Debs offered.

'We don't know them, Debs and he was taking photos of me in the street!'

'And, as well as tailing a woman I think might be having an affair with my step-dad, I'm meant to be researching singles in the city,' Debs reminded.

Ava unlinked her arm from her friend. 'I much preferred the Christmas markets task... and I'm coming round to disguises.'

'Why? Because you're scared you might enjoy yourself? I know I have a family crisis going on but I still have work to do and getting social is very much part of the remit.'

Ava looked into the brasserie and watched the two men being directed to a table a little further away from the window but still in view. Was Debs right? And if she was, why? Why was she closing herself off to possibilities? Hadn't she just told Leo she was embracing her change in status? She had told him her life was going to be all France and Camembert.

'It was Leo on the phone, wasn't it? Did he upset you?' Debs asked.

Ava shook her head. 'No. I told him straight. I don't want to hear from him again.'

'Good,' Debs answered. 'Then let's go and have dinner and research two twenty-something Frenchmen while we're eating.' Debs' gaze went to the brasserie. 'The friend looks a bit like Thierry Henry, don't you think?' She nudged Ava's arm with hers. 'Remember him?'

'Tottenham's arch rivals Arsenal,' Ava replied a little stiffly.

Debs relinked their arms. 'Come on. I suggest completing that number one on your wish list.' She grinned. 'Let's get a little bit drunk.'

Ava let Debs take the lead and she followed her friend into the deliciously warm brasserie. There was a heady fragrance of cinnamon and caramel in the air and, as they stamped their wet feet on the matting at the door, Ava caught sight of gorgeously sugar-coated, brown-topped crème brûlées being delivered to tables. She suddenly realised she was famished. She manoeuvred herself around tables of diners following Debs' path to the table Julien Fitoussi and his friend were sitting at. There was a candle in a crystal bowl glowing at its centre and sprigs of mistletoe hanging from the beams.

The photographer had his coat off now and he was wearing a dark blue jumper, the collar of a white shirt just visible underneath. Dark denim jeans were below that. He had a short crop of dark hair and Ava had to admit Debs was right, he *was* attractive, if you liked tall, dark and aquiline-nosed. And you weren't completely off men altogether.

'*Pardon*,' Debs began. 'Would it still be acceptable to join you for dinner? It's so bitterly cold, we really couldn't face trekking over to the Eiffel Tower.'

Both men got to their feet and Julien's friend immediately started organising some chairs.

'I am Didier,' he greeted, dragging one chair towards the table with one hand and beckoning a waitress with another. 'Didier Bonnet.'

'It's very nice to meet you,' Debs said, relieving herself of her coat and sitting down. 'I'm Debs and this is—'

'I'm Ava,' Ava announced. 'I don't need a fanfare.' She looked to Julien. 'It's not like I'm Madonna.'

She watched a smile cross his face and he pulled his chair out for her. 'Please, sit here.'

Ava shrugged off her wet coat and before she could do anything with it, Julien took it from her and passed it off to the waitress who was arriving with another seat. She sat down, the warmth of the room beginning to revitalise her extremities. She watched Julien take the chair from the waitress, position it between her and Debs and then he sat down. Immediately she felt self-conscious, tugging her top down over her jeans.

'We have ordered red wine,' Didier announced. 'You like French red wine?'

'Oh yes,' Debs answered. 'And there's nothing quite like drinking it in Paris.'

Ava rolled her eyes. Debs really was going for it on the singles front. She shifted in her seat, fingers going to the serviette in her wine glass and taking it out.

'You like red wine, Ava?' Julien asked her.

'I like it a whole lot better than I like photographers,' she responded. She winced at her own remark. That hadn't been funny, it had been stroppy. She looked to him and quickly made another response. 'I'm sorry, I do like it... Merlot, Beaujolais...'

'We have ordered a little Bordeaux,' Didier told her.

'Bordeaux is nice too,' she said quickly.

Debs jumped in. 'You'll have to excuse us. I know there isn't much of a time difference and we're only a tunnel away, but travelling is so tiring, isn't it? We're still getting accustomed to our new surroundings.'

'This is your first time in Paris?' Julien asked, looking to Ava, then Debs.

'No,' Debs said. 'Or should I say *non*.' She laughed, flashing earrings shaking. 'I've been several times with my job. I'm a writer... freelance for lifestyle publications.'

'A writer!' Didier exclaimed. 'So creative!'

'One tries,' Debs said with a giggle.

Ava looked at her friend, naturally vivacious, comfortable and completely in her element. Already Debs was settled in this new situation – a new city with new acquaintances.

'You would like some water?'

It was Julien again. He hovered a glass jug over the tumbler sat in front of her place setting.

'Thank you,' she answered gratefully.

He filled up her glass and spoke again. 'So, you have come to Paris for Christmas?'

'No,' Ava answered. 'Just for... well... I'm not sure how long we're staying at the moment. Debs'—' Visions of Gary strolling along the *rue* arm in arm with someone called Francine came to mind. She swallowed. 'Debs' writing job has brought her here and I'm...' Her mouth moved again, just about to say the word 'hiding'. She would have pitched it as a joke but it was a little too close to the truth and not something she should be admitting freely to strangers on her first night.

'Trying to relax?' Julien suggested. 'Away from the paparazzi perhaps?'

She smiled and nodded. 'Yes, something like that.'

He returned the smile and put down the water jug. 'It is a good time to come,' Julien continued. 'Not as busy as the summer but still as beautiful.'

'If you do not mind frostbite,' Didier chipped in. 'I wear two pairs of gloves and still I have hands like igloo bricks.'

Debs laughed at this comment, her hair shaking, her flashing earrings moving.

'You must excuse my friend, Didier,' Julien started. 'He does like to exaggerate... about a million times a day.'

Ava smiled. 'Debs, who knew your long-lost twin was in Paris.'

'I do not exaggerate,' Debs said.

Didier folded his arms across his chest. 'And neither do I... two hundred per cent *non*!'

Julien raised his palms to the ceiling in a gesture of hopelessness and made everyone laugh.

'My friend, Julien here,' Didier began, 'see how he behaves like he is a doctor.'

Julien shook his head. 'I have no idea what you mean.'

'Around his neck,' Didier said, pointing. 'His camera. Just like a stethoscope, no?'

Ava watched Julien begin to remove the device still hanging from his neck, embarrassment coating his expression.

'I apologise,' he said, settling the strap over the back of the chair and straightening his jumper.

'*Non*,' Didier said. 'It is nice to see. For a while I think I may not ever see this again.'

Julien's mouth dried up instantly and he felt igloo bricks start building a wall in his stomach. He looked to Didier, almost pleadingly. This wasn't the place, in front of these women, to make any comment about his reintroduction to photography.

'That sounds totes intriguing,' Debs answered, turning her gaze to him.

The bistro's warmth was evaporating and instead a cold blanket was trying to shroud him.

'No,' he said quickly. 'No intrigue.' He had to move this conversation on. 'Just a slight change of direction.' He willed moisture into his mouth. 'And… helping a little with my father's wedding.'

He could see Didier's eyes pop out of his skull at that comment but he'd needed anything to avoiding talking about *that night*.

'A wedding! How utterly brilliantly fantastic!' Debs exclaimed. 'Is it soon?'

'Christmas Eve,' he responded, restoring a smile.

'Are you taking the photos?'

The question came from Ava. Vivienne had asked him several times to take the photos of the special day and several times he hadn't been able to bring himself to answer.

'Pa!' Didier jumped in, 'Julien does not take photos of weddings. That is a hundred times too ordinary.' He picked up the little display of fir cones, ivy and holly on the table, holding it in his palm. 'See this?' Didier asked, as if waiting for everyone's full attention. 'A *Noël* decoration, no?'

No one responded and Julien had to wonder where his friend was going with this.

'Come on,' Didier encouraged. 'This is just a Christmas ornament, yes?'

Julien watched the women nod their heads.

'But imagine,' Didier said, waving his free palm over the arrangement like he was about to perform a magic trick. 'Imagine it in the wrinkled hand of a war veteran… or on the bridge over the Seine surrounded by love locks, one of which is open to represent lost love… there is the moonlight, the snow cascading down.' He pulled in a dramatic sigh.

'That is the most beautiful thing I've ever heard,' Debs breathed, her hand propping up her head as she gazed at Didier.

'It sounds ridiculous,' Julien stated. 'Please, let us get him some food before all that is talking is the vin rouge.'

Didier put the display down, laughing as he picked up a menu.

'So, you consider yourself an artist really?' Ava said quietly. 'Not a photographer.'

He looked to her, green eyes showing less vulnerability now and a lot more interest.

'I do not draw or paint, but yes… I would consider my photographs as art.'

He watched her absorb the information, fingers moving lightly over the rim of the wine glass.

'But modelling is art too, no? Every new shoot has a different aim,' he suggested.

'I wouldn't call it art,' she responded straightaway.

'Why not?' he countered. 'It is performance art. Giving an attitude or pose to the camera to channel a vibe or to show a certain situation.'

'And if the model's heart isn't in it? If she's being manipulated and forced to project an image she doesn't agree with?'

Her eyes were flashing with passion now and he wondered just what or who had hurt her so much she now couldn't separate one thing from another. She then suddenly seemed to cool and picked up the menu as if she hadn't entered into a debate with him at all. For a second he thought about filling the silence with a food recommendation, but then she looked back to him.

'In my opinion most art is manufactured. And with photographs it's even easier because the photographer never has to give anything of themselves.' She took a breath. 'I find it can be deceptive and manipulative. *You* might not airbrush or use Photoshop but using war veterans and love locks or… sick children and puppies… it's all about trying to provoke a reaction.' She sniffed. 'And that's about making headlines and nothing to do with art.'

He felt like he had been slapped. He looked at her, chest rising and falling, eyes bright and confronting, cheeks rouged, words bitter. Before he could even think about making a reply Debs had spoken.

'Shall we have coq au vin, Ava?' She smiled. 'I know it's terribly British to have something a little plain but, let's face it, who doesn't love a bit of *coq*?'

THIRTEEN

Ava didn't do dignified silences or smiling sweetly and saying the right thing. No, she opened her mouth and put her red Converse straight into it. Now, filling her mouth with a delicious chicken dish she knew was probably a day's calories in one meal, she was feeling a little guilty about her comments to Julien Fitoussi. He hadn't said a word to her since she had insulted his work and she didn't blame him. She hadn't really meant it. Not all of it. He had just pushed the button and she had remembered how she had felt under the lights, a lens trained on her, a photographer telling her nothing she was doing was right and her mother agreeing with him. That wasn't Julien's fault.

And here she was with Debs, two strangers from England, interrupting his evening with a friend and declaring his work manipulative. She chanced a glance sideways and immediately caught his eye. It was too late to pretend she hadn't looked, but she forked a shallot into her mouth and hoped that would signal she was engaged with something other than conversation.

'So, if you do not model any longer what is it you do now?' Julien asked.

Ava picked up her serviette and dabbed her mouth with it. 'I sell flats.'

'She sells luxury apartments!' Debs butted in loudly, her cheeks fuchsia from the red wine. 'She's so good at it she got a promotion after only two weeks and now it's all penthouse suites for totes affluent business types.'

Ava nodded. 'Like she said.'

'And this satisfies you?' Julien inquired, observing her.

She didn't catch herself quickly enough not to hesitate. 'Yes,' Ava answered.

She watched Julien nod as he picked up his glass of red wine.

'She's brilliant at it,' Debs said, to Didier more than anyone else. 'I've seen her in action.' Debs breathed in the aroma of the Bordeaux in her glass. 'Ava can get someone who, you can just tell, has absolutely no intention whatsoever of buying an apartment, and she presents the information in such a way that in the end they can't wait to sign on the dotted line.'

Suddenly Ava felt a little uncomfortable, almost sensing what was about to come. 'It isn't quite like that, Debs.'

'No?' Julien asked, turning his body in his chair, his chest parallel with hers. 'You would not woo these potential buyers with talk of the lifestyle if they bought one of your apartments?' he asked, eyes fixed on hers. 'There was no "imagine sitting on your balcony with a glass of wine, enjoying a little *dejeuner* with friends" or "*regarde*, the lights of the London Eye, spectacular... and a panoramic view of the whole of the capital to show off to your colleagues."'

She didn't respond, couldn't. She was watching his tight body language, the way his fingers were curling around his glass.

'Julien,' Didier spoke up, 'you have an apartment just like this.' He smiled at Debs. 'Julien has an apartment with a view of the Seine.'

Ava opened her mouth to make comment. To say that sounded nice and so much better than something in Canary Wharf, but then Julien spoke again.

'You paint a picture for the buyers,' he told her. 'You sell them something that is not there. Something fabricated. A dream lifestyle that may or may not come true.'

She swallowed. This was payback for her earlier outburst and annoyingly, he was absolutely right.

'You invent the wine and the sunsets, you miss out the smog and the property opposite that perhaps overlooks the balcony a little, you tell them what they want to hear,' he said. 'You show them fantasy and let them believe it can be theirs.' He tipped the contents of his wine glass into his mouth and deposited the glass back on the table. 'It is just like Photoshop but with words.' He got to his feet.

'Come, Julien, what are you doing?' Didier asked as Julien began to pull on his coat.

'This was a mistake,' Julien said. 'I should go.'

Ava looked up at him, hastening to get his arms into sleeves. 'Why?' she asked. 'Because the conversation has turned into a debate? I thought the French enjoyed a debate.'

He turned then, his demeanour softening slightly. 'Is this what it is?' he asked.

Ava shrugged. 'I think that would be the most effective resolution.'

'To call a truce,' Didier suggested, clapping his hands together. 'To put aside our differences for the sake of good wine and good times.'

'I like that idea more than I like *coq*,' Debs hiccupped, '*au vin*.'

'No,' Ava said. 'Differences being put aside won't work.' She sniffed. 'That's like asking France to give the UK maximum points at Eurovision.'

'We do not do this?' Didier asked, looking genuinely interested.

Julien was still standing, both arms now in his coat. She could just let him go. He had photographed her and wound her up. But she couldn't help thinking that just maybe she was the guilty one. Making assumptions. Being too sensitive. Letting Rhoda Rhinestone, Leo and this new information about Gary blight everything. She looked at Debs, goggle-eyed over Didier with a Bordeaux glow on her cheeks. Debs had so much more going on with her life than she had realised and she needed to start being a better best friend, and quickly.

'Sit down,' she said, tilting her chin to regard Julien. 'Please. We can have a healthy debate, can't we?' She saw him wavering, caught between doing up the buttons of his coat and taking it off again. She smiled. 'A debate about why I'm right and you're wrong, obviously.'

Didier let out a laugh. 'A challenge, my friend.'

Ava now wanted him to sit down more than she didn't want to follow a woman around Paris tomorrow. Still he stood, looking as if he were weighing up his options.

'Please, sit down,' she tried again. 'Before your *coq* gets cold.' She couldn't quite believe she'd said that and her cheeks began to flame.

Finally, Julien removed his coat and hung it around the back of his chair, being careful not to dislodge his camera before re-taking his seat.

Debs picked up the near-empty wine bottle. 'Shall we order some more wine?'

'Yes, *absolutement*,' Didier said, waving a hand with a flourish to beckon a waiter.

'So,' Julien said, his eyes on Ava again, 'are you to begin the debate or am I?'

FOURTEEN

Julien watched Ava put a spoonful of tarte Tartin into her mouth and ponder on the question he'd just asked her. Around them the brasserie had started to empty, other patrons leaving for a night of music or the ballet or simply heading home. The earlier storm had ceased and now gentle flakes of snow floated past the window a few tables away, creating the perfect backdrop for the white and gold fluffy Christmas baubles hanging in chain formation against the glass. Next to him Debs and Didier were playing some sort of game that involved the corks of wine bottles being balanced on their noses.

'I don't know how old I was when I started modelling,' Ava admitted. 'Four, maybe?'

'Four,' he said, shaking his head.

She nodded. 'I think so. But I suppose there's a chance I might have done baby commercials that I don't even remember.'

She looked to the window, gazing through the snow flurry as if trying to recall. 'Although, knowing my mother, I'm sure she would have brought those prints out to embarrass me at dinner parties if I had.' She could almost hear the comments now. *Agnes, look at Ava there, so adorable, her neck like a swan and probably the only time she's ever been a size zero.*

Julien nodded. 'Now I can see somewhat why you would not want to always be photographed.'

'But I shouldn't have been rude.' She put down her spoon. 'I just haven't had a great relationship with photographers.' Almost on instinct she sucked in her stomach and pulled back her shoulders. Old habits died hard.

'Because they have made you behave a certain way?' he asked softly.

'Yes,' she replied wistfully. 'Because that's their job.' She sat back in her seat. 'And to them I was just a clothes horse or a mane of hair for a new, thickening product or someone giving the right expression to advertise sport or... sex.'

He watched her swallow then, as if the word had fallen on her like hard rain.

'And I was never good enough. They told me that most of the time, too.' She sighed. 'It was a lot harder than selling apartments and dream lifestyles to bankers,' she concluded. 'But then I never did the modelling for me.' She shook her head. 'It was always about my mother.'

He watched her make her hands into fists. Not perhaps the reaction you would expect from a woman who was talking about her mother, although it *was* one he was familiar with. Lauren had done the very same thing when *their* mother came up in conversation.

'She keeps trying to get me to start again – just shift a few pounds, just one trip to the dentist. She can't accept that I couldn't cut it then, and I couldn't cut it now.'

A cork bounced onto the table and Debs shrieked with laughter as Didier frantically tried to claim it back and reset it on his nose. It was enough to jar the conversation and Ava retracted, both physically and emotionally. Julien watched her smile and restore the very British exterior.

'I'm sure you didn't expect to have to listen to any of this when you left your apartment overlooking the Seine tonight,' she said, toying with the napkin on her lap.

'No,' he agreed. 'I expected to have to listen to Didier telling me about every conversation he had this week and an update on the Kardashians.'

Ava laughed and he smiled, watching the way her short blonde tendrils almost shivered with the motion.

'I hear everything you say,' Didier answered, his face upturned, the cork resting lengthways on the bridge of his nose. 'I am right here.'

'I went to a party once and we didn't balance corks, we balanced After Eights,' Debs informed, steadying her head as she put another cork between her eyes.

'After Eights? I do not know what these are,' Didier answered, shifting in his seat to try and maintain balance. 'English cigarettes?'

'No, silly,' Debs said. 'They're chocolates.'

'So, are you taking the photos for your dad's wedding?' Ava asked him. 'You didn't say.'

Now he was on the spot. But he could lie. He could just say yes or no, make an excuse.

'I do not know yet,' he admitted.

'Why not?' Ava asked, without pause.

There was no taking time to get to the point with this woman. He could feel her eyes on him, waiting for his answer.

'Perhaps it is a little too close to home,' he suggested. 'You would think there was a lot *less* pressure with family but, in truth, there is a lot more.' He looked to her then. 'I would want the photographs to be perfect... Without war veterans and love locks.'

Ava smiled. 'I think that's a good plan.'

'So, tell me, Didier and Julien, where are the hot spots for singles in Paris?' Debs asked as one foot slipped on the icy pavement and she had to make a grab for a lamppost.

They had left the brasserie and were now at the mercy of the icy night, Ava's breath visible in the air as she shoved her hands

into her pockets and stamped life back into her high-top encased toes. She was tired. A yawn was crawling its way up inside
her but she held it in. Debs obviously wasn't ready to end the
evening yet.

'I know the perfect place!' Didier announced, a wide grin on
his mouth. 'A club called Showcase!'

'Let's go!' Debs responded, linking arms with him.

'I will catch up with you later, Didier,' Julien called to his
friend who was already two paces along the street.

'You're not coming?' Ava asked, looking first to Debs and
Didier and making sure their skipping off had come to a halt
and then back to Julien.

He shook his head. 'No, Showcase... it is not really my scene.'

'Is it awful?' Ava mouthed, leaning a little closer to him. 'Bad
music and even worse dancing?'

Julien smiled and shook his head. 'It is fine. If you like nightclubs.'

'Julien, come on,' Didier called. 'Live a little, *non*? It is only
Cinderella who turns into a pumpkin if she is out later than
midnight.'

'I plan to be up early in the morning,' he said.

'That is new,' Didier commented.

Ava watched Julien's features shift just a little and then he
directed a smile at her. 'If I thought you could maybe put aside
your preconceptions about photography I would invite you to
join me tomorrow.'

'Doing what?' she asked.

'I am thinking of having another photography exhibition.'

The way he had said the sentence was as if it had taken every ounce of energy in his body. His shoulders hunched a little
awkwardly and he was moving on the spot like he couldn't stand
still. He blew out a breath then continued. 'Nothing is certain. I

am just thinking about it... forming an idea at the moment.' He swallowed. 'But... I will need photographs.'

'Ava!' Debs called. 'Hurry along will you! I need to ensure appropriate research is done before I start drinking pastis!'

Julien began again. 'Perhaps it would give me a chance to show you that not all photographers are the same.'

He was looking at her with openness and honesty in those dark, hazelnut-coloured eyes, the snow falling down around his face, his breath a fine mist in the air between them. Was she considering this? Making a date to see a stranger she had only known a few hours, someone who had pressed all the right buttons and reignited her rage against the modelling regime? Was this her idea of opening herself up to possibilities in Paris? Number one on her new wish list? She swallowed.

'What time?' she found herself asking.

'Well, I was going to start early... at sunrise... but we could meet later...'

'I can do early,' Ava told him. Debs needed time to work on her articles and she could use this to obliterate Leo from her mind entirely.

'You are sure?' Julien asked.

'Do you regret asking?'

'*Non*, of course not,' he replied.

'Tomorrow then, sunrise, outside my hotel,' Ava said, indicating the Hotel Agincourt.

'Tomorrow,' Julien repeated.

'Wish me luck,' Ava said, walking backwards a few steps as she prepared to catch up with Debs and Didier. 'Or at least a free pass to the VIP area to avoid the paparazzi.'

She waved a hand and turned around, snowflakes hitting her cheeks and then she heard, '*À bientôt*, Madonna! Until tomorrow!'

FIFTEEN

Hotel Agincourt

It was almost six a.m. and the first fingers of light were creeping over the horizon turning the dark, wintry, cloud-heavy sky into something a little more hopeful. As Debs let out a snort in her sleep, Ava padded in night socks to the balcony doors of their room and pressed her nose up to the frosted-on-the-outside glass. She should feel tired after dancing until three a.m. to songs she had never heard before while Debs asked anyone within a fifty-foot radius if they were single – in pigeon French. Then had come the sobbing about Gary's affair as soon as Didier had left them. But somehow she wasn't tired. The almost three hours' sleep she'd managed to slip in seemed to have refreshed her enough that she was actually excited about the day dawning. More excited than she could remember being in such a long time.

Not worrying about the cold, her favourite red plaid shirt nightdress over her body, she whooshed the balcony doors open. There was no blast of icy air like the wind on the city streets the night before; this was more a gentle gush, a trickle of cold gently falling on her face as she stepped onto the balcony.

Her socks dulled the frosty concrete under her feet and she stepped right up to the black iron rail and the most amazing scene. It was breath-taking. Here, up high, above the grey, dark slate, cream and biscuit-coloured tiles, she had a bird's eye view of the entire city. Little windows set into roofs, tiny terracotta chimney pots, everything speckled with snow. She could see the

Eiffel Tower, the triangular icon looking over the city, standing strong, its lights still aglow as the sky started to turn pink.

And down below, on the street a few storeys under her, French city-life was beginning. Cars were crawling down the street, dog walkers, a man carrying a huge tray of baguettes. Ava sucked in the fresh air, notes of coffee, fresh bread and cheese in the air. Her stomach rolled. She hadn't had any Camembert yet. Delicious, high-in-saturated fats, creamy gorgeousness. Perhaps today would be the day. Right now she would happily eat a whole one to herself. And that was one of the great things about being single again. Not having to share.

Julien was early. Having slept for as long as he had slept in months he had woken at four-thirty feeling a little different. He didn't know what it was exactly, he just knew he felt somewhat lighter. It was as if his head was clear, his body weighed less and his thoughts were completely unclouded. Even in the dark, when he had regarded the river from his living room window, he knew today was not going to be as bleak as others.

Now, he was on the street of Ava's hotel, his vision on something creeping along the edge of the road, eyes glistening in the half-light. A fox. It was the very first time he had seen one in the city. His camera close, he moved like a trained assassin, settling each footstep into the thin layer of snow carefully, making no noise. He wanted to capture its beautiful colours – a bright, russet glow amid the white of the frosting on the ground and in the air. He watched the fox settle, its nose sniffing at a black sack discarded outside a restaurant. Steadily, Julien drew up his camera and prepared to take a shot.

'*Pierre!*'

The shout from a man coming out of a café had the fox running up an alleyway and away from Julien. Deep frustration began to coat his insides. He swallowed down the feeling. He was used to this, it just hadn't been in his life for a while. At the height of his career he had spent hours watching and waiting for that perfect photograph. Most days there would be good and bad pictures, but perfect took a lot longer. He couldn't expect everything to fall back into his lap like nothing had changed.

He turned his gaze across the road to Hotel Agincourt. What was he doing meeting with a woman he didn't know? A woman who hated photographers? It wasn't his job to make everybody love this choice of career. He wasn't even sure he had the enthusiasm to take part in a crusade to defend his art. Perhaps Ava was just like his father and blinkered to everything but her own opinion.

He raised his camera up and took a snap of the hotel. It had some interesting lines and shapes, patterns in the brickwork and swirly iron railings across the balconies. As he shifted his position slightly he saw her. Even three floors up, she was unmistakable. The bright white hair, spiked up like a snow queen, a red shirt on her body and... were they long socks? He was caught now. Instinct was telling him to take a photograph. She had the most amazing presence. Just standing there, against the glowing sky, isolated, a lone figure amongst the cityscape. And then it happened. Almost as if she were taking his direction, she stretched her arms out, face tipped up, the beginnings of the sunrise catching her skin as she put her palms to the sky. He couldn't help himself. He started to take photos. As the shutter clicked, as he repositioned himself slightly, changing the angle, he only hoped she didn't look down.

SIXTEEN

'Don't wake up properly,' Ava whispered. She had moved the hair by Debs' ear to bid her a quick goodbye now she was dressed and ready. But Debs was coming to, snorting like a warthog who had overdosed on roots. 'I'm leaving now but I have my mobile and maybe we can meet for lunch.'

Debs yawned – more lioness than hog, baring teeth. 'Where are you going? What time is it?' Her eyes remained closed.

'It's early, Debs,' Ava answered. 'And given you were still drinking shots only a couple of hours ago I think you ought to get a bit more sleep before you think about continuing research of singles in the city or Christmas markets.' Ava sighed. 'And do not, under any circumstances, do anything about this Francine. No more hacking, no phone calls under an alias, nothing until I get back.'

Debs made a noise akin to someone being poked in the eye by a Christmas tree needle.

'I'm glad you agree,' Ava said, stepping back from the bed.

Debs began snoring again before she had even got to the door. Ava checked her phone as she opened the door and saw a text message from her mother sent late the previous night.

Managed to upgrade the flights to Goa to first class. Delightful chickpea salad on the inflight menu. I've left several messages...

She couldn't face reading any more. She deleted the message, slipped her phone into her trusty messenger bag and left the room. As she walked down the maroon-carpeted hallway towards the bank of lifts her phone beeped again. She unzipped her bag and pressed the button for the lift with her other hand: *Leo*.

There was no message but a photograph. A corporate one of them both taken at a work function. It didn't seem like he gave up easily either. Perhaps she had meant more to him than she'd thought. Not that it mattered now. A betrayal was a betrayal. She locked her phone and put it back in her bag. Both these people problems were the English Channel away and that's where they were going to stay.

She could see Julien standing outside before she reached the revolving doors at the hotel entrance. He was wearing a thick, dark coat over black trousers, brown leather shoes on his feet. His camera raised at eye level he seemed to be focussing on workers erecting a Christmas tree on the building opposite. She pushed at the glass and travelled forward at the speed of the doors until she landed on the pavement.

'*Bonjour*,' she greeted.

She watched him drop the camera, the strap breaking its descent as he turned to face her. 'Good morning,' he answered. His eyes went from her face down to her Converse.

'What's the matter?' she asked, lifting her feet up and down in the slush. 'Is there some photographers' dress code I don't know about? Because most of the ones I dealt with turned up looking like David Walliams' Mr Stink.'

'Mr who?'

'Or *Dr* Who,' Ava said. 'You're right. Good call.'

'I was just...' Julien began. 'These are the only shoes you have?'

'No,' Ava said. 'Just the only ones I brought with me.'

'No boots?' he asked.

'I packed in a rush and didn't think about it being winter.' She sniffed. 'Anyhow, you're not wearing boots.' She observed his leather shoes.

'I am wearing three pairs of socks,' he admitted.

'Oh.' Almost instantaneously her toes began to numb and she stamped her feet quickly. 'Well, let's walk somewhere and restore the circulation,' she suggested.

He slipped a hand into his pocket and drew out a beanie. She watched as he put it over his dark hair. 'You have a hat,' she stated.

He nodded. 'Yes, it is winter, in Paris.' He looked at her coat as if it were made of flimsy cloth. 'You do not have boots *or* a hat?'

She shrugged. 'I wanted to show off my new hair?'

With one move, he had pulled the hat from his head and offered it to her.

'Oh, no, you don't have to do that. I'll be fine.'

'Did you know most of the body's heat is lost through an uncovered head in the winter time?'

'I do now,' Ava answered.

'Take the hat, s'il te plait.' He shook it closer to her, giving her little choice.

She accepted the offering and put it over her spikes, enclosing them and shielding her scalp from the elements. 'I take it wherever we're going isn't indoors.'

It then occurred to Julien that he hadn't actually thought about where they were going to go. That wasn't how he worked. Usually he would head out with no plan, just the camera around his neck and the day in front of him.

'Where would you like to go?' he asked her as they started to walk.

'Well, the last time I was in Paris I went to all the places *Time Out* suggested for romantic weekends.'

'Ah, so you wish to relive these?' Julien asked.

'God no!' The exclamation was severe.

'You wish *not* to go to them?'

'Oh no,' Ava said, kicking at half an abandoned Christmas cracker on the pavement.

'Then…?'

'I want to go to them all again without the burden of expectation.' She sucked in a breath. 'Just looking and seeing and not wondering what I'm meant to do to keep people happy.'

Her sentence was almost heart-breaking. It caused him to steal a glance at her. She had closed her eyes, was kicking the inappropriate high-tops at the slush, swinging her arms like a child, as if her ungloved hands were feeling the breeze. He wanted to capture it. Take a photo of it. His fingers went to his camera on instinct and then…

She snapped her eyes open and turned her head to look at him. 'Sorry, that was way too much information sharing.' She shoved her hands into the pockets of her coat. 'Which I also did last night. Honestly, I don't always hate the world.'

'No?'

'No,' she said again. 'Just most of the people in *my* one.' She smiled. 'So, let's go somewhere really touristy, before all the tourists get there, and you can show me what magic you do with that camera.'

He smiled at her. 'So I am allowed magic? Just nothing… how you say… forced?'

'Yes!' Ava answered. 'No rabbits in hats or—'

'Sick children and puppies?'

'Yes.'

'Which I have not or will not ever do,' Julien said. 'That was just Didier being… Didier.'

Ava stopped walking and put her hands on her hips. 'Is he gay?'

'What? Didier?'

'Not that it matters... except... well, I know Debs had quite a lot to drink last night but I think she might quite like him.'

Julien smiled and shook his head. 'No. Didier might be flamboyant and crazy but he is definitely not gay.'

'And he's single?'

He couldn't answer that question. It had been such a long time since he had paid any interest in anyone else's life, even his best friend's.

'Yes... I think so.'

'Good.' She began to walk again. 'And you? Are you single like me?'

'Just attached to my camera,' Julien confirmed, holding it up.

'*Bon*,' Ava said, breathing in. 'Because it's the best way to be, you know.' She laughed. 'Now where can I get my hands on some Camembert at this time of the morning?'

SEVENTEEN

Latin Quarter – The Panthéon

They had got the Metro to Maubert Mutalité and Julien had found an eatery that could fulfil Ava's need for the French cheese. Strolling past Place Maubert, only the market-stall holders setting up around them, Ava had devoured the gorgeous gooey Camembert infused with garlic and topped with fresh rosemary. It was like nothing she had ever had before. Now, lips still a little slick with olive oil, her stomach full, they carried on down Rue Valette towards the Panthéon.

'Where they are setting up the market, it used to be a place for torture,' Julien remarked, indicating the *place* in front of them.

'Wow,' Ava said. 'I know I said I wanted to ditch the romanticised idea of Paris with couples and hearts and flowers but I wasn't thinking of touring all the places they once did waterboarding.' She pulled Julien's hat down a little on her head.

'The guidebooks will tell you this was a place for scholars, for debating,' he continued. 'But that is only part of the history.'

'The board of tourism is loving you right now.'

'You like the truth,' he reminded, smiling. 'Nothing fake.'

She nodded. 'I do.'

'So, there we have it,' Julien said, pointing. 'The place where people were burned in the sixteenth century.'

'Fascinating. Take a photo. Debs can use it for one of her articles... or maybe she could pitch it to *Medieval Murder Month-*

ly.' The thought that perhaps Sue could cut off Gary's balls here if the rumours were true crossed her mind.

She refocussed on Julien, watching him look through the viewfinder trained on the scene behind them.

'So what made you want to be a photographer?' she asked. 'Or should I say, an artist?'

'I do not know,' he answered, falling back into step with her.

'I wasn't expecting that,' Ava admitted.

'Why not?'

'Well, the way you talked about it last night, I thought it was bound to be something you'd wanted to do from an early age. Perhaps you started off taking Polaroids at the Arc de Triomphe and selling them to tourists?'

'Polaroids?' he stated, a grin on his lips. 'How old do you think I am?'

'Polaroids are still cool.'

'Maybe at wedding parties or—' He stopped. 'I cannot think of anywhere else.'

'Then, if taking photos wasn't a long-held dream, how did it happen?'

He thought about her question, knowing if he told the truth he was going to have to speak about Lauren. And if he started talking about Lauren then where would it stop?

'Sorry,' Ava jumped in after a few seconds of silence had passed. 'I'm being very intrusive and—'

'*Non*,' he said. 'It is fine. My sister is the reason. She entered a photo I had taken into a competition.'

'And you won?'

He nodded. 'Yes.' He smiled, remembering. 'It was a contest to win a year's supply of apple juice.'

'What?!' Ava said, laughing.

'And my photo was of my sister, she was thirteen at the time, eating an apple on a picnic we went on in Bretagne. For a year she was the face of *Héros d'Apple*. On every carton in every store in Paris.'

'Wow,' Ava said. 'So, she was a model.'

'No,' Julien said, shaking his head. 'She works at a department store, ladies' fashion.' He should have said *worked*.

'But her face was your big break?'

'No,' Julien said again. 'It just made me take more of an interest in photography. I began to use the camera differently. Not just to catalogue events like holidays or parties but to capture smaller moments.'

'And you did this after school or did you have a proper job first?'

He laughed at the irony in her tone. 'Yes, I worked for my father in the financial sector. It did not go so well.'

'Numbers didn't appeal to your artistic nature I'm guessing.'

He nodded. 'So I went out on my own, took work where I could. I have done many weddings and baptisms and fortieth-birthday parties... corporate events... to pay the bills. But then I started to look at things from a new angle. Try to see things that other people do not see.'

'And that pays the bills now?' she asked.

He breathed out, waiting a beat before turning to her. 'My last exhibition is still paying the bills. I sold one photograph for fifty thousand euro.'

He watched her blink, green eyes staring almost as if she was deciding whether or not to believe him, hot breath leaving her mouth until, 'Wow.'

'Yes, this is what I said too,' he agreed. 'And then I took the cheque and hoped it would last until I sold another one.' He smiled. 'And here we are,' he stated. 'The Panthéon.'

He watched Ava turn to the building in front of them, the newly risen sun catching the cross at the top of its dome. It was a beautiful building, its façade inspired by the Panthéon in Rome. It never ceased to amaze him how huge the building was, the colonnade like a row of stone giants.

She was still and silent as if she was intently soaking up the scene. Seeing her reaction to it was like he was seeing the building for the first time himself. And then she spoke.

'Leo brought me here because it was modelled on St Paul's Cathedral,' Ava said.

'This is true,' Julien said in response.

'I asked whether it was because of the dome or the pigeons.'

Julien laughed, his eyes creasing at their corners. Ava smiled and indicated the clucking birds pecking at bits on the grey snow-smeared concrete.

'And what did he say?' Julien inquired.

'He didn't say anything,' Ava answered. 'Not even a laugh.'

'Well,' Julien began, 'we are here for you now, not for this Leo.'

'Exactly,' Ava agreed. 'So, choose your subject. Take your photo.'

Ava watched him, the sharp wind blowing his dark hair as his fingers went to his camera.

'What do you see apart from the columns and the dome and the pigeons?' she asked.

She continued to look at him, staring at the building, then to the sky, then to the ground, slick with wet from the melting snow. He seemed to be taking in everything. Not just the grand structure the tourists came to see, but all the nuances and details most of them would miss. Then *she* saw something.

'The light,' she exclaimed without even realising it. 'It's changing.'

'*Oui*,' he agreed.

'It's warming the stone. Look!'

'I can see this,' Julien agreed.

Ava walked forward, looking at the ridged markings on the stonework altering as the sunlight hit them. She wanted to touch them, run her hands over the mammoth columns and feel small in their presence. She headed up the wet, shiny steps, sludge wetting the canvas of her Converse wanting to get to the pillars before the effect was gone.

Sunlight fell on the top of the colonnade, the bottom still in darkness, creating the illusion of a second set of pillars like a mirror image. Ava put her hand on the first pillar she came to in shadow, her fingers cold against the stone. And then she closed her eyes, waiting.

Julien's camera was at work the second she had moved away from him. She had her back to him, her hand stretched up on one of the columns in the centre of the structure, reaching as high as her body would allow and he was photographing every second of it praying she didn't turn around.

He knew what she was waiting for. He had seen it too. The light was taking its time to come around the building but it was happening quickly as it rose to the east. Right now the Panthéon was half shrouded in darkness, partially lit up with the morning sun. Ava was waiting for that first warmth to hit her fingers, pressing into the brick.

He held his breath, primed for the second when it happened, feeling a little like he was intruding on her experience. He swallowed. That had never bothered him before. Covert photography to capture the natural simplicity of life, like that first picture of Lauren and the apple, was what he did best. He was all about opportunity.

He clicked another shot, just before the light reached the tips of her fingers and then again, the second it caught her hand.

She moved her fingers, spanning them out like she was trying to catch the sun. He snapped again, feeling an intense energy fill him up.

'Julien!' she called. 'Do you see?'

He dropped his camera down as she turned her head. 'Yes, Ava,' he answered. 'I see it all.'

EIGHTEEN

Notre Dame

There was a text from Debs when Ava checked her phone.

> *I thought I was going to feel better before now but actually I feel a hundred per cent worse. Just pondering about lunch is making me totes queasy. I will definitely feel better by dinner time. Phoned Mum and she's fine. Gary called from 'Toulouse'. I really need access to his Find My iPhone. Would you mind taking a few photographs of Christmassy things or singles in the city things? Or perhaps ask the handsome photographer to take some for me? Xx*

Ridiculously, she was blushing and she shielded her phone screen as if Julien might see. They were sitting on a wall at the very edge of the Seine, the Notre Dame behind them. They had walked around the impressive Gothic cathedral, strolling through the central nave, admiring the high altar and all the sculptures and paintings in between. Ava remembered the last time she had visited there were pickpocket warning signs up at the entrance. This visit though was different, there weren't so many crowds, and the experience was far more pleasurable because Julien didn't seem to feel the need to fill every gap in conversation with chat about the price of real estate. They were just two people enjoying the sights, here together but separately and not feeling the need for anything more.

Ava turned to Julien, saw he was focussing his camera out over the water. She couldn't tell if he was looking at the nearby bridge, or the people tramping through the sludge a little nearer to their position, or a solitary boat making its way up the river.

'Am I holding you up being here today?' Ava blurted out.

He let go of the camera then and it swung down, resting on his chest where the strap had stopped its motion.

'Holding me up?' he queried.

'Do you have somewhere else you need to be?' she asked.

'You are bored with me?' he asked. 'I have yet to convince you of the magic of photography?'

She smiled. 'Not bored and no, you haven't done that quite yet.' She kicked her feet, the backs of her trainers hitting the stone wall. 'It's just Debs is still ill from the local alcohol she had last night and can't make it for lunch.'

'You are hungry?' he asked.

'No... I mean a bit but... I just didn't want to outstay my welcome if there are other things you need to do.' She stopped talking.

'You worry too much, Madonna,' he said, shaking his head. 'It was I who invited *you* remember?'

'I know but I also know the photography is your job and I'm just here—' What was the right word to use for what she was doing in Paris?

'Sightseeing?' he offered.

'Ticking things off my wish list,' she said.

'A wish list,' Julien said, a hint of amusement in his expression.

'What's funny about that?'

'For somebody who does not believe in making things perfect you have a list of wishes to try to ensure your trip is how you need it to be.'

'It's not that exactly,' she countered. And she hadn't actually written a new one yet. God this man was as irritating as he was handsome. If she wasn't completely embalmed in eau de singleton he might just be a little bit intriguing.

'*Non?*' he asked.

'It was Debs' idea. She thinks I need cheering up.' Ava sniffed. 'She thinks finding out my boyfriend has been cheating on me this close to Christmas is going to send me into a meltdown and I might do something really crazy like cut off all my hair and dye it blonde.'

'Ava,' he said, his voice soft, 'this man from England was dating another woman? When he was dating you?'

The way Julien had said it made the infidelity sound like the worst treachery – something to be tortured for in Place Maubert. And it was, she guessed, and at the moment it seemed to be contagious.

She readjusted herself on the wall before answering. 'I'm not sure he was *dating* her as such. Just getting naked with her in the penthouse apartment with views of the docks.' She shrugged. 'He probably gave her the full champagne experience he gave me the first time. Cava, chocolates and John Legend on Spotify.'

She swallowed, looking down towards the dark, blue water, a slight mist coming from it. She didn't feel sad any more, just a little stupid that she had believed the things Leo had told her. *You're so beautiful, Ava. I love you, Ava.* All lies.

She looked up from the river to see Julien shaking his head.

'This man,' he said. 'This *person*, is the very worst kind. To betray both of you is the behaviour of a dog.'

'Yes,' Ava sighed.

'And he is on the telephone to you, here in Paris, asking for another chance!'

'What?'

Julien hated cheats, loathed them with his every atom. Lauren had had a boyfriend called Charles and he had never liked him. He always seemed a little too good to be true. He bought flowers every week, he bought expensive jewellery for no reason at all and he never really could work out what the man had in common with his beautiful, life-loving sister. But, Lauren was happy with Charles and having her happy was all he had ever wanted.

'What did you say?' Ava asked him again.

He swallowed, coming back into the moment. 'I am sorry. I heard you, last night, outside the hotel, on the telephone.'

Ava folded her arms across her chest. 'Was that before or after you started taking photos of me?'

'Somewhere in between?' he offered.

'Don't tell me,' she started. 'My face was the perfect mix of angry and angelic.'

'You knew this? You saw me and posed?' he teased.

She hit him on the arm and he laughed, shifting slightly to lessen the impact.

'Has someone cheated on you?' she asked.

'*Non*,' he said, shaking his head. 'But someone cheated on my sister.'

'Lauren?' Ava asked.

He nodded. 'They were together almost a year and she found out when a hotel called the apartment they shared together, to remind her about a booking Charles had made for that night.' Julien sighed. 'He came home, made up lies and she followed him... you can imagine the rest.'

'Yes,' Ava agreed with a swallow. The following someone around Paris was also hitting a nerve.

'These people, Ava, they have something inside them that is never satisfied,' he told her. 'I cannot speak for someone I do not know, but Charles, he was looking for adoration not love and there is a big difference.' He smiled. 'But what I do know is that everything you said to this man on the telephone is right... what was it? The possibility of possibilities and Camembert.'

She smiled. 'Now you know why I had to have it first thing this morning.'

'Do you think you might like to try something a little different for lunch?' he asked.

'You know a place?'

He nodded. 'I know a place.'

NINETEEN

The Marais – L'As du Fallafel

The bright green exterior of the shop-cum-eatery was the first thing that struck Ava as they approached the building. Some of the paint was peeling and there were posters and notices in the windows of the frontage that could be seen. The part of the frontage that *couldn't* be seen was down to a large queue coming out of the door and a gathering of people to its left, all cramming food into their mouths like they hadn't eaten since the previous December.

'You like falafel?' Julien asked her.

Her stomach seemed to be begging her to answer. 'Who doesn't like falafel?'

'My father,' Julien stated. 'It is far too exotic in his opinion. And, of course, it is not traditionally from France.'

'What is he having at his wedding? A cheese board? Snails and frogs legs?' She put her hands to her mouth. 'Sorry, that sounded really insulting.'

Julien laughed. 'We French can laugh at ourselves, Ava.'

'Sorry,' she answered. 'But I'm sure most Parisian taxi drivers beg to differ.' She blew on her hands and rubbed them together as they joined the queue. 'So what is on the menu for the wedding breakfast on Christmas Eve?'

'I am not sure,' he admitted.

'You haven't been involved in that bit of the planning I'm guessing.'

'No, my step-mother, she has most things under control.' He scratched the back of his neck where the camera strap sat.

'I'm a bit surprised my mother hasn't got remarried,' Ava admitted. 'Not because I think she's the perfect candidate to make someone very happy for the rest of their life, but because she would love a good wedding event. All that opportunity to dress up and show off.'

'Maybe she realises the wedding is not about dressing up and showing off,' Julien suggested.

Ava laughed. 'No, she thinks that is the meaning of life.'

'And how does she stand on the subject of falafel?'

'Well, she's eaten in every corner of the globe in the presence of princes and sheikhs,' Ava answered. 'But only things that are under three hundred calories per portion.'

'Well,' Julien said. 'I cannot promise to this.'

'And now you know another reason why I hated modelling. Never being able to eat what you want when you want.' Ava looked at him. 'Does this queue take long to go down?'

He had purposefully chosen a table near the fire exit and made suggestions on the menu. Now, watching Ava eat, it was yet another photo opportunity he didn't dare capture. She had started making appreciative noises the second the food touched her tongue and her enjoyment was compelling. He had in fact spent more time observing her expression as the falafel, cabbage, roasted aubergine and hot sauce met her taste buds than he had eating his own portion.

'So, I know London is supposed to be the most diverse city in Europe with restaurants from every country there is, but I've never eaten anything quite like this,' Ava said through a mouthful of fried chick peas.

'Better than Camembert?' Julien asked her, a grin on his mouth.

'Let's not go too far,' Ava answered.

He smiled, watching her move her hands from pitta bread to the Israeli beer he had suggested they have. And then it hit him, as he carried on looking at Ava, her bright, white hair unleashed from his hat now they were indoors, chilli sauce speckling her lips, life and light in her eyes: he felt *normal*. And that's when the guilt started to seep slowly into his conscience. He bit into his lunch.

'Do you think you'll do it again?' Ava asked him, eyes wide, concentration on him not her food.

'Do what?'

'Sell a photograph for an extortionate sum of money?' She grinned.

'I do not know. Perhaps,' he mused. 'Perhaps not.'

'It must be hard, not knowing what people want to see,' Ava said. He saw her eyes go from the animated, cosy vibe of the restaurant to outside where the people queuing were shielding their heads from the snow that had started to fall again.

'*Non*,' he replied. 'Despite what you think, I already tell you I do not take photographs all the while wondering what people *want* to see.' He took a sip from his beer bottle. 'But, there are times when I might take a photo of something and know that the majority of people will *not want* to see it.'

He watched Ava prop her head up with her hand, elbow on the table, looking at him with deep interest.

'Like what?' she asked.

He was a fool. He had started this conversation and now he was going to have to get himself out of it. He couldn't tell her the truth. He couldn't say he had gone out after the Paris attacks and taken photo after photo of the devastation as tears rolled down his cheeks. He couldn't tell her that he had photographed a child and his father laying flowers at the base of the apartment block where Lauren had died. Admitting to all that was going to force a conversation he wasn't ready to have about a time of his life that was still so raw.

'The homeless,' he said tentatively. 'Lauren...' He swallowed. 'Behind the department store where she works... there is shelter where they keep empty boxes before they are recycled. On some nights there are as many as twenty people crowded into the space, keeping each other warm, getting out of the cold.' He looked up at Ava. 'People do not want to see that.'

He had done it again. He had spoken about his sister as if she were still here... and it had felt so much better than using the dark, sad, desperate words he had had to use these past months.

Ava nodded, picking up her beer. 'Well, they should see it.'

'*Pourquoi?*'

'Because closing your eyes to reality doesn't make it go away.'

He smiled. That was what Lauren used to say.

'So did you just take photos of the homeless or did you do something to help?'

He shifted in his seat, leaning a little over the table. 'Sometimes when I meet Lauren from work we take them what is left from the patisserie department.' He took a sip of his beer. 'At the beginning they think we are mad, refuse to take anything, then, when we keep coming back, finally they begin to trust us.'

'That's a lovely thing to do.'

'It was Lauren's idea,' he replied.

Ava's phone began to ring from inside her bag, the theme from *CSI Miami* blaring out above the hubbub of the café.

'Sorry,' she apologised to Julien. 'Maybe Debs has recovered. Maybe she can get the Metro over here. She would love this place.' She pulled the phone from her bag and looked at the screen: *Rhoda Rhinestone*.

'Oh, bloody hell,' Ava said, putting the phone on the table and watching it vibrate its way over towards the salt and pepper.

'It is not Debs?' Julien asked.

'No.' She shook her head. What was she going to do? Pick up or let it go to voicemail? Could she bear more texts throughout the day delivering ultimatums?

'It is the man who cheated on you?' Julien guessed.

'No, much worse. Someone I can't shake off no matter how hard I try.' She scooped the phone up and pressed to answer.

'Hello,' she greeted, sounding a lot more buoyant than she felt.

'Ava, this is urgent,' Rhoda spoke. 'You didn't get my message, did you?'

'Which one?'

'What do you mean which one? *The* one. First class to Goa... crab salad... It's perfect – *you'll* be perfect just in time for the Azores gig.'

'Mum, I'm actually in France right now.'

There was silence and Ava looked to Julien who was doing his very best to concentrate on eating his lunch.

'Ava, this is a terrible line.'

'No, Mum, it's not. I'm really in France.'

'But you can't be?'

'Actually it's not far on Eurostar these days.'

'But... why?'

'Debs invited me and I needed a break.'

'But *I* was offering you a break in Goa.'

'I'm going now. I'm in the middle of a rather tasty super falafel meal with quite an interesting Frenchman I met last night.'

'Ava, this is silly—'

'Bye, Mum.' She ended the call and put her phone on the table, a breath rushing from her.

'You are OK?' Julien asked. 'You are certain you would rather be in cold, snowy Paris than on a beach somewhere right now?'

She nodded. 'I'm pretty sure Goa or the Azores doesn't have falafel, or Camembert.'

'But they have sunshine and palm trees,' Julien added.

'Seen one palm tree you've seen them all,' she said with a shrug.

'Unless you are a photographer with a good eye,' Julien said.

'How about instead of palm trees you try to make the Mona Lisa look a bit different?' Ava suggested.

'Well, Madonna, that sounds like another challenge, *non*?'

Ava held up her empty bottle of beer. 'One more beer first?'

TWENTY

The Louvre

Just to the right of the museum there was a band playing Christmas music, all dressed up in sparkling red-and-white uniforms, a conductor waving his arms to keep them in time. A small crowd was watching, their hands around paper cups of coffee. Julien looked to Ava, watching her excitement grow as they walked towards the Pyramide du Louvre, the fountains gushing up cold water into the snowy air around the glass triangular structure at their centre.

'It's like something out of *The Crystal Maze*, Julien!'

As soon as she was far enough in front of him he held his camera up and snapped. She jumped up onto the ledge at the edge of the pool and for a second he thought she might run right into the water. But she stopped, bending to put her fingers in, just like with the pillars of the Panthéon it was as if she wanted to touch and feel, be part of it.

'Julien!' she called. 'What are you waiting for?'

Every time she turned he had to drop the camera and pretend he wasn't photographing her. Perhaps he should ask her permission. She might agree. It wasn't the same as modelling. He wasn't planning on exploiting her but... he *did* know how she felt. She had told him often enough and now, with her mother on the phone, it was even clearer. He slowed his pace. He should stop taking photos of her altogether. Then he wouldn't be conflicted... but her delight in everything, seeing all these places with new eyes... it was an opportunity, like she had said, there was a possibility of possibilities.

'Julien!' Ava called again. 'I'm sorry! I dropped your hat into the water!'

He laughed and carried on towards her.

'This is more like how a museum is supposed to look, not like the crystal dome out there,' Ava said as Julien led the way to an entrance away from the crowds.

The building was a creamy, biscuit colour, all arches and soft lines with dark grey roofs of different shapes – dome, rectangle and another Ava hadn't quite decided about. Above every arch along the frontage was a statue overlooking the Square.

'It is a pyramid,' Julien said. 'Not a dome.'

'It's too modern,' Ava complained. 'It doesn't fit.'

'It is art,' Julien reminded her. 'Not all art has to fit together. Inside the museum you will see all different kinds of pictures.'

'*I* know that, but most people who come here just want to see the Mona Lisa, don't they? It's the most well known.'

'You don't have to know what every one of the exhibits is to enjoy them. That is one of the great beauties of art. What one person finds appealing, another will find—'

'Awful?'

'I was going to say not to their taste.'

'And what is to your taste in the Louvre, Monsieur Fitoussi?'

'I like the temporary exhibitions, the variety of this. Sometimes there are contemporary pieces, sometimes older work,' he said. 'There is a new one every few months.'

'But what's your favourite?'

He smiled. 'I do not know yet. Last time I came here I fell in love with an oil painting of a dog. Before that it was a landscape of lavender fields in pastels. To have a favourite would be to shut out the opportunity to fall in love with something else.'

She shivered at his words. 'I'm a bit cold.'

'Come,' Julien said, taking hold of her hand. 'The entrance isn't far.'

She hesitated, his touch a surprise, his skin warm against hers. He had taken hold of her just like that, without thought, without a hidden agenda, just to connect them. It was nice.

'I'm sorry about your hat,' Ava said through juddering teeth.

'Do not worry, I have others.'

She quickened her pace to match his and ducked her head against the flurrying snow.

'Do you think she's beautiful?' Ava asked, leaning over to her right, hands on her thighs for balance, squinting at the Mona Lisa.

'Do *you* think she is beautiful?'

'I'm asking you.'

'And I am asking you.'

'You first... if you can see properly past the guy with the longest selfie stick in the world.'

'Yes, I think she is beautiful,' he answered.

'Why?'

'Because she is perfect,' Julien replied.

'Perfect?' She squinted again at what she thought was quite an ordinary-looking woman dressed in nothing more than sackcloth.

'Although you say you do not like modelling, you are looking at her with a model's eye,' Julien told her.

'I'm not,' Ava insisted.

'No?' Julien asked. 'You are not thinking... her smile is not wide enough? Or maybe her hair is not helped by Elnett? Or perhaps the clothes she is wearing are not exciting enough?'

'All right,' Ava said, nudging him. 'You had me pegged at Elnett.'

'But, look at it again,' Julien encouraged. 'It is beautiful in its simplicity. No airbrushing, no filter.'

Ava stared at the woman with the long dark hair and half-smile. So her hands might look like they were encased in latex gloves and scarily she had no eyebrows, but there was something about her that drew you into the picture. What was she thinking when she sat to be painted? There was no way she would have known that hundreds of years later people would come from all over the world to gaze at her.

'I used to draw,' Ava said absentmindedly.

'You did?'

'A bit.'

'Landscapes? Portraits?'

'No.' She shook her head. 'Cartoons mainly or caricatures. I used to draw our teachers at school.' She smiled, remembering a pretty good drawing she'd done of Mr Morton.

'And you did not want to follow this up in your career?'

'No, I mean they were just doodles really.'

'But you enjoyed this?'

'Yes, but I don't draw them any more.'

'Why not?

She shrugged. She didn't have an answer for that one.

'There are lots of careers you can have with a talent for drawing,' Julien told her. 'Take Didier. He is a graphic designer.'

'He is?'

Julien nodded. 'But there are other ways. Illustrators for books and work for movies. Designing the sets, creating the storyboards. It is not always about creating a picture to hang on the wall.'

'I never really thought it was an option for me.' She looked at the painting in front of her. A memory spiked at her. She had spent every spare minute of her sixteen-year-old life working on art – her GCSE coursework. Lessons, lunch breaks, long into the night, wanting it to be perfect. Wanting to show her teacher, the examiners, the whole world that she was something other than her mother's protégé. She had thought if everyone saw... if her *mother* saw... that there was another career path open for her, something she truly enjoyed, something she was completely passionate about, that things would change. But, despite getting an A*, despite her teacher recommending her for an art foundation course, there was only one option open. Doing what Rhoda told her to do. These last few years she'd managed to avoid modelling, but she hadn't really put her foot down. She'd let her mother think she'd go back to it eventually and maybe by doing so she'd left herself half-believing it too. Even though she didn't want it – wasn't good enough anyway – she'd allowed it to stop her from thinking about what she really *did* want.

'She is another Madonna,' Julien commented as Ava finally stepped back.

'What?'

'Mona,' he said. 'It is a shortening of Madonna in Italian.'

'Is it?' Ava asked. 'You know what my mother would say? "This one is missing a little lipstick and a conical bra."'

'And in my opinion she is all the better for that.'

Ava nodded. 'I agree completely.'

TWENTY-ONE

Hotel Agincourt

After the Mona Lisa they had looked at a temporary exhibition by Hubert Robert. According to the information and Julien, the artist was best known for his landscapes and picturesque depictions of ruins. Ava had spent as much time watching Julien looking at the paintings as she had observing them herself. She liked the way he stood in front of them, took a deep breath and then stilled as if he was standing in front of a person, waiting for them to start a conversation. It was like he was giving them space to breathe, to tell him their story. There weren't many times in her life when she had been given space to breathe. Instead of always worrying about standing up straight and keeping her neckline fluid perhaps she should have thought about standing up for herself and discovering what she wanted from life.

Now, as it neared five p.m. they had arrived back at Ava's hotel, the streets busy as people navigated the city on their way home from work. It was continuing to snow and she was still cold, her Converse damp as she stamped her feet into the growing layer of white on the pavement. Over the beeps of taxis and mopeds the sound of carol singers filled the crisp air. The fragrance of peppermint, candy and fir cones emanated from the fabric of every building.

She smiled at Julien. 'Thank you for today,' Ava said. 'It was fun.'

'Yes.' He nodded. 'It was fun.'

'Did you get some good photographs?' she asked. 'Maybe one to sell for the price of a small country?'

He swallowed. 'Maybe. Who knows what people will like this season?' He smiled. 'It is a bit like fashion, no?'

'Madonna Lisa has done all right for herself,' she answered.

A silence descended and Ava didn't know what to do. What was protocol for saying goodbye to someone you hadn't known yesterday but had spent the whole day sharing perfect moments with? Someone you might not necessarily see ever again? Was it two kisses on the cheek in France or one? His eyes were on her. He didn't have hat hair. Leo would never have even considered wearing a hat no matter how cold the air. She shuddered. Why was she thinking about Leo?

'I should let you go in out of the cold,' Julien said.

'Yes, I should do that,' she said. 'Try and dry my shoes out before Debs takes me clubbing again.' She took a hand from the pocket of her coat and was about to hold it out to him when he leant forward and kissed first one cheek and then the other. Each touch warmed her entire face and she was blushing by the time he stepped back.

'À *bientôt*, Madonna.'

'À *bientôt*, Julien.'

She swallowed. *She didn't want him to go*. How ridiculous was that? Of course he had to go. They were just two people who had sparred over dinner and spent the day sightseeing because Debs was too hungover to do anything with her.

'Goodbye,' he said, waving a hand and smiling.

'Goodbye,' she repeated, watching him turn. He was walking away now and that's what casual acquaintances did.

His dark coat and his even darker hair were getting speckled with snow as he moved down the street against a backdrop of flashing gold and crimson bulbs on the buildings and flickering headlights on the street. Today had been the best day she'd had in so long... Paris, France, Camembert, falafels, the Mona Lisa... and someone genuinely nice to share it all with.

'Julien!' She shouted above the street sounds, moving forward a few steps and almost colliding with someone dressed as a fairy. Had he heard her? She looked down the road, still chasing his form with her gaze. He turned around and she took that as her cue to catch up with him, muttering apologies as she went against the flow of walkers.

She was out of breath by the time she stopped in front of him. 'Sorry… you probably have loads of better things to do but... I was just wondering… if you might like to do this again.' Her teeth started to chatter. 'If it's a no, just say it quick before I turn into an ice sculpture.'

'You want to see more sights?' Julien inquired.

She thought about it for a second and then answered. 'No, I actually just want to watch you take photographs. I need more convincing of this magic you talk about.'

He nodded, a smile on his lips. 'The problem with magic, Madonna, is that it has to be believed in before it lets itself be seen.'

'Who are you, Mr Fitoussi? Walt Disney?'

'The most famous cartoonist of all, no?'

She blushed then watched as he smiled, unable to stop herself from looking back into those raisin-coloured eyes.

'Tomorrow?' she questioned.

'You do not have places to go with Debs?'

She did. In the morning. Stalking Francine and hoping to God she didn't see Gary.

'Sorry, you're busy aren't you? And I've been an interruption rather than a help and you're far too polite to say anything.'

He smiled, shaking his head. 'No, not at all. I am meeting someone in the morning so...'

'Lauren?' Ava asked.

He nodded. 'But... um... we could... meet maybe after lunch?'

'Great!' Ava said, clapping her cold hands together.

'But you most promise me one thing, Ava,' Julien said.

'What?'

He pointed at her feet. 'Much better shoes and a hat.' He reached out and touched her hair, gently brushing a few snowflakes from the blonde spikes. Her breath caught in her chest and she dropped her eyes from his, taking a step back.

'Tomorrow, then? Say two o'clock? Where?' she asked.

'The Sacré-Coeur,' he suggested. 'You will like it there. There are real artists not photographer wannabes.'

She waved a hand. 'À *bientôt*, Julien.'

'À *bientôt*, Madonna.'

TWENTY-TWO

Ava's fingers were still numb as she fumbled with the key card. She was just about to try for the third time to get it into the slot when the door was whisked open and there was Debs, full make-up on her face, long purple and green bauble earrings in her ears and just a Fair Isle jumper covering the rest of her.

'Please tell me that isn't a dress,' Ava said, stepping into the room. 'It's about minus four degrees outside. If it *is* a dress you're definitely going to need seventy-denier tights.'

'It isn't a dress, silly, I'm just starting to get ready for dinner. Then we're going to an event. I did text you.'

'I didn't get it.'

As Ava continued into the room her eyes were drawn to sparkling, foil garlands that now hung all around their room. There was a miniature Christmas tree on the desk and a furry snowman. It was like a team of Christmas window dressers had been in and arranged everything like a display at Selfridges.

'What's happened?' Ava asked, plumping down on the bed and taking her bag off her shoulder.

'Do you like it? I felt better this afternoon so I went for a little mooch around and got the decorations. It makes the room so much cosier, doesn't it?'

'If you like Christmas kitsch.'

'And I totes do,' Debs said, laughing.

'You didn't go anywhere near Gary's Paris office did you?'

'No.'

'And you didn't phone up the Paris office and pretend you were someone who needed access to this Francine's diary, did you?'

'Well...' Debs began, looking a little sheepish.

'Tell me you didn't!'

'I didn't but... Mum called and she'd just spoken to Gary in "Toulouse" so I phoned the Toulouse office...'

'Oh, Debs...'

'What? I had to and—' Debs stopped, catching a sob in her throat.

'Oh, Debs, what is it?' Ava asked, standing up and moving close to Debs, taking hold of her hands.

'He wasn't there.'

'He wasn't there?' Now she was worried. Perhaps Debs was right about all this. Her stomach started needling her, the French cheese and falafel moving around like they were being mixed by a KitchenAid. She didn't want this to happen to her friend again. And Sue. Poor, lovely, surrogate mother, Sue.

'They said he was in a meeting,' Debs said, wiping her eyes with the sleeve of her jumper.

The mixing in her stomach abated slightly. 'He was in a meeting?' Ava clarified. 'Well, that's good, isn't it? Because that means he's in Toulouse.' Ava looked at Debs. 'Doesn't it?'

'No, don't be stupid. They're obviously lying for him. I rang seconds, *seconds*, after Mum put the phone down to me. You don't just put the phone down to your wife and leap into a boardroom.'

'I know you're worrying, Debs, and I'm worrying too, but I really don't think the employees of Cosmos Protection would be covering Gary's tracks if he was having an affair. I really don't,' she said, squeezing Debs' hands.

Debs looked at her, wide-eyed and still teary. 'You really don't?'

'I really don't,' Ava said again. 'I really think he was in a meeting.'

'I'm totes going mad, aren't I? It's just tomorrow feels so far away and I have these articles to fret about. I'm practically chewing my hair out with the worry and the waiting.'

'You have to stop worrying,' Ava said, pulling her into a hug.

'I know.'

'Because if you don't stop worrying you're not going to be able to focus on your writing.'

'I know,' Debs said, sniffing and stepping back from Ava's embrace.

Ava pulled her phone from her pocket to check her messages. *Leo.*

Against her better judgement she opened the text. There was no writing again, just another photo. Her, at the top of the Eiffel Tower, with him, smiling for a selfie like two people in love. No hat. Well, it had been spring. She looked happy. He looked happy. She had been happy, for a time. But how would she ever know if anything he had felt was genuine when he had been able to dump her so easily?

'You're not reading *my* text,' Debs said, moving over to Ava. 'It wouldn't make you look like that. Is it Leo? Her hands went to her mouth.

Ava shrugged. 'Nothing I can't handle.'

'You don't have to handle it on your own though, Ava. I'm here,' Debs reminded.

'I know, but you've got all this stuff going on. You don't need me adding to it.'

'You let me be the judge of that. I'm quite happy to report some of his posts on Facebook or phone up and complain about his poor customer service or anything you need me to do to get him back for being an utter arse.'

'You don't need to do that,' Ava said softly, smiling at her friend. 'But thank you. I'll bear those offers in mind if anyone crosses me in the future.'

'Good,' Debs answered, reaching for her compact mirror and widening her eyes at her reflection as if looking for imperfections. She snapped it closed again and looked directly at Ava.

'But now I want to hear all about your day with the charismatic cameraman.'

Heat hit Ava's cheeks and she looked away, focussing on her damp and grubby Converse. She bent down and started to unlace them.

'Ooh, silence and not making eye contact. This is going to be good,' Debs said, clapping her hands together. 'Did you do the getting drunk bit or was he the random man you decided to pucker-up with?'

Ava sighed and sat up. 'Those were two items from my old wish list. The one you got me to rip into bits because it was juvenile,' she reminded. She still had the pieces in her coat pocket.

'That isn't a thorough enough answer,' Debs said in a sing-song voice.

Her eyes went to her cold hands and she remembered holding the stone pillars of the Panthéon, dipping her fingers into the water outside the Louvre and wrangling with falafel. All to the backdrop of Advent in Paris and with Julien... smart, funny, intriguing Julien who seemed to understand her perfectly when no one else in her life had the first clue.

'We had a nice time,' Ava said eventually. *Nice* didn't cover it at all but it was all she had. Tiredness was creeping in now after a late night/early morning.

'You weren't mean to him again, were you?' Debs asked. 'Cameramen aren't a brainwashed tribe, you know, they're all individuals.'

Ava pulled at her shoes, revealing one soggy sock after another. 'I was very polite all day.'

'Good,' Debs said with a contented sigh as she stood up and headed for the wardrobe. 'Because I need you both tonight.'

'What?' She ripped her socks off and watched water slowly drip from the toes.

Debs tutted. 'You still haven't read my text, have you?'

'Just tell me, Debs, you're right next to me...' She blinked and blinked again. 'Holding something that looks like clothing, but also something you might wrap a Christmas turkey in prior to banging it in the oven.' The micro-mini in tinfoil silver was going to blind her if it caught the light.

'Do you like it?' Debs asked. 'I bought it today in a little vintage boutique. It's genuine 1970s.'

'I think I've seen someone wearing it on *Top of the Pops 2*, but I like it. Now tell me about tonight!'

'Well, I've booked a table for you and I to have dinner at this darling little bistro near Pont Neuf I saw earlier and then we're meeting Didier and hopefully your Julien and—'

'He isn't *my* Julien. I hardly know him, Debs.' She huffed a sigh. She was heavily doused in man repellent. She had no interest in anyone being hers or her being anybody's.

'Fine, but tonight we will be getting to know them a little better... and everyone else at the party,' Debs carried on.

'Party?' Now she was a little bit scared.

Debs clapped her hands together. 'I found it online almost straightaway, the minute I typed "single in Paris" into Google.'

Ava swallowed. This wasn't sounding good. This was sounding like something she definitely didn't want to have any part in. She was praying it just involved market research or dressing up as a Babybel.

'We're going speed dating!' Debs exclaimed, shaking the foil skirt like it was accompaniment.

'No,' Ava said, her head shaking like someone had delivered news of a death. 'No, Debs, we're not.' She stood up on her freezing feet and looked for somewhere to hang her soaking socks.

'I know what you're thinking...' Debs started.

'No, you really don't.'

'You're thinking it's going to be all cheesy and full of totes desperado middle-aged divorcees looking for a second chance at love and—'

'No, that didn't cross my mind.' Ava hung her socks over the radiator.

'Well, it isn't like that at all. It's very classy,' Debs continued. 'It's all done online through an app to begin with and then they have an actual meet-and-greet once every two weeks. I watched a video of last fortnight's party and it looked so much fun. There wasn't any of this ringing bells malarkey or moving on to the next person in five minutes. You pick a name... I thought I might be Florence. You could be—'

'Nightingale?'

'Don't be silly!'

'And the Machine?'

'Ava...'

'I won't be choosing a name because I'm not going. I don't want to be labelled as a single looking for love, because I'm not.'

'It's just for my article,' Debs said. 'That's why I asked Didier and for him to ask Julien, so I can get a male point of view too.'

'That's fine, three people's points of view is plenty, you don't need mine.' She walked into the bathroom and closed the door behind her, shutting her eyes and leaning against the wood. Why was Leo still texting her? What was it with Christmas and Paris and her best friend? Why couldn't Debs be writing an article on wine or *saucisson*? She wouldn't mind researching either of those. Just not love and dating. Not now.

'Ava,' Debs called, knocking gently on the door. 'I'm sorry. It was silly of me to suggest it. I should have known better and I shouldn't have been so scathing about Leo. You loved him, didn't you? And he's been such a bastard.' There was an intake of breath. 'And if I find out Gary has been just the same then...'

Ava shook her head. She needed to stop letting that excuse for a man... that dog... creep into her psyche with old photos in messages.

'Well, let's just say dating is the very last thing I really want to be researching but... I'm a little bit desperate.'

Ava opened her eyes and took a breath. A dating party would be easy when she had no designs on getting a date. She could just drink and watch and feel sorry for anyone who believed true love was going to come from a fake name and a few minutes of conversation.

'But that's totes OK, I'll go on my own,' Debs said.

'No,' Ava said. She whipped open the door and faced her friend. 'No, you won't. I'll come,' she said decisively. 'And I'll talk to any desperate middle-aged man you push my way in the name of research.'

Debs smiled. '*Formidable!*'

TWENTY-THREE

Bettina's, Rue De Turbigo

The moment Julien walked into the bar he knew this wasn't the work thing Didier had sold it to him as. There were tens of people milling around a group of women wearing matching T-shirts and carrying clipboards. There was more than the usual pre-Christmas décor of tree and garlands, there were posters he couldn't quite read from this distance and pink straws in everyone's drinks.

'A drink, my friend!' Didier said, slapping him on the back and leading the way to the bar.

'Didier, why are we here?' Julien asked, following his friend.

'I told you,' Didier said, not elaborating further.

'And now I do not believe you.'

Didier smiled, pulling a cigarette from the packet in his hand with his teeth before replying. 'If I tell you, you would not come.'

He couldn't deny that. He was tired. After months of not doing anything, an early start and a day touring the city had been as exhausting as it had been exhilarating. He strained his eyes to look at the poster.

'Dating?!' he exclaimed. 'Didier, dating?!'

'You say the word like you are frightened of it.'

'What are we doing here, Didier? I am not looking for a date.'

'And I still do not know why.'

'Because...' he began.

'Because?' Didier asked, eyes fixed on him and waiting for a reply.

'Because... I am not looking for a date.'

'It has been a year since Monique.'

Julien said nothing, stood still and hoped Didier would get them both a drink. He knew how long it had been. He had ended the relationship a few weeks after Lauren's death. Monique said she wanted to be there for him, but in other ways it was apparent that she did not. She wanted to talk and he *didn't* want to talk and when he'd undressed at night she'd turned away from the scar he'd been left with. There was too much compromise needed on both their parts and neither of them could, or wanted, to do it.

'It is time you embrace things again, Julien.' Didier winked. 'Embrace women.'

'*You* are looking for a date?' he quickly asked Didier.

'I am always looking for a date,' he said, smiling.

'I thought that you and Debs might be...'

Didier smiled. 'I thought you and Ava might be...' He left the sentence open-ended and waggled his eyebrows.

Julien shook his head.

'Why not?' Didier inquired. 'Did you not spend the day with her? She is very nice, no? If not a little challenging.'

'She is...' Julien admitted. He couldn't find an appropriate word but he was pretty sure he could create an entire exhibition of photographs on the colour of her eyes alone.

'Then?'

'She is not looking for a relationship,' Julien said matter-of-factly. 'And neither am I.' He sighed. 'And two people can be friends without anything else getting in between them.'

'Like hot, hard body parts?' Didier worked a hand around and down his chest, mouth open, posing like an actor in a porn film.

Julien thumped his arm. 'Just get the beer.'

'You are staying, then?' Didier concluded.

'Only to watch you make an idiot of yourself.'

'And to help Debs,' Didier stated.

'What?'

'That is why we are here, my friend. We are the male singles in the city. Debs and Ava will be here any minute.'

He suddenly wished he had changed his clothes.

'Ow! Stop rushing me!' Ava said, falling off the boots she was wearing and struggling to keep her balance. Having nothing else suitable for her feet in her case and with her Converse drying out under the heater in the hotel room she was wearing a pair of Debs' boots. They were plain black knee-length suede and a size too big. Even with three pairs of socks on – she had taken Julien's lead on that – she was having a hard time navigating the Paris cobbles slick with snow. Plus the only thing she had that went with the boots was a black cotton dress that was far more summer than winter wardrobe. She was thinking about staying in her coat even when they got indoors.

'It's very busy outside,' Debs said, looking at the crowded pavement tables, people wrapped up against the weather drinking their beer and wine under a bright red awning, fairy lights along its edge. 'And it looks busy inside too.'

'Great,' Ava said sarcastically, putting one foot gingerly in front of the other. 'I mean, yay! Brilliant for your research,' she said with more feeling. 'Lots more eligible men to benefit from my singular charm.'

'You are going to try, Ava, aren't you?' Debs asked.

Was that worry she saw in her usually unflappable friend's expression?

'Yes, of course,' she said. 'I told you I would.'

'Good,' Debs said.

Ava didn't miss the shift in tone. Something was afoot here and it had nothing to do will her ill-fitting boots.

'What's wrong, Debs? Is there something else you're not telling me?'

'Of course there isn't, silly,' Debs said, normal service resuming.

'Out with it,' Ava said, stamping the boot into the snow and putting her hands on her hips.

'We should get inside,' Debs deflected. 'It's totes cold.'

'I'll stamp harder if you don't tell me. Might even break the heel of this no doubt expensive boot.'

A panicked look coated Debs' face. 'There's another writer,' she said in little more than a whisper.

'What?'

'I've always been the go-to girl for lifestyle, travel, fashion, the one everyone calls first, the one in demand.' Debs put her hand over her cherry-red lips and stifled a sob.

'God, Debs, what's going on?' Ava asked. 'Tell me!'

'There's someone else who's getting the best pieces. Her name's Trudy. I mean, what sort of a name is Trudy? Is it even a real name,' Debs asked, almost hysterical. 'She's gazumping me... for everything. She's coming up with these new ideas and totes exciting takes and different angles and people have stopped calling me, they're calling *Trudy*.'

Ava reached out and drew Debs into her embrace, Father Christmas earrings, hair infused with glitter spray, the Fair Isle jumper and that Bacofoil skirt. 'But the article on Christmas markets and singles in Paris. The magazine you're writing them for wants you.'

Debs sniffed. 'No they don't. I've not been commissioned to write anything.'

'What?'

'I haven't written something somebody wanted for months. I've been trying to come up with new ideas like this Trudy woman, but no one's bought anything.'

'But the trip and the hotel. I thought...'

'I'm hoping to email a piece on the markets to a friend at Loveahappyending Lifestyle and she's going to try and get it into their Christmas edition, but that won't pay next month's rent.' Debs sighed. 'And the singles and hens thing... if I can manage to get photos without Christmas decorations in I was going to pitch it to *Diversity* for their summer edition.' She sniffed. 'I could really do with Sarah Jessica Parker and the gang coming back on Netflix or something.'

Ava patted her friend's back before holding her a little way away and making her look at her.

Debs carried on. 'And then there's all this stuff with Gary and my mum. It seemed to come at the right time... well, not at the right time but... I decided to come here and check up on him and I thought I could kill two birds with one stone, make something out of these themes and hopefully keep a roof over my head... and maybe my mum's head, too... because if Gary is playing away then I don't know what's going to happen with their house.'

'Right, stop,' Ava ordered. 'Stop and listen to me. You have to put your mum and Gary out of your mind for tonight. Focus on this. Focus on the fact that this Trudy has nothing on you. I mean where was she when you were telling the world that they were all going to be wearing harem pants?'

'That *was* inspired,' Debs said, a twitch of a smile on her lips.

'Exactly,' Ava said. 'And so is the singles in the city idea. And we're going to make it work.'

'Do you really think so?' Debs asked, poking at the corner of her eye like she was worried her make-up might run.

'Yes, I do and I'm going to give it my all,' Ava said, straightening her form as if she was ready to do battle. 'Even if every eligible man here looks like Napoleon Bonaparte.'

Debs took a deep breath and nodded her head.

'Come on,' Ava encouraged. 'It just so happens I know a photographer who is going to adore Photoshopping out Christmas décor.'

TWENTY-FOUR

Ava had to admit the bar was packed and everyone seemed to be having a good time, including her. It was the ultimate chance to people-watch without anyone worried you were watching them. Everyone here *wanted* to be observed... and to have their fake name written down on a postcard covered in love hearts.

She watched Julien at work. His camera around his neck, his face a picture of concentration, dark hair jutting a little over his forehead as he snapped another shot. When she had asked him to take photos of the event for Debs' article he had been only too happy to oblige. She was sure he had seen it as an 'out' from having to take part in the dating games until Debs had thrust a postcard in his hand and reminded him of the schedule.

'*Bonsoir!*'

Ava turned from where she had been putting the drinks for their party onto a tray and faced the woman who had spoken. She was dressed immaculately in a dark-grey trouser suit, a bright-red silk blouse, long dark hair that reached past her shoulders.

'Hello,' Ava greeted with a smile.

'Ah, you are English,' the woman announced, still smiling.

'Yes, sorry, my French isn't very good either.'

'But your hair is very striking,' the woman said. She shot her hand out. 'I am Caroline.'

'Hello,' Ava said, taking the woman's hand. 'I'm Ava.'

'Ava,' Caroline said. 'Such a beautiful name.'

Ava smiled, her hand still encased in the woman's palm. She inched it back as politely as she could until the woman eventually had to release it.

'So,' Ava said. 'You are a member of this group. On the app?'

'Yes,' Caroline answered, her eyes not leaving Ava. 'And you?'

Ava shook her head. 'No, I'm here to help my friend.'

'To find her a date?'

'Something like that,' Ava said, not committing.

'And you, Ava,' Caroline began, 'you are looking for a date?'

Ava shook her head. 'No,' she said determinedly. 'No… not at the moment.'

'You are just out of a relationship?' Caroline asked, leaning a little closer, her hand on the bar.

'It's complicated.' She sniffed. It wasn't complicated but she wasn't about to share the crap end to her relationship at a dating event. 'Men, eh?' she added, forcing a laugh.

'Perhaps that is where you are going wrong,' Caroline said, her hand resting on top of Ava's.

'Oh,' Ava said, her eyes going to Caroline's hand and then up to her eyes. She smiled then gently moved her hand away, reaching for her beer bottle. 'I'm sorry, but I'm straight. Not into men at the moment but definitely going to be back into them in the future… if I can find one that isn't a liar or a cheat.'

'You are sure?' Caroline asked, a playful smile on her lips.

'Yes,' Ava said. 'Sorry, I know I might be rocking the *Ellen* look at the moment but I'm definitely on the *coq au vin* side of the fence.'

Caroline nodded and raised her glass of wine to her. 'Such a shame.'

'But good luck,' Ava said. 'Plenty of other lovely ladies here tonight… not that *I'm* looking… in that way.' She took a swig of her beer as Caroline walked along the bar to another group.

'Having fun?'

Ava almost dropped the beer at the sound of Julien's voice close to her.

'I got you a drink,' she said, passing a bottle to him. 'Just before I got propositioned by a lovely lady called Caroline.'

Julien smiled. 'Didier has been speaking to a man called Horatio for twenty minutes now.'

'And I now realise I have lesbian hair.'

Julien laughed. 'There is no such thing.'

'Oh there is.'

'Everybody is different, Ava. Because someone looks a certain way you assume them to *be* a certain way?'

'No, but... OK, yes, maybe, sometimes. That's kind of what I'm used to.'

'Shame on you,' he said, sitting up on a bar stool.

'Help me get up on there,' Ava said, holding her arm out to him and setting one foot on the metal footrest. Using Julien to lean on she sprung up onto the stool next to him.

'I have taken a lot of photographs,' he said. 'I focussed on the interaction between the guests, not the Christmas tree or the garlands.'

'Thank you,' Ava said. 'This article means a lot to Debs.'

'And Debs means a lot to you,' Julien said.

'Yes, she does.'

Julien was glad Ava hadn't asked to see any of the photographs he'd taken, because as well as getting the partying people he had got quite a few of her. It wasn't just her heart-shaped face or the way she held herself – shoulders straight as if she was eye to eye with the world and making no excuses – it was something indefinable, an essence, something uniquely just *her*.

'So, Madonna, how is your card?' he asked, indicating the dating postcard they had all been given.

'Madonna isn't my dating name,' Ava said with a grin.

'No?'

'No,' she said. 'I'm Jacqueline. I thought it sounded a bit French. What are you?' She grabbed the card from his hand. She scoffed. 'Pascal!' She laughed. 'That's so bad.'

'What is bad about it, *Jacqueline*?' he asked.

'You don't look anything like a Pascal.'

'No? What then do I look like?' he asked, eyes on her.

'A Julien of course.'

'Thank you, Madonna... I think.' He watched her smile.

'So, have you marked your card at all?'

He saw her drop her eyes to the dating card and he snatched it up quickly, then held it above his head, high and out of reach. 'I believe these are supposed to be confidential.'

'Come on, I thought we were friends.' Ava tried to stand on the footrest of the stool and reach up higher. He laughed as she flailed her arms around like a desperate, unbalanced tightrope walker.

'You will fall,' he warned her as he held the card higher.

Ava plumped back down, a frown on her face. 'I don't know why it has to be secret.'

'You have marked yours?' Julien asked.

'I might have,' Ava replied. She folded her arms across her chest.

'With men or women?' he teased.

'Very funny.'

He brought the card back down then and held it out to her. 'I think you might have been right about Pascal.'

Ava looked up at him. 'You haven't written anything.'

'I *have* been taking photographs.'

'I know, but we ought to try for the sake of Debs' article.'

'We could... just talk to each other,' he suggested.

'I'm not sure that's going to count,' Ava told him.

'The purpose of the article is to capture the dating scene in Paris, non?' That's what Didier had explained eventually.

'Yes.'

'Then here we are,' Julien said. 'Two single people in the middle of the dating scene.'

'Not looking for a date,' Ava added.

'Oh, Madonna...'

'Jacqueline.'

'Where is your love of role play?' he asked, smiling.

Ava was on her second bottle of beer and being at a singles night in Paris was starting to feel a little less than bizarre. The fairy lights and Santa Claus paper coasters on every table were also grating less and she had Julien as company, not someone totally new and desperate for love.

They had settled at a table for two halfway down the room, a heart-shaped balloon on a stick as the centrepiece. She leant forward a little in her chair and spoke over the piped music playing love songs from the Eighties. 'Favourite pop band?'

Julien shook his head. 'You have asked me about films and breakfast cereals and now you ask me about pop music?'

'Well,' Ava started, 'These are things I would ask if I was looking for a date.' She grinned. 'Remember this is all for Debs.' She hitched her head backwards. 'My best friend who is currently practising her chat-up lines on someone dressed as The Grinch.'

Julien laughed. 'I don't know,' he replied. 'I do not believe in having favourites. I hear something, I like it, I watch something, I enjoy it.' He smiled. 'I do not feel I then have to collect every song from this band or watch every film the lead actor has been in.'

'What is wrong with you?' Ava exclaimed. 'No wonder you're single. Your previous girlfriends must have found you intensely annoying.'

'And your boyfriends? They all answer these questions?'

'The good ones did.'

Julien nodded, sitting back in his chair. 'In that case...'

Ava leaned forward again. 'Yes?'

'I like Coldplay,' he admitted.

Ava nodded and tightened her hold on her beer, her stomach spiking a little as she digested the information. He said he'd liked some French films she hadn't heard of, but then he'd mentioned *X-Men*... and chocolate cornflakes... and now Coldplay. If this was real, if she was looking for love, he'd be scoring high on compatibility. And the eyes were getting more Cadbury's by the second. Perhaps she wouldn't have a third beer. She put her bottle back down on the table.

'There is something wrong with Coldplay?' Julien asked.

She shook her head. 'No, of course not. Chris Martin is a song-writing genius.'

'You are a fan?'

'I might have everything they ever made on Spotify,' she admitted.

He smiled then. 'And what about *your* favourite film?'

'*Taken*, obviously. Closely followed by *Taken 2*.'

'Ah, a film set in Paris,' Julien remarked.

'The first time I saw it I was on a flight to New York with my mother. It scared her to death. She had the concierge at the hotel on the phone every time she saw someone she deemed looked like a kidnapper.'

He laughed. 'I think I would like to meet your mother.'

Ava shook her head. 'No, you really wouldn't.' She took a breath.

'So if you liked to draw at college, why did you not look further into this?'

She sighed. 'I told you. I never dared to think I could do anything like that. My mother had her plans and I just did whatever I could for a quiet life. When her and dad were rowing all the time, all I wanted to do was anything to make things... less fraught.'

'But now? You have time to make your own choices.'

She nodded. 'Except now I have the choice it's all a bit overwhelming. I mean, where do I start?' She looked around her, taking in the people drinking, laughing, getting on with their lives, looking for romance, all seeming to have everything pegged.

'It takes just that first brushstroke,' Julien said softly. 'Like with the Mona Lisa.'

Ava nodded. 'I know. But for me it's all about the pens. I have a favourite brand.' She smiled. 'I'm a Bic girl. I always sketched in Bic blue, nothing else did it for me. I drew my friends and the teachers when I was supposed to be studying... deforestation or... World War I... and I was good at it.' She sighed. 'But when school finished, even though I got that A* for art, my mum had lined up assignments for the summer and that was it. No more pens. No more drawing. What was the point?'

He smiled. 'The point is I believe you can be whatever you want to be.'

'What about you, Julien? Not tempted to go back to the financial district?'

'No,' he said. 'I'm finding there is even more to discover about photography than I thought.' He smiled. 'Another drink?'

'Just one more,' she answered, then whispered, 'And I'd avoid the man wearing red velvet. He's had at least five glasses of wine and he's been looking at you intently for the past twenty minutes.'

'I will take my chances,' Julien said rising from his seat.

Ava smiled, watching him make his way to the bar. The nicely fitting jeans he had on earlier were still nicely fitting, as was the white shirt he was wearing with them. There was no doubt, the French certainly did style better than anyone else.

'How is it going?'

Debs dropped her body into Julien's chair and looked across at Ava.

'Good,' Ava said. 'Yes, lots of research being done like I promised, and Julien's taken some photos.'

'Have you spoken to anyone else apart from Mr Kodak?'

'Yes,' Ava said immediately. 'I've spoken to a rather nice lesbian called Caroline. And if I was that way inclined I would definitely have given her my number. She was very Ginnifer Goodwin.'

'Didier is doing sterling work,' Debs said, looking across the room. 'And he's told me about a Christmas market we must go to. Apparently it's *the* place to get all things Noël in Paris. But, Ava, it will be your duty to help me write about it rather than purchase everything in it.'

'Really? The last time it was my job to stop you buying things, I had to handcuff your wrists to your bag... the really deep one you couldn't get your purse out of.'

'I gave that one to charity... by the way, it's ten minutes until the half hour chatathon.'

'That sounds like speed dating by a different name, Debs.'

'Think article. My name on a big feature in *Diversity*. Because you totes love me.'

'Fine, but I'm expecting lunch at this French market.'

'It's a pact.'

TWENTY-FIVE

Outside Bettina's

The streets were quiet when they eventually left the dwindling singles scene in Bettina's. Having had one beer too many Ava was even more unsteady on her feet. She linked arms with Debs and leant her head on her shoulder, eyes closing.

'Oh no you don't,' Debs said, shifting so that Ava had to raise her head. 'I need you fully alert for tomorrow morning.'

'Oh yes,' Ava said, widening her eyes and trying hard to stifle a yawn. 'Our stealth mission.'

'It isn't funny,' Debs reminded.

Ava tried to force the fug of alcohol away and turned to face her friend. 'I know. I'm sorry. I wasn't thinking.'

Debs took a breath, pulling her coat a little closer. 'And I'm oversensitive. What with Mum and Gary and this bloody Trudy...'

'So I will call a taxi? To Showcase?' Didier asked, arriving at their side, Julien in tow.

'No,' Ava and Debs said together.

'Sorry,' Debs said. 'That was a little bit rude. What I should have said was, thank you so much for coming tonight and helping me with my articles.'

'You are welcome,' Didier answered with a bow. 'We shall escort you back to your hotel, yes?'

'No, that's OK,' Debs said. 'We can get the Metro.'

'I think we should go too, Didier,' Julien agreed. 'We all have things to do tomorrow... like work.'

'My hours are flexible,' Didier answered. 'Like my dancing limbs.' He proceeded to elongate his leg like he was Louie Spence.

'Well, Debs and I have to be up early to...' Ava saw Debs' expression issue a warning, '...check out the Christmas markets and...' – she looked to Julien – 'you're meeting your sister.'

Julien felt the blood drain from his face. This was what happened when you spoke about someone in the present tense and didn't make the situation clear. He should have said something earlier, when Ava had just assumed that was who he was meeting up with. Instead he had failed to contradict her. But how could he say anything now? In front of Didier and Debs? And what was Ava going to think of him? Spending all day and all evening with her, talking about Lauren like she still lived in her apartment only a few streets away.

'You are meeting who?' Didier asked.

'We should go,' Julien said, taking Didier's arm. 'I do not believe that Didier's working hours are quite as flexible as his limbs.' He quickly waved a hand, ushering his friend away from the women. 'À *bientôt*, Debs. À *bientôt*, Ava.'

'What is going on, Julien?' Didier asked as they moved away. He was fighting for his arm, attempting to relieve it from Julien's grip.

'Nothing. Come on, we will share a taxi.' He increased his pace down the street, facing the stream of snow flashing through the night.

'Ava said you were meeting your sister tomorrow,' Didier repeated.

On instinct Julien looked behind them, saw the two women heading in the opposite direction, arms intertwined. 'Sshh.'

'Julien,' Didier began tentatively, 'Lauren is dead.'

Julien stopped walking, closed his eyes for a moment, then opened them again, setting them on his friend. 'I know,' he whispered.

'Then who are you meeting tomorrow?'

'My father,' he breathed. 'It isn't like you think.'

'I do not know what it could be like.' Didier folded his arms across his chest.

'I told Ava about Lauren. Talked to her about the apple juice photograph, the great times we had, her job, Charles... all the memories I have... except I didn't actually tell her she wasn't here any more.'

Julien heard the air leave Didier's nostrils. 'Julien...'

'I know. I should have told her, but everything we talked about had nothing to do with death and everything to do with the happy life she had. I don't know.' He shook his head. 'It didn't seem right to mention that.'

'So how did you go from talking about the good times, to Ava thinking you are meeting Lauren tomorrow?'

He sighed again. 'I told Ava I was meeting someone and she just assumed it was Lauren and... before I could say anything else I'd nodded and... it was too late to go back.'

Didier shook his head. 'And you worry about how *your father* is dealing with his grief.'

'I will tell her,' Julien stated. 'Of course I will tell her. I just need the right moment.'

Didier eyed him with suspicion. 'Are you sure that this is really about Lauren? Or is it perhaps about you still not wanting to speak about the fire? The fire you ran into. The fire you almost did not make it back from?'

'Don't,' Julien warned.

'You tell me you think your father does not care what has happened but you are just the same. You are always so focussed on Lauren, I think you have forgotten that this happened to you too.'

Julien swallowed, his abdomen tightening as if the tainted skin there was still burning. He took a breath. 'Trust me, Didier. I have not forgotten.'

TWENTY-SIX

Julien Fitoussi's apartment

Julien hadn't been able to sleep. Didier's words had crawled around his brain all night and his real concern was that perhaps everything his friend had said was right.

He looked out of the window as he fastened up his pale blue shirt. The sky was azure, the sun low in the sky as it woke up, a golden sheen across the water of the Seine. He could see the Hotel de Ville, its dark-grey rooftops, the stone statues below and that tall turret at its centre standing proud. Still it was snowing, but a light flurry, like God had opened up a pillowcase and was sprinkling feathers down over the city.

He checked his watch again. He had an hour before meeting his father. Shirt on, he walked across the bare boards to where his Macbook was showing a black screen. One shake of the mouse and there was Ava. Her head was turned away so you couldn't see her face, just her body, encased in her dark coat, bright white hair unleashed after she'd dropped his hat, hands flicking up drops of water from the fountains at the Louvre, the sky a moody grey behind the pyramid of glass. The thought that no one would get to see this, that not even his subject would get to see this, felt wrong. This was beauty, the resilience of human nature, finding joy in everyday life.

He leant forward, clicking his mouse on the next image. Ava again, last night, looking into the mid-distance at Bettina's. The contrast of her hair against the black of her dress, those high boots she didn't seem comfortable in, the expression on her face somewhere between lost and hopeful...

He should stop taking her photo... or ask her if he could take more. But he knew what her answer would be and right now, he wasn't ready to give up his new muse. But photos or no photos, maybe as soon as she found out he had lied about his sister, he would lose whatever choice he had.

Ava sat on the balcony, one of the hotel's gold-and-red bed-spreads on the seat of the chair, another one wrapped around her. She was gazing out at Paris at nine a.m., coming to life fuelled by café and crossiants to the soundtrack of car horns, bicycle bells and Christmas carols played by accordions. She breathed in the scent of snow, winter air and the faint aroma of freshly baked baguettes, trying to wake herself up.

She hadn't slept well. Debs had snored loudly and, after she had rolled her friend gently onto her side to make sure none of her hair blocked her airway, Ava's mind was working overtime on just about everything. Last night had been more fun than she could have imagined until it was over... rather abruptly. One minute they had been saying goodbye, talking about what they were going to do today and the next... Julien had looked slightly flustered. Didier had seemed bothered about something too and then they had left, with a wave of hands and little else. She pulled the bedspread tighter around her. What more had she been expecting? Just because she and Julien had shared beers and talk of Chris Martin's attributes didn't mean... well, it didn't mean anything at all. Men were all the same. A big testosterone-filled ball of confusion she didn't need in her life. Except she had one man-sized problem to fix here. One she needed to figure out for Debs and for the woman who had mothered her properly when Rhoda was still trying to nurture her with Rimmel.

She shook her head, looking through the wrought-iron railings at the Parisians below, rushing through the snow in their winter boots and wool coats. She couldn't believe Gary would do this. She wanted Debs and Sue to have got the wrong end of the stick because the thought that he could be deceiving them made her sick with fear. But, no matter what was or wasn't happening, she was going to get to the bottom of it and be there for her best friend. Just like she had the first time when Debs' dad had packed and left and Debs had turned up at Ava's house looking like she had rubbed coal under her eyes. Rhoda had taken one look at the make-up horror and almost closed the door again until Ava had whipped it out of her mother's grasp, taken Debs by the hand and led her three streets down to the café that did the best and biggest lattes with squirty cream on top. Ava had drawn a caricature of Jon with Devil's horns and it had made Debs laugh and then she had drawn a picture of Debs and her mum with Ava in the background eating a giant ice cream and that drawing had made Debs cry. Ava had held her then and whispered gently that everything was going to be all right. And everything was going to be all right now. It just had to be.

'Ava!' Debs called from inside. 'Have you seen my hairband with the reindeers on?'

TWENTY-SEVEN

Saint-Honoré

At just after ten a.m. Julien stood outside the boutique Vivienne had messaged him the details of. In the window was a pale-grey suit with a matching waistcoat, a pink handkerchief in the top pocket of the jacket. Next to it was another mannequin dressed all in black, long tails on the coat. It looked like something someone would wear to a ball… or to a funeral. He sighed, watching the snow settle on the front window of the shop. There was no getting away from this. He may as well put his best foot forward and face it head on. Taking a breath, he pushed at the door.

A bell rang as Julien entered and a tiny man dressed in a green checked suit sprang forward, a tape measure wound around his neck. He held out his hands, just catching a Christmas wreath as it fell from the pane of glass on the door.

'My apologies. We have yet to fix this on correctly,' the man said, cradling the pine cones, holly and spruce as if it were a new born baby.

'It's OK,' Julien answered. 'I am—'

'Monsieur Fitoussi,' the man said, nodding. 'I am Jean-Paul. Your father is already here.'

Of course he was. A couple of minutes past ten and his father would make comment that he was late. Julien swallowed his irritation and nodded to the man.

'This way please,' the man said.

Julien followed Jean-Paul past rows and rows of different suits in every shade imaginable, past a large Father Christmas with eyes that lit up and a fat tree decorated with hanging ornaments and strings of sparkling tinsel. And there was his father dressed for business as usual. Julien stopped walking a little short of the space and just observed. Did Gerard look a little thinner? His hair a little greyer at the temples? He swallowed. Perhaps Vivienne was right. Maybe his father was dealing with his grief in a different way, but feeling it just the same.

'Monsieur Fitoussi,' Jean-Paul greeted. 'Your son is here.'

Gerard turned then and faced Julien before dropping his eyes to the expensive watch on his arm. 'You're late.'

Julien stepped into the room and spread his arms wide. 'Then we had better get started.'

They had begun being measured almost in total silence, apart from comments from Jean-Paul and the scribbling of his pencil as he noted final adjustments down. Julien swallowed as the tape measure was held to his groin and then down to the floor.

'Stand up straight, Julien,' Gerard ordered. 'Vivienne wants this wedding to be perfect.'

He closed his eyes and willed the measuring to be over. 'So, how is business?' he asked.

'Why would you want to know that? You have no interest in my business.'

'That isn't true,' Julien responded.

'You left the company, remember?' Gerard stated gruffly.

'I am well aware of that. I didn't realise that this meant I could never enquire about the business in pursuit of conversation.'

Jean-Paul stood up and urged Julien to stretch out his arms. Had his father always been this difficult to talk to? When had he turned so hard, so unreachable? The man Gerard used to be smiled and laughed and shared conversation around the dinner table. He showed interest, listened intently, gave opinion but never judgement...

'You were not interested in my business when you stormed out of the party the other night,' Gerard snapped.

He had to give his father that one. It had been immature and he had behaved without respect, he could see that now. He swallowed down any urge to be drawn into another combat he was sure neither of them wanted.

'I apologise,' Julien spoke. 'I should not have done that.'

'No, you shouldn't,' Gerard responded tightly.

'So,' Julien said. 'The wedding. It is an exciting time, no?'

'Hold still,' Jean-Paul said, the tape measure poised.

A sigh came from his father and Julien lifted his head from watching the tailor to look at Gerard. There were definitely more worry lines, an aura of vulnerability about his father that had never been present in the past.

'Everything is on course?' Julien asked. 'That venue for the reception... the caterers...'

'I told Vivienne to hire a wedding planner,' Gerard said, his hands at the lapels of his jacket. 'But she seems to want to do everything herself.'

Julien smiled as Jean-Paul turned him around for more measurements. 'She is a very capable woman. And this means a lot to her. It is a brand new start for both of you.'

'I do not see the point,' Gerard stated softly, almost under his breath.

'What?' Julien asked.

'All this stuff,' Gerard said, arms flying up then down again.

Jean-Paul looked up, addressing Gerard. 'Monsieur Fitoussi, you would like to try on the suit now?' He wrapped the tape measure back around his neck. 'I will pin and make final adjustments.'

'Let's get it over with,' Gerard responded, resigned. He plumped down onto one of the plum leather banquettes, another sigh escaping.

Julien smiled at the tailor and waited until he had scurried off before taking a seat next to his father. He removed the camera from around his neck and set it down on the seat next to him. He watched Gerard shift slightly, his eyes falling to the camera.

'You are taking photos again,' he stated.

Julien nodded. 'Yes.'

'Why?'

It seemed an odd question and for a second Julien didn't know how to respond. He opened his mouth to speak until Gerard spoke again.

'The other night you were adamant you were not taking photographs.'

'I wasn't then.'

'But you are now?'

'I'm not taking photographs for other people,' he said, 'like *Parisian Pathways*. I'm taking photos for me.'

'What does that mean?' Gerard asked, turning to face him.

'It means,' Julien began. 'I am taking photographs again because *I* want to. Not because anyone is telling me to.' He swallowed. He hadn't meant that statement to come out as harsh as it had. He quickly spoke again. 'I simply mean, perhaps you were correct, maybe now is the right time to move on.'

A long, slow sigh left his father's lips, his head hanging, hands pressed to his thighs.

Julien could almost feel his father's sadness. It was written so obviously in his body language. How had he not seen it before? Had it always been there? Hidden just under the surface, beneath the public face and the businessman bravado?

'I want to do another exhibition,' Julien stated.

There was no reaction from his father. Julien wet his lips and carried on. 'An exhibition to remember Lauren.'

He watched his father close his eyes then and suck in a breath that rolled his shoulders.

Julien continued. 'I want it to raise money for the Croix-Rouge.'

Gerard looked up then. 'Why?'

Julien thought for a moment before answering. 'Because that is what Lauren would have wanted.'

He matched his father's gaze, waiting for what he had said to sink in before saying more. 'Lauren would want something positive to come from her death. She would not want her whole life to be defined by the moment she died and how horrible that time was for everybody.' Julien sighed. 'Lauren was a bird on the breeze, a sweet, warm, generous person who embraced everything. We cannot forget all that.'

'You know there is nothing you can do to bring her back,' Gerard stated.

Julien nodded. 'I know that.' He sighed again. 'Just lately I have been trying instead to remember everything we shared, to make her still a part of my life.' He swallowed, thinking of Ava's mistaken assumption.

'That will not work, Julien,' Gerard snapped. 'You think you can just take a few photos and make things all right again?'

'Unlike you, I know I'm not going to focus on the Paris attacks just so I can pretend the fire Lauren died in didn't happen.'

He held his breath as the angry, bitter words dissipated. He remembered how his father had said nothing about the fire but instead had gone to dinner parties where he rallied against the state of France, picking apart the logistics of each terror attack. Meanwhile, Julien had watched as the newspapers filled with articles about terrorism, day after day, with only one small article in three papers about the fire that had taken the life of his sister.

At the time he had felt like the whole world was saying not all lives mattered, that some lives meant more than others, more than Lauren's. It was like the city of Paris, along with his father, was belittling his grief. Now, as the months had gone by, he could see that it had simply been a case of timing. There was a difference between what was important and what was deemed newsworthy. And his father had just done exactly the same as the press. Gerard had hidden his grief. He had buried the seething rage and anger he felt at the injustice of the death of his daughter and directed it straight towards the Paris attacks. The attacks had perpetrators, someone to blame. The fire was an accident with no one to point a finger at.

'I don't know why you came here today, Julien,' Gerard said, getting to his feet. 'I don't know why you are even involving yourself with this wedding. You're not moving on. You are fooling yourself. Still, now, it is all about dwelling on the past... an exhibition!' Gerard scoffed.

'I am not dwelling on the past. I am facing up to it. Trying to make something good come from it.'

'Nothing good can come from it!' Gerard barked. 'How can it?! Lauren is dead!'

His father's voice had cracked on the last word and Julien got to his feet, ready to reach out...

'Don't touch me,' Gerard hissed.

'I came here today because Vivienne asked me to,' Julien stated, putting his hands into the pockets of his jeans. 'She is worried about you. She does not want this widening gap in the family.'

Gerard shook his head. 'It is not her business.'

'Of course it is, Dad. She's a part of this family. She is about to become your wife. She loves you.'

'Who do you think you are? To tell me what should happen. To tell me what I should do and how I should feel?'

'That isn't what I'm trying to do.'

'I don't wish for your opinion,' he snapped. 'And I am certain, if it has to be this way… that a wedding can take place without a best man.'

'What?'

'You should go,' Gerard stated.

'But—'

'Jean-Paul!' Gerard called. 'Could we look at something for business too, while I am here? Something for the spring.'

Julien couldn't believe this was happening. He watched his father head towards the very back of the shop. The conversation was over.

TWENTY-EIGHT

Outside Cosmos Protection offices

Ava looked at the photo of Francine Duval on her iPhone. She had sleek, shoulder-length black hair, brown eyes and, in Ava's opinion, a little too much red lipstick for the corporate photograph. She also looked to be in her late thirties at most. It wasn't impossible but seemed a little unlikely that Gary – edging towards mid-fifties – would be having an affair with someone who could, theoretically, be young enough to be his daughter. She opened her mouth to say as much to Debs but then saw her friend was regarding the entrance to the office through a pair of binoculars.

'Where the hell did you get those from?' Ava exclaimed. 'Binoculars!'

'There's a little shop a few doors down from Agincourt, it sells all manner of winter holiday necessities.'

'I really wouldn't have put binoculars on a list of winter holiday necessities,' Ava responded.

'Shh, I'm watching,' Debs said, waving her free hand in the air then training her concentration back on the building.

'Have you thought through what we're going to actually do if a) Gary is actually the person she's meeting and b) if he's not?'

Debs sniffed. 'Well,' she began, 'if he *is* the person she's meeting I'm going to cut his balls off with the little scissors from the sewing kit in my handbag.' She let go of a breath. 'And if he's not the person she's meeting *today* then there's always tomorrow. He's in…' – she made quotation marks in the air with her fingers – 'Toulouse until Thursday.'

'Oh, Debs, seriously? I think we have to come up with a better strategy than this. Following this woman around the city doesn't seem like the best way.'

'We've been through this. Mum made me swear not to do any digging but she's got her head in the sand… and I *have* to know.'

'I know you do, but if he isn't doing anything I think he would be mortified to know you were spending your time stalking one of his colleagues and Sue was worrying herself to death over it.'

'Shh… I think that's her,' Debs said, one hand resting on the metal bike rack at the side of the street, the other gripping the binoculars as she leant forward.

'Where?' Ava asked, straining her eyes to look across the street.

'There… totes gorgeous Wang handbag… the bitch.'

'In the lemon trouser suit?' Ava asked.

'Yes! And who wears lemon in the winter apart from the French? Fucking stylish bitch.'

'Debs!' Ava exclaimed. 'Is now the point where I'm supposed to remind you that she hasn't actually done anything yet?'

'That we know of,' Debs countered. 'Gary has been coming to "Toulouse" for the past six months. She could have been parading her whole selection of stylish outfits for him… shit, is she hailing a taxi? If she hails a taxi we're screwed.'

'Not if we hail the one behind it, but you'll have to run,' Ava said, stepping out onto the road.

'*Arrêtez*!' Debs shrieked, manically flagging down the cab driver.

'What time was her mystery appointment?' Ava asked.

They were still in the taxi behind the vehicle containing Francine Duval. The driver was playing Christmas music at full volume and was humming loudly and out of tune as they travelled as fast as the Parisian traffic would allow them.

'Eleven,' Debs responded.

'So it's not lunch then?'

'She'd scheduled two hours.'

'So it could be.'

'Are you hungry already?'

'You sounded just like my mother then.'

'What if she's meeting Gary?' Debs said.

Her friend was chewing at the ends of her hair, something she had done since primary school when she was nervous. Ava would have joined in as a show of solidarity but her hair was so short there was not a chance she would get it into her mouth.

She patted her friend's leg. 'Focus on thinking about what we are going to do when she stops wherever she's stopping and meets whoever she's meeting. What's the plan?' Ava asked.

'I don't know.'

'You don't know?! I thought the girl with a sewing kit and a pair of binoculars was bound to have a plan!' Ava looked out of the window as a park flashed by. There was greenery amongst the bare trees and snow-covered cobbles. Shoppers taking in the ambience, workers heading to or from meetings… no one else in a taxi tailing someone and not knowing where on earth they were going.

'It's stopping!' Debs reached through the hatch and began patting the taxi driver's shoulder. 'It's stopping. *Arrêtez, Monsieur, arrêtez!*'

The cab driver screeched to a halt, skidding a little in the snow. Debs was pulling at the door before the engine had stopped.

'Debs, wait,' Ava urged, scrambling for her bag and her purse.

'I don't want to lose her.' Debs opened the door and jumped down onto the pavement.

'Keep the change,' Ava said, thrusting a twenty-euro note into the driver's hand before diving for the door, too.

Standing next to Debs as the cab departed, she saw her friend twisting and turning her head like she was an owl wary of predators.

'Did you see where she went?' Debs asked.

'No, I was paying for the cab,' Ava said, her eyes scanning the busy street. There were lots of people with shopping bags here. Not your Bags for Life from Tesco, but boutique bags that sang 'high-end'. 'There!'

Ava almost pointed, before she remembered this was a covert operation. Francine was turning left just up ahead, going under a dark green canopy above a shop front.

'It's a restaurant,' Debs said. 'It's a posh restaurant and Gary's going to be in there ordering oysters and chocolate and all the other aphrodisiacs there are...' She stopped, a sob leaving her.

'No,' Ava said, taking Debs' arm. 'No, he's not.' She squeezed Debs' arm. 'And if he is then you've got a sewing kit and I've got... a tube of spot cream with a really pointy end.' She looked at Debs. 'Come on, let's go.'

Fighting the fierce wind and side-stepping the other pedestrians on the street they made their way along the boulevard to the entrance Francine had disappeared into.

'It's not a restaurant,' Debs said, looking at the sign that stated only 'Sasha'.

'No,' Ava agreed. 'It's a boutique.' She sighed. 'What do we do now?'

'What do you mean?' Debs asked.

'Well, she's obviously not meeting Gary in a boutique,' Ava said. 'Gary's more Jacamo than boutique, isn't he?'

Debs pushed at the door, its glass frosted with fake snow, little gingerbread men hanging from each pane. Ava grabbed her arm, squeezing again. 'What are you doing?!' she hissed.

'Going in,' Debs responded. 'To do a bit of innocent browsing. Perhaps my articles need a little upmarket chic.'

'Debs,' Ava said again, using all her weight to try and hold her friend back. 'This is a bad idea.'

'Let me go,' Debs urged. 'Or come in with me.'

Ava looked through the glass to the shop's interior, where Francine was stood waiting to speak to the elegant lady behind the counter. She looked back to Debs and sighed. 'Do not do anything crazy.'

TWENTY-NINE

Sasha's boutique

Ava peeked out from behind a rather nice cream lace dress. It was highly inappropriate wear for the current climate but come the summer... if her back wasn't quite so broad and she had elongated fibulas. Debs was on the other side of the rail, sandwiched between a low rack of vintage shoes and mannequins dressed in winter woollens.

'Can you hear anything?' Debs asked her.

'What are you expecting to hear? It's a dress shop. She's probably just here to... I don't know... buy a dress?' Ava offered.

'To parade in front of Gary in,' Debs suggested through gritted teeth.

'Stop it,' Ava said. 'We don't know that.'

'We need to get nearer,' Debs stated, sidling along the rail, holding a camel-coloured shawl up to her body like it was some sort of camouflage.

'You know this is ridiculous, right?' Ava commented.

'No, I don't know that,' Debs said with a sigh. 'And what other choice do I have?' Debs gripped the mannequin. 'What I really want to do is smack her in the face with this plastic head.'

'You can't do that,' Ava said. 'As much as you think you want to.' Her mind went back to Waitrose and the man dressed in tweed. 'Because you have no evidence that this woman has done anything.' And she really hoped she hadn't. Although Francine did have a look of Sue about her. *Gary's taste*. Slim, petite frame, hair a little darker than Sue's, feminine attire but the lemon trouser suit a little too sickly jam tart-like. She swallowed. She didn't want to think about how accurate the tart reference could be.

'This is just like Dad,' Debs said through gritted teeth.

'No,' Ava said. 'We don't know that... I'll get a bit closer.' Ava picked up the white summer dress and strode boldly forward, catching sight of a full-length mirror close to the space Francine and a shop assistant were in. It was only when she was near enough to hear their conversation that she realised something she should have realised before... they were talking in French. And her French was a whole lot worse than Debs' ...but Debs was close to holding the head of a dummy with violent intentions. She held the dress against herself and tuned in.

Spécial – that meant special.

Mariage – marriage, meant the same but said slightly differently wasn't it?

Fin de semaine – what the hell did that mean? Fin was 'end'... no idea of the rest.

Gary.

Bile flooded her throat. Was 'Gary' French for something? She begged the gods of languages that 'Gary' was a French word. Because if it wasn't a French word then Francine had just said Debs' step-dad's name in a dress shop.

Ava swallowed, her eyes flashing over to Debs. She quickly smiled at her friend. Because what else could she do right now? And had she even heard right? She didn't want to have heard right. Because what did she do now? It was fine, wasn't it? Innocent. Gary worked for the same company. He was in senior management. He could be Francine's boss.

'Mademoiselle.'

Should she tell Debs? Should she let her friend bury the dummy's head in this elegant, beautiful, Frenchwoman's face? Should she join in and batter her with the plastic arms?

'Mademoiselle, may I help you?'

Ava turned to the voice then. It was the shop assistant. Long blonde hair shining like an advert for L'Oreal. Ava almost dropped the dress in her hands. 'Bonjour... just looking... at this,' Ava said, holding the dress up to her again.

'You would like to try this on?' the shop assistant asked.

'I... er...' Ava looked to Francine. The woman was tapping her iPhone. Was that a message? A message to Gary?

'No, thank you.' Debs took the dress out of Ava's hands and strolled up towards the counter where Francine was positioned. 'But could we have a look at your purses?' Debs picked up a small red leather coin purse from a basket on the cash desk and held it out, whilst trying to discreetly look over the shoulder of the woman from Gary's firm.

'We have a wide range of purses,' the shop assistant began. 'What type are you looking for?'

'Something... very French,' Ava suggested. 'For a gift.' She moved close to Debs.

'I have something in mind,' the shop assistant said. Her attention went to Francine. '*Demain?*'

'*Oui, cinq?*'

'*Oui, au revoir.*' The shop assistant turned back to Ava and Debs. 'Now, I will look for something for you.'

Debs looked like she was hovering, torn between carrying on with their charade and gleaning information from the shop assistant, or following Francine.

Francine was at the door, about to go out and back onto the street as the shop assistant disappeared towards the very rear of the boutique.

'What do we do now?' Debs asked. 'She was writing in a book under the desk.' She leant over the cash desk.

'Get down, Debs,' Ava urged. 'You look like you're about to rob the place. They probably have CCTV.'

'There are four books here! Who has four books in this day and age?' Debs asked, picking one of the journals up.

'Er... you do! Put it down!' Ava urged.

'We should follow Francine,' Debs decided, bolting for the door. 'She had a two-hour appointment scheduled in her diary and she's been here five minutes...'

'Debs...'

'Did you hear anything? Anything at all that might incriminate Gary?' Debs asked.

Ava swallowed. Now was the moment to fess up. To say she thought... no, she knew... she had heard his name. She opened her mouth with the best of intentions.

'No, nothing... they were speaking French.' She directed her eyes to the floor.

'Come on, quick, before she hails another taxi!'

Debs pushed at the door and, all the way hoping she had said the right thing for now, Ava followed.

THIRTY

Christmas Market, La Défense

They had lost Francine. Their taxi had got stuck between a bread van and a wobbly parent and child on a tandem. The Frenchwoman's cab had sailed off into the distance and Debs had cursed the driver of the van, the driver of the taxi and the twosome on the tandem. Debs was terrified. It had been all wild eyes, even wilder hair and incantations of planning how she was going to continue with her private-investigator work. And while Debs was muttering about finding out where Francine lived and going through her bins, Ava had thought about what she had heard in the boutique. If Gary was Francine's boss it was fine. But if he wasn't... She was trying not to be scared now too. But she was. She was frightened that this had the potential to rip her best friend's heart out and devastate Sue for the second time in her life. She just didn't know what to do for the best. So instead of churning things over she had focussed on something to keep her friend's mind off things and had directed the cab driver to bring them here. And here they now were, in the midst of the most fabulous Christmas market Ava had ever seen.

The smell was heavenly and she didn't know which way to turn her nose first. One breath in gave her gingerbread and spiced caramel, another was wurst and mustard, all of it infused with sparkles, snowflakes and Christmas at every turn. But Debs, beside her, was walking around blind to all the shopping opportunities that usually would have had her practically orgasming with excitement.

Ava linked her arm through her friend's and squeezed. 'Remember the pact we made last night?'

'I can't concentrate on anything,' Debs responded. 'What are we even doing here?'

'Debs, you're writing an article on Christmas markets. This is the Christmas market you wanted to come to. Look at it!' Ava said, throwing her free arm out to highlight the goodies on offer.

'I can't concentrate on anything. Not while there's some French bint hitting on my step-dad.'

Ava sighed. This was an impossible situation. She reached into her pocket and drew out her iPhone. 'Right, that's it. I'm calling Gary.'

'No!' Debs wailed, hands flapping for Ava's phone. Then she stopped. 'You don't have his number.'

'I do,' Ava replied. 'He's given me a lift so many times it's saved under "T" for "Taxi Dad".'

'Don't call him, Ava, please,' Debs begged.

'Well, you can't go on like this.'

'I know,' Debs said with a sigh. 'I won't.' She took a deep breath. 'You're right. I need to take a time out. Regroup. Think about what to do next.' She offered a watery smile. 'And I totes promised you lunch.'

'You did,' Ava agreed.

Debs' eyes finally met with the festive wooden huts all around the open-air market as she finally came to. 'Oh my goodness. Look at those earmuffs!'

Ava let herself be dragged towards the hut with all manner of woollen goods hanging from its surrounds. There were furry things, fluffy things, animal heads and more glitter than at a Little Mix concert. The earmuffs Debs was raving about were penguin faces, with glittery red cheeks and sticky-out beaks.

'How much?' Debs asked the stallholder.

'*Combien?*' Ava added.

The reply was fifteen euro and Debs was reaching into her bag for her purse before he'd even answered. Ava picked up a hat. It was navy blue with a pattern knitted into the wool. Despite what Julien had said about having others she ought to replace the one she had dropped into the fountain. This one would suit him. She smoothed her fingers over the wool.

'That's a bit plain,' Debs remarked, leaning over her shoulder. 'How about this one?' She held up a bright pink hat with gold antlers sticking out of the top.

Ava smiled. 'I don't think it would suit Julien.'

'Ah,' Debs said, 'it's for Julien.'

'Don't read anything into it. I dropped his hat into the water at the Louvre and I want to get him a new one.'

'His and hers?' Debs suggested, picking up a red version of the hat Ava was holding.

'Only if it's on a special offer,' Ava answered.

'*Combien?*' Debs asked, taking the blue hat from Ava and holding them both up to the stallholder.

Ava sank her teeth into the heavily cinnamon-infused Stollen slice the size of a dinner plate. Her taste buds exploded as the juicy fruit, sugar, almonds and citrus all hit at once. With her new berry red hat on her head, the snow coming down around her, the most perfect mouthful of sugary Christmas goodness between her lips, she would probably consider life in Paris to be pretty sublime, if it weren't for the tears in her best friend's eyes.

Debs forked up a tiny piece of crepe and shook her head at Ava. 'Life is not fair. I don't know how you can eat something that big and end up so small whilst I have to hide what I've got under jumpers.'

'I have a concave spine and no boobs,' Ava said through a mouthful of food. 'You've got that booty Beyoncé is always on about.' She inhaled a second mouthful.

'But no one has offered to put a ring on it.'

'Yet.' Ava smiled.

'Have you taken pictures?' Her eyes went to the hundreds of Swiss chalet-style huts around them making it look like they'd stumbled upon a village high up in the Alps.

'Yes... and I might have to go back to that little stall that sold the silver jewellery,' Debs remarked.

'Debs, you have three cotton bags filled with stuff,' Ava reminded her.

'None of it is for me,' she responded, rubbing sugar off her top lip with her finger. 'They're gifts.'

'The glass shaped like the Eiffel Tower?' Ava asked, an eyebrow raised.

'My mum,' Debs offered.

'The Santa Claus pin cushion?'

'My nan.'

'The "grow your own rainbow" kit?'

'Do you think that will really work?' Debs asked with sincerity.

Ava laughed and bit into her cake. Her eyes went to the large structure at one end of the square the market was on – *la Grande Arche*. It was white stone, completely hollow, the snow coming down making it look like a giant picture frame. It was a completely different style to the Gothic and Byzantine architecture she'd seen in the capital so far. She wasn't sure she liked it. It was a little piece of modern just outside of a city with so much history.

'I haven't bought anything for Gary,' Debs muttered.

'Debs...'

'If he leaves Mum then Mum isn't going to cope and I can see the house getting sold and Mum wanting to live with me and I don't know if I'm even going to be able to stay in the house if I don't sell an article soon.'

Ava put an arm around Debs' shoulders. 'Right, well, we need to do two things in that case.'

'What?' Debs asked with a sniff.

'You need to start making notes about this market and... we need to find someone who can hack into Francine's email.'

'I thought you thought that was a totes terrible idea.'

She had. She did. Before she had heard Gary's name on the Frenchwoman's lips. But she didn't want it to be true. She was hoping to find proof of Gary's innocence. They were work colleagues. The fact the woman was in an expensive dress shop talking about him was odd, but perhaps Gary's firm were quoting for insurance for the boutique... it could be anything. And anything was better than an affair.

'I just think we need to get some facts. Facts in black and white before we worry any more.' She sighed. 'And if there are no facts to find then Gary's done nothing wrong and everything can go back to normal.'

Debs nodded, putting another forkful of crepe into her mouth. She chewed it up before speaking. 'Do you know someone who can hack email?'

'I have a hunch I know someone who can help.'

Ava's eyes went across the market square, looking through the wooden chalets, past the revolving merry-go-round to the vendors selling candyfloss and cinnamon-infused sweet treats and beyond to the street outside the Christmas fair... and there was Julien. Walking arm-in-arm with a woman.

Ava swallowed, watching. The woman was beautiful, Parisian beautiful, dressed in a stylish, tailored bright green coat, her dark wavy hair resting on her shoulders as she and Julien moved along the street. Was this Lauren? She had imagined her a little different. Younger. But she *was* pretty. So pretty. Something inside her prickled. Maybe this wasn't Lauren. Maybe it was someone else. A girlfriend. Maybe when Julien had said he was single he hadn't really meant it... or lied. She sniffed, watching the woman tighten her hold on Julien's arm, smiling up at him as she talked. It didn't look like the sort of connection a brother and sister would have, even if they were close. Did that mean she had been duped again? That all men really were bastards? Just like Leo and, potentially, Gary. She sighed, watching the two of them disappear into the distance. Not that Julien was *her* man. Not that she wanted him to be. It was just he had started to restore her faith in trust just a little bit, and now...

'Ava?' Debs questioned, pulling at her sleeve. 'Are you OK?'

She snapped herself out of it, turning her head to face her friend. 'Yes,' she said a lot more brightly than she felt. 'What's next? Back to the silver jewellery stall?'

'I thought I wasn't allowed to revisit that stall,' Debs said with a grin.

'It's nearly Christmas,' Ava reminded her. 'And I think we both deserve a treat.' And a non-male distraction.

THIRTY-ONE

Sacré-Coeur, Montmartre

Julien was going to tell Ava about Lauren. He had to. This morning with his father... he was as good as the same, hiding, pretending everything was all right. Ava deserved the truth. The only reason he hadn't told her, the only reason he had let her assume, was because he had wanted to pretend, just for a little while, that things were how they used to be. That wasn't right and it wasn't honest either. And even though he hadn't known Ava very long, he already knew how much she valued honesty.

He spotted Ava straightaway. She was standing right in the middle of the steps leading up to the Sacré-Coeur shooing away pigeons that seemed to be forming a circle around her feet. He stopped walking and held his camera up to capture the scene before she noticed him. She was wearing a red hat, not unlike the hat Lauren used to wear, her blonde spikes hidden, only her rosy-cheeked face, full lips and cat-like eyes exposed to the elements. He clicked, trying to catch a pigeon in flight, the shadow of the church as the sun hit the bell tower. Then, through the viewfinder, he saw her look directly towards him and he dropped the camera like it had turned into molten lava in his hands. He waved quickly and started to move towards her.

'Hello,' he greeted.

'Hi,' she responded, mouth downturned slightly.

'Ava... there's something—'

'I saw you at the market today,' Ava blurted out.

'You did?'

'With Lauren.'

'What?' His heart started to palpitate and his throat dried up.

'She's so beautiful. You never said how beautiful she was. All that long hair and gorgeous clothes.'

'Oh!' Julien exclaimed, almost relieved until he remembered how deceitful this all was. Now was the time to confess and make things clear... Except the words weren't coming. All that was coming was gap filling and half-truths. 'You saw me with Diane.'

'Diane?'

'She is someone I know through my work. She runs a gallery I have had a few paintings displayed at... I met her on the way back from meeting with my father.'

'Your father,' Ava said. 'Not Lauren.'

He swallowed. He hadn't realised just how many lies he had told without even knowing it. And before sense could prevail it was happening all over again. 'The fitting for the wedding suits are almost done.' Another lie. How could he also admit his father now didn't want him to be his best man? That his whole family was so messed up she ought to be running away fast in the opposite direction.

'That's good,' Ava answered with a sigh.

'There is something wrong?' Julien asked her.

She looked unsettled, a little shaken. Had she found out about Lauren from Debs? Had Didier decided to tell the truth Julien couldn't face up to? Or maybe it was something else. Had Ava seen him taking photos of her just now?

'I've just spent the whole morning chasing someone across Paris who Debs thinks is having an affair with her step-dad.'

He tried to catch up with what she was saying but all the words were completely different to what he had being expecting. Relief and guilt flooded him simultaneously.

'I thought I heard something in the boutique but I can't be sure. Not sure enough to tell Debs and then... we lost her. And I don't really know what to do next,' Ava admitted.

'Ava,' Julien said, moving in front of her eye line to attract her focus.

'I shouldn't be telling you this. Debs wouldn't want me to tell you this, but there's no one else I can tell and I think you'll be honest with me... I really hope you'll be honest with me.'

His stomach turned. *Honesty*. Just as he thought. Crucial to her.

'Debs is panicking and I'm panicking for her and it's almost Christmas and no one likes life-changing things happening at Christmas... What do I do?'

He looked at her, gazing up at him like his answer to this question could change her world.

'Ava,' he said softly, 'take a breath.'

'I don't do that in-through-the-nose, out-through-the-mouth stuff. It ended my parents' marriage.'

'Just trust me,' he said. 'Keep still and just breathe.'

She huffed a sigh then closed her eyes. He watched her unable to keep still, stamping her Converse up and down in the snow, sending pigeons into flight.

Her chest was rising and falling quickly, like she'd just competed in an Olympic event, then slowly, as every second ticked by the rapidity lessened until she was breathing more steadily, less anxiously.

She flicked open her eyes. 'Sorry,' she whispered.

'You have nothing to be sorry for,' he said. 'If you want to explain I am here to listen.'

She nodded. 'OK. But you have to promise, when I get to the part about hiding behind a dress, you won't laugh.'

He smiled. 'I promise, Madonna.' And, for now, the moment for telling her the truth about Lauren was gone.

She told him everything Debs had told her about her suspicions about Gary, about Debs' father's infidelity and how wonderful Sue and Gary had been to her when she was growing up. By the time she had finished, her bum was numb and damp from the concrete step she had sunk down onto, pigeons still attacking her feet.

'You think we're mad, don't you? Like something out of a really low-budget comedy film,' Ava said.

'I do not think that. I think it is a very difficult situation.'

'Well, what would you do? If you were me or if you were Debs.'

'Am I you? Or am I Debs?' he asked.

'We're kind of in this together.'

'Well, I think I would talk to Gary.'

'Noooo!' Ava exclaimed. 'That's because you're a man. You don't think like a woman. You can't see how awful that would be.'

'Why would this be awful? Debs calls him. She says she is worried about her mother. She says there are rumours...'

'Rumours?'

'You would like to say that Debs' mother thinks he is cheating on her because of some secretive phone calls and what her first husband has done in the past?'

'Definitely not.'

'Rumours then... and you simply ask him.'

Her stomach was already tightening at the thought. It was the simplest way but... it didn't feel right.

Julien pulled in a breath, and stood, turning his head to look at the white basilica towering over them. 'When in doubt, stop for a moment,' he said. 'Look at this place, Madonna.' He threw out his arms. 'Sometimes you just need to remember the bigger picture. It helps to put everything into perspective.'

'The church?' Ava asked. 'Debs has never really been a church goer. Only the one time when she had a crush on the curate.'

'*Non.*' He shook his head. 'Not the church. Everything here. The whole area of Montmartre. The vibe of the place, the artists, the tiny squares, the view... all the tiny parts and pieces coming together.' He sighed. 'And you can almost see the whole of Paris from up here.'

Ava got to her feet. He was right and she had been so caught up in the Gary situation and shooing away pigeons who were crapping on her Converse that she hadn't looked properly. High up here on the butte there was a view over the rooftops of Paris, a patchwork of cream, beige and brown like layers of cream cakes topped with the falling snow, the slender metalwork of the Eiffel Tower in the distance.

'It is beautiful,' Ava breathed, inhaling snowflakes and not caring. She let out a contented sigh. She felt almost free here, standing with the City of Light spread out before her, miles away from her mother and the mess of the fallout from Leo. She just needed to resolve Debs' family crisis. She refocussed.

'Whenever I need to think I come up here and I look at the city... and somehow it always grounds me,' Julien said. 'It reminds me that no matter what the issue, no matter how big you think your problems are, they are always just a speck on the map... a tiny blip on one of the paths of a whole world waiting to be explored.'

Ava sighed. 'I have wasted so much of my life,' she said, vision on the city scene. 'Doing things. *Not* doing things. Travelling... but travelling with my eyes completely closed.' She shivered. 'I don't want to do that any more.'

Julien swallowed. Standing there, watching Ava soak in the city, seeing and feeling everything as if it were the first time, was moving him in ways he hadn't been moved in a long time. She had just confided in him too. Asked his advice. And here he was still holding onto that sad truth he needed to let go of before she asked again. He wanted to be honest with her. Just like she had been with him. 'Ava,' he began. 'There's something—'

Ava yelped as suddenly a pigeon flew up from the ground, its wings scuffing her shoulder and sending her leaping to the left with a scream.

'Argh! Ugh! Bloody pigeons!'

Julien laughed at her batting her hands around and stamping her feet, causing a whole flurry of feathered animals to take flight.

'I don't like them,' Ava moaned.

'Not even with a little wild mushroom and red wine gravy?'

'Bleurgh, no!' She laughed, then smiled. 'But I could probably make light work of some more Camembert though.'

'You are hungry?' he asked.

'Ah, a late lunch, Monsieur Fitoussi, what a good idea,' Ava said, slipping her hands into her pockets and looking like she was preparing to move up the steps. 'Oh,' she said. 'I almost forgot.'

Julien regarded her quizzically and watched as she produced a paper bag from the pocket of her coat and held it out to him.

'I bought this for you,' Ava said.

'A gift, Madonna? What did I do to deserve this?' He took the bag and smiled at her.

'Don't go overboard,' she answered. 'It isn't a new camera or anything else that gets photographers excited.'

He smiled, watching as her cheeks heated up at her comment.

'Open it,' she encouraged.

He unfurled the end of the paper bag and slipped his hands inside, drawing out the dark blue knitted hat. He looked up, smiling. 'Thank you, Madonna.'

'Personally, I think it's a lot nicer than the one I dropped at the Louvre.'

'I agree,' he answered, running his fingers over the wool.

'Put it on then,' she ordered.

He pulled the hat down over his head and adopted a pose he thought might make her laugh – index finger and thumb to his face, his chin resting in the V.

'Come here,' Ava said. 'Your hair is sticking out all wrong.' She stepped to him and slipped her fingers under the hat, carefully selecting sections of his hair to be exposed and others to be hidden away. Her face was so close to his there was nothing in his sightline but her perfect eyes and tickling his nose was the faint scent of her – cocoa butter and lip gloss. It was hard not to move or react as his body told him how pleasurable her attention was. And then she stopped, looking at him as if she was now pleased with this appearance.

'There,' she almost whispered.

He couldn't answer her, he was too busy being hypnotised by her beauty. He inched forward, holding his breath, not really knowing what he was doing until his hand connected with hers. Momentarily jolted by the touch he stilled, continuing to look into her eyes, still unable to read her expression. He was caught. Between two frightening places. The one where he did something and everything changed and the one where he did nothing and regretted it for the rest of his life.

He wrapped his index finger around hers tentatively, his chest tight… then Ava stepped back and broke the connection.

'So,' she said, her fingers at the rim of her beanie hat. 'Where's best for lunch? And who do you know that can hack email?'

He forced a smile, knowing how close he had come to making a complete fool of himself. 'What would Mademoiselle care to eat?'

'Something very French,' Ava replied. 'With plenty of garlic.'

'Very well,' he answered. 'This way.'

THIRTY-TWO

Place Du Tertre, Montmartre

When the sun came out and the snow slowed to no more than a few wisps in the air, the temperature could almost have been considered warm. Only a few days ago Ava would never have imagined herself here in Paris, surrounded by the domed and turreted Sacré-Coeur, sitting at a table outside, a tiny Christmas tree at its centre flashing red, blue and white like the national flag. To her right, across the restaurant, were artists braving the cold, their easels out, some painting the scene, others painting tourists who were posing for them. Would she have been here, creating caricatures for visitors if she had cut industry ties with her mother? There was an accordion player too, a small grey kitten at his feet, squeezing the boxy instrument in and out, playing a festive tune. Ava dipped another slice of warm bread into garlic-infused butter and bit off a mouthful. Her first reaction was to make a noise, claim the bread was the best food she'd ever tasted and share that joy with Julien. But ever since he'd touched her hand fifteen minutes and a bottle of beer ago her stomach had been fizzing like its only contents were Coke and a strong peppermint. She chewed down on the bread, almost wishing it didn't taste so utterly divine.

'What?' Julien asked. 'No comment on the bread and the garlic?'

Shit. He'd noticed. He knew her already. She smiled, swallowing the fluffy goodness down and picked up her bottle of beer to avoid saying anything straightaway.

'I am a little disappointed,' Julien said, his fingers at his water glass.

'Why?' Ava asked, setting her bottle back down. 'Did you really enjoy me snorting all over falafels?'

'Actually I did,' he answered, with a smile.

There was that school science experiment already, popping and whizzing around her gut. He had such a lovely smile, perfect teeth, full, thick, lips, that strong jawline… But men weren't to be trusted. She sensed there was still something going on with Julien he wasn't telling her. Lauren. Diane. His father. Who had he really met this morning? Was this Diane an ex? A friend with benefits he didn't want to admit to? The fact she cared was also worrying her.

Ava grabbed another slab of bread from the basket on the table and sunk the edge into the white porcelain pot of garlic butter. She put it to her mouth and let the savoury hit cover every single taste bud. She groaned, closing her eyes and moaning as the deliciousness overtook her. This was seriously good, simple food, it deserved to be relished with as much gusto as in *that* scene in *When Harry Met Sally*. She half-opened one eye to see Julien staring back at her, his fingers tight on his water glass.

'Too much?' she asked with a laugh, wiping her mouth with a serviette.

'*Non*,' he answered. 'The bread is the best in Paris.'

'So why haven't you eaten any?' Ava asked, indicating the basket she had been tucking into.

He smiled again. 'Because they also do the best mussels and snails in Paris and I am saving myself.'

She looked to the outside and the crisp snow on the ground, a hyacinth sky above, the painters and their easels in a line across the cobbles. A man in his fifties with shoulder-length white hair sat closest, sketching with just charcoal, his fingers working quickly, his strokes firm and definite then softer as he smudged the edges to create tone. That could have been her passion if she had been strong enough to stand up for herself.

'Ava?' Julien said.

She looked back to him. 'Did you say mussels *and* snails?' Ava said, clapping her hands together. 'Now you're talking.'

'It is *escargots de Bourgogne*... mussels in a snail butter,' he elaborated.

'Snail butter?' Ava looked at him with scepticism in her expression. 'Do you mean those horrible silvery trails they walk all over cabbage leaves?'

Julien laughed out loud, shaking his head. 'I do not know what bit of what you say to laugh at more.'

Ava blinked, not knowing what she had said to cause such amusement. 'I think you think of... What is the word in English? The snails without shells,' Julien said.

'Homeless snails?' Ava asked. 'Worms?'

'Bigger,' Julien said, his fingers to his temple as if racking his brain.

'Caterpillars? James Corden?' She shook her fingers as reality dawned. 'Slugs!'

'Yes!' Julien said.

'Mussels and slugs?'

He laughed again. 'No, Madonna, mussels and snail butter for lunch, the slugs on your cabbages in England.'

'I have eaten a lot of cabbage in my time,' she admitted with a sigh. 'And when I say eaten I mean that very loosely.'

Rhoda had a whole A4 file filled with interesting soups, shakes and other liquidised treats designed to keep the weight off/down/anything but up.

'You like cabbage?' Julien asked.

'Only on Christmas Day,' Ava replied. 'Sat next to half a dozen roast potatoes, swede, sausages wrapped in bacon, a large helping of turkey all swimming in thick gravy.' She smiled. 'So are you having a big family Christmas this year? Your dad and your step-mum and Lauren?'

He nodded quickly then picked up his beer bottle and took a swig. 'How about you, Ava?'

'Two Christmas dinners. One low-carb, low-cal, practically Paleo and the other full-fat, calorie-laden, gorgeousness.' She smiled. 'Guess which one is with my mother?'

'She does not squeal when she eats something nice?' he asked.

'She squeals if something nice even touches her plate, let alone her palate.'

'Think how this must feel,' Julien began. 'To worry about everything you want to put in your mouth.'

'I think George Michael and Monica Lewinsky had this same problem.'

'There are lots of different things to eat at the Luxembourg Quarter Christmas Fair. We should go there,' Julien said.

The 'we' gave Ava a shiver down her spine and she quickly straightened up, trying to tell her mind and body not to be so easily seduced by the lure of French food and the hot guy sat opposite her.

'For Debs' research maybe,' Julien added.

'That sounds nice,' Ava admitted. 'With everything else she has going on she really needs something positive to focus on.'

'Then it is a date,' Julien said.

He'd said 'we' and now 'date'. Why was she getting excited? There was still that itch there might be something he wasn't telling her. Her hands flew to the bread, picking up another slab and tearing off a white fluffy segment to push into her mouth.

'Tonight?' Julien asked.

Ava made a grab for her beer bottle and raised it in the air. 'Tonight, Monsieur Fitoussi.'

THIRTY-THREE

Julien Fitoussi's apartment

As he got ready for the Christmas fair, Julien hated the fact he still hadn't told Ava about Lauren. Why had he spent the afternoon with her, talking about everything *except* the fact his sister was dead? *Those* words were the only ones that should have been coming out of his mouth today, not invitations to Christmas fairs. And with his fingers aching to grasp the camera and take photographs of her too, he felt like the biggest fake in the city. And on top of all of that there was his failure with his father too. Vivienne had wanted him to help and all he had done this morning was make things even worse.

He fastened up the top two buttons of his shirt regarding his reflection in the mirror. How had things got like this? When had he turned into such a hypocrite? Preaching at Gerard to deal with his grief, move on, when he was pretending to someone that Lauren was still alive, needing to talk about her as if she was still here.

A knock on the door drew his attention away from the mirror and he moved to open it.

'Julien! Come! We are late!'

He pulled open the door to greet Didier. His friend was wearing a Santa-red long-sleeved shirt beneath his dark coat, a jade green woollen hat covering his head.

Julien hesitated for a moment. 'I do not know if I should come.'

'What?!' Didier exclaimed, pushing the door and barrel-ling forward. 'This was your idea. And it was a good idea. Why would you not come?'

Julien shrugged.

'What is going on?' Didier asked, hands on hips, eyes boring into him.

'Nothing... I...'

All at once Didier seemed to know. His friend's eyes narrowed and he threw his arms up in the air. 'My God... you have still not told Ava about Lauren, have you?!'

Julien felt himself shrink under Didier's scrutiny. Hearing the exclamation from his friend made it all the more real. Brought home his absolute dishonesty.

'I tried... I wanted to... but I couldn't.'

'Julien!'

'I know... I know... I am pitiful. I am contemptible. I am—'

'Still hurting,' Didier offered a little softly.

Julien nodded. 'Yes.'

Didier put a hand on his shoulder. 'There is nothing wrong with that, my friend.' He drew in a breath. 'But there *is* something wrong with lying to someone.'

'I know,' Julien said, nodding. 'I know that. I definitely know that. It is just, every time Ava talks about Lauren... it makes me remember and... remembering feels so good.'

'Julien, you can remember the past *in* the present. You don't have to *make* the past the present to keep Lauren's memory alive.'

He nodded soberly.

'You have to tell Ava,' Didier stated. 'And you have to tell her tonight.'

Debs looked at her phone, shaking it in the air as if the motion would make unexpected things happen. Ava sucked in her stomach, the button on her jeans a little tighter to fasten after indulging in all that delicious French cuisine. If Rhoda were here she would be rationing by now, counting grams of fat and measuring things by the fist.

'No,' Debs said. 'Definitely no messages from Mum.' She breathed in what sounded like a relieved sigh. 'I guess no news is good news. I did suggest Mum should ask Gary what the weather is like in Toulouse, because I've checked and it's not snowing there and it's totes warmer, so if he mentions snow and minus temperatures then he's not in Toulouse.'

Ava put an arm around Debs' shoulders, nearly knocking over a glittery penguin on the desk she hadn't seen earlier. 'You need to stop worrying, Debs, just for tonight.'

'I know,' Debs said. 'I will... in a minute.' She forced a smile. 'So, how was your afternoon with Julien?'

At the mention of his name Ava's insides started mixing like Mary Berry was in there with a wooden spoon, concocting the world's biggest, richest Christmas cake, scattering dried fruits like she was throwing rice at a wedding.

'Fine,' she answered.

'Fine?' Debs queried. 'It must have been more than fine for him to arrange a trip to this fair tonight.'

Ava swallowed. 'I think he has a girlfriend.'

'Oh.'

And now she had said the words they pinched even more. Which was completely stupid.

'I mean, he said he was single when I asked, when we first met, just as something to say really but—' She stopped talking.

'But?' Debs queried, scrutinising her.

'But I saw him with someone at the market this morning and when I asked him about it he said it was just someone he knew from a gallery but—'

'But?'

'But it wasn't his sister who he *said* he was meeting and...' She sounded ridiculous to her own ears.

'And?'

'He said he'd met his Dad to have a suit fitting... which he hadn't mentioned before and...'

Debs raised her eyebrows as Ava reached for her messenger bag and started to rifle through the contents – lip gloss, an empty to-go coffee cup, her hat – finally she pulled out a piece of paper.

'And I drew this.' She shoved it over to Debs then put one hand to her mouth and began to chew the nails as her friend unfolded the paper.

Debs let out the kind of gasp someone made when they were being proposed to by surprise. She followed it up with an 'Oh my God!'

Ava bit her nails harder.

'This is...'

'Awful? Terrible? Stupid?' Ava offered.

'It's brilliant is what it is!' Debs exclaimed. She turned the paper around so Ava could see it. 'Look at it, Ava. It's a totes beautiful, perfect drawing.'

Ava took her hand away from her mouth and looked at the sketch she had done of Julien. She had sat out on the balcony when she'd returned from Monmartre, her eyes on the street – the team of bell ringers outside the department store opposite, the man pushing a barrow of Christmas toys – and before she had known it she had picked up a pen and started to draw. And this one wasn't a cartoon. Julien didn't have oversized eyes or a nose that dominated the picture. It was just him, gorgeous him, drawn from her mind... because he was on her mind... too much.

'It's bad,' Ava said, sighing. 'Because I don't really draw any more... but I drew him. And that means I like him. Which I shouldn't. And I know that. And... I think he has a girlfriend.'

'But you don't *know* he has a girlfriend. He told you he was single.'

'And I shouldn't care either way, should I? Because men are all the same, aren't they?' Ava looked to her friend for the confirmation she was expecting.

'I should say yes,' Debs answered. 'With my dad as an example and with... Gary...' She sighed. 'But... Didier is nice and... well... I'd quite like to give him the benefit of the doubt.'

'You would?' Ava asked.

Debs nodded. 'Not anything serious but, just, you know, having fun, no strings attached.'

'I guess,' Ava said, still doubtful.

'Why don't you give this picture to Julien tonight,' Debs said, passing back the drawing. 'And ask him again if he has a girlfriend. Or,' she began. 'I could ask Didier for you.'

Ava shook her head. 'How old are we? Eleven?' She smiled. 'No... I'll ask him... not that it matters to me really... because we're just friends.'

'Of course,' Debs said, nodding.

Ava blew out a breath. 'OK, then, let's go and get you some Christmas-fair-in-Paris research done.'

Debs smiled, linking arms with her. 'It's going to be totes amazing!'

THIRTY-FOUR

Christmas Fair, Luxembourg Quarter

Julien could see Debs and Ava standing underneath the tall chestnut trees, the old, faded, green metal chairs underneath the leafless boughs still occupied by old Parisian men playing chess, even in the cold, darkening evening. There were fairground rides and lines of stalls everywhere you looked. From food sellers to fortune-tellers, the fair was buzzing. To his right a family played boules, trussed up in bright winter coats and hats, fingers inside gloves.

As Didier walked on ahead, Julien's hand went to the camera around his neck and he lifted it to his face, eye lining up with the viewfinder, capturing the mother, father and two sons as they laughed, golden lights from the carousel behind them, the outline of the Fontaine de Médicis just visible.

And then he focussed on Ava. Her hat was on her head, her hands in the pockets of the denim coat, those red Converse still on her feet. He liked spending time with her. More than he had enjoyed spending time with anybody over the past twelve months. But how was she going to feel when she knew about Lauren... about the fire... He would no longer be just Julien Fitoussi, the photographer; he would be a victim in her eyes, reliving things again.

But that was what he had to deal with. That's what he had to face head on. Moving forward. Not dwelling like his father had accused him of. Reminiscing but no longer mourning.

'Julien!'

Didier's voice carried across the gardens and he stepped forward.

Ava stamped her feet into the snow knowing that Julien was approaching and feeling like she was on a first date. Why did it matter to her so much that he didn't have a girlfriend? Why was her stomach churning up her insides like a snowplough munching through slush?

'*Bonsoir*, Madonna,' Julien greeted, arriving at her side.

'*Bonsoir*, Monsieur Fitoussi.' She couldn't ignore the chestnut eyes and her fingers wrapped around the picture in her coat pocket, remembering how she had traced the outline of them with her biro.

'I am dying for some churros!' Didier announced. 'Please, before we take photographs and get involved with being sold overpriced sparkly items we would never look twice at in the summertime but are must-haves for Christmas, I need to coat my stomach with sugar.'

'That sounds like a fabulous idea,' Debs agreed, grinning.

'Churros for four, yes?' Didier said, looking at each of them in turn.

'Come on,' Debs said, linking her arm through Didier's. 'We'll get these.'

Ava reached out quickly, attempting to claw at her friend's retreating coat but she missed. And that left just the two of them. And she had to ask Julien if he had a girlfriend. She looked up at him.

'Ava,' he said. 'There is something I have to...' He paused. 'Something I must tell you.'

'You've got a girlfriend,' Ava stated bluntly. 'I know.'

'What?' Julien exclaimed.

'It doesn't matter… because we're just friends and everything but… when you sort of held my hand today I thought… if your girlfriend had seen that… she might have thought it was something… not that it was something but…'

'Ava—'

'But I don't get why you would say you were single when you're not, because I thought we were friends and somehow I dissected my awful love life and home life for you and—'

'I *am* single,' Julien interrupted.

Ava blinked, confused. 'You don't have a girlfriend?'

He shook his head. 'No.'

'But the woman at the market.'

'I told you that was Diane from the gallery.'

'You did but… I thought you were meeting Lauren so…'

Julien shook his head. And this is where everything had sprung from. Him talking about his sister like she still worked not far from here, still lived in the apartment with the blue door.

'Ava, there is something I have to tell you… and it is about Lauren.' Every part of him was telling him to stop, fight against the words he didn't want to say, but he needed to do this for so many reasons.

'Please understand this…' He sighed. 'I did not mean to be dishonest with you.' He took hold of her hands as she just looked back at him, expression now confused. He swallowed. There was no going back now.

'Ava, Lauren—' There was no easy way. There were no soft words or a gentle way to put it. He took a deep breath and held it for a moment. The last moment before Ava realised he'd deceived her. 'Lauren died,' he said in no more than a whisper.

Her hands fell from his and one went to her chest as she rocked back a little. 'What?' she exclaimed. 'What d'you mean?

God, I feel sick. Julien… What d'you mean she died? I don't understand.'

'No. Ava, it is not now, not today.' He shook his head. This was so much harder than he could ever have imagined. 'It was… it was a year ago,' he said, swallowing. 'Ava, when I was talking about her to you, I just—' Nothing he said sounded appropriate. He tried again. 'I am so sorry, I… don't know what I was thinking. I just—'

'I don't understand,' Ava stated. 'Because you definitely said… you said yesterday that you were meeting her this morning.' She wet her lips. 'And…'

'I did not make it clear… I should have made it clear… I don't know why I did not but…'

He saw her absorbing this information and as each piece of knowledge hit her he watched every small part of the relationship they had built up begin to crumble. He had lied to her. Just like the boyfriend she had travelled the English Channel to leave behind.

'When did you say this was?' she asked. 'How long ago?'

'A year ago,' he repeated.

'A year.'

'Yes,' he said.

'She has been dead a year… we talked about her and it slipped your mind that she was actually dead?' Ava snapped.

He shook his head. 'It did not slip my mind… it never slips my mind… I just… said the wrong thing and then, once I had started saying the wrong thing it was just harder to put right.'

'I knew there was something wrong. When you said you had met your father… it just didn't seem right…'

'Ava, I didn't want to lie to you,' he said, wanting to take her hands but fearing it was too much now. 'It was just so… so wonderful to be able to speak to someone who didn't know what had happened… to talk about Lauren and to remember her like she was alive.'

'How did she die?' Ava asked, her tone a little softer.

He swallowed. 'It was an accident... a fire in her apartment block.' He paused, his skin prickling. 'It started in the roof and it ripped through the whole building. When I got there the whole place was engulfed in flames and...'

She gasped. 'You were there?'

'Too late,' he answered.

Her hands went to her mouth then and he saw tears building up in her eyes. He didn't want that. He didn't deserve her pity or her sympathy after he had kept it from her and tried to pretend it hadn't happened. And now she knew. Now he was the man who had lost his sister in a fire and hadn't been able to save her.

'Ava, from the bottom of my heart, I apologise for not telling you straight away. It was just so refreshing to be able to talk about her, share memories without pain, when for so long everyone around me seemed to want to forget her. I—'

'Julien,' Ava interrupted.

'No, please, you do not have to say anything. I know you will not want to see me again. I know how important honesty is to you and—'

'Julien... it's OK,' Ava said. 'I understand.'

'What?'

'I said it's OK,' she said. She moved her feet in the snow, crunching it underneath her soles. 'From what you've told me about Lauren, she was a big part of your life. Losing someone like that... I can only imagine...'

He nodded. 'She *was* a big part of my life.'

'Then... you had better tell me some more about her,' Ava said.

He smiled. 'Really?'

She nodded. 'Really, Monsieur Fitoussi.'

'Churros! Ava! Come on before Didier eats them all!' Debs called from the stall a few feet ahead.

'Ava,' Julien said, catching her arm before she could move away, 'there is something else you should know.'

'You do like Coldplay, don't you? You haven't lied to me about that?'

He smiled. 'Yes, Madonna, I do like Coldplay.' He wet his lips as he looked at her. 'And you should know... I really do not have a girlfriend.'

THIRTY-FIVE

'Have you been here before?' Ava asked as they walked behind Debs and Didier, taking in the sights and sounds of the Christmas fair going on all around them.

'Yes,' he answered. 'Many times. It is something of a tradition.' He breathed in the scent of sizzling sausage, caramelised onions and toffee-coated apples. 'Didier and I and—' He stopped talking, his sister's name on his lips.

'Lauren?' Ava added. 'Please, Julien, I meant it, I want to hear about her.' She watched Didier and Debs pause by a stall selling silver jewellery. 'I don't have any brothers or sisters but that girl with the hair like a Yeti... she's pretty much everything to me.'

'Lauren liked to come here to buy Christmas presents for the family,' Julien told her. 'She bought a special brooch for my step-mother here once.'

'Well, I hope she wasn't a kleptomaniac magpie like Debs. If we don't catch up to her and Didier, she's going to have bought enough silver to reconstruct the Eiffel Tower.'

'Ava, I want to have another exhibition of my work.'

She stopped walking and turned to face him, her full attention right there.

'I have this idea that I hope is going to help my family as well as a lot of other people.'

She didn't respond, as if waiting for him to give her more. What more was there yet? Just the spark of an idea, the hope that people would want to come, the frightening thought that he no longer had what it took, that the photographs he had sold in the past were the pinnacle of his career.

'I want to raise money for the the Red Cross.' He wet his lips. 'Ava, I have been so angry with everyone.' He breathed. 'That needs to change.'

He looked directly at her again then, watching for the reaction in those green eyes. She was just looking back at him, unspeaking, unmoving, barely breathing.

'I want to celebrate Lauren's life and the lives of all the others lost in the fire on Rue Auzenne and I want it to do some good. Raise money. Show the resilience we all need at this time.'

Her hand was on his arm then. 'You told me you were looking for a focus for your work.'

'Yes.' He nodded.

'And for your exhibition these would be photos *you* want to take, not photos other people have *told* you to take.'

He nodded again. 'Yes.'

'Then, all round, it's a wonderful thing to do,' Ava concluded.

He felt as if someone had just filled his chest with helium... or hope. Could this really work? Without the photographs he had taken of her? There was no way he could ever use them now. Not after he had already broken her trust.

'Do you have a photograph of her?' Ava asked. 'Of Lauren?'

'*Oui.*'

He slipped his hand into the pocket of his jeans and drew out his phone. Tapping at the photo app, he found one of his favourites. Him and Lauren, a selfie from an ordinary Friday night out in their last summer together. Her long blonde hair shining in the sun, her wide smile and the sparkle of mischief in her eyes dominating the snap. He held it out to Ava who took the phone, looking to the screen.

'She's blonde,' Ava said, shaking her head as she remembered thinking Diane at the market could be Lauren. This was more like the woman Julien had described. 'And so beautiful.'

He couldn't bring himself to reply.

'And she looks so happy.'

'She was... almost all of the time.'

Ava passed back the phone and as he took it from her she connected his free hand with hers. The warmth and sentiment kick-started a chain reaction inside him.

'I will need help,' he said quickly, trying to ignore the feelings cascading over his body like a shower set to scalding. 'To decide on the photographs, to arrange the event... I thought you might like to use your artistic eye again... but I understand, if, after everything you feel you cannot...'

'Oh, Monsieur Fitoussi, of course I'll help,' she responded, giving his hand a squeeze. 'Just as long as I'm behind the lens and not in front of it.' She smiled. 'Seeing as Paris *is* the most photogenic city in the world. I'm sure you'll have no problem conjuring up some great shots.'

'*Magique*, Madonna?'

'Just this once,' she answered with a smile.

'And perhaps some snail butter?' he asked.

'My life would be poorer without it,' she replied. 'Come on, let's catch up with Debs and Didier before she gets to those snow globes over there.' She dropped his hand and headed off.

He watched her, bowling up to their friends, arms flying, snatching something from Debs' hand and it was then he knew. He knew that really the only thing he wanted to photograph in Paris was her. And that now, more than ever, she was completely off limits.

THIRTY-SIX

Hotel Agincourt

'These eggs Benedict are totes amazing,' Debs announced, scooping up another forkful of egg and sauce, a little drizzling down her chin as she missed her mouth.

They were in the corner of the dining room, next to the window with a view of Brasserie Du Bec across the street – the restaurant they had eaten in with Julien and Didier again last night. The Christmas fair had been so much fun. They had ridden the carousel, watched a winter-themed puppet show, drank spiced wine and ate churros. They had all added snippets of observations for Debs' articles that she noted down or dictated into her phone. Then they had eaten a late dinner before departing just after Debs had tried to balance truffle chocolates on her face and ended up getting one stuck up her nose. They had all laughed so much. It was simple, relaxed, just so... Paris at Christmas. And later there would be more of that to come. Ava was meeting Julien to help him take photographs for his exhibition.

'Aren't you hungry?' Debs asked. 'Is it because of Julien's sister?'

'No,' she answered.

'It was a bit of a shock, wasn't it?'

Ava shrugged. It *had* been a shock, but Julien had been so apologetic last night. Lauren's death had hit him so hard, how could she not forgive him? You couldn't be mad at someone who was still mourning.

She *was* hungry but it was Goa Day. Her mother was on her mind and when her mother was on her mind the only other thing in her head space was calorie counting. Maybe she should have gone to Goa. The Azores client would have taken one look at her and put her straight back on the plane. She would have done what her mother had wanted and not had to face the dreaded camera. Christmas was coming and although she hated the low-calorie version Rhoda knocked up she always went through with it. Because you didn't leave your mother alone on Christmas Day no matter how much she blighted your life. But she didn't know if she could take another *silent* Christmas this year. She'd had one of those the year she first skipped out on modelling and it had taken until the next one for a thaw to begin.

She reached into her bag and picked out her phone. Looking at the black screen she realised she was too scared to actually switch it on. She knew what would be there. Another five text messages from her mother and a couple of voicemails. Rhoda still wouldn't have given up hope that Ava would 'come to her senses' until the boarding gate closed. She put the phone on the table.

'You don't mind doing this, do you?' Debs asked. 'Because say if you do. This is my problem really and I know you think I'm totes nuts but—'

'Debs, we're in this together, remember,' Ava stated.

'I would do it myself but if Gary's at it with her then he might have mentioned me... Well, probably not I suppose because why would you mention your step-daughter when you're in the middle of shagging someone who isn't your step-daughter's mother... that would kill the passion, wouldn't it?'

'Just a bit,' Ava agreed.

'Unless he has a fetish... which I don't want to even consider, but seeing as I apparently do not know this man at all...' Debs ended the sentence with a high-pitched sob.

She wasn't going to mention the fact that there was a possibility Francine would remember them both from the boutique. Instead, Ava reached across the table and stabbed at Debs' eggs with her fork, pinching some and putting it into her mouth. 'It's fine. It's going to be easy.' She put the fork back down and pulled Debs' shiny notepad and fluffy pen towards her.

Debs nodded, dabbing at her eyes with a serviette. 'So, last night was fun. You and Julien seemed to be getting on well.'

Ava nodded. 'He still likes Coldplay, he doesn't have a girlfriend and we can be friends again.'

'*Just* friends?' Debs queried.

She nodded, not looking up from the notepad. Even as the pen hit the paper and she tried to concentrate, she couldn't stop recalling how Julien had looked last night. Those lithe limb-hugging jeans, the shirt that skimmed his body, his rich dark hair, and how intense his eyes became when he was listening deeply.

'What am I saying?' Debs asked. 'You're about to bust into the office of a woman who is probably cheating with my stepdad. Men just can't be trusted as anything more than friends.'

'Not even Didier?' Ava countered. 'I thought you were giving him the benefit of the doubt.'

Debs blushed and picked up her cup of tea. 'He's totes sweet.'

'And good-looking,' Ava added.

'Don't think I don't know what you're doing,' Debs stated. 'Classic reversal technique to try and throw me off the scent of something going on with you and Julien.'

'Nothing's going on,' Ava stated. 'Friends.' She hadn't given him the picture.

'What are you doing?' Debs asked, looking to the notepad.

Ava looked too. She had just sketched a caricature of her mother, giant earrings hanging from ear lobes, teeth set in an overbite she didn't have any more thanks to the Croatian dentist, hair like the creamy quiff of a Mr Whippy.

'You're drawing again,' Debs stated like Ava had discovered a cure for the common cold. 'First Julien, now your mother.'

Ava put down the pen.

'It's very good,' Debs said, pulling the notebook towards her. 'But I'm not sure I want you to draw me.'

Ava smiled. 'Why don't I draw Francine?'

Debs passed the book back across the table. 'She might have a teeny tiny waist but she has quite a blunt chin. Totes emphasise that.'

THIRTY-SEVEN

Cosmos Protection offices

For the second time since they had been in Paris, Ava and Debs stood outside the Cosmos Protection offices. It was freezing today, too cold for snow and Ava was actually relishing getting inside the building for a little warm relief.

'So, you know where her office is?' Debs said, binoculars to her face.

'Yes.' They had looked on the website, and Debs had somehow found schematics for the building when it was renovated. 'Francine is on the third floor.'

'It looked like they all had names on the doors of the offices if the Christmas party 2014 photos are still reliable... but if it's open-plan now?'

'I ask... in my best French.'

'No!' Debs exclaimed. 'Play dumb.'

'As I said... my best French.'

Ava was still very much believing that Francine had said something other than 'Gary' in the boutique. It could be any number of things. Barry – someone else's husband she was cheating with – Larry – ditto or a cute Christmas lamb – marry – maybe Francine was getting married. It would explain the expensive dress shop. But what if her fiancé was Debs' step-dad?

'I just want this all to be over... one way or the other... I need to concentrate on getting my writing career back on track. I can't have a family crisis right now – things are bad enough.' Debs sucked in a breath. 'That sounds totes selfish, doesn't it?'

'No,' Ava stated. 'Of course it doesn't.' She steeled herself, standing up straight and looking at the entrance of the building. 'Right, give me the parcel and remind me what I'm looking for.'

Debs handed over the small box, brightly wrapped in gold and red paper. 'Anything at all that looks suspicious. I will make a telephone call for her to come down to reception as soon as you're in the building, so you're going to have to be quick. Check her emails, poke around in her drawers and her handbag. If she's having an affair then there's going to be evidence somewhere.'

'OK.' She wasn't OK really. She was worried someone was going to catch her in drawers and handbags and the gendarmerie were going to take a very dim view of it. This was, on the face of it, completely insane. But after breakfast she had had her best friend in floods of tears because Sue had found a number of euro purchases on Gary's credit card. Sue knew the password to the account. Sue also knew these items weren't attributable to the usual overnights in Toulouse or the airport restaurant – but they were all French.

Even if the name 'Gary' hadn't been spoken in the boutique, something was off. Confronted with the credit card information, busting into Francine's office had seemed like the only logical thing to do.

Ava swallowed. 'And if she comes back and I'm still there?'

'You've set the ring tone for my number to the theme from *Star Wars*, haven't you?'

'Yes.'

'And you have actually turned it on?'

'Yes, two voicemails from my mother I refuse to listen to.'

'Then as soon as Francine leaves reception to go back upstairs I'll call you and you'll totes get a Darth Vader sense of urgency.'

'OK,' Ava said, taking another breath and rocking up and down onto her tip-toes. 'But, just say, she comes back and I'm still there.'

'That's why you have the parcel,' Debs reminded. 'But please don't give it away unless you absolutely have to. I really want to try that grow-your-own-rainbow kit.'

'OK,' Ava said. 'I think I'm ready.'

'OK,' Debs said, a shaky breath leaving her lips. 'Thank you so much, Ava, for doing this.'

'Please say that again, with bail money in your hand, if all this goes wrong.'

'Good luck.'

Clutching the box to her chest, Ava prepared to cross the street.

Her plan was to say absolutely nothing unless she had to. She had considered borrowing a helmet from the back of a line of mopeds parked just outside and refusing to remove it while she carried the highly confidential, not-to-be-opened-by-anyone-else package up to the third floor, but then she thought better of it. Knowing her luck, a woman refusing to remove headwear would spark a security alert.

This was just a role to play. Exactly like a *modelling* role. She was a delivery girl. Tasked with the job of getting this private package to Francine personally. She just had to slip into that part. Give it the right attitude. No one at the insurance office would ever suspect what she was really doing.

She pushed open the glass door and was hit by the emptiness of the reception area. There was a Christmas tree to her right, but no lights, no decorations, just a bare tree in a pot. She almost felt sorry for it. *Delivery girl.* She looked to the pristine white desk in front of her and behind it two immaculately presented women oozing Parisian office chic. They looked efficient as they typed away on keyboards that barely made a sound, they would be able to smell her fake story a mile off. Eyes shooting left she picked out the elevator. That's where she was heading.

Stepping confidently forward she stopped at the sound of someone's voice. '*Pardon, Mademoiselle.*'

Why hadn't she had the foresight to slip her earphones in before she entered the offices? She could have continued walking, nodding her head to inaudible music and making for the lift. Instead she was stood still, caught between running for the stairs and facing someone she didn't really want to speak to.

Ava waved a hand. She could pretend she was mute. Had only heard the voice because of the vibration in the air. She walked a few steps more, willing the lift not to be up on the fifth floor. Perhaps someone was on their way down... but not Francine just yet, not until she was halfway to the third level... but someone who would force the lift doors open just when she needed them.

'*Madame,*' the receptionist called again.

She wasn't stopping. Not now. Not for anything or anyone. She waved again then sprinted past the elevator and through the door that had a sign of a stick man going up some stairs.

Receptionists didn't run, did they? Ava was quite sure, in all her twenty-four years, she had never seen a receptionist run. But, just to be sure, *she* ran. Taking the stairs two at a time and hoping, when Debs' call came through that Francine didn't decide to be health-conscious and not use the lift.

Powering up the steps she stopped when she got to a door indicating it was the third-floor entrance. This was it. Francine's level. It was time to be the delivery girl/private investigator.

She pushed open the door with one foot and stepped through, trying to act confident. Shit, it *was* all open plan and now she was faced with glass screens and dozens of people talking into headsets at their desks, moving around the floor looking like they were performing important business, and she had no idea where Francine's desk was.

But she was a *delivery girl.* She had the ultimate excuse in her hands. An important package. And she needed to be quick.

She swallowed and stepped forward, tentatively at first until she remembered she was acting and needed to be convincing. 'Excuse me,' she addressed a woman in a navy pantsuit. 'I'm looking...' She tried again. '*Je cherche* Francine Duval.'

The woman pointed. But to nowhere specific, just to the main clump of desks in the centre of the room. Ava supposed it was a start. She nodded and moved on, walking past employees of Cosmos Protection and trying to appear nonchalant.

When she got a fair way into the mire of wood, pleather seats and paperwork she addressed someone who looked young enough to be a school leaver. 'Francine Duval?' Suddenly aware of how weak and non-authoritative she sounded she put her shoulders back. '*Un cadeau.*'

The young man smiled. 'She has gone to see a client but I can take this for you.'

And he spoke excellent English. Fuck.

'Oh, no, *non*, thank you. I have instructions to put this... right on her desk,' Ava said, her cheeks reddening.

'You do?' the man asked.

'I do.' She cleared her throat. 'So, if you could just tell me where her desk is then...'

Her phone erupted then. The *Star Wars* theme tune blaring out for the whole floor to hear. It couldn't be time for her to get out of there already. She held the box in one hand and disabled her ringing phone with the other, smiling at the man. 'Francine's desk?'

He furrowed his brow but pointed. 'By the window.'

He had barely got the word 'window' out of his mouth before Ava was skipping over to it way too eagerly for a *delivery girl*. She didn't want to draw any attention to herself. When she was rifling through Francine's belongings she needed everyone to be looking at something else other than her.

The desk was neat. *Very* neat. With a pristine keyboard and computer screen, not one Post It note stuck to it. There were no coffee rings on the desk or escapee paperclips and not a crumb on the clean mouse mat.

This was a woman who kept things tidy. How likely was it that she was going to keep evidence of an affair here? A dirty secret was going to clutter up her work surface no end.

Ava wrenched open one of the drawers. Francine had perfumed liners and little wooden trays housing everything. There were highlighters in four different colours, beautiful tapestried notepads and envelopes sorted by size. It was actually Debs' dream drawer of stationery – that was ironic.

Star Wars erupted again and it made Ava jump, frantically pushing her hands into the pockets of her jeans to get her phone out and stop it.

'Can I help you?'

Shit. She knew who that was without needing to turn around. *Francine.* No more than a few yards behind her. She could practically feel the breath on the back of her neck. *Confidence.* She had to play a role.

'Yes,' Ava said, spinning around and pretending she was chewing gum. She had no idea why she felt the need to do that but the up and downward motion of her jaw was stopping her blurting out things best kept to herself. 'I have a parcel for you.' Debs was going to have to be parted from the grow-your-own-rainbow kit after all.

'A parcel?' Francine looked immediately suspicious. Why would someone look immediately suspicious if they had nothing to hide? Or maybe it was because she had neat eyebrows as well as everything else and they could only express suspicion.

'A present,' Ava continued, eyes roving over the desk, looking for anything, *anything* that might be evidence of an affair with Gary. '*Un cadeau.*' She was really rocking the French language.

'Really?' Francine exclaimed, her voice a note lighter, eyes showing a little excitement. 'Who is it from?'

Who *was* it from? She really hadn't thought this through. Who could it be from? It was so tempting to say Santa. She swallowed. 'I don't know... perhaps a client.'

She handed the box over to Francine and watched the woman begin to tear at the paper. She didn't need to be here to see Francine discover that someone had given her a grow-your-own-rainbow kit... but she needed every second to try and see something of use while she was here, living out this charade. And then it happened, just as Francine was pulling the gift from its box, the woman's computer binged and a notification popped up on the screen. An email. From Gary Lyons. Debs' step-dad Gary.

Ava expelled air in shock, then quickly scrutinised the screen looking for the subject of the message. Would it be a love heart emoji? A saucy 'hey babe'? Something dirty?

It said 'private'. And then there was the very first line. 'Francine, the other night was amazing...'

Ava stepped back, walking into a metal bin that fell, scattering an empty plastic bottle and a takeaway coffee cup over the carpet. She had to get out of there.

'There is no card... no message...' Francine called to Ava's retreating form.

She shrugged. 'Sorry... I'm just the delivery girl.' And then she turned towards the door to the stairs, desperate to escape, even though she knew what came next would be harder.

THIRTY EIGHT

Eiffel Tower

She hadn't told Debs anything yet. 'Francine, the other night was amazing.' She swallowed. What did you read from that? She knew exactly what conclusion Debs would jump to. But it couldn't be that, could it? Maybe Francine was working on a joint French project. Maybe they had Skyped through an 'amazing' new insurance concept. Ava had come out of the offices trying to look nonchalant and told Debs she had found nothing. But she had, and even if the email wasn't as incriminating as it appeared, it did seem to indicate that Gary was in Paris not Toulouse. And no one lied about where they were unless they were covering up something really big, did they?

She had left Debs – worried, frustrated, dying for answers – heading off to research a new coffee shop afternoon for singles and Ava only hoped the coffee and the need to write something Trudy couldn't would distract her friend until Ava worked out what to do next.

'You are here, Madonna?'

Julien waved a hand in front of her face, his voice just loud enough to hear above the sound of a brass band playing to tourists who, even in the cold, were congregating around Paris' most famous landmark. Some were waiting to ascend the tower, others just sipped hot chocolate and munched on crepes, browsing the stalls of tacky souvenirs, of which there seemed to be many.

'Here,' she replied, nodding.

The trouble was, now she was here she remembered the last time she had been here. She'd squeezed Leo's hand tight and almost burst with excitement when she saw the fountains and the trees, the infamous tower like an upside down ice-cream cone. She'd turned to him, ready to say this was the best place she'd ever been and then she saw in his free hand he was holding his mobile phone, tapping out an email to work or... perhaps even then he was sending messages to someone else... someone like Cassandra.

'Look at them all,' Julien stated. 'Everyone always wants to take photographs of the tower.'

His voice dragged her back to the present and she turned to face him. 'Of course they do. This round-the-wrong-way Cornetto is what most people come to Paris to see.'

'And you too think this is beautiful?' Julien asked.

'I think it's iconic, yes,' Ava admitted.

'Why? Because everyone tells you it is?'

'Monsieur Fitoussi, you really are cynical about everything, aren't you?'

'It is simply an iron building.'

Ava sucked in a breath. 'You can't say that! It's your national symbol!'

'You know that most of the French people think this is ugly, no?'

'They can't!' Ava said, appalled.

'Why not?' he asked her. 'It is too big, it towers over the skyline and looks out of place.'

'I'm outraged and am deeply offended on its behalf,' Ava said. She turned to face the tower and raised her hands in the air. 'Madame Eiffel, don't listen to the crazy photographer. You are not just a pile of girders, you are an icon... a beacon of solidarity for all the not-quite-perfect models out there. So what if your lines are metal? You're sleek and original. Who cares if your lifts are always going out of order? You're special!'

'You are crazy,' Julien stated, laughing.

'So, if you come here and don't take photographs of the tower, what do you take photos of?'

She watched his eyes come away from the tower and she tried to follow his line of sight.

'You know the Musée Rodin?' he asked.

She shook her head. Until this trip she hadn't set foot in a museum here or anywhere else. Most holidays she'd been on involved lastminute.com.

'There is a sculpture,' he said. 'It is called... *The Kiss*.'

She swallowed, her cheeks heating up. 'You take photos of a sculpture?'

He shook his head. '*Non*.'

'Then what?'

He spread his arms wide, indicating the snow-covered grass between them and the Tour Eiffel, the trees lining the avenues leading the way to the structure. 'Look around you,' he said. 'You said it yourself, people come here to see the ugly tower.'

'I didn't call her ugly, *you* did,' Ava protested.

'So, tell me, what type of people come here the most?' Julien enquired.

'I've seen quite a number of Japanese.'

'Not the nationality,' Julien stated.

'Students?' Ava guessed again.

'Couples,' Julien said. 'Men and women, women and women, men and men... lovers.'

At the word 'lovers' Ava's stomach paraglided down to somewhere near her Converse. What was it with the French accent? She regrouped quickly. She had been part of a couple in Paris before, high on the romance and the lure of plastic statues and key rings of the tower. This time she was completely, utterly immune. With a two-timing rat as an ex and Gary's alleged infidelity in the air she didn't need to look hard for reminders that single was better. Single was simple. She cleared her throat. 'What does that have to do with a sculpture?'

'Well,' Julien started. 'I like to watch the lovers. I watch how they interact with each other... look at each other... kiss each other.'

A shiver ran through her as those dark eyes met hers and she quickly screwed her face up. 'There's a name for people like you and it almost rhymes with Sacré-Coeur.'

'Photographer?' he asked, blinking.

Ava shook her head and let out a laugh. 'I think you need to show me, Monsieur Fitoussi.' She breathed in. 'Show me what's going to make the cut in your charity exhibition.'

'*D'accord*,' he answered. '*Regarde.*'

Julien had taken her across to one of his favourite spots, a bench with a view of the comings and goings around the bottom of the tower. Usually, in spring, the trees would be in blooms of pink and white, now there was no foliage, just dark boughs sprinkled with snow, tourists not in shorts or summer dresses but thick coats, hats and scarves. Ava cradled the coffee she'd bought, looking at passers-by as if she expected some sort of revolution to occur. Already he knew patience wasn't her strong point. If he wasn't able to find the couple he had described he feared she would be bored. And what would her boredom say about his idea for beauty, simplicity and life going on as the backbone of his exhibition?

'What are we looking for?' she whispered as if they were part of some top-secret covert mission.

'It is not as simple as that,' he answered.

'You *don't know* what you're looking for, do you?' she guessed.

'You are finally understanding my work,' he stated, smiling as his eyes still scanned a crowd congregating around the carousel. Old-fashioned painted horses rose sedately up and down on gilt poles, piped fairground music accompanying them, riders red-cheeked and smiling.

'I don't know how you do it,' she admitted.

'Do what?'

'Go out with your camera and not know if you're going to find anything.'

'Oh, Madonna, that is the very best part of my job.'

'It would drive me mad. Particularly if I planned on having an exhibition.'

'Is it not a little like selling apartments?' he asked.

'How?'

'You do not sell an apartment every day?'

'Actually most weeks lately I've sold *at least* one every day.'

'But until that sale, perhaps when the clock is ticking around to the end of the day. Maybe you are tired and you think there is no possibility of anyone coming to view and then... a rich sultan arrives and buys a whole floor.'

She smirked. 'There's only been one rich sultan in Canary Wharf and unfortunately Milo got the commission on that one.'

'But you understand what I am saying. When we wake up, when we greet the day, none of us know exactly what is going to happen... good or bad.' He quickly smiled. 'The only thing we do know is that *something* is going to happen.' He caught hold of her arm quickly. 'Look!'

'Where?' she hissed.

'The couple there.' He moved his camera up to his eye.

'What? The man with the grey hair in jeans and the elegant woman who looks like she wants to punch him in the face? Are they even a couple?'

'Yes,' Julien breathed, taking another shot. 'They are a couple.'

'But they look like they've had an argument,' Ava stated. 'They're walking three feet apart.'

'I know,' Julien stated, sitting forward on the bench. 'Wait.'

'The look on her face tells me we could be waiting a very long time for her to thaw. When I look like that it's usually days.'

'Unless someone buys you food?' Julien asked. 'Or perhaps strong coffee?'

Ava folded her arms across her chest. 'Maybe.' She sniffed. 'Is that what's going to happen? Is he going to buy her a bag of *madeleines* and a Java and all will be forgiven?'

'Sshh,' Julien said, one eye on the couple through the camera.

'I'll sing if you shush me again.'

'Please, not the 'La Marseillaise'. You sang all the wrong words last night.'

Ava concentrated on the couple Julien had pointed out. They looked to be in their forties. The man had shoulder-length grey hair swept back behind his ears, a brown leather three-quarter-length coat buttoned up to the neck, smart dark blue jeans and he was carrying a large bag with thin handles that looked like it came from a boutique. She shuddered. She didn't want to think about boutiques or *cadeaux* any more today.

The woman's hair was ebony, her glossy red lipstick a stark contrast to her pale skin, a short coat belted at the waist stopped at knee-length boots with heels higher than the pair Ava had worn to Bettina's. Even from this distance she could clearly see the woman's expression was fixed somewhere between sad and angry, not interacting in any way with the man who walked next to her. Ava didn't know what Julien was thinking, picking this couple for his 'the kiss' moment. If they ever kissed again it would be some sort of Christmas miracle.

'He's had enough,' Ava remarked, watching as the man walked away from the woman. 'I'm really not sure they were even a couple in the first place.'

'You are not watching closely enough,' Julien responded.

'I can see that she's pissed off with him and he's leaving her.' She took a swig of her coffee, swallowing then blowing the steamy breath out into the air.

'And where is he going?' Julien asked her.

She looked back to the scene, her eyes finding the man and following his movement across the avenue to a stallholder, two buckets sat on the concrete in front of him. *Roses.*

Ava let out a laugh. 'He isn't really going to do what I think he's going to do, is he?'

'What?' Julien asked.

'Roses,' she stated. 'From a street seller?! The woman looks like she's walked out of a chic boutique. She is never going to fall for a rose from a street seller when she looks as mad as she does right now.'

'You really have no faith at all, Ava?' he asked. 'Now who is the cynical one?'

Ava swallowed at his words. Why should she have faith in love? Two words. Leo. Gary. Two more. Her parents. She had every right to be cynical.

'Ava,' Julien said, 'look.'

She concentrated back on the man in the leather coat who now had a single red rose in his possession. The woman was standing a few yards away, her gaze on the Eiffel Tower, the winter sun reflected off the grey steel. Ava was holding her breath. Part of her wanted the woman to knock the rose to the ground and stamp her feet at his weak attempt at reconciliation. The other part of her wanted the woman to take the rose and smile, perhaps lift it to her nose and inhale the sweet, velvety scent. She wet her lips, eyes almost hurting as they focussed.

Ava could hear Julien's camera clicking away as the man approached the woman, the rose hidden behind his back. The man said something, making the woman turn and give him her full attention. Then he bowed to her before reaching out and taking one of his hands in hers. The woman was looking at him, the expression on her face a work in progress. The rose was presented and Ava watched the woman transform. Her whole body softened to the man, her face lighting up with surprise and utter excitement at this single stemmed flower with red petals. Ava swallowed, tears pricking her eyes without her even realising it, watching intently as the woman threw herself into the man's arms, the rose held tightly in her hands as she embraced him with everything she had. Ava couldn't look any more. Love. Simple. Honest. Not for her.

She quickly got to her feet, heading for anywhere with a little breathing space.

THIRTY-NINE

Ava couldn't go back. She was going to stay here, hands almost freezing to the metal railings, staring at the Eiffel Tower until it got too dark to see. Then and only then might the embarrassment start to lift. Getting emotional over a single rose and two strangers kissing in Paris. What was she thinking?!

'You left your coffee,' Julien said.

'Give it to the woman with the rose. If she went bat-shit crazy over a flower, who knows what she'll do over a coffee.'

She sensed him stand alongside her, then watched him put his hands to the railing, his index finger rubbing at the layer of snow on the upper rail.

'I am sorry,' he said softly.

She closed her eyes. She was done for. Now he was offering sympathy. She opened her eyes again. 'What for?'

'For not realising that perhaps you do not want to think of love at this time.'

She turned slightly, offering him a glance. 'I have a friend writing about the singles scene in Paris whilst hunting down a woman she thinks is sleeping with her step-dad. Like that theme song from *Four Weddings and a Funeral*, love is... all around... whether I like it or not.'

'I was insensitive.'

'Don't be ridiculous, Monsieur Fitoussi. I'm a big girl.' She let out a sigh. If that was the case, if watching the scene play out in front of her hadn't affected her, why had she run away and started hugging a fence?

'I was lucky,' Julien said, turning around and leaning his body against the railings and holding her coffee cup out to her.

She took it and it immediately warmed her fingers. 'What?'

'It does not always work that way,' he said. 'With the woman and the rose.'

'No?'

'No. Sometimes I could sit for days and not find any one giving me the emotion I want to capture.'

'You're just saying that to be nice.' She sniffed. 'You said it yourself. Paris is full of lovers. A whole city obsessed with love.'

'A city that needs all the love it can get right now,' he added. He was right.

'New beginnings, Madonna, like we talked about last night.'

New beginnings. Change. If she just found the courage to tell her mother 'no' once and for all she could finally be in control of her own destiny. She could change things in her life.

'I want to buy a love lock,' Ava stated, looking up at him, wide-eyed.

'What?' he asked, brow furrowing in confusion.

'I want to change things. I want to make a new beginning.'

She looked around the snow-spotted area around the base of the Eiffel Tower – the band still playing Christmas tunes, the stallholders holding flashing hats with models of the Tour Eiffel on them, the silver-painted human statue dressed like something from a Dickens' novel. 'Where do they sell them?'

'Ava...'

'Do you know? Do they have them on the merchandise stalls? I bet they do.' She deposited her cup in the nearest bin and began to walk towards a stall. Suddenly she was stopped, strong fingers gripping the sleeve of her coat.

'Ava, love isn't just about having another person in your life,' Julien stated. 'The man in England... he...'

'Oh,' Ava said. 'It's nothing to do with Leo.'

'No?'

She looked up at him, taking in the dark hair spiking out underneath the hat she had bought for him and those beautiful eyes. 'Have you ever been in love, Monsieur Fitoussi?'

She watched his expression cloud over in perfect time to the darkening of the Paris sky above then. She waited for his response.

'Yes,' he answered. 'Once.'

She spoke quickly, feeling the need to stifle the churning feeling in her stomach. 'What happened?'

'Nothing,' he said. 'And then everything.'

She watched a whole collection of emotions appear in his eyes, cover the firm jawline and drop down into the full lips. In her coat pocket her hand ached to come out into the cold and trace the contours of his face. She scrunched her hand up around the paper inside. Her wish list. Talk of dogs and plastic surgery and getting drunk. She held the torn paper between her fingers.

And then Julien smiled. 'Perhaps I should have bought more roses.'

'Or a love lock,' Ava suggested. 'Come on, Monsieur Fitoussi,' she said, threading her arm through his. 'Who says that love locks have to be for couples? What do you have in your pocket I can use to scratch my name with?'

They had climbed over six hundred steps and joined the winter crowds in the double-decker lifts, windows steaming up as they headed skywards, until they had reached the very top of the Tour Eiffel. Now, standing a few paces behind her, Julien watched Ava taking in this scene, his camera at work.

She had hurried over to the balustrade without concern for the nine hundred and five foot drop below her, as if she was determined to be at the front. She put her hands to her hat and removed it, slipping the wool covering into the pocket of her coat then putting her hands to the metalwork in front of her. The blonde spikes were immediately buffeted by the harsh, freezing air and he watched her straighten her arms, bracing herself against the force but remaining stoic. He snapped a couple more photos then joined her, gazing out over the city, the visibility stretching almost fifty miles.

'Like at the Sacré-Coeur it makes everything else seem that little bit less significant,' Ava said, breathing in deeply.

'Yes,' he answered. 'Up here you can see everything much more clearly.'

'I thought you said most of the French hated the Eiffel Tower,' she reminded.

'I said nothing about the view,' he answered.

She sighed. 'Up here I feel as though I'm bigger than anything else but also—'

'Smaller than everything else,' he interrupted.

She turned to him. 'Yes, that's exactly it.'

'And then you remember that, despite the vastness of this city' – he spread his arms out to indicate the size of what they could see – 'this is just one city... just one place.'

'But at night Tim Peake could see us from space,' Ava reminded.

'Not *us*,' Julien stated. 'Just... the light.'

There was that feeling again, squeezing his insides as Ava's green eyes looked up at him, her cheeks and the end of her nose a little pink, that bright hair meant as a statement only succeeding in her making her appear more vulnerable.

'Do you wish *you'd* bought a lock?' she asked, grinning as she pulled out the golden padlock she'd purchased.

'You do know, Madonna, the place to lock yourself to is the Pont de L'Archevêché.'

Ava flapped a hand. 'That's where *everyone* puts their lock,' she dismissed. 'I want to be different and' – she looked around – there isn't many up here... maybe thirty or so.'

'You know why this is?' Julien asked.

'Because lovers are too lazy to climb the steps or put up with that slower-than-snail-butter ride in the lift?'

He smiled. 'No. I am afraid to say that periodically the authorities cut them off.'

Ava clamped her hands to her chest. 'What?!' She was wide-eyed. 'The city of love destroys the hopes and dreams of hundreds of tourists?!'

'In reality it is vandalism.'

'Speaks the man who photographed them.'

'Just because I take photographs of something does not mean I support it.'

He watched Ava scowl, her fingers curled around the lock in her hand. 'So you're really saying *you* don't believe in true love either.'

'That is not what I am saying at all.'

'So you're saying you don't believe in the power of the love lock.'

'The power of the love lock, Madonna? Really?'

'It's a statement, isn't it? It's someone saying, "This is how I feel right now, here in this place."'

'Usually with another person,' Julien stated.

'Ah ha,' Ava said. 'But it doesn't *have* to be with another person.' She held her hand out. 'Give me the little baby camera screwdriver you said you had.'

Snowflakes were settling on her hand as she waited, watching Julien dip his fingers into the pocket of his coat and take out an almost microscopic tool. He placed it in her palm and she closed her fingers over it, moving it around until it was in her grip and ready to use like a pen.

'What are you going to write?' Julien asked.

'*Now* you're interested,' Ava said, pressing the padlock to her thigh and bending over, the tool in her other hand, attempting to etch into the metal.

'Have you done this before?' he inquired.

'Etched? No, because I'm not from the fifteenth century.' This was hard work. It was a good job her name was only three letters long or they might be up here long enough for the astronauts to wave at them.

'I mean a love lock,' Julien said.

She looked up then and shook her head. 'No.' She was about to drop her head and resume, then she spoke again. 'Have you?'

'*Non*,' he answered.

'Because you think they're a little bit like graffiti?' she questioned.

'No,' he said. 'Because locking yourself to something or someone... it's like...'

'Marriage?' Ava asked with a grin.

He shook his head. 'No, it's like... trying to get the world to stay the same. Trying to control Fate.'

'Wow,' Ava said. 'You really do think deeply about everything.' She started to carve out a 'V'. 'I think most people who lock their initials onto a bridge are just trying to make a gesture of love... or reassurance... a statement of togetherness. It doesn't matter if all of them stay together for the rest of their lives, the important thing is, at the time, they believed they could.'

Had she just said that? Had she really spoken up for love? She couldn't bring herself to look at Julien. He was probably grinning, knowing she had shone a shaft of light down onto the 'true love' camp.

'You are writing your name,' Julien said.

'Yes. Just *my* name and, if my fingers don't go numb, I was going to scratch the date on the back. Because my love lock is all about me and no one else.' She took a breath. 'I did a drawing this morning.'

'You did?'

'Yes, without even really realising it. Debs was eating eggs Benedict and I was thinking about Goa and there I was, scratching out a rather impressive evil caricature of my mother.'

'And how did that make you feel?' Julien asked.

'Like I could probably get a job with *Marvel* if I wanted.'

He smiled. 'New beginnings, Madonna. The possibility of possibilities.'

She nodded. 'Yes... so this love lock... this is about me, believing in myself,' she stated, scratching the last leg of the final 'A'. 'This is about me, sending a message. Not to anyone else. Just to myself.' She drew in a long breath, her eyes going from the padlock in her hands to the view down below, the white speckled greenery of the open space in front of the tower, the hundreds of roof tops, the cars and people far below all looking no bigger than the snowflakes rushing through the sky towards them. 'This is about me loving me. Standing here, independently, not on a plane to Goa to please my mother, not doing a boring job or being cheated on.' She raised her head to meet his eyes then. 'Just being here in Paris, maybe single, but with everything out there within my reach.' The sigh that left her made a high-pitched noise of delight and she felt a thrill run through her. 'That's why I'm doing it. Just for me.' She smiled. 'To celebrate me.'

She meant it. A new start was needed and whether Julien thought the idea was silly or not, attaching her lock at the top of the Eiffel Tower was going to be life-affirming. She hooked the metal catch through the wire of the barrier and clasped it on with a definite clunk.

'There,' she said, pulling at the lock to ensure it was fixed. 'It doesn't matter if it stays here for a week or for a hundred years... I'll remember the moment I fixed it on.' She smiled. 'You think I'm being selfish, don't you?'

He shook his head. 'No, Madonna.'

'Well, maybe I am, a bit.' She sighed. 'But I think this time I have to be a little bit selfish.' She looked out over the city. 'I've spent my whole life doing things for other people and not doing things for me. It's time I took control of my life.'

Julien smiled. 'I do not think that is selfishness, Madonna. I think that is just waking up.' He put his hand into the pocket of his coat. 'And that is a good thing.' He drew out another padlock.

She gasped. 'You *did* buy one!'

'Maybe.'

'Maybe? I can see it, Julien.' She held out the screwdriver to him.

'I do not know why I am doing this,' he admitted. 'Because in reality it is pointless.'

'But you believe in the magic of photography and true love. Why can't you invest a little in this?'

'I am, Madonna,' he said, scratching out his name. 'Only so your poor love lock is not hanging all alone for decades, stray cats and master etchers looking at it in sympathy.'

She punched him on the arm. 'Don't you put a *pity* padlock next to mine,' she warned.

'There,' he said, blowing the small shavings of metal from his lock and admiring the word.

Ava looked at his name, perfectly formed, not a large scrawly mess like hers. 'You've done this before!'

'What?'

'Look how neat it is!' she exclaimed. 'You etch... in secret... when you're not taking photographs.'

He laughed. 'I promise you I do not.' He smiled. 'May I lock myself next to you?'

'On one condition,' she answered.

'Yes?'

'When I go back to England, you have to come up here at least once a week and make sure the locks are still here.'

He shook his head. 'You are serious?'

'Yes! I know I said it didn't matter how long they survived up here but I don't want to think about a burly council worker with bolt cutters breaking apart my celebration of me.'

'You are crazy,' Julien stated.

'Promise,' Ava said. 'If we were stood in England, halfway up the Blackpool Tower, then I would do it.'

'I thought you said you live in London.'

'I do.'

'Blackpool is not close to London. I know this.'

'Promise me,' Ava said again.

'Very well,' Julien said. 'I promise.'

'OK,' Ava said, satisfied. 'You can loop it through next to mine.'

She watched him push the silver metal of the catch through the fence and then secure the lock in place right next to hers. She sighed and looked at their locks, the backdrop of a wintry Paris behind them. 'I wonder what people will think when they stand here taking their selfies. Do you think they will look at our locks and think about who we are?'

'Not if they are from the *conseil* with tools to remove them.'

'Stop it!' she said, laughing.

'What would you like people to think, Madonna?' Julien asked her.

Ava rested her elbows on the barrier and gazed out over the city. 'I want people to think, Ava and Julien stood here once and they loved this place.' She took in another breath. 'And they'll be imagining me looking like Anne Hathaway and they will imagine you looking like... who is the most famous Frenchman? Still David Ginola?'

'Seriously?' He raised one eyebrow.

'Who do you want to be?' she asked. 'I know... one of Daft Punk.'

'For one moment I was thinking you might say Jean-Michel Jarre.'

'Who's that?'

Julien laughed, shaking his head.

'Eric Cantona!' Ava countered.

'Do you only know footballers?'

'You can blame my dad for that.'

'So, what if I am Jean-Paul Gaultier,' he suggested. 'The designer of that conical stage outfit, Madonna.'

Ava laughed. 'Very funny.'

A sharp wind came out of nowhere and Ava made a grab for her hat, the strength of the wind blowing her off-kilter. Julien reached out to steady her, his hand connecting with hers.

'You are OK?' he asked.

She nodded, tingles spreading up her arm as his fingers remained intertwined with hers. She should let him go. She wasn't looking for anything romantic here. She was voting for the Single Party. She wanted a T-shirt that said Young, Free and Not Yours. Men were all the same. She had oodles of proof. Didn't she?

But then her fingers tightened around his and she let his much bigger hand envelop hers. Daring to look up, she met the dark hair spiking out from under his hat and those gorgeous eyes looking back at her. Julien wasn't Leo. He was a man standing at the top of the Eiffel Tower with her, a man who listened to her opinions, shared his but never told her what she felt was wrong. Never judged.

Her heart was pummelling her chest wall, the wind whipping around her cheeks, her hand still in Julien's, flakes of snow hitting her exposed skin. She swallowed, still looking into his eyes, unmoving and then... she saw him inch forward, just one inch, barely noticeable unless you were fixed on noticing like her. It was just enough to tip the balance.

Ava closed the gap between them quickly, before she could think about what she was doing, and raised herself up on tiptoes, pausing just before she made any connection. She held herself there, eye to eye with him, the heat from his breath warming her cheeks, the rise and fall of his chest only inches away from her own. Time seemed to stop and she was almost ready to drop down and retreat until...

He claimed her mouth with his, almost gathering her up in his embrace, his hands on her face, his beautiful lips pressed against hers. He tasted of snow and cinnamon coffee and a hot sweetness she couldn't immediately define. With closed eyes she tried to savour every second as his tongue sent shockwaves of longing through her, right down to her Converse. She held on, her hands pulling his hat away from his head, her fingers weaving through his thick dark hair. Right now she wanted to stay here in this perfect moment forever.

And then Julien ended the kiss. Ava opened her eyes, blinking, almost scared she had imagined the whole thing. Julien was looking back at her, his fingers at the camera still around his neck, body language giving off mixed signals.

'Did I break it?' she asked on a breath.

Confusion coated his expression as he looked back at her. 'What?'

'Your camera,' she said. 'You know... when I threw myself at you like a desperate ex-model pretending to be Anne Hathaway.'

He shook his head. 'No... to both things.'

'Good,' Ava said. 'Because we should... we can forget that ever happened. I mean, it was just a moment. I blame the love locks.'

'You do?' Julien asked her.

'Don't you?'

'*Non*,' he answered. 'I blame the fact I have not been able to take my eyes off you from the moment we met.'

FORTY

Julien couldn't believe he had said that out loud. What was he thinking? Why had he let himself kiss her? He had wanted to... more than anything... but... it wasn't right. Ava didn't need the complication of a romance for numerous reasons she had spelled out to him since they had met... and he wasn't ready either.

'Oh,' Ava answered. 'Really?'

He nodded, despite his internal protestations. 'I do not know if it was your hair or your eyes or the way you hated me with such passion when we first met but—'

'This is a bad idea though, isn't it?'

He swallowed. She was right, of course, he thought so himself, but the words pinched all the same. And how did he respond?

'Would it help if I tell you I believe, in life, there is no such thing as a bad idea. Only ideas that work and ideas that do not.'

'I'm not sure that *does* help,' she answered.

'What if I tell you I do not want to hurt you.' He swallowed.

'What if *I* said you are thinking about things too deeply again.'

'Madonna...'

'Monsieur Fitoussi.'

She had lifted her head up to meet his gaze again, her jaw set to defiant and all he wanted to do was take that petite frame into his arms and never let anything bad touch her. And that was half of his conflict. He couldn't promise her that. Life was life. And he was still so at odds with it.

'We should go,' he said, the chill of the wind finally making it through to his bones. 'Find somewhere for another coffee, no?'

The look on her face said he had already hurt her by making such a feeble response. 'Ava...' he tried again.

'You should put your hat back on,' she said, pressing the wool to his hand.

The route they had taken up to the summit of the tower seemed twice as long coming back down again. Ava felt stupid. She didn't know what to say to Julien. The first person who really seemed to get her and she had buggered it up by kissing him. To be fair he had kissed her back but now, at least a foot between them on the descent, even small talk was difficult. She wished she could take back the kiss... the best kiss she'd ever had... one that had made her toes curl and her head fizz.

'I am concerned about my father,' Julien spoke, continuing to step downwards.

He had moved the conversation on. It was for the best. 'He isn't well?' she asked.

'No... it is not an illness... well, perhaps it is.' He sighed. 'Ava, my whole family has not dealt with Lauren's death very well. My father, the one who pretends to be strong and untouchable... he is not coping and I worry for my step-mother,' he admitted.

'What are you going to do?'

'I would like my exhibition to take place before the wedding.'

Her jaw dropped then and she gripped the rail of the stairs. 'You told me the wedding is on Christmas Eve.'

'*D'accord.*'

'But if you plan to put something together and advertise it and get lots of people there you're going to need more than a week.' She leant against the barrier as tourists filed past them.

'I want to do this for Vivienne and my father. To try to get our family back in one piece before the wedding,' he said. 'A new start for us all.'

She swallowed. Of course that's what he wanted. Because he was a nice person who had so much more going on in his life than her and a kiss he hadn't asked for.

'Well, you know I'll help,' Ava said. 'In between trying to find out if my best friend's step-dad is a philanderer.' She gave him a half-smile.

'I have skills on social media, you know,' Ava said, taking another tentative step downwards. 'And Debs has loads of contacts at magazines... most of them are in the UK but it's only a Eurostar stop away and I'm sure there's a few favours she can try and pull in for some shout-outs in art magazines in particular.'

'You think she would help me?' Julien asked.

'Of course! You're helping her by taking photos for your articles aren't you?'

'Yes,' he answered.

'There we go then.'

He nodded. He hated this. He didn't want to be talking about her helping with the exhibition. He wanted to be talking about how it had felt to kiss her. The last flight of stairs was just coming up. What happened then?

'So, I'll go back to the hotel now and I'll tell Debs what you want to do and... do you have a venue yet?'

He didn't have anything yet. He had hoped Diane's gallery would have space but she was fully booked. He shook his head.

'Well, if Paris is anything like London, this close to Christmas, everything is going to be booked,' Ava stated.

'Yes,' he sighed. 'Perhaps it is impossible.'

'Aren't you the man who told me I could be anything I want to be? That anything is possible?' Ava asked, smiling. 'There are only things that are easy and things that are more difficult.'

'If you believed that, Madonna, you would believe in magic,' he reminded her.

'Well,' she began, descending the final steps onto the ground. 'Perhaps I am coming around to the idea.'

He stepped off the final stair behind her and set his feet onto the snow. 'I am glad to hear that.'

She was looking at him now, bright hair sprinkled with snowflakes, cheeks flushed from the descent and the sharp wind, green eyes shining, lips pink. The taste of her mouth flooded his as he watched her, his insides quaking, hinting that, internally, putting his feelings aside wasn't going to be easy.

'Thank you for bringing me here.'

'You are welcome,' he answered. 'I got some good shots.'

'So, shall we meet tomorrow?' she suggested. 'To talk through the exhibition?'

'Tomorrow,' he agreed.

'OK, Monsieur Fitoussi. I will text you.'

She turned away, ready to leave, and the concern that there was this slight awkwardness between them made him call out.

'Ava.'

She turned back, beautiful cat-like eyes appraising him. He swallowed. There was so much he wanted to say. So much his body was telling him to do. 'You should put on your hat,' he offered.

She smiled. 'You're right,' she replied. 'Someone told me it's very important.'

He watched her dig her hand into the pocket of her coat and pull out the red beanie. She slipped it over her spikes and he stepped forward, his fingers pulling at the wool and rearranging her hair underneath it. His hands lingered a little on her skin and he stepped back again.

'See you tomorrow,' Ava said, waving a hand.

'À *bientôt.*'

He watched her turn away from him and as she did so there was something on the ground where she had been standing. He bent down, retrieving the piece of paper before the snow wetted it any more. It was lined paper, slightly ripped at the bottom and he turned it over to just see one line of writing.

7.   *Climb the Eiffel Tower and kiss a random man at the top of it*

He blinked at the words then lifted his gaze, looking for the retreating form of Ava. This was the wish list she'd talked about. The celebration of her. And he was just a tick in one of the boxes.

FORTY-ONE

Hotel Agincourt

Ava pushed the key card into the door and watched the red light flash again. This time, the third time of trying, she hammered on the door with her fists.

'Debs! It's me! The sodding key card won't work! Can you let me in?'

There was no response but, putting her ear to the door, she was sure someone was in there. She sniffed. Was that smoke she could smell? She hammered again. Surely if it was a fire, some detector would be going off already.

'Debs!'

The door was whipped open and there was Didier, wearing nothing but one of the white Hotel Agincourt towels around his waist. '*Bonsoir!*'

Ava slapped her hands over her eyes. 'Now I really want there to be a fire.'

'Come in,' Didier invited. 'Debs, she is very busy.'

'Invited into my own room... wow... thank you.' Ava stepped past the Frenchman and into a grey fog. She coughed, the scent of heavy perfume strangling her lungs. Squinting she saw Debs sat at the table by the window, fingers hammering at her laptop, two glowing incense sticks and the flashing and vibrating snow-man also present. Debs waved a hand but didn't speak, fingers working over the keys like she was setting up a code to solve all EU problems.

'She had emails,' Didier announced, like he was delivering a royal decree.

'That's nice. What are Paperchase offering in their pre-Christmas sale now?'

'From Nigel,' Didier stated, wide-eyed, chest expanding.

'I have no idea who "Nigel" is and' – she turned to face Didier – 'was this before or after you took all your clothes off?'

Didier grinned. 'The first one a little before, the second one sometime after.'

Ava shook her head. 'I shouldn't have asked.' She threw her hat down on the bed and attempted to move across the room. Didier caught her arm, the other hand securing his towel. 'You must not disturb her.'

'What? Are you joking?' Ava asked. 'I've only been out for a few hours. This morning I left her heading to a singles coffee afternoon and ready to carry on buying tacky presents for her whole extended family, now she's battering her computer through a mist that smells like Katie Perry's last perfume.'

'I tell you,' Didier whispered, 'she is busy. She has emails... from Nigel.'

'That means nothing to me! You may as well be speaking French!' Ava exclaimed.

All she really wanted to do was lie down and let her mind stop for five minutes. Here she feared if she lay down she would become a victim of death by incense inhalation.

'It's OK, Didier,' Debs called, eyes still firmly fixed on her screen.

Ava turned her head to what she could see of her friend. Was that a Father Christmas hairband she was wearing? And a jumper embroidered with liquorice allsorts?

'When I got back here from Cosmos and met Didier I had an email from Nigel.'

'Farage?' Ava asked.

'No,' Debs said, still tapping away. 'Nigel from *Diversity* magazine!' She drew in a breath, finally shifting a little in her seat and turning to Ava. 'You won't believe it, Ava, but he's offered me a job!'

'Oh my God! That's fantastic!' She was thrilled for Debs. This was the turnaround her friend needed. And it also sounded as though her thoughts were far away from hacking Francine's email account. 'So, you're putting a few ideas things together accompanied by eau de yoga retreat?'

'Not quite,' Debs answered.

'I'm sensing this good news has a payback,' Ava said.

'I need to get him these articles to him a little quicker than I had anticipated.'

'I don't know all that much about magazines but I do know they have tight deadlines,' Ava said.

'You are right,' Didier chipped in, hands on hips.

'Please, put some clothes on,' Ava begged.

'I have to have these to Nigel by five o' clock tomorrow.'

'What?!'

'And I don't have nearly enough time to make them good enough and I really, really need this job, Ava.'

'I know, but... what does that mean? You won't be able to come to dinner? You won't be able to leave this room?' She wanted to leave this room. She felt like she was being asphyxiated.

'All of the above, I'm afraid, times a thousand,' Debs answered. 'And there's more... I need a favour.'

Ava bit her lip. Whatever is was she had to say yes. Debs had got her out of London, away from her mother, put her up at her home more times than she could count, had plied her with wine when things got tough, done her hair when she had hair to do...

'Go on,' Ava said.

'You will like this,' Didier announced, splaying his arms out. 'I like this!'

'Are you still here?' Ava asked, turning her attention to the half-naked Frenchman.

Didier smiled and headed off in the direction of the bathroom. Ava waited until she could hear the shower running before she faced her friend again.

'What do you need?' Ava asked, plumping down on the edge of the bed. She crossed her fingers, hoping this didn't involve putting a tracking device on Francine's car.

'Well,' Debs said, 'Nigel doesn't just want singles, he wants couples too. We are talking a six-page spread here, Ava. So, allegedly... according to the internet and everyone I've called this afternoon who has knowledge of these things... the most romantic thing for couples to do in Paris is a dinner cruise on the Seine.'

Ava's stomach started to bubble as a cold dread started to weave its way around her. She could sense where this was going. She had to hope she was wrong.

'I've booked you on one tonight.'

'With Didier?'

'No, not with Didier, with Julien. Didier is going to be out researching the gay scene for me. I can't just write about heterosexual singles in the city, can I?'

'You do know Didier's not gay.'

Debs smiled. 'Of course I know that. Why do you think he answered the door in a towel?'

Ava coughed, the incense smoke making her eyes sting.

'He has a lot of gay friends who are going to help him research a couple of the bars and clubs tonight.'

'What about Francine?' Ava asked. 'You sent me a text about some gala thingy you wanted to spy on her at.'

'Francine is going to have to wait,' Debs said. 'This is the job of my dreams. If my family is about to be blown apart at least let it happen when I'm in secure employment.'

'Are you sure, Debs?' Ava asked softly, the words 'Francine, the other night was amazing' going through her mind.

Debs looked up, eyes a little teary. 'I can't think about that right now.'

Ava squeezed Debs' shoulder and tried to drag her thoughts to where Debs wanted them: the romantic cruise she had just booked with Julien, the man she had kissed at the top of the Eiffel Tower and then pretended it hadn't mattered.

'You do remember Julien and I aren't a couple,' she said. 'And he might not be free tonight.'

'Didier's messaged him.'

'And he said it was OK?' Did she want the answer to be yes or no? It was too soon to be put in a situation like that, wasn't it? Or perhaps it was the perfect time. They could throw themselves into Debs' research and talk about the photography exhibition and forget the kiss had ever happened. Just good friends was safest. But then again, that kiss... and what he had said about not being able to take his eyes off her! Perhaps this date that wasn't a date could be a chance to test the romantic waters.

'I'm sure he will,' Debs said. She checked her watch. 'You have an hour.'

'What?! With a Frenchman hogging the shower?! I don't know if I can...'

'Ava, this means so much to me. A permanent job... at *Diversity*. They're new, they're funky, they're going places... and they could take me places too.' Debs swallowed. 'And if things go bad for Mum and Gary it's a guaranteed monthly income.' Her voice had wobbled at the end. 'I'm not meant to be thinking about that now... every time I do my creativeness just dries up.'

Ava nodded. 'You know I'm going to do it. It's just... if Julien doesn't come along I'm going to stick out like a sore thumb.'

Debs grinned. 'If Julien doesn't go for it then eat and drink as much as you can and listen to other people's conversations...

and take lots of photos.' Debs sighed. 'The boat is going to be full of couples. All I need is a taste of the ambience, a flavour of the romance... and I can fill in how much, what time and the map from the website.'

'And what are you going to be doing while I'm in the middle of the hand-holding capital of Europe?'

'I'm going to have steam coming out of my ears trying to write the best articles I've ever written.' She held aloft her cup. 'You think this is tea?'

FORTY-TWO

Julien Fitoussi's apartment

Julien stared at the text on his phone, then his eyes went back to the piece of paper he had pressed flat on his desk. Showered, wearing fresh black jeans, he was sat in front of his laptop, the light of his desk lamp highlighting Ava's words.

> 7. *Climb the Eiffel Tower and kiss a random man at the top of it*

He shook his head. It kicked him every time he reread it and what was worst of all, he knew it shouldn't matter so much. They had both agreed it had been a moment that meant nothing. But it *had* meant something to him. It had meant a lot of things. That he had the ability to feel again. That he was thinking of something else other than Lauren and what they had both been through. That he was beyond Monique.

He looked down at his body and his fingers found the scar on the left side of his abdomen. A red angry welt of ugly skin. That was what had repulsed Monique. She might have said it was his inability to open up to her but he knew better. Who would want to look at that for a lifetime? He didn't. Grabbing a black shirt from the top of the sofa he slipped it over his body and began to fasten the buttons with haste. He was making too much of this. He had got too close, inviting Ava to see how he worked, taking her all over the city, asking for

her help with the exhibition. He needed to take a step back...
a few hundred paces back... not go on a romantic cruise up
the Seine. He swallowed, checking his reflection in the mirror. But Didier had practically begged. It was for Debs. He
should look at it as work. He could take some photos of the
sights for the exhibition – he needed something if he was going to pull it off. He could make sure they both knew where
they stood.

From the desk his mobile phone erupted into life and his
step-mother's face blinked on and off in the half-light. Picking
it up, he answered.

'Hello.'

'Julien,' Vivienne greeted, her voice tense.

She sounded nothing short of pained. 'What's wrong?'

'It's... your father, he came home from work and he drank
and then he drank some more and he... smashed the photographs.' Vivienne let out a sob that made Julien want to reach
down the line and gather her up in his arms.

'I tried, Vivienne, at the suit fitting,' Julien began. 'I tried to
make things right like you asked but... he is still too far away.'

'What am I going to do?' It was an almost desperate plea. 'I
don't know what to do.'

He didn't know either, but he did know that his step-mother
didn't deserve to shoulder this worry alone right before her wedding. How could he tell her that his father didn't even want him
to be his best man any more?

'I'm coming over.'

'I don't think you should right now – not while he's like this.'

'Perhaps he should see someone,' Julien stated.

'Someone?'

'A counsellor?' He swallowed. Vivienne had suggested this to
him and Gerard shortly after Lauren's death and both of them
had flatly refused.

'Oh, Julien, you know how he is with that subject,' she said. 'The very same way you are.'

'I told him I wanted to do another exhibition. To honour Lauren and the other families who lost people in the fire.'

'Oh, Julien,' Vivienne exclaimed. 'That is a wonderful idea.'

'Dad didn't think so.' He sighed. 'He said whatever I did nothing would bring Lauren back. As if I didn't know that already. As if I didn't already realise that nothing will be the same.' He paused. 'Vivienne, I just want to do something positive. Something I think Lauren would approve of. I know that locking myself in my apartment and hiding wasn't solving anything. And I know Lauren would have hated that.'

'Will you come over? Not now but later this week?' Vivienne asked. 'For dinner?'

'I do not think he will want me there.'

'I want you there, Julien.' She sighed. 'I *need* you there.'

His heart ached as his step-mother's tone pinched at him. He had to help her, and his relationship with his father was at a point where it couldn't really get any worse.

'I'll come,' he agreed.

'Friday?'

'Fine,' he agreed. 'Vivienne,' he started, 'you are OK for tonight?'

There was a pause before... 'He shut himself in the bedroom and cried himself to sleep.'

Julien closed his eyes and held his breath before continuing. 'If you need me, Vivienne, for anything, please just call me.'

'I will.'

He heard her inhale deeply. 'I am so glad you are taking photos again, Julien. So very glad.'

'Me too,' he responded. His eyes went to his computer where the images he had snapped of Ava at the Panthéon, outside her hotel and at the Sacré-Coeur, slipped left and right. Why was he torturing himself with the images when what they had shared today was all about numbers on a list to her?

'Do you have a theme for the exhibition yet?'

'Beauty,' he answered. 'Beauty in every day.'

He took the mouse on the desk in his right hand and clicked the button to shut down. Ava's picture disappeared and finally, as he said his goodbyes to Vivienne, the screen went black.

FORTY-THREE

Notre Dame boarding point

Ava was wearing Debs' boots again and still her feet were cold. She was also wearing a bright red dress she had found in her case that had only made it in there because she'd thought it was her favourite Hollister sweater. She hadn't thought about romantic dinners on a riverboat when she was grabbing things for a trip with her best friend.

She checked her watch again. Julien should be here already if they were going to get on board before the boat set sail. Maybe he wasn't coming. She wouldn't blame him. After the kiss today it was a little cliché that they were now being pushed into another couples' event. And there were couples galore on the dock, accepting complimentary champagne from wine waiters dressed in pure white suits, even the snow looking a little beige in comparison. Other cruisers were already on board the long vessel, its inside completely encased in glass from which the travellers were going to experience the magic of Paris by night. Didier had shouted the information through the bathroom door to her while she was grabbing a five-minute cold shower after he had used all the hot water.

From her vantage point she could see the elaborate interior, well-dressed guests standing, nibbling at canapés, beside a gold-and-purple-decorated Christmas tree, while around them the immaculately dressed staff put the finishing touches to the tables set close to the full-height windows. The sound of violins started up and Ava looked to her left where three young men in black jackets, white shirts and red bow ties had begun playing festive music. Everyone was happy. Everyone was relaxed. Except her.

From inside the bag on her shoulder her phone vibrated. Perhaps it was Julien, making his apologies. She unfastened the zip and pulled it out. Before she saw who the message was from she saw the photograph. A selfie she had taken. A selfie she had deleted from her camera roll only a few days ago. Her and Leo underneath the Arc De Triomphe. She pressed hard on the off button and waited for the phone to shut down. He could text her a hundred photos, nothing was going to change.

She looked at her watch again. How long before she had to make a decision? Should she get on alone or leave?

Julien held his breath the moment she came into view. The bright red of her dress beneath her coat, those knee-length boots again and the silver blonde of her hair made him come to a standstill a few feet away. What was he doing here? Torturing himself? His whole body was telling him just how he felt about her. His brain, in comparison, knew there were plenty of reasons to keep his distance, not least the fact that their kiss had just been something to accomplish for her.

He couldn't help himself. With the golden glow from the streetlamps, the silvery patterns on the water to her right, the violinists, the snow on the ground and the bateaux lit up in lilac and white, it was a perfect Parisian scene. He lifted his camera to his face and snapped. Zooming in he saw her look at the watch on her arm. He dropped his camera down, his fingers touching the strap around his neck. Was he really doing this?

* * *

Just at the moment Ava was certain Julien wasn't going to turn up she spotted him across the quayside. Wearing dark jeans, a black shirt visible under his woollen coat, his camera around his neck, her insides dipped like the mercury in a thermometer on a really cold day. She waved a hand and watched him walk across the snow-covered pathway towards her.

'*Bonsoir*,' she greeted, with a grin. 'Here we are again.'

'Here we are again,' he responded. 'Pretending to be something we are not, *non*?'

Ava looked up at him then, the tone of his voice a little off. 'Yes... I'm sorry about that. Debs... these articles and being worried about her mum and—'

'Didier told me the details,' he responded. 'Shall we go on? I can take photographs of the *real* couples.'

He walked past her then, stepping onto the short gangplank where someone was waiting to greet them. She slipped her hands into the pockets of her coat, gathering the material around her and following him.

'*Bonsoir, Mademoiselle*,' the woman at the entrance said as Ava struggled on her heels down the three steps that led onto the boat.

'*Bonsoir*, we have a reservation,' she began, her eyes going to the retreating form of Julien who was already on the boat snapping photographs. 'In the name of Devlin, I think.'

'*Oui, Mademoiselle*,' the woman replied.

'Ava!' Julien called. 'Come. It is this way.'

'Sorry,' Ava quickly apologised before heading onto the boat.

She stepped through the main door onto dark wood flooring, mahogany-coloured tables covered in white linen, sparkling glasses and perfect china set in place on each and every one of them. In the centre of each table was a large glass bowl, a selection of festive decorations in each – red and green baubles, a handful of white fluffy balls like clouds of snow and a fresh

orange spiked with cloves. In the furthest corner, cleverly positioned so as not to block the views from the windows, was a
band – a guitarist, a singer and a man on the keyboard – lightly
playing something by Frank Sinatra.

'Ava,' Julien called again. 'We are here.'

She swallowed, looking at the table where Julien was standing. It was right up against the glass, set for two, a candle glowing next to the bowl of festiveness. If this was a date there was
no denying this would be a particularly spectacular setting. She
would make a mental note of that for Debs.

Julien pulled out the chair for her.

'Thank you,' she said, dropping down into it and watching as
he moved to the seat opposite and sat down too.

A waiter appeared with menus and quickly poured them
both a glass of champagne, topping it off with a strawberry that
floated on the bubbles. Ava smiled as he departed.

She took a sip of the champagne. 'Ooo, this is lovely. Do you
like it?' she asked him.

He waved a hand in the air. 'It is OK.'

She smiled again. 'Do I sense a little French champagne
snobbery, Monsieur Fitoussi? I know we aren't exactly connois-
seurs in England.'

'I am not really a great fan of champagne,' he admitted.
'Sorry.'

'You don't have to be sorry. We'll just order beer when he
comes back,' Ava suggested. 'Or maybe a bottle of wine?'

'Whatever you like.'

He was being brusque and not holding her gaze. She reached
forward across the table towards his hands. He withdrew, moving his hands and sitting back in his chair. This was odd. She
knew the vibe was a little edgy after the Eiffel Tower moment,
but they had left each other on good terms earlier, friends like
they had been, aiming to plan his exhibition.

'Is something wrong?' she asked.

'No,' he answered a little too quickly.

'Are you sure?' she asked. 'Because—'

'I'm fine, Ava,' he responded. 'Everything is fine.'

His tone was sharp and she withdrew her hands, picking up her napkin and looking out of the window at the choppy Seine, the winter breeze blowing the snowflakes across the water.

'I am sorry,' he said a little softer. 'I am just a little tired that is all.'

She looked back to him. 'It was all those steps. Up and down the Eiffel Tower.'

The second she had said the name of the landmark she had kissed him at the top of, a charge ran through her and her lips reacted like they could still taste him. She reached for her champagne glass and inhaled the effervescent liquid.

'What are you going to order?' Julien asked.

'Oh... I haven't even looked at the menu,' Ava said, putting her glass down and looking at the cream card she had laid down next to her side plate. It was all in French. As it would be, being in France. The only words she recognised was *legumes* and *boeuf*.

'You would like me to translate the menu?' Julien offered.

She shook her head. 'No, it's OK.'

'You understand this?'

'I'm not fussy when it comes to food. I'll just choose one.'

Julien put down his menu. 'I will have the cat I think.'

She smiled. 'I'm not that gullible... and I know the word for cat.'

'Ava, let me translate it,' he offered.

'I've found snails,' Ava said, still looking at the card.

'For starter there is foie gras, snails, salmon or crab,' Julien said. 'For the main course there is sea bass, beef fillet, duck or veal. And for dessert there is apricots and cherries, chocolate concerto...'

'Concerto? A whole orchestra of chocolate! You really don't have to read any further.'

He put the menu down and picked up his champagne glass. 'We will set off soon.'

Ava glanced out of the window, across the width of the water, taking in the rows of twinkling lights woven into the trees and French life passing by – a family on a selection of bicycles – a man and a woman and two little girls trying to catch up, taxis and lots of Renaults...

'Have you been on one of these cruises before?' Ava asked.

'A sightseeing cruise,' he responded. 'In the day time.'

'Is it good?' Ava asked, excitement coating her words.

'It is a nice way to see the city. Everything is so much slower on the water. We drift, we take in the hurrying of others, the lights, the landmarks looking different in the dark.'

'Everything is different, isn't it?' Ava said. 'You look at something once and you never see it all the first time around.'

Julien shifted in his chair, his fingers curling around the stem of his glass. That was how he had felt about Ava. Before the piece of paper had fallen from her pocket.

'It's like filo pastry or... those last few layers of pass-the-parcel when you're a child. You expect it to be more of the same then... wow, chocolate fondant or a colouring book.'

He couldn't help but smile at her analogy. This was the Ava he had got to know over the past few days, not someone who would make such a thoughtless, weak wish list.

'What's your favourite place here, Julien?' she asked. 'In Paris I mean. What do you like best?'

Her eyes were fixed on him, those beautiful, clear green eyes full of interest for whatever he was about to say. He swallowed. 'I like the Place des Vosges,' he answered.

'What is that?'

'It is a square in the Marais district. And surrounding this are buildings that have been the home to many famous people of interest. Poets, painters and writers.'

'What makes it special to you?' Ava asked him.

'I do not know... perhaps the fountains... or maybe it is just the peace. It is a big square, closed off from the rest of the city.'

'Will you take me there?' Ava asked.

'It is near the Place de la Bastille. You have been here, *non*?'

'*Non*,' she said, sipping at her drink. 'The only places I have really been are with you.'

His heart suddenly felt so heavy. He took a swig of his drink. He couldn't take her to the Place des Vosges any more than he could take her anywhere any more. It was all too complicated now. *He* had complicated things by buying a love lock, by kissing her, by sharing so much of himself with her, by being here tonight...

'Maybe I am not the best tour guide,' he offered.

He watched Ava fold her arms across her chest and hit him with a dark look of suspicion. 'What's going on? Why are you being like this?'

'I do not know what you mean. We should order the food,' he said, raising his hand and beckoning the waiter as the boat began to move.

'Not until you answer one question,' Ava said.

He was scared to ask but there was no way out. 'What?'

'Why haven't you called me Madonna tonight?'

FORTY-FOUR

Ava held her eyes on Julien, waiting for him to give her an answer. He had coiled his napkin up in his hand and was just looking back at her, no words forthcoming.

'*Monsieur*,' the waiter addressed Julien, giving a little bow. He said something else in French Ava presumed meant he was asking them if they were ready to place their order.

'Ava?' Julien asked. 'What did you want to eat?'

'Crab, duck and chocolate,' she responded, draining the contents of her champagne glass. She put the glass back down on the table and listened as Julien told the waiter their order.

When the waiter headed off again Julien cleared his throat and looked to the full-length window. 'The lights of the Eiffel Tower,' he began.

Ava cast a glance to her left, looking out and up, seeking the very top of the structure. It was coated in a bright amber glow, spiralling up from its legs to the pinnacle, bands of silvery white lights at the two lower levels and small dots of red nearer the spike. It did look beautiful and Christmassy. She turned back, her humour unimproved.

'I asked you a question,' she repeated.

He let out a sigh. 'I will call you Madonna if you want me to, Ava.'

'Not like that,' she responded. 'Not like you can't bear to have the word on your lips.'

He shook his head.

'Have I done something wrong?'

'No,' he said immediately.

'Something's changed,' she stated sadly. 'If this is about what happened at the top of the tower... well, I thought we were forgetting about that.'

'Of course,' he answered. 'Now that is has been ticked off the list for you.'

She furrowed her brow. 'What?'

'Your wish list,' he spat. 'What was it exactly? Number 7. Kiss a random man at the top of the Eiffel Tower.'

Ava watched as he drew something out of his pocket – a piece of paper – and put it on the table between them. She looked at it. Her writing. Her wish list. The one she had torn up almost as soon as she'd got here. She looked up from the piece of paper and set her eyes back on Julien, anger curdling inside her.

'That's what you think, is it?' she questioned, a little louder than she'd anticipated.

'It is yours, *non*? A list of wishes. Things you want to achieve in this new beginning in your life?'

'Yes, it's mine,' she answered.

'Then?'

'Then you really haven't been listening to me at all these past few days,' she rushed out. 'Julien, I've confided in you... I've confided in you about how I feel... about what I really want from my life... about how much I want to start everything over again. About Debs' family problems.' She was breathing erratically now, her body caught between fight and flight responses, not knowing whether to shout or to cry, to hit out or run away. 'And I kissed you at the top of the tower because, at that moment, it was the only thing that made sense. You and me, standing by two separate love locks but totally connecting in every other way... at least... at least I thought so.'

'Ava...'

'And *I* felt something up there. Despite everything I said about striking out on my own and being independent from men, from my mother, from everything that might want to clip my wings... I felt something... something I hadn't felt before and... when I said I wanted to forget it... it was because I thought *you* wanted to forget it and I didn't want to lose what we already seem to have... this friendship... this bond... this connection... after only a few days.'

Tears were pricking her eyes and she got to her feet quickly, looking for a way out.

Julien stood. 'Ava, please wait. We can—'

'We can what, Julien?' she asked, shaking. 'Because you've just presented a scrap of notepaper like it's the ultimate truthteller and that everything that's gone before doesn't matter to you.' She swallowed. 'And let's not forget, just a few days ago *you* were the one who lied to me about something huge... and I listened and I understood and now... here you are... throwing Exhibit A down like I've been indicted.'

'I—'

'If you look at that piece of paper... if you really look at it... you'll see it's ripped,' she stated, her voice a level above the band playing in the corner. 'Because that whole stupid list was torn up the second I got to Paris.' Tears were springing out of her eyes now and she hated herself for showing him how much this hurt her. Another man who was causing her upset. Hadn't she learnt her lesson? She pressed an index finger to each eye in turn and straightened her body, standing tall. 'The other things on that list were buying a dog to irritate my mother, drinking myself into renal failure and getting plastic surgery,' she informed him. She dug her hands into the pocket of her coat she'd slipped around the chair. 'I wrote that wish list when I was eighteen and stupid and had no idea what life was all about. I haven't written another one.' She sniffed. 'I decided to take every day as it comes at me here in Paris, nothing forced, nothing planned... just like we talked about.' She threw the rest of the pieces of the wish list onto the table and watched one land a little too close to the candle, immediately catching on fire. 'And if you really knew me like I thought you did, Monsieur Fitoussi, you would have just asked me, not immediately jumped to conclusions.'

'Ava—' he tried again.

'No... I've heard enough and I'm getting off this boat.' She grabbed her coat from the back of the chair and headed for the exit.

FORTY-FIVE

Before Julien could even react, a waiter was over at the table pouring a whole jug of water over the burning paper. He shifted his chair back to avoid getting a soaking and looked at the staff member, offering him an expression of apology as he rose out of his seat.

He had been a fool. He should have known. In his heart. Deep down. He knew her. Just like she had said. So why had he done this? Been so accusing? Not asked before assuming the worst? Because of the alternative? Because now, having heard her speak about their kiss as if it was something she was never going to forget, not a throwaway minute, he was more frightened than ever about what came next. The camera around his neck knocked over his empty glass of champagne as he made to leave the table. She wouldn't jump off the boat, would she?

The very first thing Ava had discovered when she'd made it to the outside was how very small the boat was. The second thing was, there was no way off that didn't involve leaping from the bow and swimming to the tall concrete banks of the Seine.

Her eyes were still spilling tears as she stood against the metal barrier, looking out across the water, everything in her vision a little blurry. What was upsetting her the most? The thought that Julien had such a low opinion of her he could believe that list was who she was now? That he thought she was fickle, a dumb model, stupid – all the things she'd heard behind her back a hundred times before and externally shrugged off but internally worried about constantly? This was cutting deeper than anything before. What he thought mattered to her. Because *he* already mattered to her. And now she had to let him go. Because their trust was truly broken. Just like with Leo... but worse. Worse because Julien already meant so much more.

Along with the rhythmic rushing of the water beneath the boat the clicking of a camera invaded her quiet. She turned her head and there was Julien, his lens focussed on her, taking shot after shot the more her body moved. She wanted to strangle him with the strap, just like she had the very first time they'd met.

'Stop it!' she hissed, putting her hands in front of her face and advancing towards him.

'*Non*,' he replied, continuing to take photos as she took another step over to him.

'I said stop it!' Ava repeated, her hands on the camera, attempting to drag it away from him. Her fiery eyes met his and she noted a stubbornness in his expression.

'I said no,' he said again, even more firmly.

She tightened her hold on the camera and didn't move.

'I have tried to stop, Ava and I cannot.'

Still she would not remove her hands from his camera. His heart was thundering inside him. He had to tell her now. She had said she didn't want to see him again and the thought of that was overriding anything else. 'I have been taking photos of you since the very first night I saw you.'

'No... no you haven't,' she stuttered.

'Yes, Ava, I have.'

'But... I told you I didn't want my photo taken.'

'I know,' he breathed. 'But I had to.'

He saw the confusion on her face, her small hands still gripping his camera like she wanted to wrench it from him. How did he begin to explain this?

'Ava, when we met... just before we met... I had only just picked up this camera again,' he said. 'I had not taken a picture since that night... the night we lost Lauren.' He took a breath. 'Then, the day we met, I had a reawakening and I went out and I took some pictures, decided I would try and step back into the world again.' He wet his lips. 'And then I saw you.' He bent his head a little, ensuring he had her full attention. 'You came striding out of your hotel, talking loudly into your phone, so full of life, so full of harsh words and angst and then... Do you remember? You faced the sky and you embraced the night like it was your best friend.'

Julien watched her swallow, her eyes refreshing themselves as she looked back at him.

'I took your photo then, several shots... good shots... and you caught me and made me promise not to take any more.'

'And you promised,' Ava reminded. 'You knew how I felt about it.'

He nodded. 'I know... but then we were at the Panthéon and you were holding onto those stone pillars like you were wrestling with the world, the sunlight just breaking through the dawn, one moment so happy, the next moment so sad, and I had to capture it.'

Ava let the camera go and reached for the metal railing again, facing the water.

'I took more at the Louvre,' he continued. 'And the Sacré-Coeur and I cannot imagine my exhibition without you at the centre of it,' he stated. 'I do *not want* to imagine an exhibition without you at the centre of it.'

She shook her head. 'No,' she said. 'You think I'm someone who kisses random men.'

'I do not.'

'You did!' Ava exclaimed. 'Until I told you the crazy person who wrote that wish list was eighteen and desperate for an escape from the life she had. The warring parents and a mother who would probably have fed her laxatives with her breakfast if she could. "You got a tattoo, Ava?! Your life is over!"'

'I am sorry,' Julien said, touching her arm. 'I was stupid. I should have known.' He paused. 'I did know.' He patted his chest. 'I *did* know. In here.'

'Careful there, Monsieur Fitoussi, don't dislodge the granite.'

'Look at me, Ava,' he ordered.

She shook her head. 'No.'

'Look at me,' he said again.

'I don't want to.'

'Please,' he said softly.

She turned her face a little, refusing to look up. 'At first I took photographs of you because you are the most beautiful woman I have ever seen,' he whispered. 'Then, the more time we spent together, I realised that you were even more beautiful on the inside.'

'Don't,' Ava croaked. 'I'm not beautiful. I'm average. Not perfect. Never good enough.'

'No,' Julien said forcefully. 'That is not true. None of it.' He grabbed her hand in his, turning her body and making her look at him. 'Ava, I made a stupid mistake at the top of the Tour Eiffel,' he said, moving his fingers to gently brush the blonde spikes on her head. 'But the mistake was not kissing you.' He held his breath, taking in her delicate features. 'The mistake was pretending it did not mean anything and then letting you go.'

Ava was shaking and it had nothing to do with the snow settling on the deck around them as the boat cruised up to the Institut de France. She looked away from Julien, needing a minute, trying to focus on the building bathed in golden light, its blue-grey dome standing tall above the bridge they were about to go under. Her mind was whirring.

'Ava,' he whispered, his mouth close.

'I can't... I don't... this is too much,' she breathed. 'We can't, Julien.' Her body was telling her the exact opposite. Every sense she possessed was telling her what she craved was standing no more than an inch away from contact.

'Ava, these past months, my whole life has been on hold,' Julien said. 'It has all been such a terrible waste and... I don't want that one night when we lost Lauren to own my future.' He took his hand in hers. 'Even my immediate future. These days. With you.'

He was caressing her fingers with his and his hand was so warm, his skin so soft, it was making gravy out of her.

'I was scared, Madonna,' he admitted. 'I was scared at the top of the tower, I was scared tonight and I am scared now... terrified that all that I have done has hurt you so much that I may not ever be forgiven.'

She needed to say something.

'Do not say anything yet,' he begged, as if sensing what she was about to do. 'Just, let me finish.' He brought her hand to his lips and kissed her knuckles. 'I don't want to live with regrets any more, Ava,' he started. 'I want to... be able to go into a bistro and not sit near the fire exit. I want to go to a rock concert and not scrutinise every other person there. I want to live life, freely, wholly.' He sighed. 'But most of all, I want to feel confident enough to tell you that, yes, we have known each other just days, but the thought of not having you in my life is the most terrifying thing of all.'

A sob left her then and she squeezed his hand in hers, nodding her head. 'It scares me but... I feel that too,' she admitted.

'You do?' he asked.

'I did.' She sniffed. 'Until you decided you were just number seven on my wish list.'

'Am I too late?' he asked. 'Can I make you trust me again?'

She turned her body fully towards him then, relishing what she saw. His angular jaw, that aquiline nose and dark eyes, the black hair a little messy.

'That depends, Monsieur Fitoussi,' she replied.

'On what, Madonna?' he inquired. 'Right at this moment I will do almost anything.'

'An exchange,' she said, inching herself closer to him.

'Go on,' he urged, dark eyelashes blinking.

'Give me the camera,' she said, her fingers moving back to the Canon around his neck.

He shook his head. 'I cannot. That is like asking a Frenchman to give up garlic.'

'I thought you said you would do literally anything to earn my trust?' Ava said. 'Or perhaps I don't mean anything to you. Maybe I am just a number on *your* wish list?'

He smiled at her, then very slowly he took the camera from her and lifted it, plus the strap, from around his neck. He held it out to her. 'But you must promise me something,' he said. 'You must not drop it into the river.'

She shook her head. 'Don't be silly, Monsieur Fitoussi. I'm not going to drop it into the river,' she said, putting the viewfinder to her eye. 'I'm going to take pictures with it.' She snapped off a shot of him.

'You know,' he said. 'There is one type of person who hates their photograph taken more than someone who used to be a model.'

'Yes?' she asked. 'And just turn a little to the left.' She took another photo.

'Photographers,' he replied. He made a grab for the camera and took it from her hands, hiding it behind his back while she screamed and tried to reach.

'Stand still, Madonna,' he ordered.

'No more photos of me, Monsieur Fitoussi!'

'I'm not going to take your photo,' he said. 'I'm going to kiss you.'

Ava barely had time to still before his lips stole the breath from her and she gasped, a half-step back bringing the railing into her spine. She closed her eyes and let the heat from his mouth overwhelm every other thought and feeling. As his tongue frisked hers with an obvious passion, she let his body mould against hers, the weight pleasurable, desire arriving fast. She brought one hand up to his cheek and smoothed her fingers over the slight roughness.

Then there was a bang, quickly followed by another and her eyes went to the dark sky and she caught hold of his hand, holding him close.

'It's fireworks, Julien,' she said quickly. 'Fireworks. Look!' She directed his gaze to the water in front of them where spirals and colorations of fizzing, zipping colour were working their way across the night.

He slipped an arm around her shoulders, drawing her near and kissing the top of her head. 'I see them, Madonna,' he whispered.

FORTY-SIX

Hotel Agincourt

Holding Ava's hand in his, Julien stopped outside the Hotel Agincourt and faced her. High on the romance of the night, his stomach full from the delicious food, a little buzzy from the alcohol, he looked at her, wanting to drink in the moment.

'When I came out tonight I had no idea this was going to happen,' Ava said with a sigh.

'No idea?' Julien asked, smiling a little.

'Well, I don't know if you've noticed but I'm not the kind of girl to get weak at the knees over Parisian boats.'

'And Parisian men?' he inquired, teasing.

'Monsieur Fitoussi, that is the Stella Artois talking.'

'I promise you it is not.'

He pulled her towards him then, his lips on hers, warm, soft, wet, the snow trickling down around them, the only light from the moon, the hotel sign and a solitary street lamp. Ava's fingers ran through his hair, then down to his neck. The top button of his shirt under his coat unfastened, he stole a breath as she moved onto the second.

'Ava,' he said.

'I like it when you call me Madonna,' she whispered.

'I should go,' he said, his hand finding hers as she made contact with his chest.

'I know this is soon and I know, in my heart, that we are not like Debs and Didier but... what if I asked you to come in?'

His heart was already thumping but her suggestion had other parts of him kicking into action. The thought of her, undressing, being bare, looking at him... a mix of longing and fear settled in him.

'I should go,' he repeated.

'It's too soon, isn't it? And now you think I'm a slapper.'

'A what?'

'Someone who jumps into bed with someone she's only just met.' She sighed. 'I really shouldn't try and be European now Britain is leaving the EU.'

'I do not think this,' he reassured. 'I think that thinking about this, hearing you say this is making me want to say yes but... I want to do the right thing.'

'Kiss me again,' she purred.

'This I can do,' he answered, moving his lips to hers again.

He kissed her slowly, his tongue softly swaying with hers until he knew he had to end the moment before his libido started making choices for him. Choices he wasn't ready for.

'Goodnight, Madonna,' he said, dropping a final kiss on the tip of her nose.

'Goodnight, Monsieur Fitoussi,' Ava said, holding his hand and squeezing it in hers.

Ava didn't want to let him go. She wanted to take him into the hotel, up to her room – perhaps not *her* room if Didier was still there or Debs was still thundering at her keyboard in a fog of patchouli – to spend the night with him. She held onto his hand, unmoving on the pavement.

'Tomorrow,' Julien said. 'I will show you the Place des Vosges.'

'Really?' she said. His favourite place. He wanted to show her his favourite place.

'*Oui*,' he said. 'But for tomorrow to come... I need to go.'

She smiled and loosened her grip on his hand.

'Goodnight, Madonna,' he said again. He brought her hand up to his mouth and dropped a kiss on the skin.

'Goodnight,' she replied, taking a micro step backwards.

He waved a hand and she watched him walk into the night, the snowflakes an almost fluorescent white against the darkness of his coat. Ava sighed and let her eyes roam to the city line of Paris. The dark sky, the Christmas lights flashing from brick-work along the street, the hotchpotch rooftops, small loft windows hiding tiny city pads, balconies and balustrades in front of large, airy apartments with a view to the Eiffel Tower, shop fronts and restaurants getting ready to close. It was a heady mix of Christmas, capital city and French romance. Who knew this had all been waiting for her when she got here?

She took a breath of the cold air and turned to the hotel entrance, pushing at the revolving doors and looking forward to dreaming about what tomorrow might bring.

Her boots had hardly touched the carpet of reception when she stopped walking and her stomach dropped to be-low basement level. At the front desk, talking to the con-cierge, was someone wearing jade pixie boots with a six-inch heel, a silver sequinned dress and a three-quarter-length fox fur coat she really hoped was a fake. The urge to creep silently like a ninja towards the bank of elevators was so tempting, but one wrong move and the game was up. And then the op-tion was taken out of her hands. Her mother turned around and faced her.

'Ava,' she greeted. 'I was just telling this awfully rude man behind the front desk that you were staying here and he was refusing to believe what I was telling him.'

Ava took a step forward, body still braced for combat. 'What *were* you telling him?'

'That I was here to see you and... never mind what I was telling him! Look at you! You look radiant! Is that a Vera Wang?'

Ava felt her mother appraising her from the heels of Debs' boots to the red dress she hadn't really wanted to wear in the first place.

'What are you doing here?' Ava asked, standing still and watching Rhoda pull along her Louis Vuitton case until she was only a few feet away.

'Listen, darling, I know how you felt about going all that way to Goa but—'

'Are you still on about Goa? Seriously...'

'Shh! Decorum, Ava. We are in public,' Rhoda reminded her.

'Why are you here?' Ava asked. 'Shouldn't you be face deep in skin-firming mud from the Ganges?'

'As I was saying... I know how you felt about going all the way to Goa and the assignment in the Azores, so I'm here to offer an alternative,' Rhoda continued.

Ava's blood was humming through her veins wondering what direction to take. Her mother was stood in front of her, she hadn't even attempted an air kiss or a false hug, and she was already talking about modelling assignments.

'It's late,' Ava said, looking at her watch even though she knew the time. 'I really ought to get to bed.'

'Let's have a drink,' Rhoda suggested. 'I'm sure that lovely little man behind the front desk can get us a nice cognac or something.'

'So he's a *lovely* little man when you want something.' Ava shook her head. 'How did you find me?'

'You told me you were in France.'

'I remember I didn't tell you I was in Paris or the hotel I was staying at.'

'No, but a quick look on Facebook at Deborah's page, a photo of her in a ridiculous Christmas jumper and the hotel location tagged and I had my answer.'

'You stalked my friend!' Ava exclaimed.

'I obtained a little information that's all,' Rhoda said almost sternly. Then the expression changed again. Her mouth widened into a smile and her eyes lit up. Those whitened teeth on display and the nose altered to look like Nicole Kidman shifted to side profile. 'Anyway, that's by-the-by and you are going to love me when I tell you what I've managed to line up.'

Ava put her hands on her hips. She had to be imagining this. This couldn't be real.

'This new job is so much better than the Azores,' Rhoda continued.

'I thought the Azores was going to be the pinnacle of my career.'

'I'm pretty sure I didn't say that.'

Ava sighed. 'Mum...'

'Ava, this is Fate. And it isn't far. It's actually in Paris.'

She clenched her hands into fists and dug them hard into the corners of her pockets. Forget dreaming about tomorrow, this was the nightmare of today.

'Mum, please listen to me...' She swallowed. Could she actually say the words? Her mind went to the life-affirming love lock. The celebration of her hanging from the Eiffel Tower. Julien. Gorgeous, sweet, Julien who had told her she had her whole life to make new choices. She took a deep breath.

'Mum, I'm not doing *any* modelling any more.'

Rhoda shook her head like Ava was an irritation she could do without. 'Don't be ridiculous, Ava. What else are you going to do with your life? You've shot yourself in the foot with Leo, you need to focus on your career.'

Leo. She gritted her teeth, not rising to the bait. 'I know that,' Ava said. 'But why can't I do anything I want to do?'

'Because modelling is what you were *born* to do.'

'No, Mum, modelling is what you *forced* me to do. You were the one that wanted that life. I never did.'

'That's madness,' Rhoda said. 'You have a gift. You can't just waste it.'

'You don't even think that. It's always been *a size six isn't a size zero, your hair needs to be straighter, your legs need to be longer, your lips need to be wider.* Well, I'm happy *this* way. I'm fine with what I see in the mirror. I'm not a supermodel – not you, not the bloody photographers, not the pictures in the magazines, have *ever* made me think I was beautiful. But you know what? *Tonight* I feel beautiful. For the first time.'

'Ava, I don't think you understand,' Rhoda said, exasperated. 'Hazel Yashenko has had to drop out of Katya De Pierrot's fashion show tomorrow night. You're taking her place.'

FORTY-SEVEN

Ava opened her eyes as the laptop tapping became too noisy to ignore. The smell of ylang-ylang infiltrated her nose and she suddenly wanted to be sick. She coughed and pawed at the duvet wrapped around her legs.

'*Bonjour!*'

Didier sprung up from the twin bed next to her like a jack-in-the-box on speed and Ava screamed, a hand going to her heart.

'For God's sake! You nearly gave me a heart attack!' She tried to breathe again as her eyes blurred into focus.

'I apologise,' Didier said, grinning. 'You would like some fruit tea?' he offered.

'No... no I don't.' She looked over to the table where Debs' fingers were still moving faster than *The Flash* on a mission, her hair muzzed up like Chewbacca. 'Am I allowed to talk to Debs yet?'

'I can hear you, you know,' Debs called, eyes unmoved from the screen.

'Good, so—' Ava started.

'So I want to hear everything about romantic cruises up the Seine in thirty minutes. I've ordered room service to bring us breakfast.'

'My mother is here,' Ava said.

Debs knocked her teacup off the table and it hit the carpet, slopping fruit tea into the shagpile. 'What?!'

'Yeah,' Ava answered. 'Surprise!' She sensed now wasn't the time to get annoyed that Debs' Facebook posts bearing their pinpoint location were somewhat to blame.

'That is so nice,' Didier said, still grinning. 'Family coming to visit.'

'It isn't nice, Didier, it is totes terrible,' Debs answered, spinning around in the chair and facing Ava. 'What is she doing here?'

'She's got me another job,' Ava said, tone coated in mock excitement.

'That is wonderful!' Didier stated, eyes bulbous, belt of the dressing gown he was wearing slipping a little as he stood up.

'It isn't wonderful, Didier,' Debs snapped. 'Ava's mum is... difficult.'

'Eloquently put,' Ava agreed.

'I hope you told her what to do with her job,' Debs said. 'I take it it's another modelling event.'

Ava nodded. 'Yes, probably the biggest, most prestigious one I've ever been offered.'

'What?'

'One of the models for Katya De Pierrot.'

'*Zut alors*! She is very famous!' Didier exclaimed.

'Fuck,' Debs stated. 'That's huge!'

Ava nodded. 'I know. She must've sent them shots from when I was a teenager. Ava, eighteen, pre-tattoo, the reluctant anorexic. How she thinks I could even get into shape in time... She's delusional.'

Silence reigned and Ava looked to Debs, waiting for her to comment further. Nothing was forthcoming and Ava pulled the covers off her T-shirt-clad body and stood up.

'You are thinking of *not* doing this?' Didier asked.

Ava let out a breath. Everything she held dear was screaming at her to run in the other direction but it was Katya De Pierrot's brand new collection. She loved her clothes – the whole time Ava had been modelling she'd thought it might just be bearable if she got to wear the clothes of someone she truly looked up to as an artist. And then there was the money. She had longed to work with someone of her magnitude the whole time she had been modelling. But if she said yes, what did it mean? This was a step back into the modelling world and her mum's chance to regain control.

This was the problem. She always buckled in crucial moments. She'd given into the personal trainer last spring and then it was the acting class the previous summer when she'd just recovered from a 'nasty sprained ankle' that had got her out of one of those awful industry fairs. It wouldn't end here. It never ended here. There would be job after job, a treadmill of little sleep, red-eye flights and calorie-controlled everything until she got too old and saggy to get jobs for anyone other than SAGA holidays. She wasn't the same person who had got on the Eurostar to the French capital. She now had it in her mind she might really think about doing something with her drawing.

'What do you want to do, Ava?' Debs asked. 'What do you really want to do?'

'Right now?'

'Right now,' Debs asked.

'I want to go to the Place des Vosges,' she said with a sigh.

FORTY-EIGHT

Place de la Concorde

Neutral ground was best. Ava had been repeating that mantra to herself ever since she snuck out of the hotel before calling her mother and setting the meeting place. Before that she had recounted the romance of the riverboat sail up the Seine for Debs to turn into Shakespeare-esque magazine fodder, leaving out the bit about being kissed in front of the Assembelée Nationale. Her friend was on a deadline and Ava didn't want her relationship with Julien dissected just yet, not while it was still so new to her.

She bit into a brioche and found when the chocolate hit her tongue she was already wondering how many calories she was ingesting. She put the pastry down. That's what a few hours with her mother had done already. She sipped her hot chocolate – about four hundred calories with the cream – and put her eyes on a taxi that had pulled up outside the café. She knew before the tan-stockinged legs even appeared in perfect formation that it was her mother. Used to living in London with the Tube at her disposal but always calling a taxi, there was no way Rhoda would have got on the Metro.

Ava wiped the crumbs from her hands and took a deep breath. It was just one job. The biggest job she had ever been up for. It was a huge deal. Was she really ready to do this?

As Rhoda walked through the door, Ava got to her feet and waved. If ever there was anyone inappropriately dressed for the weather, and her age, it was her mother. A white linen dress skirted her mid-thigh and she was wearing only a slim-fitted cardigan, no coat. Hair and make-up looked like they had been provided by a stylist.

Rhoda wrinkled her nose as she pulled out the chair opposite Ava. 'Ava, is that a chocolate brioche?'

Ava nodded. 'Yes, would you like one?'

Rhoda looked like she had been Tasered. 'Is that a joke?'

'No it's a rather delicious French bread. I'm sure you've had one before... well, I mean, at least given one half a glance.'

'You can't eat that sort of thing, Ava. How many times? Bread bloats and... is that hot chocolate?'

'With cream,' Ava answered, taking another sip and ensuring she got the white fluffy topping on her lips.

'You are aware no one working for Katya De Pierrot is larger than a size six.'

'Really? That's a shame. I'm usually about a ten these days.'

'We can fix that,' Rhoda said, moving her hot chocolate cup. 'We have three days. Granted it's not going to be a full detox in Goa but—'

Ava nodded. 'The thing is, Mum. I don't want to model for Katya De Pierrot.'

'Now you're just being ridiculous. Last night—'

'Last night you railroaded me,' Ava stated. 'Last night you turned up at my hotel, without warning and—'

'Ava, I left you several messages and a voicemail.'

'I know but I only got them this morning. I turned my phone off last night because I was sick of getting emotional blackmail from you and from Leo.'

Rhoda's eyes lit up. 'Leo is still messaging you?'

Ava sighed. The voice was coated in so much glee it was almost a cover version of a Justin Bieber song. 'Leo and I are over. Dead in the water. Absolutely no going back.'

'Until he sees you dressed in Pierrot.'

'Mum, stop!' She sighed. 'It isn't a case of wearing six-inch heels and having my hair rolled up like Princess Leia...'

'At the moment we're going to have to get you a hairpiece.'

She wanted to scream. She wondered if she just let her lungs produce the kind of noises that Bjork could make, her mother might actually stop and listen. And then she remembered all the soft, kind, reassuring things Sue had said to her before they left for Paris. That Leo wasn't good enough for *her*, not the other way around.

'Last night you were on board with the idea,' Rhoda stated.

'No, last night I listened to you and then I went to bed. This morning I've realised that this opportunity is just like all the ones before it and I don't want it, or them... *any* of them... any more.'

She hadn't quite screeched like a dolphin but the gentle festive music and the chatter from the other customers was definitely now muted and there were pairs of eyes on her. She made a grab for her hot chocolate and hid her face in the cup.

Rhoda shook her head and Ava looked across at her mother. There was something about her expression that was different. This wasn't a woman ready for battle; this was a woman on the verge of tears.

'I don't know what else to do,' Rhoda stated. 'I mean I thought Goa and the Azores would do it, I really did but then... then I had to pull out all the stops. I've been up for days, Ava. Days and nights searching for the opportunity of a lifetime and then... well, I wouldn't wish an accident on anyone but it seemed like Fate. Hazel Yashenko breaks her femur and here you are, already in Paris.'

Ava wasn't sure if her mother was aware tears were springing from her eyes, threatening to undo all the Max Factor she had been liberally applying from the birth canal to today. She swallowed, just watching and waiting for Rhoda to carry on.

'I want you to want what I want, Ava,' Rhoda spluttered, her head shaking, her hand batting the marble of the table in search of something. Ava used her index finger to push a metal square of serviettes towards her.

'Mum—'

'No, I didn't mean that. I just... want you to want *me*.'

Ava almost dropped her cup of hot chocolate. Steadying the porcelain until it found the tabletop she tried to decipher what exactly Rhoda was saying.

'Your *father*' – she said the word like she'd ingested Dettol – 'he seems to just pick up the phone and... you're there... with that Thai bride.'

'Mum—' Ava began.

'I mean who does he think he is? Hugh Hefner?' Rhoda wrestled a serviette from the holder on the table and dabbed at her eyes with the edge of it.

'Mum... what are you saying?' Ava asked.

Rhoda shook her head. 'I just want... things to be how they used to be.' She sniffed. 'Before you joined the estate agency and didn't come home for weeks on end.'

Ava furrowed her brow. Was she hearing this right? Were her mother's attempts at getting her back in the modelling profession nothing to do with modelling but everything to do with wanting to spend more time with her?

'Don't get me wrong, I liked Leo,' Rhoda said. 'He was always clean and he took care with his hair and...'

'Mum, he cheated on me,' Ava reminded her.

'And I thought if I convinced him what a mistake he'd made and he said he was sorry then you would be happy and you'd thank me and... we'd maybe have low-carb Asian some Saturday nights again.'

Ava shook her head. Was their relationship really so fractured that Rhoda felt she needed an excuse – or several excuses – to spend time with her? Why hadn't she just talked? Or had Ava been closed-off to listening?

'Did you ask Leo to send those picture messages of us together?' Ava asked.

Rhoda sobbed and nodded her head. 'You were meant to be with me, in Goa, when they came through, so I could comfort you and... well I thought he hadn't done it and...'

'Oh, Mum,' Ava said. 'I'm not twelve.'

'Your father... he has...' Rhoda was ugly crying now, boulders of snot blocking her every breath. 'He has the season ticket at Tottenham and the exotic holidays. All I have is things you used to be interested in... like… *America's Next Top Model* and—'

'Herbal Essences?' Ava offered.

'You think this is funny?' Rhoda asked.

'No, Mum,' Ava said. 'I'm sorry.'

'You never want to be at home.'

'Because I'm twenty-four and because you always threw modelling work at me,' Ava responded, sighing. 'If I'd known you just wanted to find some common ground then I would have suggested—' She stopped talking, her mind racing to think of things they actually had in common.

'Yes?'

There had to be something, didn't there? She quickly thought about things they'd done other than spend time in front of cameras. She smiled. 'Horse riding.'

She watched her mother's usually strained over-Botoxed face lose its rigour slightly, the corners of her mouth moving up. 'Ava, don't be silly, we haven't done that in years.'

'Well, maybe we should have,' Ava said. 'I liked it.' She breathed in, getting the glorious ginger-and-coffee-infused air but remembering the scents of countryside in the summer – grassland, ragwort and eau de pony. On board her favourite chocolate brown mare, nothing but the sun, the outside and the sound of the gentle clopping of the horse's hooves.

'Why did we stop going?' she asked Rhoda.

Rhoda raised her shoulders in a shrug. 'We always had something else to do.'

'Modelling?' Ava asked.

'You started going to football with your father.'

'Oh, Mum, that didn't mean I didn't want to spend time with you too.'

Rhoda dabbed at her eyes again. 'Divorce is an ugly thing, Ava. It turns you into someone else... someone you never imagined you would be.'

She swallowed, her mind going to Sue and Gary. She didn't want her best friend going through another parental break-up. She responded, 'But it's been a long time now and...' – she chose her words carefully – 'is it worse because Dad's moved on? Because he's with Myleene?'

'No, of course not,' Rhoda said a little too quickly.

'He was sad to begin with,' Ava told her. 'But I think he knew, deep down, like you did, that you were never going to stay happy together.'

'I was too young,' Rhoda stated. 'I leapt into something instead of thinking about my career. That's why it's so important to me that you don't do the same thing.'

Ava smiled and reached across the table for her mother's hand – onyx, opal and diamante rings on each finger. 'I won't,' she said. 'But it doesn't mean I have to follow the same path you did.' She hesitated. 'Not that it wasn't the right path for you... I mean you have your business and you enjoy the glamour and everything, but it isn't for me. I'm not sure it ever has been.'

'Oh, Ava,' Rhoda said, still teary-eyed. 'But you are so good at it. So much better than I ever was.'

Ava squeezed her hand. 'I'm good at selling luxury apartments too but I don't see my future there either.'

'So... where do you see it?' Rhoda asked.

Her drawing came to mind. It was a possibility but she wasn't confident enough to share that yet. 'I don't know,' she said. 'But that's OK. Because I don't need a wish list with things to tick off. I'm just going to take every day as it comes.'

She felt her mother shudder, as if the very thought of not having a schedule to keep to was going to send her heart into abnormal sinus rhythm.

'Honestly, Mum, once you get started it's a lot easier than it sounds.' She smiled. 'And you hardly ever have to check your phone.'

Rhoda shook her head. 'You never used that calorie-counting app, did you?'

'No, Mum,' Ava admitted. 'And neither should you.' She waved her hand in the air. '*Excusez-moi,*' she called to the waitress. 'Another hot chocolate with extra cream and another chocolate brioche.'

'For me?' Rhoda asked tentatively.

'Yes, for you,' Ava said. 'And while you sit there and enjoy every fat-laden morsel I'm going to tell you about something I need your help with.'

FORTY-NINE

Place Des Vosges

Julien was late and he had cursed the traffic the whole way across the city. A cab had slowed right in front of him and he had taken it, thinking it would be faster than heading to the Metro. He had been to see a possible venue for the exhibition. It was a light, bright dance studio with a view of Pont Neuf. On the floor were bare wooden boards and the walls were natural brick, one half of them lined with full-length mirrors. And it was available next week. He had closed his eyes as he stood there in the middle of the room, thinking about where to position his work, working out if there was room enough for guests to be comfortable weaving in and out of the artwork. And then he had opened his eyes and looked out at the river, Parisian life, moving along, heading towards Christmas, the end of another year and a new start when 2017 arrived. He'd turned and looked at the woman showing him around and booked it. He had a matter of days to get this together and he was both exhilarated and scared to death about it.

He skidded through the snow into the square, looking for Ava. They hadn't said which part of the park they were going to meet in. At a jog he rounded one of the fountains and began scouring the benches under the row of trees, bare-branched for the winter.

'You're late, Monsieur Fitoussi!'

He turned around at the sound of Ava's voice and saw her. He smiled, waving a hand, and began to hurry towards the bench she was sat on, red hat covering her hair, Converse still on her feet. He was so excited to tell her he had a venue, that they could begin to get things going, that he wanted her to meet his parents... Dinner tonight. He hoped getting both Vivienne and his father to see that this exhibition could not only be a reality but also be their chance to draw closer as a family and start the much-needed healing process. And he wanted Ava with him.

She stood up as he got nearer and he took the last few paces slowly, drinking her in, remembering how close they had been last night. He stopped just in front of her, his breath catching in his throat.

'You were right about this place,' Ava stated, looking around.

'An oasis, *non*?' he said. 'A little piece of quiet away from the city.'

'And you never mentioned there was more than one fountain,' Ava spoke. 'You know how I love a fountain and there are *four*!'

'Already I am fearing for my hat,' Julien said, putting his hand to the hat she had bought him.

She smiled and he couldn't wait any longer. He took a step forward and took her into his arms, his lips finding hers, wanting to wrap her up against the cold weather.

'I missed you,' she whispered, looking into his eyes.

'We have only been apart for fourteen hours... or so,' he answered, his fingers straightening her hat.

'You counted too,' Ava said, grinning.

He shook his head, laughing. 'Walk with me?' He offered her his hand.

'Ooh, to celebrate Louis XIII and Anne of Austria?' she asked, slipping her fingers between his.

'Someone has been reading a guide book,' he teased.

'I might have had a quick look on Wikipedia to find out more about your favourite place,' she admitted.

'There was a celebration here when they married,' Julien told her as they began to walk. 'A *carrousel*.'

'Do you think it still looks the same as it did then?' Ava asked him.

'I know there were not so many trees then... see, the linden trees,' he stated, indicating the trees around them so spiky without their greenery. 'In the summer, when everything is green, there are people on the grass and beneath the trees seeking shade and a little quiet. Reading, sleeping...'

'Eating?' Ava asked.

'The French love to picnic,' he reminded. 'A little *vin rouge* and...'

'Camembert.' Ava smiled.

Julien squeezed her hand. 'I have something to speak with you about.'

'Me too,' she replied.

'Please, you first,' he said.

She shook her head. 'No, Louis XIII, this Anne of Austria isn't abiding by how things were done in the seventeenth century. You first.'

'OK.' He breathed deeply. 'I have found a place for my exhibition.'

'You have!' Ava exclaimed. 'Where?'

'It is a large, open, studio with a view over the Seine, by Pont Neuf. It is a blank canvas but one with character and the light there... it is just right, there are mirrors and...' he said, full of enthusiasm.

'How many people does it hold?'

'A hundred,' he replied. 'I know it will be tight, but if I use mounts in the middle of the room together with the walls and—'

'A hundred,' Ava stated, swallowing.

'You think I will not fill the room? That it will look empty?' *That no one will come.* He kept that thought to himself.

She laughed. 'No, actually, the exact opposite. I'd better tell you my news.'

He stopped walking and turned to face her, expectant.

'My mother is here.'

He hadn't been expecting that. 'Oh... that is... a surprise.'

'Yes,' Ava answered. 'And when I saw her I thought about jumping on the Eurostar back to St Pancras International. And then...' She sighed.

'Then?'

'Then I actually told her, really told her that I was never modelling again.' She let go of a tight breath. 'And we talked... we talked, Julien. We actually had a conversation that didn't only involve her telling me goji berries were the in thing for your digestive tract... and it turns out... she misses *me*. It hasn't really been about the modelling... well, not all of it and... I think we understand each other a little better.'

He smiled, squeezing her hands in his. 'I am so pleased for you, Madonna.'

'But, the thing about my mum is... she's not someone who can be idle.'

'No?'

'No. I mean, I can't remember the last time she took a holiday... probably her honeymoon twenty-five years ago.'

'So...' His core was tightening preparing for the worst. Ava was going to leave. Return to England with her mother. He knew she was going to have to go eventually, but now?

'So *I've* given *her* a job,' Ava stated. 'I know I should have asked you first but I just jumped at the opportunity. Seized the day.'

'Madonna, what have you done?'

'I asked her to use every contact she has to get people here for your exhibition,' Ava announced. 'She just needs a date and a time and all the other information and, Julien, if there is one thing I know about my mother's contact list, it's that it includes some very, very rich people who are going to want to buy your photographs for a great cause.'

He was speechless. He really didn't know what to say. No one had ever done anything like that for him before.

'God, are you cross? Was it a step too far? I'm sorry, I can call her and I can tell her—'

He silenced her with a kiss, her lips warm against his as the snow flurries cooled every other part of them. He touched his palm to her cheek and watched her blink back at him. 'I do not know what to say,' he finally spoke.

'I did a good thing?' she queried.

'You are not sure?' he inquired. 'Do I need to kiss you again?'

She laughed. 'I think I'd like you to do that anyway.'

He moved towards her again but this time she stopped him, putting the flat of her hand against his chest.

'But first I think we need to rethink this venue,' she said. 'Because with Rhoda Devlin on the case we need to be thinking more in the high three-figure range.'

'Really?' Julien asked.

'Really.'

'Then I need to take some more photographs.' He kissed her lips again, then held her away from him, just enjoying watching her expression. 'There is something else,' he stated.

'Didier is moving in with you?' she asked. 'That was a hopeful plea.'

He shook his head. 'No... my parents have invited me to dinner tonight and I would very much like you to come with me.'

'Oh,' Ava said.

He noted the visible swallow and he reached for her hands again. 'You do not have to, if you feel it would be... not right. I just thought...'

'Are they going to ask me lots of difficult questions about French history or the euro or anything to do with opera?' Ava inquired.

Julien laughed. 'I hope not or I will not last past the first course.'

'There's going to be more than one course?'

'My step-mother makes a wonderful clafoutis.'

'I have no idea what that is but it sounds delicious.'

'So you will come?' Julien asked her.

She nodded. 'I will come.' She pulled at his hands, dragging him along the path. 'Now, treat me like a queen and get me my next caffeine fix.'

He smiled at her. 'Very well, Madonna. Café it is.'

And then he saw her stop smiling, her face whitening as she gazed across the park.

'Ava?' he queried. 'What's wrong?'

'It's that man...' Her voice was weak, uncertain, perhaps a little afraid. 'That man over there.' She lifted her hand in an attempt to point.

He looked to where she was indicating and saw a tall man wearing a navy blue winter coat and carrying a briefcase.

Looking back to Ava he saw her swallow. 'It's Debs' step-dad,' she said. 'It's Gary.'

FIFTY

Ava couldn't quite believe it. He really was in Paris. The silent phone calls, the Skyping, the mention of his name in the boutique, the email on Francine's PC, everything she had put down to something else, to her not hearing properly, to something work-related, and here, now, when he was supposed to be in Toulouse, Gary was in Paris.

'Should we do something?' Julien asked her.

She couldn't speak. She was just watching Gary, making his way through the park, heading towards the fountain just ahead of them like he didn't have a care in the world.

'Ava,' Julien stated.

'We need to follow him,' she responded, shaking herself back into the moment.

'We could catch up to him,' Julien suggested, holding his hand out to her.

She shook her head. 'No, I don't want him to see us. I need to see where he's going.'

'But if you speak to him...'

'Julien, don't you know anything about the work of private investigators? It's called "private" for a reason.' She took his hand in hers. 'Come on or we'll lose him.'

They followed Gary to a restaurant and watched him being shown to a table for two they could just about see from the street. Ava had tears in her eyes. A table for two. In Paris. When he was meant to be somewhere else. There was only one person he was going to be meeting. Debs had been right all along. Sue was right to be concerned about her marriage. History was about to repeat itself.

'You are OK?' Julien asked.

She shook her head, unable to commit to an answer.

'You should not worry,' Julien said. 'Nothing has happened.'

'What d'you mean?' Ava asked.

'Well, he has just gone into a restaurant. There are many reasons why he might do this.'

'Like for lunch?' Ava suggested. 'Or a coffee... on his own... in a city he isn't even meant to be in.' She looked through the window, hat pulled low on her head. 'I can't believe he's doing this. He knew what Sue and Debs went through before. He promised them forever. A new beginning.'

The words felt bitter as they left her mouth. Here she was, having stood up to her mother for the very first time, with a man she had deeply fallen for, on the brink of breaking out into the exciting unknown, and her best friend was about to have her whole world turned upside down.

'I need to go in there,' Ava stated.

'I thought you did not want him to see you.'

'That was before he waltzed in there and sat down... with a newspaper for God's sake... reading it like he's relaxed... like he's waiting for a lover.' She stepped towards the entrance. 'I need to just go in there and ask him what he's doing here when he's meant to be in Toulouse.'

'Maybe,' Julien began, 'maybe you should call Debs.'

She shook her head. She didn't want to do that for so many reasons. The first involved her friend hammering out an article to get this job she craved for professional reasons and would now need more than ever to support her and her mum. The other reasons were because she didn't know how she was going to tell Debs that Gary was here. That Gary was a cheat. That although Gary had been seemingly love-struck on his wedding day waltzing Sue around the floor to 'Everything I Do, I Do It For You', everything he was now doing was for someone called Francine.

'I can't,' Ava admitted. 'What do I say to her?'

'Madonna, I am here for you, whatever you want to do, but if you really do not want him to see you, you need to move away from the door.'

Ava stepped back and there was a shriek. Someone's foot was underneath her Converse and when she looked up into the owner's face she saw it was Francine.

'Sorry,' Ava said on autopilot. She wasn't sorry. She wished she'd stepped back twice as hard.

'I know you,' Francine replied. 'From my office. A rainbow I can grow at home.'

Ava's blood was boiling. This woman was about to walk into the restaurant and sit down for a tryst with Gary. She wished she had a Waitrose shelf of things to throw at her.

'Here to see your boyfriend?' Ava spat.

'Ava,' Julien said, taking hold of her arm.

'*Pardon?*' Francine said, taken aback but pushing by, trying to ignore her.

'Your boyfriend,' Ava repeated as Francine moved past, eyes glued forward. Her hand was on the restaurant door. 'Are you going to share some vin rouge and plan your first Christmas together? If it *is* your first Christmas together? I mean we don't really know how long this has been going on.'

But Francine had already gone through the door.

'You make me sick!' Ava shouted. 'I hope you... choke on the bread basket.'

'Ava,' Julien said, pulling her back.

Ava shook his arm off and pressed her nose up against the glass of the eatery. She watched, stomach dropping piece by piece, as Gary stood up, embracing Francine.

'Ava,' Julien said, softly. 'What do you want to do now?'

'Now,' Ava began, 'now we call Debs.'

FIFTY-ONE

Ava was chewing her nails, pacing up and down an alley next to the restaurant and waiting. She'd positioned Julien so he could still see the door to the eatery. Around her, city life was going on as usual. Pedestrians trampled snow, mopeds beeped horns, Christmas lights flashed from every building and her stomach was performing a winter Olympics triple Lutz. No one else here had their best friend's feelings on a knife-edge. She was feeling hopeless – desperate to protect her and knowing she couldn't.

'It's the Parisian traffic,' she muttered, vaguely directing the moan at Julien. 'The bloody Parisian traffic.' She about-faced and marched towards the bins again. 'We can't let them leave if they try to leave.'

'It is Didier,' Julien announced. 'With Debs. They are here.'

Ava shot to the alley entrance and her eyes went to the moped careering down the street towards them. No helmets on their heads, the Frenchman drew the moped to a stop and Debs was clambering off, her face a weird mix of pale and intense, eyes like Frisbees.

Ava took a breath then stepped towards her friend, throwing her arms around her and holding her close, tears smarting in her eyes. 'I'm sorry,' she whispered. 'I don't want this to be true. I don't want you to get hurt again.'

'It's OK,' Debs answered, in perhaps the shortest sentence she'd ever uttered.

'It's not OK though. It's so far from OK. I want to punch her. And I want to punch him and...' Ava said, stepping back and wiping her nose with the sleeve of her coat.

'I think that's my job,' Debs stated sadly.

'Can I just say that we do not know if anything has happened?' Didier said.

'No,' Ava and Debs said together.

'But your step-father may be entirely innocent,' he continued.

'He's here in Paris, Didier,' Debs said. 'Meeting a woman who isn't my mum, when he's meant to be working in Toulouse.'

'And there might be another explanation for this,' Julien joined in.

'Like there was another explanation for Leo and Cassandra?' Ava asked, looking to him. 'Or for Lauren and Charles?'

'They're in there?' Debs checked, glancing towards the window of the restaurant.

'Yes,' Ava answered.

Debs looked to her, swallowing. 'Would you... come in with me?'

'You're sure?' Ava asked. 'Because if Gary starts giving you grief or *that woman* says anything then I won't be responsible for my actions.'

'We could all go in,' Didier suggested. 'Julien and I could have coffee.'

'No,' Ava and Debs answered together.

'We would sit at a safe distance,' Didier said. 'For support... to stop the owner calling the gendarmerie if things get a little – how do you say? – heated.'

Ava was about to open her mouth to protest again when the little bell above the door signalled its opening and there, right in front of them, coming out of the restaurant and on to the street was Gary and Francine.

'Ava?' Gary exclaimed in shock. His head turned left. 'Debs?! What are you both doing here?'

'You bastard! You absolute bastard! How could you?! How could you?!' Debs flung herself at Gary, thumping his chest with her fists like he was King Kong threatening to crush her off-spring.

'Debs,' Didier said, stepping forward and taking hold of her shoulders.

'Get off me!' Debs ordered, trying to push him off.

'Who are these people, Gary?' Francine asked. 'A delivery girl and—'

'Don't you speak!' Ava ordered. 'Don't you dare speak! We... are his family!'

'Perhaps we should all take a moment... go back inside... sit down?' Julien suggested.

'Debs, what's the matter, love? What's going on?' Gary asked, trying to avoid another thump and finally catching hold of Debs' arms.

'Yes!' Debs exclaimed. 'That's exactly what I want to know! What the fuck is going on? With *her*!'

'Francine?' Gary queried, looking confused.

'I think we should call her *the bitch*,' Debs suggested viciously. 'Or maybe *the homewrecker... the marriage-breaker... the divorce-maker*.'

'*Pardon*?' Francine gasped.

'I said don't you speak!' Ava yelled, pointing an accusing finger. 'I heard you talking about Gary in a boutique and I had convinced myself I'd misheard... and then I saw an email from him on your computer. It said "Francine, the other night was amazing".'

'You did?' Debs asked, dropping her arms from Gary's grip like she had just been sapped of all energy. 'It said that.'

'I... couldn't tell you...I didn't want to tell you,' Ava admitted. 'I wanted to believe that it wasn't true and now...'

'I don't know what you girls think is going on but—'

'We know what's going on,' Debs attacked again. 'You're having an affair with this... with *her*... because you're not meant to be in Paris... Mum thinks you're working... in Toulouse!'

'An affair?' Francine exclaimed.

'Now, hang on a minute—' Gary started.

'Don't speak to her like that,' Ava ordered, taking a step towards him.

'Ava,' Julien said.

'Let the man speak?' Didier suggested.

'You're just like Dad... you said you loved Mum and me and... now Mum isn't good enough and I'm not good enough,' Debs continued. 'And all those things you said, all those promises you made about family and sticking together—'

'Debs, I'm not having an affair,' Gary said.

'...and my job is totes shit and I've had to spend a whole twenty-four hours writing until my fingers burn to try and get a gig *Trudy* will probably have land in her lap and... What did you say?' Debs asked.

'I said I'm not having an affair,' Gary repeated.

'This is all... *la erreur*?' Francine offered.

'A mistake,' Didier translated. 'A misunderstanding.'

'But it can't be,' Ava stated as Julien slipped his hand in hers. 'I saw the email. I heard you talking about him in the dress shop.'

'Mum said you'd been secretive... that you were Skyping... travelling even more.'

Gary put his hands to his head, shaking it. 'It doesn't look like I've been quite as discreet as I'd hoped.'

Everyone was now waiting with bated breath for someone to provide all the missing pieces.

'Debs, Francine has been helping me with a surprise... for your mum.'

'A surprise,' Debs stated, lips trembling.

'Yes,' Gary said. 'She loves Paris. She told me that on our very first date together all those moons ago. I wanted to organise a special weekend for her big birthday next month. And I wanted to splash out a bit, treat her.'

Ava felt sick and she gripped hold of Julien's hand, her eyes going to her best friend.

'What?' Debs said, tears already falling.

'Francine works for the Paris office of Cosmos. We met at the conference last year. She's been helping me put together a whole weekend of things for me and your mum to do when we're here... and I wanted to get her a dress... an expensive dress from a French boutique.'

'I am about your mother's size, *non*?' Francine said tentatively.

Ava opened her mouth to tell the woman not to talk again but quickly shut it. It was true. Now she thought about it, Francine was the same shape and height as Sue.

'As I was in Toulouse already, I nipped over here on the way back to London to pick up the dress.' Gary picked up the boutique bag that was by his feet. 'And Francine needed my signature on a couple of things. And the other night... the other night was amazing because Francine told me about this great show in Toulouse to take my clients to.'

'Oh God,' Ava exclaimed. 'Oh, God, Gary, we're so sorry!'

Debs was just crying, her face becoming a red crumpled mess as she began to heavy breathe.

'Debs, come here, love, don't cry,' Gary said, opening his arms and pulling her into an embrace. 'You're my girl,' he whispered. 'I love you, you know that, and I love your mum more than anything. I'd never do anything to hurt either of you.'

'And I am not a... *divorce-maker*?' Francine said, looking to Ava. 'I have a boyfriend called Luc.'

'I'm sorry,' Ava said to Francine. 'I'm very sorry for everything... particularly the grow-your-own-rainbow kit.'

'All right, love?' Gary asked, easing Debs back from his shoulder and looking at her with concern. 'You know if there's anything you're ever worried about you just need to talk to me.'

Ava felt Julien squeeze her fingers at that comment and she didn't dare look at him for fear of looking into a knowing, slightly told-you-so expression.

Debs nodded. 'I was just... scared that's all and worried for Mum and...'

'It was my fault really,' Ava said. 'I had this crazy idea of just, you know, trying to hack emails and following Francine around Paris... it was me who lost faith, Taxi Dad, not Debs.'

Debs shook her head. 'Don't listen to her. She's just covering for me.'

Gary smiled at Ava. 'Being her best mate like always.' He turned back to Debs then. 'Listen, you've got to promise me you'll keep this quiet from your mum, it's been months in the planning and I want it to be complete surprise.'

Debs nodded, smiling. 'Of course I will.'

'So, now, apologise to Francine and then tell me what you're doing in Paris and why your job is totes shit. I think Taxi Dad needs to hear about that.'

FIFTY-TWO

Hotel Agincourt

Despite everything that had happened that day, even after coffee and macaroons with Debs, Gary, Julien and Didier in a warm and gorgeous little café, the high emotions, sugar and caffeine weren't enough to distract Ava from being nervous about what was to come. Dinner with Julien's parents.

'He's had my email an hour and three minutes now,' Debs said, hitting the refresh button on her laptop again.

They had both talked to Sue before Debs had hit 'send' on her articles and eased her anxieties about Gary. Using a 'top secret insurance project' they had together explained Gary's behaviour and all the incidentals along the way and Gary had been briefed to go along with that until the big reveal for Sue's birthday. Now the full focus was on Debs' potential job.

'I know he has,' Ava replied. 'But, in the scheme of things, with your mum and Gary being solid and off for a saucy week-end in Paris soon, this job... well, it isn't *everything* any more. You're good at what you do, Debs, *great* at what you do. And if this Nigel can't see that then he isn't worthy of you.' She looked at herself in the mirror. Usually right now she would be asking herself if she should wear her hair up or down. There wasn't a lot you could do to change platinum spikes.

'I need to know tonight,' Debs moaned. 'Before seven or I will be on tenterhooks at the circus and won't be able to enjoy it.'

Ava turned her head from looking into the full-length mirror on the wardrobe door. 'The circus?'

'Didier's taking me. He texted. It's one of those upmarket circuses with lots of people who can turn their bodies inside out and do magic with chainsaws. No animals... well, apart from a poodle who can breakdance,' Debs informed.

'Wow, could you video that?' Ava asked.

'Anyway,' Debs announced, one eye on the computer screen, 'I know I've been completely caught up in these articles and the whole Francine and Gary thing...' She patted the edge of the bed next to her. 'What's been going on with you?'

'You mean apart from my mother turning up?'

Rhoda was having a spa treatment in the facilities at the hotel followed by a specially prepared room-service meal. Her mum had been complaining the brioche had tampered with her fine digestive balance since she had finished eating it and Ava hadn't dared suggest perhaps it was a reaction to good food rather than chemically enhanced stuff.

'How did that go?' Debs asked.

'Surprisingly well,' Ava answered. 'I can honestly say I won't be modelling again and I won't be hearing from Leo either.'

'Goodness, I missed a lot while I was going blind writing about singles and penguin earmuffs.'

Ava let out a sigh. It was no good. She was pent up about this dinner and she needed Debs' advice. She pulled at the sheer cream top she was wearing over leggings and finally sat down.

'I'm meeting Julien's parents tonight,' Ava rushed out. 'His dad and his step-mum and... I've never met a dad and a step-mum before... only my own.'

Debs clapped a hand over her mouth, almost knocking out one of the flashing Santa's sleigh earrings she was wearing. 'You're not just friends, are you?! Something's happened, hasn't it? Was it the cruise up the Seine? I thought there was rather too much about the chocolate pudding and totes not enough feels.' Debs sighed. 'I made some feels up by the way... for the article.'

Ava shook her head, a smile on her face. 'I can't describe it, Debs. I've not had anything quite like it before.'

'Makes you feel weak? Want to look into his eyes every second you're together? Practically *need* to slather him in mincemeat and lick it all off?' Debs asked excitedly.

Ava swallowed. 'Actually nothing like any of that.'

'Oh.'

'But in a good way,' Ava added. 'When I'm with him it's as if... I'm wholly me and... he's wholly him but somehow we're together too.'

'No,' Debs said. 'I've never had anything like that before.'

'And he makes me feel...' She sighed. 'As if I could do absolutely anything.'

'Goodness, Ava, that sounds very much like... love.'

Ava shook her head. 'It can't be though, can it? Because it takes a long time to love someone and you have to have a first argument—' She stopped herself from talking, remembering their misunderstanding about Lauren and the burning wish list on the boat. 'Well, you at least have to... enjoy the same foods.' The taste of falafel was in her mouth before she could force it away.

'And cover each other in mincemeat,' Debs added.

'I really don't think that's a thing.'

'Didier understood,' Debs answered.

Ava stood up. 'Don't say any more or I'll be looking for dried fruit in my sheets.' She brushed down the front of her shirt again and turned her body to the side to check out her profile. 'Does this look OK? And can I borrow your boots again?'

Debs got up from the bed and stood behind her friend, hugging her close. Ava regarded their joint reflections in the mirror. Debs with her Disney Princesses sweatshirt and multi-coloured Yule log necklace, her with butterflies in her stomach.

'You look amazing,' Debs stated.

'But what if they think their son must have lost his mind to be spending time with me?'

'Then it will be the very last time you spend with them,' Debs said. 'And he will feel the same.'

She hoped so. She really wanted to make a good impression. She also knew how important the exhibition and Julien's parents' role in it was to him. He had told her that afternoon that he wanted them and other families who had lost someone in the fire to play a part in the night.

And then the laptop made a bing. Ava looked to Debs, her heart in her mouth. 'What does that noise mean?'

'I don't know,' Debs admitted. 'I've never noticed it do that before when I've got new mail.' She fled over to the desk.

'Debs...'

'Nigel's replied,' Debs gasped, her hand working overtime on the mouse.

'God, what did he say? It's all good, right?'

Debs was silent, her eyes scanning the screen, her head moving left to right.

'Debs! Say something! Even if it's bad news, just tell me. It's not everything, remember. Sue and Gary. Together forever.'

Debs turned to face her, eyes downcast, bottom lip trembling.

'Oh shit,' Ava said, stumbling up and off the bed in a bid to cross the room as quickly as possible. 'I'll stay in. I'll call Julien... I have his number now and I'll tell him I need to be here with you.'

'No you won't,' Debs said stroppily. And all at once her demeanour changed, her smile lighting the room like the night-time display at the Eiffel Tower. 'Because we're totes celebrating tonight. Me and the breakdancing poodle and you with Julien,' she screamed. 'I got the job!'

FIFTY-THREE

The Fitoussi's home

Even though Julien was holding her hand she was shaking both with the cold and her nerves. The sheer blouse was a mistake. She should have asked to borrow one of Debs' jumpers. And this house they were standing in front of reeked of elegance, towering to the night sky, a blue slate roof somewhere up near the stars.

'How many storeys is it?' Ava asked through juddering teeth. 'And are we w-waiting for a butler?'

'You are cold,' Julien remarked, putting an arm around her shoulders and drawing her into his body.

'You h-haven't answered my question.'

'No butler,' Julien responded. 'And it has three storeys. The top floor has the bedrooms, the middle floor the living areas and the bottom level for the maids.'

'What?!'

'I am joking with you,' he teased. 'It is just a simple town house.'

'In a very nice area of P-Paris,' she said.

'And we do have another house in the countryside.'

Ava didn't get time to respond before the door was whisked open and a beautiful woman with dark hair was standing there dressed elegantly in a black short evening dress, a diamante brooch of a cat on the front of it.

'Julien,' she exclaimed. She directed a smile at Ava. 'Hello.'

'*Bonsoir,*' Ava responded, a hesitant smile at her lips.

'Vivienne, I would like you to meet Ava Devlin,' Julien introduced. 'Ava, this is my step-mother, Vivienne.'

'It's very n-nice to meet you,' Ava said, stepping forward and offering out her hand.

'It is so wonderful to meet you,' Vivienne greeted. The woman ignored the hand and instead kissed Ava first on one cheek and then the other. 'And Ava is such a pretty name.'

'Thank you,' she answered, still shivering.

'You are cold! And I am leaving you here on the doorstep. Come in,' Vivienne ushered. 'Julien, you know where the coats go, then bring Ava through to the drawing room, I have lit a fire.'

Julien took Ava's hand in his and nudged her forward and into the house.

'You would like some wine, Ava?' Vivienne asked. 'I have white open or some red.'

'White please,' Ava said, warming her hands in front of the fire.

For Julien it was strange being in his family home again. It had probably only been months but it all felt a little different. Nothing much had changed. The oil paintings on the wall bought for investment, the large ox-blood-coloured leather suite, the mahogany-coloured coffee table were all relics from his childhood but they seemed foreign to him. His eyes caught some photo frames on the mantelpiece he didn't remember. He moved next to Ava, looking at the pictures inside them.

'We just freshened up the photographs,' Vivienne said, as if in explanation. He knew then why the change. His father, smashing the ones that were usually there.

'Is that you?' Ava asked, pointing at one of the photographs. He was dressed in dungarees riding a tyre attached to a metal bar in a play park.

He nodded. 'Yes. I had a good sense of fashion, no?'

Ava laughed. 'No, is the right answer.' She picked up the photo. 'And that's Lauren with you.'

Julien looked at the photo. Lauren standing with her arms stretched up to the sky on the very top of the climbing frame.

'Now, she is wearing a much better outfit,' Ava remarked.

Julien smiled and looked at his sister wearing a tangerine playsuit and flip-flops on her feet, her blonde hair blowing in the summer breeze.

'And this is her too,' Ava said, indicating a photo in a silver frame a little further down the cream-coloured shelf.

'Yes, just a few years ago,' Vivienne said, coming over to them and plucking the picture up. 'She was such a beautiful girl. This was from a photo shoot we had done together. We laughed so much that day.'

Julien could sense the emotion flooding from his step-mother and he gently took the picture out of her hands and set it back on the shelf. He turned to Ava. 'Lauren was always laughing.'

'And she had the most infectious laugh,' Gerard answered.

Julien shifted around quickly, seeing that his father had entered the room. He offered Gerard a smile as he neared them, dressed casually for him in grey flannel trousers and a pale blue shirt, no tie. He looked tired, strung out, vulnerable.

'I will get the wine,' Vivienne said, taking steps towards the door.

'Dad, this is Ava,' Julien introduced. 'Ava Devlin. Ava, this is my father, Gerard.'

'*Bonsoir*, Monsieur Fitoussi,' Ava said. 'It's so nice to meet you.'

Gerard nodded, then looked to the departing form of Vivienne almost as if she were abandoning him in unfamiliar territory.

'So, Dad, how is business?' Julien asked, trying to keep the conversation moving.

'Excuse me for one moment,' Gerard said, stepping back. 'I will get the wine.'

'But, Vivienne is—' Julien began.

'Please, excuse me,' Gerard said, retreating fast.

Julien could do nothing more but watch his father leave.

FIFTY-FOUR

Ava couldn't eat another thing if she tried. She had said that after pudding but still managed to eat three different kinds of cheese and some biscuits. Now Vivienne was trying to encourage her to have tiny homemade chocolates from the bushy, very real, huge Christmas tree that almost dominated the dining room.

'I really can't eat anything else,' Ava said, her hands on her stomach.

'Ava, you really must taste these,' Julien stated. 'Vivienne makes the most wonderful chocolate.'

'Julien, honestly, you remember how stuffed I was on falafels?' She bulged her eyes at him. 'I'm more stuffed than that.'

She watched Julien take a chocolate from Vivienne and sit back in his chair. 'OK, Ava really has had enough,' he said, biting into the sweet.

'But could I maybe take a couple back to my hotel?' Ava asked with a smile.

Vivienne laughed. 'But of course.'

She chanced a glance at Julien's father. He had barely said more than a few sentences throughout the whole dinner. He had eaten far less than any of them and he was on his second bottle of wine. She knew how much this dinner meant to Julien and how he wanted the fundraising evening to be a step forward for his family.

'So, we're going out to take some more photographs tomorrow,' Ava stated.

'Ava...' Julien said, his cheeks reddening.

'Before... well it seems like a lifetime ago really... I used to do a bit of modelling and I thought I knew everything there was to know about photography but watching Julien work... it's so different to what I've been used to.'

'He is a wonderful photographer,' Vivienne responded, smiling. 'Isn't he, Gerard?'

'There's no need—' Julien started.

'And what he's doing with the exhibition, for the Red Cross... it's going to be an amazing night.'

Gerard shifted his chair back and got to his feet and Ava stopped talking, realising she wasn't going to get the reaction she had hoped for.

'Dad,' Julien said, getting up too as his father headed out of the room.

'Leave him, Julien,' Vivienne urged, voice coated with anxiety as the door shut behind Gerard.

'Not this time,' Julien said decidedly. 'Excuse me.' He put his napkin down on the table and followed his father's lead.

'I'm sorry,' Ava said as the door shut behind Julien.

'It is not your fault, Ava,' Vivienne insisted. 'I do not know how much Julien has told you but...'

'Pretty much everything I think,' she answered. 'Eventually.'

Vivienne shook her head, her fingers going to the brooch on her dress. 'I am so worried about the whole family, Ava. Gerard, he has always been the strong head of the family. A leader... the foundation stone... he hates to be this way, feel how he is feeling. He believes that grief is just weakness and weakness is not in his nature.' She sniffed back tears, screwing up her napkin in her hands. 'He blames himself for Lauren's death. For being too caught up with work. For her moving out to her own apartment. I mean, it is crazy, she was a grown woman, she was always going to make her own way, live in her own place... and it was an accident... it could have happened anywhere at any time.'

'Julien misses her very much,' Ava spoke softly.

'And I worry about him too. Not opening up, not accepting that this accident happened to him too. Living with the memories of the trauma and his injury.'

Ava swallowed. 'His injury?'

Vivienne topped up Ava's wine glass before filling her own. 'He has not told you either.' She shook her head. 'It is not really my place to—'

'Please,' Ava said. 'Please, Vivienne, he's the best man I've ever known. I want to help him.'

When Julien reached the kitchen Gerard was leaning over the sink, weight on both hands, head hanging. He flicked on the light and his father moved, sinking his hands into the bowl of washing up and play-acting.

'Dad, you don't need to pretend for me,' Julien said lightly. 'You have never washed up.'

Gerard slammed a plate down onto the drainer. 'What is going on, Julien?' Gerard asked. 'Who *is* she?'

'Ava?' he queried. 'I told Vivienne on the phone. She's—'

'I know that she is not Monique,' Gerard snapped.

His father's words burned and it took every bit of self-control he had to not react.

'No,' he responded on a breath, 'she is not Monique.' He sighed. 'And, if you like, we can have a conversation about Ava not being Monique. And then when you have finished telling me whatever it is you think you need to tell me maybe we can talk about the reasons I'm here for dinner. To help you. To hope that you will help me.' Tension was performing rope tricks in his stomach now but all this needed to be said now, before it was too late.

'I want you and Vivienne to be part of this exhibition. I don't want it just to be about the best pictures I can take of the landmarks of Paris, I want it to be about real people, the real France, the best parts and the darkest moments but with an unending string of hope and beauty running right through the middle of it.' He took a breath, his eyes not leaving his father's. 'I want all the loved ones who lost someone in the fire to contribute something. A photographic memory, about loss, recovery, beauty in life and life going on. I want this exhibition to mean something. To achieve something. I don't want it to be about me and my photos. I want it to be about Lauren, about you and Vivienne, about resilience.'

His heart was drumming hard but he had to get this message across.

'I need your help, Dad. Not the help of your business or your contacts, although that would be appreciated. I need you. I need you to do this for Lauren, to remember her not with pain but with joy in your heart.' He let go of a breath, watching his father's expression. 'You don't have to pick up all the pieces alone, Dad. We are in this together.'

Gerard shook his head. 'Sometimes I feel like I am one of the missing pieces. The piece that has got lost under the sofa somehow. The one that longs to fit back in place but can never seem to be found.'

Julien reached forward and squeezed his father's forearm. 'The jigsaw will never be whole again until that piece is recovered.'

'Even if the puzzle might be better off without the old, rough, sharp-cornered edge?'

'Never,' Julien replied.

Gerard sighed. 'I do not know where to start.'

'Well,' Julien began. 'I think we both need to start talking... to each other... to Vivienne... maybe to a professional.'

'I do not like that idea,' Gerard answered.

'Neither do I,' Julien agreed. 'But the idea I like less is that we are never again how we used to be.'

Gerard nodded.

'So, do you think you will be able to help me? With the exhibition?' He swallowed. The whole night, if it was going to be as perfect as he wanted it, hinged on what Gerard was about to say. He could do it without him but it wouldn't be right.

'I think,' Gerard began, 'that perhaps I should have remembered I had a son as well as a daughter.'

Julien swallowed the poignancy as his father clasped hold of his hand, giving it a strong, reassuring squeeze.

'I will help,' he answered, nodding.

'Thank you, Dad,' Julien replied. 'Thank you.'

Gerard cleared his throat of emotion, wiping a hand at his eyes before straightening his stance. 'So, Ava...'

'Who isn't Monique.'

'Yes. That has been established.' Gerard waited a beat. 'So?'

'Well, if life was not so short I would possibly sit back and contemplate my feelings for her.'

'But life *is* short,' Gerard reminded.

'Indeed,' Julien agreed. 'So, that being the case, I need to tell you now that I am in love with her.'

FIFTY-FIVE

Julien Fitoussi's apartment

'Ah!' Ava exclaimed, her eyes looking up from the screen of her phone as they walked along the snow-speckled streets. It was after midnight and she was following Julien's lead, no idea which arrondissement they were now in.

'What is it?' he asked.

'My mum,' Ava said. 'She reckons she's had over eighty people respond to her emails about your exhibition saying they would like to come or send a representative from their company.'

'This is a joke, no?'

'No,' Ava said, excitedly. 'It's not a joke. We need to design some proper fliers tomorrow but Mum hashed together a mailshot with your website link and reviews of your last exhibition and said it's for the Red Cross and told them Lauren's story and... they're coming... eighty of them already.'

'I... this cannot be real.' He stopped walking and blew out a breath.

'It is real and it's going to get bigger and better and... we really need to think about another venue,' Ava offered.

'I just... I don't know what to say.'

'How about you start by telling me where we are?' Ava asked, looking around the unfamiliar street, not another soul around.

He took her hands in his, gently caressing the skin and smiling at her. 'We are at my apartment.'

Her eyes left him then and went to the building to her right. It was tall, wide and built in a lovely cream stonework with Juliette balconies at each front window. Black iron gates covered the door to the entrance.

'Coffee?' he asked her. 'Or I can call you a taxi to...'

She turned back to him. 'No. Coffee sounds good.'

Behind the iron gates and the door into the building there had been a communal entrance hall with gunmetal post boxes for all the apartments. Julien had told her he was number 34, which, to Ava, made it feel like there were far too many people living in one block. But this was Paris and Paris was known for making the most out of every available space.

Glass doors, a wooden surround in green and then a choice of an old-fashioned looking elevator or the stone stairs upwards. She had insisted on taking the stairs and when she'd arrived, puffing and panting and wishing she'd stepped inside the circa 1930s lift relic, Julien had no sympathy.

Now she was standing inside his apartment, marvelling at the minimalism and the view across the rooftops and an unobscured picture of the Seine.

'Ava?' Julien asked. 'You would like some coffee?'

She shook her head. 'No. I would like to open these windows.' She stepped forward towards the folding doors and began to fiddle with the key in the lock.

'It is minus temperature outside,' he reminded her, coming close.

'I know but I want to see the river and the moon and I think if I lean out far enough I might be able to see the Sacré-Coeur.'

'I am afraid you will not,' Julien told her.

'How do you know?' she asked.

'Because I have tried this many times.'

She pressed her face against the glass, taking in the perfect solitude of Paris at this time of night. Here they were in the very midst of the city but somehow completely separate from it. There was something she had been thinking about since Julien had kissed her on the boat. Something that had been rolling through her mind all over dinner and when she had got the text message from her mother. There was something she needed to do. For him and for her. Something she needed to let go of once and for all.

She turned away from the window and faced him. This gorgeous, intricate man who had literally picked her up from her lowest point and taught her how to be strong again. She sighed as pure passion ripped through her.

'Julien,' she whispered. 'I want you to take my photo.'

She held his eyes, wanting to see just what that sentence was going to do to him. He did not disappoint. She watched his pupils dilate, confusion etched across his face, those full lips set to neutral. She watched the rise and fall of his chest and longed to just reach out and steady the motion. But she wanted the timing to be perfect.

'Ava...' he began.

'Julien, I really want you to photograph me,' she repeated. 'And I want you to photograph *all* of me...' She paused. 'Apart from my clothes.'

Her breath was caught up in her chest as he looked back at her, his eyes unmoving. The air between them was charged and she was scared to move or to not move, afraid of breaking the intensity. Her cheeks were heating up and suddenly she felt both so alive and excited and yet so desperately vulnerable and terrified.

'Ava, I know how you feel about being photographed,' he spoke.

'By other people... not by you,' she answered. 'Because I know that you're not going to tell me my shoulders are uneven or my legs are too short or I should hold my breath and smile less.'

He shook his head.

'Please,' she begged, reaching for his hands and holding them in hers. 'Please, Julien, I want you to take my photo. I want you to make me look as beautiful and as liberated as the woman of Rodin's sculpture.' She wet her lips. 'No one has ever photographed me *that way* before.'

'It is not usually the way' – he paused – 'for a photographer to take pictures... *like that*... of someone he cares about.'

'Well,' Ava began, 'it would be unusual of me to want a photographer I *don't* care about to take pictures like that.'

He was still holding her hands, his eyes so expressive, projecting a million different things she didn't even know how to start to translate. And then he let her go.

'You really want this?' he checked again.

'I really do,' Ava answered.

'OK,' he agreed.

'OK?'

'But it is a professional shoot,' he stated.

'Of course,' she replied a little uneasy about the truth of her reply.

'Let me move some of the furniture.'

Her heart skipped a beat.

FIFTY-SIX

Julien hadn't been able to watch as Ava undressed. But he knew she was doing it because he heard almost every button unfasten, the sliding down of her trousers, the taking off of the boots, even the unclasping of her bra. He just carried on setting up his equipment, choosing the right lens, ensuring the batteries were charged, anything to keep his mind on the job and not on the fact the woman he loved was about to be completely naked in front of him.

Ava let out a breath that put every part of him on high alert. He dropped a memory card and quickly bent down to retrieve it, eyes focussing on the floorboards.

'I'm ready,' Ava said, her voice thick.

He swallowed. She might be ready but he wasn't sure he was. He had to dig deep, be professional. She wanted photos of herself she had never had before. It was important to her. And it had never been more important to him.

He turned then, his vision drawn to his sofa, the corduroy cushions plumped at one end and Ava's beautiful form resting there, completely nude.

He cleared his throat, trying to beat down the rising heat that was taking a stranglehold on him. This was both exquisite and unbearable. 'OK.'

'Is this OK?' Ava asked, propping her head up with one hand, legs together but elongated along the length of the settee.

Julien moved behind the camera, hoping that looking at her through the viewfinder would dampen his arousal a little. He took a breath, allowing the camera to focus. No, he was definitely still very much aroused.

'Just hold very still,' he directed softly. 'Nothing more.'

'I am holding very still, Monsieur Fitoussi,' she answered. 'And your cushions are a little itchy. I can guess you probably haven't had many naked girls on this sofa before.'

'Really?' he asked. 'Perhaps your skin is just more sensitive.' He pressed the button on the camera.

'And I asked for that,' Ava responded, smiling.

He looked up from behind the camera, a serious expression on his face. 'Being honest, you are the first naked woman I have had on my sofa, Madonna,' he assured.

'I knew,' Ava whispered.

He went back behind the camera, changing the focus a little. She was undeniably beautiful and what made it even more endearing was the fact she didn't even truly know that. She had been a model, someone who was held up as *the look* to aspire to, yet he saw her self-consciousness and susceptibility. Despite being brave enough to strip herself bare in front of him, he could see it hadn't been without a lot of consideration. And there was that tattoo, a circle and two triangles making a ten-pointed star on her right side, just above her hip bone.

'I can't hear the camera, Monsieur Fitoussi,' she called. 'This isn't the Moulin Rouge you know.'

He smiled and took another shot, then watched her adjust her stance, her eyes coming back from looking out the window and resting on him. He snapped another shot.

'Did you design your tattoo?' he asked her.

'Does it show?'

'I like it.'

'It isn't just a drawing. Each point means something,' Ava spoke. 'Courage, power, destiny...'

'Beauty?' he asked.

'Yes,' she replied. 'Although I never quite believed in that one. Is this position OK?' she asked.

He could barely breathe as it was. Professionalism had never felt so hard to maintain. 'For the moment,' he answered. 'Ava...'

'Yes,' she replied.

'I would like you to pretend you are wearing the most expensive perfume you can imagine.'

She sighed. 'My mum spent most of her money on perfume... and jewellery... and a boob job.'

'No,' he stated. 'This is... something different. Not expensive... more like rare. This perfume has never been worn before, it is delicate... it is yours alone... an individual fragrance just for you.'

He watched her, instinctively knowing what was going to happen to her body. He had used this technique once before when his subject was particularly unrelaxed. That time he had suggested they were wearing a dress made of the finest silk.

The tension seeped from Ava's body and every part of her was now alert and completely connected in the moment. She thought she was modelling the fragrance as if she could show that to the world, but really she was baring her inner beauty to the lens of his camera.

'That's good,' he spoke, knowing his tone was giving away how much this was affecting him.

'Maybe,' Ava said, moving her body a little. 'Maybe, it would work even better if you came a little closer.'

He watched her through the viewfinder and closed his eyes. What did he do? His body was singing with arousal and his heart had been lost long ago. But getting close in the way she was referring meant letting her truly in. Baring himself, literally. And the very last time he had done that everything had fallen apart.

* * *

Ava was starting to shiver. Not from the cold, because the room was warm, but from all the delicious feelings that were rolling over her. She had never felt so alive or as comfortable in her own skin as she did right now. But taking off her clothes had been so much more than giving permission for Julien to photograph her, it had been wanting to let him know how she felt about him. It was crazy that it had happened so fast but the truth was, it *had* happened. The unthinkable, the very thing she had sworn to avoid in Paris – a man in her life.

'Julien,' she called.

His face was behind his camera so she couldn't see his eyes.

'Julien, look at me,' she begged.

He raised his head then, his eyes going to her and she quaked.

'Ava,' he began. 'There is something you should know.'

She shook her head. 'No, there isn't.'

'Ava...'

'I know, Julien,' she replied. 'I know what you're afraid of and you don't need to be.'

'You do not understand,' he insisted.

'I do,' she said, putting her feet to the floor and standing up. 'Vivienne told me tonight. When you were in the kitchen.' She took steps to close the gap between them.

She watched him drop his head. 'What did she tell you?' he whispered.

Ava reached him and palmed his face, forcing him to meet her gaze. 'She told me you were injured the night Lauren died. She told me she thinks you never took time to get over that because you were too focussed on mourning your sister.'

He looked down at her. 'Did she tell you I have a ten-inch scar on my left side that will never heal?'

'Only ten inches, Monsieur Fitoussi? I was really hoping for fifteen.'

'Look at you,' he breathed. 'Perfect in every way.'

'No,' she stated. 'I'm not. But for the first time in forever I am happy with that.' She moved her hands to the buttons of his shirt. 'And a lot of that is down to you.'

She unfastened the first button and moved on to the second, watching him watching her.

'Before you came here, Ava, I was not good to be around.'

'I don't believe it.'

'It is true,' he whispered. 'I was sad and I was angry and sometimes I wished to not even be here any more.'

'And now?' she asked, as she made light work of the other buttons.

'Now,' he began. 'Life is beginning to feel different.'

She pulled the shirt from his body and smoothed her hands over his shoulders. 'This week, you've shown me so much, Julien... the real, uncovered Paris. With the best food, the best wine, the best museums, the best tower, the most annoying pigeons...'

'Camembert,' he whispered.

'Falafels,' she breathed, tracing a fingertip across his chest.

His mouth met hers then and she rocked back on her bare feet as the force of his desire came at her. His hands holding her close, he moved her back, towards the sofa, his mouth hot with hers.

She fell against the cushions, coming apart from him and he stood in front of her, his eyes appraising. Her breath tight in her chest, her eyes roved down his torso, acknowledging his taut physique, until they reached the scar on his side. She swallowed, following the mark to its end, just above the waistband of his jeans.

Reaching out gingerly, she made contact with the mark, her fingers softly tracing the dips and lines in the flesh.

'Madonna,' he whispered, his hand finding hers as if to shield her from it.

'No,' Ava said, dismissing his touch.

'Please,' he said.

'There's nothing wrong with it, Julien,' she insisted firmly. 'All it says to me is that you're here. That you are in one piece.' She brought her lips to the tender skin and kissed him gently. 'That you survived.'

She felt him flinch a little then relax as she drew away, her hands at his hips, tugging him towards her.

She was looking up at him, her cheeks a little flushed, her eyes wide, her hands at the button of his fly. He had never wanted to connect with anyone as much as he wanted to connect with her... on every level.

He unfastened the buttons of his jeans, dragging the denim away, all the while keeping his gaze on her. He wanted to see her regard him, all of him, and to know that she was not going to look away.

His hands dealt with his underwear too until there was nothing left between them but a little floor space in front of the couch.

'If you touch me now, Julien, I feel like I might—' She couldn't seem to finish the sentence and the sentiment hit him low.

'I *know* I might,' he whispered, dropping his body a little lower, inching a little nearer. 'But I also know that if I do not, then I will regret it for the rest of my life.'

He moved over her, his torso perfectly aligned with hers, keeping them apart by just inches, eyes locked together. His composure was weakening as every second passed by, longing to touch, to taste, to lose himself in her completely. And then she moved, just a fraction, arching her back and ensuring her breasts touched his chest. In that instant everything else was forgotten.

Julien slipped his hands behind her, scooping her up in his arms and drawing her form close until nothing separated them.

'Julien,' she breathed.

'Ava, I want to honour you every single moment we are together.'

Tears started to leak from her eyes as she gazed back at him.

He spoke again. 'You have become the most special person in my life and I do not know what I have done to deserve this.' He dropped a kiss on her throat as her head momentarily tilted back.

She breathed hard, then looked back at him, kissing his mouth and pressing her body hard against his. Taking his hand she placed it between her legs.

'Ava,' he moaned.

'Madonna,' she corrected.

'Madonna,' he whispered.

'Make love to me, Monsieur Fitoussi.'

FIFTY-SEVEN

Ava nuzzled her head into the space between Julien's shoulder and neck, breathing in the scent of his slightly damp, dark hair. Every tiny particle of her was still exploding like a fireworks display. He had slowly skimmed every inch of her with his hands, his mouth, his tongue and made her feel things she never even knew existed. She blinked into the dark, holding onto him, the flashes of snow on the windowpane outside reminding her that there was a world going on away from this room but that right now there was nowhere she would rather be. She was happy to be cocooned here, possibly forever.

'Madonna?' he said, shifting slightly and drawing her tighter into him.

'I'm still here,' she answered.

'I know this.'

She turned then, a tricky manoeuvre on the edge of a sofa people should really only be sitting on, until she was facing him.

'I never want to get up,' she stated.

He smiled, brushing her hair with his hand. 'I think this will be difficult.'

'Why?' she asked.

'For many reasons.'

'Like?'

'Like how would we get falafel?'

'They must have a delivery service.'

'I would never take another photograph.'

Ava leaned back a little, stretching her arm as far as she could manage. 'I think,' she said, her voice under strain, 'if I just move a little bit more... I could reach your camera...' She dropped her arm and stilled. 'No. Can't reach it.'

He smiled at her, latently brushing her skin with his fingers. 'It is late,' he whispered.

'No,' she replied. 'It's early. A brand-new day. And in a few hours the sun is going to start coming up and cafés are going to start serving coffee and all those pastries stuffed with chocolate and Paris is going to come alive again and...'

'Then we should get some sleep,' Julien offered.

'I can't sleep,' Ava answered. 'I hate to tell you this, Monsieur Fitoussi, but what we just did... it was like drinking six espressos.'

'You have had six espressos at one time?' he queried.

'I had four once and spent the rest of the day feeling like Batman.'

'You know Batman personally, Madonna?'

She punched his arm. 'I meant the crazy take-on-the-world-with-funky-gadgets kind of vibe.'

'Batman,' he repeated, smiling.

'And you can be my Robin.'

'I do not think the tights would be my thing.'

He pressed his mouth against hers, delivering another soft, sensual kiss that warmed every part of her. Their lips still together, she drew herself closer to him, feeling him wrap his arms around her.

'We should get some sleep,' he said again.

'We should talk about the exhibition,' she countered.

'I have taken on too much, do you think? To try and do something like this before Christmas? Before my parents' wedding?'

'No! I think quite the opposite. And believe me, with my mum on the case, if anyone can plan an event within a tight deadline it's her.'

'I need more photographs,' he told her. 'I need to get in touch with the other families, ask for their help.'

'And I can help you,' she said, connecting their hands.

'Madonna,' he spoke. 'You are the most amazing person. I hope you know this.'

She nodded. 'I'm getting used to that idea but,' she said, circling her arms around his neck, 'I think I need a tiny little bit more convincing.'

'Really?' he asked, moving his face nearer to hers.

'Yes,' she said. 'And I'm not talking about your long-range lens.'

'No?' He kissed her.

'I'm talking extreme close-up.' She squealed as his fingers found a ticklish spot.

'How about 4D?' he inquired.

'Oh, Mr Fitoussi, ooh la la!'

FIFTY-EIGHT

Hotel Agincourt

Ava could hear her mother's voice the moment she stepped through the front doors of the hotel. She had left Julien at the brasserie after crepes and two espressos. He was going to try and contact the other relatives who had lost loved ones in the fire and endeavour to get their support for the exhibition. She had other things to organise, like the invitations and the guest list. She didn't have the first clue about event planning but it was all for Julien. Gorgeous, hot Julien, the mould of his fit body still ingrained on her fingertips.

'I got a text message that said eleven o' clock,' Rhoda said.

'Yes, me too,' Debs answered.

'She did not text me,' Didier responded.

'I don't think she has your number yet, sweetie,' Debs said. 'Oh, Gary's just texted me. He's at the airport, heading home.' She sighed. 'I hope he doesn't feel he has to tell me his exact location all the time. I don't want him to feel like I'm an electronic tag or anything.'

'I want to know why Ava isn't in her room,' Rhoda continued.

Ava watched Debs look at Didier and Didier look back at Debs and no one dared looked at Rhoda.

'I'm here!' Ava announced, striding closer. 'Sorry I'm a bit late.'

'Where have you been?' Rhoda asked. 'It's all very well sending messages asking us to be down here but—'

'I popped out... for croissants,' Ava stated.

Rhoda looked at her with suspicion. 'The breakfast here is superb... even for those with special dietary requirements.'

'I know but... when in France.' Ava shot a look at Debs.

'So, where are they?' Rhoda asked.

'Where are what?'

'The croissants,' Rhoda said, her eyes on Ava's empty hands.

'Ah!' Ava exclaimed. 'I must have left them in the boulangerie! Never mind, we'll order some with coffee, yes?' She smiled at the three of them and headed off towards the bar-cum-snug area where the roaring fire awaited.

'We really need some proper art work,' Rhoda stated. 'It's all very well me sending out emails but we need to follow them up with professional invitations, it's how things are done.'

Ava's brain was bursting. Despite telling Julien this was definitely something they could achieve in double-quick time, she was starting to realise just what was ahead of them – very closely ahead of them.

'I can do the artwork,' Ava said before she had thought about it.

'Don't be ridiculous, Ava, you need a professional,' Rhoda dismissed.

'Ava's great at drawing,' Debs commented.

'Not so good at bubble writing though,' she admitted with a smile.

'I can help with this too,' Didier piped up, cream from his coffee on his top lip.

'You don't draw,' Rhoda stated, looking at Ava.

'I do.' All she could think of was the caricature she had done of her mother only a few days ago. 'Cartoons mainly, but sometimes, I do something real.'

'Well, we won't want Mickey Mouse,' Rhoda told her. 'The people I work with have a very discerning taste.'

'How about Pluto,' Didier suggested. 'Or maybe a large profile of Wreck It Ralph.'

Rhoda screwed up her nose and opened her mouth.

'He's joking!' Debs assured. 'Totes joking, aren't you, Dids?'

Didier laughed. 'I apologise, Mrs Rhinestone.'

Ava froze as her mother's nickname hit the air.

'Devlin!' Debs jumped in quickly. 'Silly boy, it's Mrs Devlin.'

'But I thought—' Didier began.

'Anyway,' Ava said far too loudly. 'Didier and I will design the invitations then you will pass them out to all the contacts who have accepted and start to go through the "maybe" list. We need to get the invitation document to Julien's father too and... shit,' Ava said, slapping her hands to her forehead. 'This isn't going to work yet.'

'What? Why not?' Rhoda questioned. 'And don't swear like that, Ava. You're not on the terraces at White Hart Lane now.'

'Well, Julien's booked this venue but with all the people you've got coming already, hopefully the families Julien is speaking to, plus Gerard's contacts and the press and officials from the Red Cross, it's never going to be big enough.'

'Not having a venue is a pretty big thing,' Debs remarked.

'I know that,' Ava said. 'Didier, where in Paris can we accommodate up to say... five hundred people?'

'And remember it is very close to Christmas, so try and think a little outside the box and preferably somewhere that will give it for free because it's charity,' Debs added.

'Five hundred people,' Didier said. He blew out a breath and elongated his body in the chair, hands clasping his shorn head. 'I do not know.'

'You must know somewhere,' Rhoda scoffed. 'You live here.'

'Mum, please,' Ava said.

'Five hundred people... you are looking at a small concert hall,' Didier stated. 'Or perhaps a park.'

'A park!' Rhoda exclaimed. 'In winter?! The kinds of clients I have do not want to spend their evening wrapped up in coats. They will be wearing cocktail dresses and eveningwear.' She tapped into her iPad. 'We must make the event black tie.'

'A park,' Ava said, her mind almost careering at motorway speed. Could they really make that happen?

'What are you thinking?' Debs asked her.

Ava smiled. 'I'm thinking I know the perfect venue... but I think we're going to have to phone the council.' She looked to Didier. 'Is that a thing in Paris? The council? The people that run the city.'

'*Absolument*,' he answered, grinning. 'And I have a friend there.'

FIFTY-NINE

Jardin des Tuileries

'Don't look at me,' Julien stated. 'Look anywhere, Madonna, except at me.'

She laughed and ignored him, looking directly down the lens of his camera and pouting a little. She momentarily glanced to the left and took in the wintry scene of the garden. All around them people were walking through the park as the sun began to set, the glow from the streetlamps, together with the flashing Christmas displays on the neighbouring buildings providing an atmospheric scene.

'You did spend too long performing in front of the camera. You are ruined,' he announced, dropping his camera so it hung from his neck.

'That is extremely rude,' she announced, jumping down from the bench she had been sat on and stomping towards him.

He put his hands in the air. 'What? I am supposed to retreat? Be afraid of you just because you have *that* look on your face?'

She stopped mere inches away from him. 'What look?'

'The one where you try to make your beautiful eyes move from perfect circles to angry lines,' he began. 'Then your lips come down and you pretend to be mad.'

'I'm not pretending anything,' Ava stated. 'You insulted my modelling skills.'

'I did not.'

'Did so.'

'I was simply saying that photography this way is different to what you are accustomed to.'

'Maybe, but *this* was my idea.' She held aloft the piece of white card in her hands. 'And you have to admit it was genius.'

She watched him read the words again, and the same thing that had happened the first time happened again. He looked a mix of sad and joyful, his emotions written all over his face but none of them daring to spill. She watched a sigh leave him.

'I just hope it is enough,' he stated. 'To be special enough that people will want to buy the photographs.'

'Listen, my mother is charging people two hundred euro each to attend. If you are someone who has that sort of money you are going to be buying photographs. I mean it's going to look great on their social media profiles and a few thousand euros is a drop in the ocean for sheiks and professional footballers.'

'You are right,' he agreed. 'It is just I suppose I do not want to think that the photographs are to be bought to enhance somebody's public image. I always hope they are bought because they mean something to someone.'

'Oh, Monsieur Fitoussi, in this case you must make an exception. When we're talking about raising a lot of money for charity and getting everyone to remember Lauren, I don't think beggars can be choosers.' She pushed the placard towards him. 'You hold the sign up.'

'I am no model,' he insisted, holding onto his camera.

'I agree,' Ava said, making a grab for the camera. 'The bone structure is pleasing but you slouch a little sometimes.'

'Really, Madonna? I slouch?' he asked, moving the camera away from her.

'Yes, you do,' she responded, laughing.

'Well, you are not the perfect muse I first thought,' Julien told her. 'Why can you not be like the Mona Lisa, just look into the mid-distance, that enigmatic expression on your face?'

'For one because I'm not wearing something medieval and rather drab and two...' She pulled the camera towards her, forcing him to move with it. 'Because when you're taking my photograph I can't help but remember last night,' she breathed. 'And all I can think of is you and me, wearing nothing but a Mona Lisa smile.'

He moved his face a little closer to hers, dark eyes heavy just below the edge of his woollen hat. 'Is that so?'

She nodded. 'It's very distracting,' she continued. 'And, I'd go as far to say that it is you who has ruined me for modelling, Monsieur Fitoussi, not the other cameramen with their SLRs and MTFs.'

'*I* have ruined you,' he said as a statement.

'Yes,' she agreed, swallowing, as his gaze grew even more intense.

'What should I do about your accusation?' he inquired.

'Well...' she began, his lips only a fraction of an inch away from hers.

Before they could touch, Ava's phone erupted from the pocket of her jeans and she drew it out, checking the screen. *Debs*.

'Hello,' she greeted.

'*Bonsoir!*' came Didier's voice.

'Oh, wow, I wasn't expecting that,' Ava said in reply.

Julien furrowed his brow and tilted his head as if expecting an explanation.

'Surprise!' Didier continued.

'I get that it's you now,' Ava answered, backing a step away from Julien.

'I have good news,' Didier stated.

'You do,' Ava said, almost in a whisper as she bent her head away from Julien.

'We have a new venue!' the Frenchman informed.

Straightaway Ava's heart was singing and she closed her eyes, silently thanking Didier, his friend at the council or whatever Christmas miracle workers had fixed this.

'We have... I really don't know what to say,' Ava stated.

'You are forever in my debt?' Didier suggested.

'Let's not go too far,' Ava said. 'Or perhaps Debs can pay up for me.'

'We have already talked of this,' Didier answered.

She could tell he was grinning. 'Not a word then, like we said.'

'*Absolutement*,' Didier said. 'Three thousand per cent.'

Ava ended the call and slipped the phone back into her jeans before turning back to Julien. She smiled. 'Now, where were we?'

'Well,' he said. 'I was ruining you and you were pretending to be mad about it.'

'Oh yes,' Ava answered. 'So, for your punishment you must come to dinner with me tonight.'

He shook his head. 'I regret to tell you this, Madonna, but that is like saying to an alcoholic that he must bathe in red wine.'

'A restaurant of my choosing,' she added.

'O-K,' he said a little tentatively.

'And no camera,' she said.

She watched his fingers curl around the gadget like it was a comfort blanket he could not do without.

'Sounding a little trickier now?' she asked.

'*Non*,' he insisted. 'This can be done.'

She nodded. 'Good. Right. We had better get some more work done before we lose the atmospheric light completely,' Ava said, taking the placard from under his arm and heading towards one of the marble statues.

'Madonna,' Julien called. 'You are starting to talk like a photographer. Perhaps all is not lost!'

SIXTY

Hotel Agincourt

'I can't believe how much you and Didier have done in one day.'

Ava had just listened to Debs reeling off numerous jobs they had ticked off the list for Julien's exhibition. She had always known her best friend was something of a dynamo, but it seemed she had been working harder than the employees of Argos on a Christmas Eve.

'I phoned all the main newspapers and lifestyle magazines in the city and every single one of them agreed to advertise the event tomorrow or the next day depending on what space they have.' Debs stabbed at her notepad with a glittery pen Ava hadn't seen before. 'Those that didn't have publications out soon enough were going to put something on their website. Between me, Didier and your mum, we finalised the invitation using the design you did and got that doing the rounds too.'

'And we have the venue,' Ava breathed.

'We totes have the venue,' Debs said.

'I guess we need to think about marquees and drinks and nuts or something. Will people really give that stuff for free?' Ava inquired. 'I'm finding out my event-planning skills are seriously lacking.'

'I started on that but your mum seemed to think her guests would be expecting champagne so...'

'Ugh! Seriously! I mean I know she's done a lot and they are all rich list but if we can't get things for free then—'

'Ava,' Debs said. 'Don't worry.'

'How can I not? The event is only a few days away and it means so much to Julien... it means so much to *me* now.' Her stomach was skitting around like a kitten chasing after a ball of wool.

'So,' Debs began. 'On that note... you and Julien.'

'Can I counter that with *you and Didier* before I have to answer?'

'Absolutely, doubly not. We talked about that before, but with you... I think things have changed.'

Ava knew her reddening cheeks gave her away immediately.

'Ava, I haven't seen you like this about anyone before.'

It was true. What was the point in trying to deny it? She had never *felt* the way she felt about Julien with anyone before.

'I think,' she started, 'I think, even though it's been such a short time of getting to know each other.' She sighed. 'I think... no, I don't think... I know... I'm in love with him.'

'Goodness!' Debs said, slapping both her hands to her own cheeks. 'I totes didn't actually think you were going to say that.'

'You didn't?'

'No... I don't know... I just don't think I've ever known you be in love before.'

Ava nodded, turning her attention to her own reflection in the mirror, smoothing her hands over the midnight blue skater dress with a scalloped sequinned embellishment at the neckline giving her curves in all the right places. 'You're right. Because I never have been.'

'Oh, Ava, I'm caught between being completely, utterly thrilled for you and being totally two hundred per cent scared to death for you.'

'Because of what he's been through? Because of this exhibition being so intense?' Ava asked, turning back to her friend.

'No,' Debs said. 'Because he lives in France and you... don't.'

Ava shrugged. She had put that out of her mind since the moment she started falling for him. Nothing would ever work if you spent every minute analysing it. 'There's a tunnel now, we came over through it.'

'I know, but—'

'How do I look?' Ava asked, smiling at Debs.

'Beautiful.'

'Good,' Ava said. 'Because tonight is going to go one of two ways.' She sighed. 'He's either going to fully embrace it or go running up the boulevard.' She picked up her handbag. 'OK, I think I'm ready.'

Debs smiled. 'Oh, not quite.' She stepped towards the nightstand at the side of her bed and picked something off the top of it. She held the items out to Ava who instinctively opened her hand.

'Christmas baubles,' Debs said. 'Earrings, to match your dress.'

Ava looked at her palm to see (thankfully) small blue hanging earrings that did complement what she was wearing. She slipped them one by one into her ears. 'Thanks, Debs.'

SIXTY-ONE

Montmartre

Julien stood outside on the pavement just a few yards from the Sacré-Coeur, blowing hot air on his hands. He checked his watch again then looked up and down the cobbled street for any sign of Ava. Despite the chill in the air and the frost on tables outside where no one was foolish enough to sit tonight the atmosphere was warm – helped by the strings of Christmas lights wound around Juliette balconies or hanging from street lamps and awnings.

He had spoken to his father before leaving tonight. Gerard had confirmed he could make the time for the photo shoot with the other families who had lost relatives in the fire. There were two families who had declined to take part and Julien understood. It was only just over twelve months ago. It was still too hard for some, just like it had been for him until very recently. Gerard had also told him how scores of his clients would be attending, how he was paying for several people from his own company to come, and asking if he could donate anything else to ensure the night ran smoothly. It all somehow seemed to be coming together.

And then he noticed a taxi slowing down. It stopped just a few yards away and the door opened, Ava stepping out. His insides turned to mush as he looked at her, long boots on her legs, a blue dress that skirted her knees and those blond spikes as cute as ever to him. He drew in a breath, then stepped towards her.

* * *

'*Merci beaucoup*,' Ava said, paying the taxi driver and including a small tip for him managing to get her here only a few minutes late and without too much road rage.

She shut the cab door and took a step further onto the pavement, breathing in the air of this district – wine, cheese, a soupçon of ginger spice and maybe a touch of artists' oils. And then she saw Julien. His tall frame, that typically French wavy dark hair, his hands in the pockets of his coat, black jeans and brown leather shoes. He was nothing like the other men she had dated, in any way at all. Physically, emotionally, everything about him was different. Everything about him was perfect. Even the imperfect bits. She released a sigh of contentment and smiled at him.

'Monsieur Fitoussi,' she greeted.

'Madonna.'

'Am I a little late?' she asked, stepping up to him. 'Or are you a little early because you couldn't wait to see me?'

He smiled. 'I was early of course.'

'And that is the right answer,' she stated, slipping her arm through his.

'Where are we going?' Julien asked her.

'Not far,' she answered.

'Do I know it?' he inquired.

'I don't know,' she admitted. 'It's somewhere I saw when we were here together before.'

'And you did not show me at the time? Madonna!'

She smiled, resting her head against his shoulder and enjoying how it felt.

'So, the photos we took today...' he began.

'Yes?' She lifted her head up, turning to look at him.

'They are good,' he stated.

'Good?'

'More than good,' he said again, smiling. 'They are very good.'

She smiled. 'I knew they would be.'

'So much confidence,' Julien stated. 'For someone who came to Paris with very little.'

Ava smiled at him, raising one eyebrow. 'Ah, but this isn't about me, Monsieur Fitoussi. You are the star of this show. Everyone is going to be focussed on you.'

'Yes,' he agreed with a heavy sigh. 'And I really wish that they could just look at the photographs and I could hide in a corner.'

'Hey,' she said, stopping in her tracks and halting him too. 'Don't do that.'

'*Quoi?*' he asked.

'You have to think of this as just another exhibition,' Ava reminded him. 'Otherwise it gets... overwhelming.'

'This you tell me,' he stated, his breath visible in the air.

'You weren't like this before your first show were you?' she asked, holding his hands.

'Yes... much worse. I was sick.'

'Shit, really?'

'Yes, shit, really.'

'Well, you need to remember that you're the best there is,' Ava said matter-of-factly.

'Your opinion matters to me so much, Madonna, but it is a very competitive world and—'

'Wow, Julien, you really don't know the modelling industry, do you? Have you ever had someone poke you in the ear with a long range lens?'

She folded her arms across her chest and waited for a response.

'I cannot say I have.'

'Well, try having someone stick you in the ear with a bobby pin because they thought you were trying to do them out of an assignment.'

'I cannot imagine,' he admitted.

'It's for charity and there is no competition,' Ava reminded him. 'Last time it was just for collectors who loved what they had seen of your work. Now it's all about the Red Cross. There's no way it isn't going to be a success and you've got a whole mini-team of people behind you.'

'I know,' he said. 'And Lauren is the most important thing.'

'Then, Monsieur Fitoussi... get a grip,' she urged.

'A bobby pin?' he asked, a wry smile on his face.

'Sometimes I wonder if you pretend when things are lost in translation,' she said, looking up at him.

'Is that what you really think, Madonna?' he asked, matching her gaze.

The way he was looking at her made her insides tingle. 'Stop looking at me like that.'

'Like what?' he asked, edging a little closer to her.

'Like you want to... lick me all over,' she said, her thoughts spilling from her mouth.

She watched his expression as her sentence met his mind and before she could do anything else he had caught her mouth up in his and delivered another one of those hot, sexy kisses that had her pinned to the spot.

'Madonna,' he said when he had come up for air. 'You must stop saying these things in the middle of Paris.'

'Really?' she asked. 'I thought the French were well known for being liberal. I mean... Moulin Rouge near here and something about energetic bunnies.'

'*Au Lapin Agile?*' he queried.

'Like I said.'

'Yes, but mime artists are for the street, Ava, not licking people,' he said, slipping his arm around her shoulders. 'No matter how appealing it might have sounded to me.' He drew her in tight to him.

'We're here,' Ava said a few moments later. They had weaved slowly through the twisty, windy streets around the Montmartre district until the roads grew a little narrower and the tourists and resident population began to thin out. It was somewhere they had explored on their first visit here. Ava had admired the tiny doors and even smaller windows of the traditional town houses and he had enjoyed watching every bit of enthusiasm she had shown about a city he thought he already knew so well. Seeing things through someone else's eyes was always part of what he tried to do but with Ava it was even better. She was like a ball of unfettered energy, just waiting to soak life up.

'Are you listening to me, Monsieur Fitoussi?' she asked. 'I said we're here.'

He looked to the small bistro just in front of them. It was made from old, thick, grey, brick; garlands of gold lights around each window and at the edge of the scarlet red canopies. Two small fir trees sat either side of the door, twinkling the colours of the tricolour.

'Have you been here before?' Ava asked him.

He shook his head. '*Non.*'

'I thought it was the sweetest little place I'd ever seen,' Ava said, then smiled. 'And I saw someone eating the biggest Camembert with at least a pint of coffee.'

He laughed. 'I should have guessed.'

'So, shall we go in?' she asked. 'I've booked a table.'

He nodded, taking hold of her hand and stepping towards the door. 'This way, Madonna.'

The warmth from the inside hit him straightaway and it was a welcome relief from the harsh wind that had been whipped up around Paris that evening. A waiter was there to relieve them of their coats and his eyes went to Ava, the blue dress making her look even more radiant.

'This way, sir,' the waiter said, directing them to the left. He fell in step behind Ava, giving a cursory glance at other diners, enjoying food that smelled divine, heart-shaped candleholders and carafes of wine on the table. When he turned back and prepared to walk on Ava was moving into a seat even further away from the fire exit. Instantaneously his mouth dried and his palms started to feel a little damp.

'This is OK?' the waiter asked him. The young man looked completely confused as Julien found his feet were almost stuck to the floor.

'Yes,' Ava said to the waiter. 'This is OK. Can we... have a moment and... two beers and the wine list.'

The waiter nodded his approval and left, heading towards the bar.

He wanted to move. He wanted to just take a seat but it was going against every single instinct. His eyes flashed over to the back of the restaurant, looking for the fire door. Then he looked at Ava, not knowing how to resolve the situation, not wanting to appear weak.

'Julien,' she said, softly. 'I'm not moving to another table.'

He managed a nod. He had known she was going to say that. This moment she had made was all about the things he'd said before they'd made love together for the first time. Him wanting to grab life tightly, not let the past define him, and here he was failing at the very first obstacle.

'I know how you feel about it, but I want to sit in windows, Julien,' she said. 'And I want to sit in windows with you.'

Of course she did. Why wouldn't she? And before this had happened to him he had chosen to sit where he could watch the world go by too. He tried to batter the memories down. It had been an accident. A tragic accident. The chance of it happening again, of happening to him...

He looked over at Ava. She was breathtaking. The dress brought out the colour in her eyes, her bright hair like icicles, her fingers toying with the edge of the tablecloth. He wanted this new existence so much. He wanted to be the man he had started to be with her. The one he wanted to grow into and live with for the rest of his life. A courageous man, a better man. Ava's.

He took a step forward, concentrating on just getting to the seat opposite her and not really knowing what came after that. He gripped the back of the rustic wooden chair and lowered himself into it before realising his breathing was coming so short and fast it could almost be classed as hyperventilation. And then Ava's hands sought out his and she enveloped them in hers, interlocking their fingers together. He lifted his head, keeping his eyes on hers and let his focus drift back, away from 2015 and here in the moment, with the woman he loved, holding onto him. Very slowly his breathing re-established a pattern and, in his peripheral, he saw the waiter coming back with two bottles of beer. Ava squeezed his hand and he attempted to settle in the chair.

As soon as the waiter had taken the tops from the beer he reached for his, needing to get some moisture into his mouth. He took a swig and, with a shaking hand, replaced it on the table.

'You did it, Julien,' Ava whispered, smoothing his palm with her fingers.

He shook his head. 'This is not how things should be,' he stated, making sure the disappointment was obvious in his tone.

'It was never going to be easy,' Ava said. 'But it is all about making that first step towards a new start, isn't it? That's what you've been telling me since we met.'

'Look at me,' he said, frustrated. 'Scared of not sitting next to a fire door.'

'But you're doing it,' Ava encouraged. 'You're here, in the window... and look outside.'

He forced his head to the left and it was a moment before his vision caught up. In this tiny back street where the snow was starting to fall again, it was a perfect snow globe scene, a snapshot of quaint, quiet, nothing-to-fear Parisian life. He felt the tension dissipate. He could do this.

'There's something else,' Ava said, drawing his attention back to her. She smiled, squeezing his hands again. 'We have a new venue for the exhibition.'

'What?!' he exclaimed. 'But... how? Where?'

'It had to be bigger. We were never going to fit all my mother's contacts in the first one, and apparently your father is getting confirmations by the dozen already.'

He nodded. 'He told me.'

'So, we had to think outside the box a little,' Ava stated. 'And... basically all the concert halls were booked.'

'Ava, you need to tell me,' Julien said, his heart back to palpitating.

She smiled. 'It was my idea but I needed Didier and his connections at the council to make it happen.'

'Madonna, please,' he begged.

'We're having your exhibition at Place des Vosges,' she said. 'Your favourite place.'

He swallowed. 'This is not true.'

'It is true,' Ava insisted. 'I promise you, it's true.'

'But... how?' He could not believe this. He was already starting to think about the work involved – canopies, chairs, lights.

'Because it's for a great cause and everyone wants to help.'

'But, Ava, to have something like this... outside... in December.'

'I know, it's a little crazy, right? But don't worry, we're think-ing of everything. Debs, Didier, even my mother – who seems to be relishing the job – we have marquees and heaters and wine and things to eat that aren't just nuts… It's all coming together.'

He was staggered. To know that these people were all work-ing to make this event a success while he went around just trying to ensure he had photographs worthy of this night. And now she was telling him this event was going to take place in his very favourite square in the city.

'I do not know what to say,' Julien admitted. There didn't seem to be enough words to express how he was feeling.

'Say you're happy about it because I've been really nervous about telling you,' she admitted. 'Especially as I knew I was also going to try and make you sit away from the fire exit.' She swal-lowed, dropping her eyes to the table.

He smiled and tipped up her head with his index finger, until she was forced to look at him. 'Madonna, I don't want you to ever feel nervous to tell me anything. We should always trust that hearing the truth is better than anything else.'

'People have said something like that to me before but I've never thought they really meant it,' she stated.

'I mean it,' he promised her.

'OK,' she answered. 'Then, seeing as we're getting everything out in the open…' She paused, taking a sip of her beer.

He waited, wondering what she was going to say.

'My mother wants to meet you.'

She had blurted the sentence out and then closed her eyes up tight as if not seeing would protect her from something. He smiled, even though she couldn't see and waited patiently until one of her eyes unfurled slowly.

'I think I would like that,' Julien answered.

Ava's other eye opened. 'You did hear what I said, didn't you?'

'I did, Madonna.' He picked up his bottle of beer. 'And I might have been a little apprehensive about sitting in the window seat tonight but I am not afraid of meeting your mother.'

'O-K,' Ava said. 'That beer is dulling your senses.'

'I have had two mouthfuls,' he said.

'She will ask you lots of difficult questions. Sometimes it's best to say the first thing that comes into your head rather than think too hard about it. Like... if she asks, "What do you think of Kate Middleton's hair", you say...'

'It is not quite as beautiful as Ava's,' he responded, smiling at her.

She laughed. 'No! Don't say that! She hates my hair! That will score you no points at all.'

'I have to score points?'

He watched her change her expression and shake her head. 'No... you're right,' she said. 'You don't have to score points. Because it doesn't really matter what she says or thinks... My mind is made up.'

'It is?'

'Yes, Monsieur Fitoussi,' she breathed. 'I think I want to keep you.'

SIXTY-TWO

Hotel Agincourt

Ava bit her nails and started to pace. Debs had the hairdryer on full blast and it was starting to get on her already fragile nerves. She walked to the balcony doors and looked out over the street. The sky was a cloudless blue thanks to the harsh frost of the previous night. The snow on the pavement looked like it was hard and crispy just the same as that squeezy chocolate topping you put on ice cream that you had to batter with a spoon when it set. She watched workers with their coffees to go, an old man wearing a long coat and a beret on his head, thin cigarette hanging from his mouth, navigating the traffic on the road on an old-fashioned bicycle. Why was she so freaking nervous? This was just breakfast with Julien... at the hotel... *with her mother.*

The hairdryer stopped and Ava turned, the next fingernail between her lips.

'You are going to choke on one of those in a minute,' Debs said, hands in her hair, fluffing it like it was a precious lapdog.

'Good,' Ava said. 'Then I wouldn't have to have breakfast.' She checked her watch again.

'I don't know what you're so nervous about,' Debs said.

'Really?!' Ava exclaimed. 'You *really* don't know!'

'Ava, this isn't about a job in the... Cayman Islands... or a fashion shoot for ASOS. This is breakfast.'

'With my mother and the man I—' She stopped herself. 'With Julien.'

'And he is adorable,' Debs reminded, her hair now resembling a Wookie. 'Totes adorable.'

There was no denying her friend was right. The issue was, apart from Leo, who had introduced *himself* one time when he had picked Ava up from home, she had never introduced anyone to her mother before. It felt colossal.

'He isn't going to drop croissants and jam down his front. He isn't going to talk with his mouth full. He will probably pull out your mother's chair and charm her with his photography talk,' Debs suggested, throwing her head forward until she was face down to the carpet then quickly flicking it back up again. Now it was Afro Wookie.

'You're right,' Ava said, feeling almost excited. 'I don't know why I didn't think of it before. That's what they have in common. The camera! Him behind it. Her in front of it. They can talk about lighting and posing and... all the things I never talk about with him.'

'There we go,' Debs said, adding some dangling fairies to her earlobes.

'And we can't stay for more than an hour because we have the families' photoshoot and then we need to look at the photos and sort the photos and decide what goes on canvas, on block, in frames... Apparently people are into buying "moving pictures" right now.'

'Isn't that called video?' Debs asked.

Ava shrugged. 'No idea. Julien's the expert.'

Debs looked at her watch. 'You'd better go. The lift was particularly slow last night.'

Ava checked her watch. 'Shit, five minutes!'

'Good luck!' Debs called.

Ava bounded for the door.

Rhoda was already ensconced at a table for four in one corner of the dining room when Ava entered. There was no food in front of her mother, just one small white china cup and a side plate desperate to be treated to something. She was thankful Julien wasn't there. She wouldn't have wanted to leave him alone with her.

'Morning!' Ava greeted brightly, slipping into the chair opposite her mum and shaking out the napkin folded into a star shape before placing it over her lap. 'I'm going to have crepes and bacon.'

She waited for Rhoda to make comment – something about fatty acids.

'I've ordered some coffee,' Rhoda said. 'It should be here soon.'

'Bacon?' Ava asked, feeling she almost needed the criticism.

'I thought I might try the scrambled eggs,' Rhoda responded.

'Not the fruit salad?' Ava asked.

'Not today,' Rhoda stated. 'Are you all right?'

'Yes... just... really need some coffee.'

Ava saw Rhoda look at her watch – gold from Dubai, studded with emeralds. 'He'll be here,' Ava assured. 'He lives a little way from here and in the morning the Metro is really busy.'

'I was looking to see how long ago I ordered the coffee,' Rhoda responded. 'Are you sure everything is all right, Ava? You seem a little on edge.'

'I'm fine,' Ava insisted, toying with the napkin on her lap.

'So, Julien Fitoussi is someone you have been spending a lot of time with in Paris,' Rhoda said. 'Not just "an acquaintance", which you passed him off as when asking for my help with the exhibition.'

Ava swallowed then nodded.

'And how did you meet?'

'Well...' She took a breath. 'Sorry, can I stop you? I just want to know are we starting the cross examination now? Just to be clear, because I sort of had the idea that that would go down over food when Julien was actually here.'

'I'm not cross examining you, Ava, I'm trying to settle myself with this situation.' Rhoda cleared her throat. 'I didn't mean *situation*, I meant this...' She leaned a little across the table. 'Ava, you have never willingly introduced me to a boyfriend before.'

'*Willingly* is pushing it right now,' Ava said with a half-laugh.

'Is *boyfriend* the term we should be using?' Rhoda asked. 'I'm only asking because it's only been just over a week since Leo.'

'I know,' Ava said as a waitress brought them coffee and she almost snatched it from the woman's hand. 'But when you meet him properly... hopefully soon... you will see he isn't like Leo at all.'

'I liked Leo,' Rhoda reminded.

'I know you did but, even discounting the whole cheating on me thing, he wasn't the right person for me.'

'And this Julien is?' Rhoda asked.

'Yes, this Julien is.'

'One other thing,' Rhoda said.

'Just one?'

'Why didn't I know you could draw?'

Ava opened her mouth to respond.

'*Bonjour.*'

She turned her head quickly, almost upending her cup with her elbow, and saw that Julien was at their table. She stood up and got caught between embracing him and shaking his hand in an awkward move that involved a lot of shuffling.

'Hi, Julien, wow, gosh, you're here!' Ava said. 'This is my mother, Rhoda Devlin. Mum, this is—'

'Good morning, Ms Devlin, it is a pleasure to meet you,' Julien greeted, offering his hand across the table to Rhoda.

'Good morning, Monsieur Fitoussi,' Rhoda greeted, indicating the third chair at the table. 'Please sit down before Ava knocks all the crockery over. We were about to have eggs, crepes and bacon.'

Julien could feel Ava's tension as she poked her breakfast around her plate, not making any noises of enjoyment or saying very much at all. She had drunk half a cup of coffee and sipped on some water, barely any of the food touching her lips.

'So, have you always been a photographer?' Rhoda asked. 'I have looked at your work on your website and it is very good.'

'Thank you,' Julien answered. 'And the answer to your question is yes and no. I used to work with my father in the financial sector but I found it is not where my passion lies.'

'It's a steady income though, isn't it? Money at the end of the month rather than... maybe no money at all?' Rhoda countered.

'But is it not a little the same for modelling?' he asked. 'Some weeks an assignment, others not?'

'There's a great deal more to modelling than actually modelling, Mr Fitoussi.'

'Please, call me, Julien.'

'I run a very successful agency. We deal with rising stars in the whole of the entertainment industry as well as models.'

'Ava has told me,' Julien stated. 'She is very proud to have a mother with such an entrepreneurial spirit.'

He watched Rhoda's eyes fall to Ava who had the good grace to smile.

'Did you really say that?' Rhoda asked her daughter.

'I may not quite have said the word "entrepreneurial" exactly.'

Rhoda carried on. 'I had hoped Ava would take over one day.'

'Ah,' Julien said. 'You are like my father. He too thinks that I can be like him and step into his shoes when it is time for him to retire.'

'But you're not going to do that,' Rhoda said. 'You're going to carry on taking photographs.'

'Yes, Ms Devlin, that is right. And maybe one day, when I have children, I will try to remember that trying to shape their paths is only something they are going to go out of their way to rebel against when they are older.' He smiled.

'Julien didn't mean you, Mum,' Ava said quickly. 'I mean, not that *I* thought he was talking about you or anything. He's just very sure of his own path and... we're not having children yet... or at all... at the moment... or soon.' She stopped talking and hid her mouth in her coffee cup.

'I do admire people who know what they want in life,' Rhoda said, sipping at her coffee. 'My issue is that Ava has never had a clear direction of her own.'

'No?' Julien asked. He broke a piece of croissant off the crescent-moon-shaped pastry and popped it into his mouth.

'No. And that's why I thought modelling would be the right path for her.'

'You decide this when?' Julien asked. 'She tells me her first modelling job was when she was just four years old.'

'Well,' Rhoda began. 'That particular job was just something that fell into our laps really.'

'I apologise,' Julien said. 'I did not mean to sound rude. It is just, I believe everybody's passion comes at different times. For you, Ms Devlin, modelling was what you wanted to do and you knew this with all your heart, yes?'

'Well, yes,' Rhoda answered.

'For me, although I fooled around with a camera, it was not until I was in a job that I did not like that I realised what it was I wanted to do. And sometimes it is hard, sometimes, when the money is not coming in so steadily, I have to take photographs that do not make my soul sing.' He smiled. 'But, I always know now what I should be doing.'

'Apparently Ava draws,' Rhoda stated. 'I didn't know that she drew.'

'I drew the tattoo, Mum,' Ava reminded. 'The tattoo you didn't like.'

Rhoda swallowed. 'Well... that was a long time ago and... it wasn't that the tattoo wasn't good it was that it was on you.'

She cleared her throat. 'Julien, would you care for some more coffee?'

'Thank you, Ms Devlin.'

'Oh, please, call me Rhoda.'

'Rhoda,' he said, nodding.

'Now, let's talk some more about this exhibition,' Rhoda said, smiling. 'I have to admit, I do love a challenge and I think it's shaping up to be an incredible event for a marvellous cause.'

'And Ava and I, we want to thank you so much for all the work you are putting into this. We could not be doing it without you,' he said.

'Well, it isn't how I thought I would be spending the run-up to Christmas but—'

'Thank you, Mum,' Ava piped up. 'For everything.'

Julien watched a look pass between mother and daughter and very slowly he sat back in his seat.

SIXTY-THREE

Julien Fitoussi's apartment

Ava watched Julien as he slept. It was the day of the exhibition and they had spent the previous days and nights working until late making sure everything was set up to be perfect for this one night. Each day had presented a different challenge, but Ava was almost confident that all the bases were covered. So many tickets had been bought already and they were set to raise a vast amount for the Red Cross before even one photograph had been purchased.

Already showered and dressed, her hat and coat on, she sat softly down next to him and trailed her fingers through his hair. She wanted this event to be a success more than she'd ever wanted anything to go well in her life before.

'Madonna,' he whispered, his tone coated with tiredness.

'Go back to sleep,' she urged.

'What time is it?' He started to sit up.

'It's early. Not before my first coffee early but before the department stores open early. And you didn't get to bed until two,' Ava reminded.

'And you did not let me sleep until three,' he said, leaning forward and kissing her.

'You needed to de-stress,' she said, smiling.

'Where are you going?' he asked. 'You are dressed already.'

'I'm going to the Place des Vosges to meet Debs, Didier, my mother and a team of people she seems to have under her employ to set up for tonight.'

'Vivienne is making arrangements for the wedding but she said she could meet you there at two.'

'Great,' Ava replied. 'Please tell her to bring pastis. I will definitely need it by then.' She smiled. 'Sorry, my mother being strangely human lately is freaking me out.'

Julien smiled, taking her hand in his. 'She likes me.'

'And I have no idea why. You've practically shot her down every time you've opened your mouth.'

'In a very genteel way,' he reminded. 'You would like me to change my opinions to match hers?'

'No, of course not.'

'Then?'

'I think she likes you more than she likes me.'

'I see this as a positive for now.'

'I have to go,' Ava said, standing up. 'You know what you have to do?'

'Hide? Run away?' Julien asked.

'Don't you dare! I may be able to sell luxury apartments but I don't know the first thing about photographs.'

'Ava, you were a model,' he reminded. 'And now you are dating a photographer. You know everything there is to know about photographs.'

'I'm *focussing* on the word *dating*.'

'Very amusing,' he answered.

'Seriously, Monsieur Fitoussi, it's a big day,' Ava said. 'For everybody.'

He nodded. 'Yes.'

'You're going to see your dad. You're going to phone the caterers and make sure they got the lactose intolerant email so the Countess of Whatever doesn't die before she's bought a piece of art and you're going to—'

'Spend the rest of the day wishing I was here, in bed with you, and tonight was over.'

'Wishing the day away, Monsieur Fitoussi?' she asked, one eyebrow arching skywards. 'We don't wish the day away. We embrace every second. Every new sunrise brings the possibility of possibilities.'

'Madonna, I do hope that was sincere.'

'Au naturellement,' she answered.

He caught her hand again. 'I will see my father. I will phone the caterers and I will promise that the day after tomorrow I will take you to the best wedding party you have ever been to,' he stated.

'You want me to go to the wedding with you?'

'But of course.'

'I wish you'd have told me this earlier. I've only got one smart dress and I'm wearing that tonight.'

'You can wear it to the wedding also, no?'

'Are you joking? Wear the same thing in the same week, when my mother's in town? She would kill me! The gods of fashion would send Gok Wan and a plague of stylists!'

'Madonna,' he said, squeezing her hand. 'Do not worry about the dress today.'

'No, you're right. I'm too busy worrying about countesses with allergies and "moving pictures" and projectors and the fact Didier has mentioned the school of mime... Did you know they had a school of mime here?'

Julien laughed. 'I find it worrying that you might think they do not.'

'I can't even speak about it right now,' Ava exclaimed.

'You do not need to,' Julien replied. 'It is mime.'

She grabbed one of his pillows and hit him over the head with it. 'That is not funny.'

Julien put his hands up in the air and made a pretence of walking them up an imaginary wall.

'I hope you realise how completely unsexy that is,' she stated, trying to keep her expression on frustrated.

'Really?' he asked, walking his hands through the air towards her.

'And you're not funny,' she added, his fingers working up and down the air in front of her face.

'No?' he asked. 'Not funny or a little sexy?' He stood up then, the duvet falling from his body and his naked form settling a few inches away from her. Ava swallowed, immediately wanting to press herself against that gorgeous body and lose herself in him again.

'I need to go,' she said, her voice wavering a little at the strain of keeping her composure and not touching him.

'Go, Madonna?' he asked. 'Or come?'

'You can't say that!' Ava exclaimed. 'It's like... talking about licking on the streets of Paris.'

He raised both his eyebrows then as if waiting for her response.

'Oh!' she exclaimed. 'Being on time is overrated anyway.' She threw down her handbag, wrenched off her hat and pushed him back down onto the bed.

SIXTY-FOUR

Place Des Vosges

Ava eyed the sky above the Parisian park. Clouds were forming and the blue sky of earlier in the day looked set to turn into a very dirty shade of cream. The possibility of snow they were ready for, the chance of rain – cold, wet, freezing winter rain – they were not.

'What if it rains?' Ava asked, directing the question towards Didier and Debs who were both poking at an iPad and laptop.

'It will not rain,' Didier answered. 'Pierre! Where are the red carpets?'

Ava looked to the male Didier was addressing who looked no older than sixteen.

'They are on their way, Didier. There is traffic,' Pierre responded.

'There is always traffic in Paris. Why do people not realise this?'

The boy went to make off towards one of the two large marquees covering the west side of the square.

'Pierre!' Didier called again.

The boy stopped and turned back. 'Yes, Didier.'

'I want to know as soon as the photographs start to arrive.'

'Yes, Didier.'

'Who is that?' Ava asked Debs, nudging her arm.

'Pierre?' Debs said, eyes still on her screen.

'Yes!'

'My cousin,' Didier answered. 'He is a very clever boy. We can rely on him. I have Anais and David also working. At the moment they are arranging the programmes for the evening into the shapes of a dove... for peace.'

Ava shook her head. The whole tranquil setting Julien had shown her was at the moment one big circus of activity. She only hoped, when it was time to start inviting in guests, every-thing would calm down a little. She wanted it to be more sedate garden party than all-flashing Hollywood.

'Ava's right. The weather forecast says it might rain,' Debs an-nounced, eyes lifting from the laptop and looking at Ava in horror.

'It will not rain,' Didier insisted, almost appearing cross at the challenge to his previous statement.

'We're in trouble if it rains,' Ava said. 'The lighting and the projections on the buildings... it really isn't going to be the same if we have to have it undercover.'

'It's always a risk when you have an outdoor event but I'm totes confident that it won't put people off buying Julien's gor-geous photos.'

'It isn't just about the photos though, is it?' Ava sighed. It *was* about the photos and the charity, she knew that, but what she really wanted from this night was for it to be both a culmina-tion of everything she had shared with Julien and a chance for his father and Vivienne to move on towards their special day in two days' time. Perhaps it was asking too much expecting it to be all things. Maybe the predicted rain was a reminder that life wasn't perfect.

'You need another coffee,' Debs said, putting an arm around her shoulders.

'I need another coffee too, *s'il te plaît*,' Didier said, blowing air into a balloon.

'Ask Pierre!' Debs said, waving a hand and moving with Ava across one of the pathways.

* * *

'Better?' Debs asked once Ava had inhaled a mouthful of scalding, deep dark roast.

Ava nodded, taking a second sip and letting the caffeine kick in.

'Look at this place,' Debs said, satisfaction in her tone.

She had to admit, despite the chaotic moving to and fro of crates (hopefully containing Julien's work), chairs, tables, lights and cameras it was starting to look a little like a winter wonderland. The frost on the trees hadn't thawed despite the winter sun and small boxes were being tied to the branches – red, white and blue like the French flag along with glass lanterns to contain candles, newly donated by a local shop who had seen the advertisement in one of the newspapers. People walking through the park stopped to look, taking fliers from one of Didier's relatives or someone her mother had hired, that contained the website and telephone number for them to donate to the cause.

'I had no idea when I came here that I would be in the middle of all of this,' Ava said, finding the moment almost overwhelming.

'You thought you would be spending a few days running around Paris dressed as a croissant for some crazy scheme of mine,' Debs said, linking her arm through her friend's.

'Instead we spent half the time chasing after a Frenchwoman with a pair of binoculars. Seriously, how did this happen?' Ava asked with half a laugh.

'Well, I have to say, if we are really going to unravel everything, I think it all started when I suggested we took a chance and had dinner with two intriguing Frenchmen.'

'So you're taking the credit for this, are you?'

'Not for this,' Debs said. 'But maybe an incy wincy bit for you meeting Julien.'

Ava smiled. She had to give her friend that one. 'OK,' she replied. 'Fair enough.'

'And also don't forget it was my need for some romance in my writing that got you a dinner on the Seine and I think that might have been when the real magic started to happen. Am I right?'

Ava blushed. 'Sooo, about *that* article... all good with Nigel?'

'I have a salary "package",' Debs announced. 'I can't remember the last time I had one of those.'

'Wow! Free lunches? Gym membership?'

'Yes and a company that comes round and massages you at your desk,' Debs informed, shrugging as if her shoulders were stiff already.

'A desk!' Ava exclaimed. 'A desk! Not your dressing table at home.'

'I know!' Debs said. 'A proper grown-up again.'

Ava smiled. 'A proper grown-up with a proper wish list.'

'Boring aren't I?'

'No,' Ava said. 'Not boring, just very sure of what you want.'

'Still no advance on getting drunk and buying a dog?' Debs asked.

'I'm working on it.'

'Paris looks good on you, Ava,' Debs stated, observing her friend.

'Does it?' Ava asked.

'You're not the same spiky blonde I got on the Eurostar with.'

'Really? I'm not sure if that's a compliment.'

'It's meant as one.' Debs breathed in. 'I don't know, I see a change in you, that's all. Maybe it's the love in the air.'

Ava laughed. 'Or maybe it's the amount of red wine you've been drinking with Didier.'

'You know we're going home on Christmas Eve,' Debs reminded.

'I know but we have a late train, don't we? Julien asked me to go to the wedding with him,' Ava stated.

'You haven't told him you're going back to the UK yet, have you?'

'I mentioned it. A while ago. With my mouth full of cheese.' She sniffed. 'We've been sort of caught up with this event.'

'What happens then?'

'I don't know yet.'

'Well, what would you write on your wish list?' Debs asked.

'That I wish my crazy friend would live for the moment more? That they really should do strong coffee in bigger cups here? That I wish Prince was still alive.'

'Ava...'

'Ooh, look, there's a mime artist.'

SIXTY-FIVE

Julien had wanted to be early but thanks to the Parisian traffic he was stepping out of the car with his father and Vivienne only twenty minutes before the event was due to start. And in his pocket, his fingers curling around the paper, was the very best picture he had ever seen. He had found it earlier when he got out of the shower, propped up on his desk. It was a portrait. Of him. Sketched in blue biro with a message from the artist.

Monsieur Fitoussi, to the possibility of possibilities and believing in the impossible, Madonna xx.

'Oh my!' Vivienne exclaimed, her hands going to her mouth as she observed the scene before them.

This was now overwhelming. He had seen the bones of it earlier when he had supervised the setting up of his work but it had been transformed even more since then. The entire square looked like something out of a Disney film. White lights surrounded the black metal fence and hung from the trees, two large marquees were set up either side of what looked like hundreds of chairs – almost all of them filled with people – their gaze on a large screen at one end of the park that was currently lit up with a photo of his sister interchanging with the other people who had lost their lives in the fire, red, white and blue spotlights moving up and down in sequence.

'You have done all this in less than a week,' Gerard remarked, his voice thick with emotion.

'Not alone, Dad,' he answered. 'With a lot of help from a lot of friends, some people I do not even know but who wanted to help.' He paused. 'And Ava.'

He saw her then, running across the frosted grass towards him, skidding on the high boots as she attempted to stop. He put his hands out to catch her.

'Thank you, sorry, stupid shoes again but I didn't think Converse was right for the occasion.' She took a breath. '*Bonsoir*, Gerard and Vivienne, welcome to the Julien Fitoussi Fundraiser for the Red Cross. Would you like a catalogue?' She offered them out to Julien's parents.

'Thank you, Ava,' Vivienne stated. 'I am so sorry I was unable to get here this afternoon.'

'I completely understand. The wedding being... two days away. Gosh, you must be nervous... I don't mean nervous because you know what you're doing but...'

Vivienne smiled. 'You received my parcel though, yes?'

'Yes,' Ava said. 'We did. I'm really hoping we won't have to use them but, if we do, *c'est la vie,* as they say in France.' She laughed, then took a strong grip on Julien's arm. 'We really need you mingling.'

'There are hundreds of people here, Ava,' he remarked, his eyes roving the patrons in the park.

'I know. I did say you can count on my mother. We are practically out of canapés. Debs has gone begging to restaurants.'

'Julien,' Gerard said. 'You should go. We will find some seats.'

'Please, have some champagne, my mother's company donated it and I really hope none of it goes to waste,' Ava called.

'Your mother bought champagne,' Julien said, turning to her.

'I know. Don't say anything, but I really think that proves she likes you more than me.'

He shook his head, still astounded by the number of people who were here. 'Look at this place, Ava.'

'I know,' she said, breathing deeply.

There were wine waiters handing out sparkling drinks and nibbles, guests snuggling under blankets, others standing beneath large patio-style heaters in just formal wear, excited chatter filled the air... and nerves invaded his stomach.

'Come and look at your pictures,' Ava encouraged, slipping her arm through his. 'Debs and my mother have been tasked with selling them until I can get back there.'

'I do not know what to say,' Julien spoke. 'Or how to thank you. Not just for this tonight...' He breathed out. 'For my picture.'

He watched her blush a little.

'You liked it?'

'It is amazing, Madonna. You need to believe that.' He gently touched her hair. 'Thank you.'

Ava looked up at him, smiling. 'Oh, Monsieur Fitoussi, I can think of lots of ways you can thank me thoroughly later.'

'Julien Fitoussi is... an artist. No, I would go further than that and say... a photographic genius. His photos are going to be like gold dust after tonight's exhibition. If I were you I would snap up a couple of these tonight while the prices are so low... and remember it is all for charity.' Debs smiled at the guest who had stopped by Julien's photo of the Saint-Jacques Tower.

'Debs, how's it going?' Ava asked, smiling at the guest who was moving through the twisted board some of Julien's photos were mounted on to replicate the shape of the Seine.

'It might help if the photographer was here. I'm running out of things to say,' Debs admitted, snatching a glass of champagne from a passing waiter.

'He's here, he's just talking to a Red Cross representative and one of the other families... Where's my mother?' Ava asked.

'She's with the Prince of Somewhere and there was a countess at one point.'

'The countess didn't eat any of the Brie, did she?'

'I have no idea. I didn't realise I had to keep an eye on people's eating habits as well as their chequebooks.'

'Sorry. Listen, why don't you take a break? Find Didier and take your seats. I've got this and Julien will be here any minute before the show on stage starts.'

'Are you sure?' Debs asked, inhaling more champagne.

'Yes, go,' Ava urged.

'Gone!' Debs said, heading for the marquee door.

Ava gazed around the room at the people observing the pictures and then something she hadn't seen before caught her eye. Slightly larger than any of the other photos, on canvas, in the centre of the display on the back wall was another photo of her. It was one she hadn't seen earlier when she had been making sure everything was in place.

She weaved around the guests, muttering *excusez-moi*'s until she was stood directly in front of the photo. She knew then when it had been taken. The clouds had blocked out the sun and Julien had gone to get coffee. She had been waiting for him, sitting on a bench, the buckets of bright red flowers at her feet, eyes focussed on two little boys who had been chasing each other with sticks as pretend guns.

She had thought nothing of it at the time but here, looking at the dark, moody sky behind her image, the boys shouting and poking each other, the red flowers at her feet, it held a simple message... She put her hand to her chest, just soaking in the haunting image.

'Madonna,' Julien addressed her.

The sound of his voice brought her back into the moment and she turned to face him. 'I... didn't see this one.'

'It is frightening, *non*?'

'I'm not sure anyone is going to want it hanging on their wall,' she admitted.

'No,' Julien said. 'I agree. Your mother tells me the photographs of war veterans and love locks are selling the very best.' He smiled.

'So...'

'This photo is not for sale,' he stated. 'See, no price.' He touched the edge of the canvas before drawing in a breath. 'But when I saw how it had turned out I needed it to be here tonight. To remind me of what is important... the beauty of Paris... you... innocence in a changing world.' He sighed. 'Tonight isn't just about Lauren and the fire; it's about everyone that has been lost in this country this year. And what and who it affects the most. The future. Our future. The future of our children.'

There were tears in her eyes as he finished and the next thing she knew the people in the marquee were clapping their hands together in a heart-felt applause. Ava stepped back, turning to the guests and stretching out a hand. 'Ladies and gentleman, the extremely talented, Monsieur Julien Fitoussi.' She began to clap loud and hard and everyone else joined in again.

SIXTY-SIX

Julien was suffering from the same sweaty-palm scenario that had afflicted him when Ava had suggested he sat in a window seat of the restaurant near the Sacré-Coeur. On stage the lady from the Croix-Rouge was telling the audience about the charity's progress all around the world and the good work the donations received tonight was going to do.

Any moment now it would be his turn under the spotlight, gazing out into the darkness, the only light out there provided by the loops of bulbs hanging from the trees and in the windows of the buildings surrounding the Place des Vosges.

He balled his hands together in an attempt to stop the sweat and looked out into the dark.

'He looks like he might be sick,' Didier announced. 'Does he look to you like he might be sick?'

'Ava?' Debs asked.

'He isn't going to be sick.'

'He has done this before,' Didier remarked. 'At his last exhibition.'

'I know,' Ava said. 'He told me.'

'He is swaying,' Didier stated. 'Does he look to you as if he is swaying?'

'Stop it,' Ava begged.

'I don't know if I can watch,' Debs admitted, hands in her hair.

'Shh,' Ava said. 'We are all going to watch, because Julien standing up there talking about Lauren is a lot easier to bear than the night she died. I don't care if he's sick all over the Countess of Whatever as long as the night is a success and he feels a little peace again.' She shivered and put a fingernail in her mouth, biting down.

'She's right,' Debs said, placing her arm around Ava's shoulders and pulling her close.

'*D'accord*,' Didier said, his arm going around Ava too.

'...I give to you, Monsieur Julien Fitoussi.'

The noise from the crowd caught him unawares and the spotlight swinging to capture him left him temporarily blinded. He had to do this. He had to move. Just one foot in front of the other. Just focussing on the fact he was still here and he owed it to his sister to be brave right now. Sheer grit carried him to the lectern and he offered the audience a smile, waiting for the applause to cease.

'Good evening, everybody. I would first like to say thank you to all of you from the very bottom of my heart for coming here tonight. It is cold in Paris in December, no?'

There were some titters of amusement from the guests.

'I know you have all paid for the pleasure of sitting on freezing cold chairs looking at my photographs and I only hope that the champagne and food has cheered you a little.'

He cleared his throat. 'Tonight, I want to talk to you about my sister, Lauren.' He glanced to the screen behind him and another photo of Lauren appeared – a selfie with him, taken at a birthday party for one of their friends.

'Lauren Fitoussi. A sister. A daughter. A friend. But never to be a sister-in-law, an auntie or... a wife.' He took a deep breath. 'Those milestones we all take for granted will be ours. Time is endless. We can take our time. We can live our life... at a steady pace, with no worries... because we will all live until we are at least eighty.' He looked out into the crowd, not seeing anything but black. 'But that is only true if you are fortunate. You have looked after your health, you have not drunk too much red wine or eaten too much Camembert, maybe you have exercised... But does living to less than eighty years make you unfortunate? Does this mean that Lauren was not lucky? No,' he stated. 'Lauren...' He looked up at her photograph. 'She lived a life that was good, a life that was true. She drank too much red wine and she ate too much Camembert and she loved to laugh and to dance until her feet were so sore she had to walk home barefoot.' He smiled as he remembered. 'I do not think that if Lauren was asked what she would do that was different in her short life that she would make any changes... only to do more of the same.' He leant on the lectern with both hands, steadying his body as well as his nerves. 'And that is what tonight is all about. Our lives. Our choices.' He sighed. 'Tonight is about helping those in need, remembering my sister and the loved ones of so many who died in the fire on Rue Auzenne. Ordinary people. Just like you, just like me.'

The photo on the screen changed to a group shot of the relatives of all the victims of the fire, all holding placards with the name of their loved one and a photo of them doing something that made them happy, smiles, laughter, the best memories. There in the centre were Vivienne and Gerard, arm in arm, one holding a photo of Lauren, the other with the sign bearing the slogan #ForeverWithUs.

He leaned in a little closer to the microphone, before letting the next words escape in a broken whisper.

'Lauren Fitoussi, forever with us.'

The crowd were on their feet in an instant, clapping hard and Ava joined them, tears in her eyes, Julien's words battering at her heart. And as the audience applauded the heavens suddenly opened and rain began to flash down onto the square.

'Shit! Not now!' Ava exclaimed, leaping up from her chair.

'What do we do?' Debs asked. 'We don't want people to leave until they've been totes fleeced. In a charity sense obviously.'

'The boxes,' Ava said. 'The boxes Vivienne sent over. Where are they?' She flapped her arms up and down as the rain began to fall a little harder.

'Relax,' Didier said, sitting back in his chair. 'I have this under control.' He folded his arms behind his head and looked a little smug.

'Didier, you were in charge of those boxes,' Debs reminded him.

'I know,' he answered coolly. 'I delegated. Ah, *regarde*.'

Ava followed Didier's line of vision and watched as Pierre, Anaïs, David and a troupe of Didier's other relatives appeared carrying the red, white and blue Fitoussi Finance umbrellas and began a human chain, passing them along the rows for the guests to put up and keep dry under.

'You are wonderful,' Debs said, flinging her arms around the Frenchman. 'Utterly totes wonderful.'

'I know,' Didier answered. 'And now it is time for the mime.'

'What?' Ava asked. 'Mime? I don't remember signing off on mime.'

'Artistic friends of mine will mime acts based on scenes from Julien's photographs while the guests buy them all up,' Didier explained.

'Please, Didier, promise me there are no clowns.'

SIXTY-SEVEN

Julien shook hands with someone who had just paid double the quoted price for his photograph of the artists at Montmartre. It was going well. There were only now a handful of photographs without sold stickers on them. He was, however, exhausted.

'Julien.'

He turned at his father's voice and greeted Gerard with a smile. 'Dad.'

Expecting his father to speak, he was taken aback when Gerard's arms clasped around him and drew him into a heavy embrace. He closed his eyes, holding onto his dad and relishing the closeness that had been missing from their relationship for so long.

Gerard drew away and plucked the handkerchief from his top pocket, dabbing at his eyes quickly. 'You were wonderful up there tonight.'

'I do not know about that. I am not one for the spotlight.'

'You should be proud, Julien. I am proud.'

'You are?'

'I should have been prouder sooner,' Gerard admitted. 'It will be stubbornness that kills me, not red wine.'

'You are going to live to over eighty, Dad,' he assured.

'If this wedding planning does not kill me first.'

'Where is Vivienne?' Julien asked.

'Talking to someone about last-minute chocolates... What we need these chocolates for I have no idea. The wedding is the day after tomorrow.'

'I know,' Julien answered. 'It is going to be a wonderful day.'

'And... you know... I never really meant it about you not being my best man,' Gerard stated.

'I know,' Julien said again.

'There is no one else I need more by my side,' Gerard insisted.

'It will be an honour.'

He watched his father's gaze move across the marquee. 'Will you be bringing Ava... to the wedding?' Gerard asked.

'Yes,' Julien said.

'Good,' Gerard answered. 'Because we would very much like to invite her for Christmas Day too.'

Julien swallowed. Gerard's invitation brought home the matter that he knew Ava was going home for Christmas but he had no idea when she was leaving.

'I don't know if this will be possible. She will probably be returning to England and—'

'Julien, what are you thinking? You have just delivered a speech on that stage telling people to fight for want they want in life, that they only have one chance... You are going to let her go back to England?'

'It is not a case of "letting" her. She is her own person. She makes her own choices and that is the way it should be.'

'You say you love her,' Gerard said.

'More than I have ever loved anything,' he answered.

'Invite her to Christmas dinner, Julien.'

'See the way Monsieur Fitoussi has captured the light so perfectly here?' Rhoda leant forward and brushed her hand through the air near the section of the photograph she was describing.

'It's a shame there are no rabbits,' the countess answered, sipping from her champagne glass.

'Rabbits?' Ava said, almost spitting out her drink.

'I think,' Rhoda began, shooting Ava a look. 'If you tip your head slightly to the right and look past the bushes at the foreground there is just the edge of... yes, there, look, one... no, two rabbits.'

Ava watched as the countess slowly shifted her head forty-five degrees to the right, eyes zooming in on the photograph. It was a job to hold in her laughter.

'I see them!' the countess announced. 'Darling little grey ones! I'll take it. How much is it?'

'Twenty-thousand euro,' Rhoda stated. 'But all for charity. Thank you, Countess.'

'I'll send my man along to finalise the details.'

Rhoda bowed and shifted away from the countess as the woman moved off.

'Oh, Mum, and I thought I was the saleswoman of the family. Rabbits!' Ava exclaimed, a laugh finally leaving her.

'Shh! We don't want her to hear you,' Rhoda said, putting a sold sticker on the photograph.

'I am perfectly fine with embellishments, but lying about the photographs...'

'She saw the rabbits. She said so,' Rhoda bit back.

Ava caught hold of her mother's hand and squeezed it tight. 'Thank you, Mum, for everything you've done for me since you got to Paris.'

'It's a lot colder here than Goa would have been—'

'Mum!'

'I was about to say but I'm glad I came here,' Rhoda stated.

'Are you?' Ava asked.

'Yes,' Rhoda said, squeezing Ava's hand. 'Because being here has let me see exactly the sort of woman you've become and... that person is so much more than I ever was at your age.'

'Oh, Mum,' Ava said, swallowing a knot of emotion.

Rhoda flapped her hand in front of her face. 'We do not cry in public, Ava,' Rhoda reminded. 'Not even the best mascara copes well with tears.'

'Or rain,' Ava sobbed. Her gaze went outside the marquee where the rain had turned back into snow. Guests were still sitting out on the seats, snug under blankets and cocooned beneath Gerard's corporate umbrellas.

'What happens now, Ava?' Rhoda asked, adjusting her sequinned jacket a little.

'Could I have that a little more narrowed down?'

'It will be Christmas in a few days and...'

'I'm coming home,' Ava said. 'Of course I'm coming home.' She swallowed. Saying the words twice was supposed to help.

'And after that?'

She blew out a breath. 'You know how single-minded and organised I am, Mum, I've got a plan.'

'You have?'

'Don't be silly! Of course I haven't.' Her eyes drifted to Julien, embracing his step-mother. 'But I have a couple more days yet.' And she only hoped that, just as it seemed to have so far, Paris was somehow going to come up with all the answers.

Finally with a cold beer in his hands, Julien watched Ava saying goodbye to guests as if her job in life had always been event organising. It was well past midnight and most of the attendees had left for their hotels, private planes, nightclubs or bars and they had somehow raised roughly in the region of five hundred thousand euro.

Ava turned, hands in her hair, the strain finally starting to show, and he moved towards her, grabbing a chair in his free hand.

'Madonna,' he greeted. 'Sit down before you fall to the ground.'

'Monsieur Fitoussi... you still remember who I am,' she stated. 'I thought someone who was being referred to as... and I quote "a photography sensation of our time" would be far too busy rubbing shoulders with artistic types than offering exhausted ex-models a chair.'

'You are delirious. You need a drink,' he jested, offering her his beer.

'Nectar,' Ava said, taking a swig. 'So much better than champagne.'

Julien quickly fetched another seat and put it down next to her, sitting himself. Ava passed the bottle back to him.

'Ava, tonight was better than I ever could have imagined.'

She smiled, leaning her head on his shoulder, eyes half-closed. 'It was, wasn't it?'

'Thanks to you and Debs and Didier and all those relatives I did not realise he owned.'

'And he owned them,' Ava stated. 'That's for sure.'

'Almost five hundred thousand euro, Ava.'

'Actually it's almost six hundred thousand,' she said, yawning.

'It is?'

'I sold the photo of me and the two boys playing with sticks.'

'You did?'

'I said I couldn't let it go for less than a hundred thousand and one of mother's maharajas bought it.'

'A hundred thousand euro.' He shook his head. 'So much money.'

'For a great cause.' She yawned again.

'You need to go to bed,' he told her.

'Mmm, I was hoping you would say that.'

'To sleep, Madonna,' he detailed.

'Oh, Monsieur Fitoussi, I want to live every minute as if it were my last,' she said. 'I want to bathe in the fountains at the

Louvre and feed pigeons at the Panthéon. I want to eat falafels stuffed with snail butter and drink a jug of coffee at the top of the Eiffel Tower. I want to...' She snuggled into his chest. 'I'm really tried.'

He kissed the top of her head and held her close. 'Tomorrow, Madonna. We have tomorrow.'

SIXTY-EIGHT

Julien Fitoussi's apartment – Christmas Eve

'This was such a mistake,' Ava said, jumping up and down and shaking the dress she was wearing. It was one her mother had lent her, surprisingly sedate, in a light coral colour, with a neckline that didn't make her look like she was advertising Victoria's Secret.

'The dress?' Julien asked, buttoning up his shirt.

'No, not the dress... Is there something wrong with the dress?'

'No, Madonna, you look incredible,' he assured her. 'You always look incredible.'

'Even when I'm dribbling all over your pillow?'

'Even then. What is the problem?'

'It's your mirror,' she announced. 'It should be hanging on the wall, so that when you stand in front of it you can see the whole of yourself, not bits in turn, only if you jump,' she stated, leaping in the air.

'I am a man,' Julien reminded. 'I look briefly to see that my hair is in place and that the zip of my trousers is fastened and—'

Ava turned to him, grinning. 'Perhaps I should double check the mirror is correct,' she suggested, hands grabbing the waistband of his grey suit trousers.

'Ava... we cannot... we are about to go to the wedding of my parents.'

She dropped her hands and pouted. 'And I'm leaving tonight.'

They had talked about it yesterday as they were clearing away everything at the Place des Vosges. Julien had invited her to spend Christmas Day with his family and she had had to tell him she was leaving with Debs and her mum on the last Eurostar out of the capital that day. She needed to go back to London. She needed to return to some sort of normality before she could start making choices about her future.

'I know,' he answered. 'And it is not fair for me to wish that you are not.'

'Did you say the word "wish", Monsieur Fitoussi?' she teased.

'Ava,' he began. 'You are a strong, independent woman, I would never dare to try to tell you what to do.'

'I know,' she answered, slipping her arms around his waist.

'But... I will miss you,' he said softly.

'I am only going to be a very small ocean away, practically a jog through a tunnel.'

'And we can FaceTime,' he offered.

'And I will come back,' Ava said. 'Think of it as á *bientôt* not *au revoir* or *fin*.'

She looked up at him, those dark eyes studying her and she waited until she knew he couldn't wait any longer and his full, delicious lips met her mouth. She closed her eyes and savoured every second until he broke away, dropping a kiss on the tip of her nose.

'After the wedding I want to show you something,' he told her.

'Negatives in the dark room?' she asked, raising an eyebrow.

'Something much more positive,' he assured.

'I can't wait,' she answered.

SIXTY-NINE

Saint-Laurent Church

Everything about the church was beautiful. The outside had been all grey stone, at its centre a large entrance arch that sat just below an ornate section resembling a bee's honeycomb. A tower came after, followed by the one tall spire, a small cross at its pinnacle. Inside, the ancient wooden pews were already filled with people. There were urns of purple lilies and winter berries either side of the aisle giving off an extraordinary fragrance and small white and lilac flowers tied together with a sprig of mistletoe sat on the end of each row.

'You will be OK?' Julien asked as Gerard left his side, continuing to the front of the church.

'Of course,' Ava answered. 'It's a wedding. I'm going to be singing and crying and quietly drinking the take-out coffee I slipped into my handbag.'

'Really, Madonna?' he said.

'No, not really. Go on,' she urged. 'Go and be the best man with your dad.' She slipped into the pew and waved him off.

Julien carried on down the aisle, smiling at people he knew and those he didn't just in case they were distant relatives he *should* know, before joining his father in front of the altar where the priest was waiting.

Gerard blew out a breath and slipped his hands into his pockets.

'You are OK?' Julien asked him.

'Do you have the rings?' Gerard checked.

'Of course,' Julien assured. He swallowed. He didn't have the rings. He had given them to Ava, to put in her handbag.

'Sorry!'

It was Ava's voice and when he turned around she was there, the small velvet pouch between her fingers.

'I have the rings,' she announced to Julien, Gerard and the priest. 'I went in for my takeaway coffee and... wow, there they were.'

'Thank you,' Julien said, taking the pouch from her and kissing her on the cheek.

'You're welcome,' she answered. 'Backing up now, good luck, Gerard.'

Julien smiled, watching Ava hurry back to her seat and almost knock the hat off the lady sat next to her.

'One day this will be you, Julien,' Gerard spoke, hands still in his pockets, rocking back and forth from ball to toe.

'Standing in a church ready for the love of my life to join me?' he asked.

'No,' Gerard answered. 'Standing in a church ready for the love of your life to join you and wondering why the hell you waited so long.'

As his father finished the sentence the organist began to play and both of them turned to look as Vivienne came through the door.

Resplendent in a floor-length, figure-skimming ivory gown she paused, a wide smile on her face, before confidently taking her first step down the aisle.

Ava pushed another slice of cake into her mouth and groaned as the fondant exploded.

'Oh... mmm... that's so good.'

Julien smiled at her and began to unfasten his waistcoat. Now the formalities of the wedding breakfast were over he could relax a little, except that in a few hours Ava would be leaving him and travelling back to the UK.

'Julien,' she said. 'I thought you enjoyed my food noises,' Ava said.

'I do,' he said. 'You know I do.' He reached out and brushed a chocolate crumb from her lips.

'Aren't you having cake?' she asked.

'I have had two pieces.'

'How many have I had?' Ava asked, looking at her now empty plate.

'I have lost count.'

'It's happening, isn't it?' she said. 'I'm having that model's fall-out where now every food is accessible I want to coat the entire square metreage of my insides with it.'

'You have done this since we met,' he reminded her.

'Cheeky!' she said, swiping his chest with her hand.

He caught her hand in his and brought it to his lips, then she stroked his cheek before pulling her chair a little closer, so her knees were touching his.

'We only have a few hours left,' she whispered. 'And all I've done is eat.'

He smiled. 'Have you finished eating now?'

She nodded. 'I have space left but I'm really hoping we can dance to Coldplay.' She took hold of his hand.

'OK, Madonna, one dance to Coldplay and then we will go.'

'Go?' It was Vivienne's voice and Julien looked up to see his step-mother standing next to them.

'Oh, Vivienne, you look so gorgeous,' Ava announced, jumping up. 'The dress is divine on you.'

'Thank you, Ava,' Vivienne answered, smiling as Ava hugged her close. 'It was a beautiful service, wasn't it? And so many friends here today sharing the moment with us.'

Julien stood and kissed his step-mother on both cheeks before taking her hands in his and smiling. 'You look so happy.'

'I am happy, Julien, happier than I can remember being for so long and...' He watched her gaze go to where his father was gesticulating wildly, laughing with friends from his business. 'I know there is a long road ahead but, with help, I know your father is going to be well again.'

Julien nodded. 'I know.'

'And that bodes well for the honeymoon,' Ava said, grinning.

Vivienne laughed. 'We are not having a honeymoon. We have been together too long to worry of these things.'

'Really?' Ava exclaimed. 'I don't think that's a very good start to a marriage. When I get married I want to eat—'

'Camembert?' Julien offered.

'No.'

'Snail butter?'

'No, stop it, I'm talking.'

'Coffee.'

'You don't eat coffee.'

'The strength you have this, I am certain it could be eaten with a spoon.'

Vivienne laughed. 'Oh, Ava, I am so sorry you cannot stay for Christmas Day. You can stay for the dancing at least?' Vivienne asked.

'Just one dance,' Ava said.

'Coldplay,' Julien added.

'Then I will make this happen,' Vivienne said, smiling. 'Drink some more champagne,' she urged. 'I want everyone to celebrate.' Picking up the skirt of her dress she made off across the function room floor.

Julien looked back to Ava and kissed her lips, looking into her eyes. '"An Adventure of a Lifetime?"' he asked.

'That would be perfect, Monsieur Fitoussi.'

SEVENTY

Eiffel Tower

Ava stopped walking and bent double, taking a breath and wishing she had Converse on her feet and not Deb's crippling boots that were definitely not made for traversing several hundred steps.

'You are OK?' Julien asked, putting a hand on her back as she inhaled the cold winter air mixed with soft snow.

'Oh yes, I'm great, almost tasting the whole wedding breakfast again but apart from that...' She straightened up. 'You could have warned me we were going to be power-walking up here or I might not have had more than one piece of cake.'

'Ava,' he stated. 'You would not have denied yourself cake.'

'No,' she replied. 'You're probably right.'

Julien walked to the barrier and put his hands on the cold steel and she watched him. Dressed in the beautifully fitting grey wedding suit, the camera strap visible at his neck, his dark hair moving a little in the breeze, she felt her insides curl with both joy and utter sadness. She was leaving Paris. Leaving him. Just when she was starting to feel like she belonged somewhere.

She stepped forward, taking her place next to him and looking out at the city below.

'It looks like a maze from up here,' Ava whispered. 'So huge and a bit confusing.'

'A maze is only something to be worked out, Ava,' Julien said. 'A bit like a puzzle.' He took a breath. 'When I look out over here now I see all the places we have been together.'

She sighed and tipped her head a little until it was resting on his shoulder. 'Are we going to be able to work out the puzzle of us?' she asked.

'I think we can do this. I see only straight lines,' Julien said. 'By air, by tunnel, by sea.'

'I wish we had longer,' she admitted.

'I wish for that too,' he said. 'But, I have brought you here because I have got you something.'

Ava took her head off his shoulder then and faced him, watching him dig his hand into his pocket.

'What is it?' she asked, slightly excited, a little bit apprehensive.

'Hold out your hand,' he urged.

'Is it another hat?' she asked.

'No, Madonna, it is not a hat.'

Instinctively Ava closed her eyes as she offered out her hand and then she felt something quite heavy fall into her palm. She opened her eyes and looked at the golden padlock nestled there. Engraved into it was the inscription *Java*.

'Java,' she whispered, looking up at him.

'I think perhaps we could be like those celebrity couples and combine our names,' he spoke. 'And it was not lost on me that it is a type of coffee. That just made it even more perfect.'

She didn't know what to say, her heart was racing like a Eurostar train, fighting to get back into a normal rhythm while her eyes told her emotion was going to spill out at any second.

'It's the best gift I've ever had,' she said, lips trembling. She blinked back the tears and looked to the metal fence bearing the locks they had fastened on a few days ago.

Julien took the lock from her hand and slipped the end first through her padlock and then through his, until the new lock was dangling in between them.

'This is you,' he said, picking up Ava's lock. 'Strong, fearless, Ava, finding out what path she wishes to take.' He picked up his lock. 'This is me, Julien Fitoussi, living free.' He picked up their lock. 'And this is us. Connected. Strong apart. But even stronger together.' He snapped the lock closed.

Tears were streaming down her face now and she shook her head. 'The very best thing I did was come to Paris,' she sobbed. 'And the next best thing I did was ripping up that wish list... because if I made one today it would be so, so different... and every single line would have your name written there.'

'Madonna,' he said, pulling her into his arms.

'Monsieur Fitoussi.' She clung to him, breathing in the musk of his cologne, letting the warmth of his body wrap her up and realising what true love was for the very first time.

SEVENTY-ONE

Gare Du Nord

'So, things that we've missed while we've been in Paris,' Debs said.

Ava, Rhoda and Debs were standing near the Eurostar area at the station, waiting. Around them people rushed to and fro, heading for trains out of the city, others arriving with their suitcases and parcels wrapped in Christmas paper. There was music provided by a string quartet and someone dressed as a cheery, furry robin giving out leaflets. Ava checked her watch again.

'Is this a little like I-Spy?' Rhoda asked Debs.

'I'll start if you like,' Debs offered. 'I've missed *EastEnders* obviously. That BBC World War I drama everyone has been raving about on Facebook and—'

'Anything that isn't on the television?' Rhoda asked. 'Perhaps your hair straighteners?'

'I don't have hair straighteners,' Debs replied.

'Hmm,' Rhoda said. 'Ava, it's getting very close to boarding. We are going to have to go down.'

'Not yet,' Ava answered. 'Julien said he would be here and he'll be here.' She drew her phone from the pocket of her jeans. 'I'll call him again.'

'What have you missed about the UK, Rhoda?' Debs asked. 'Slim Fast?'

'You realise that is full of hidden sugars,' Rhoda snapped back.

Ava turned away from her friend and mother and pressed her phone to her ear. It was ringing and ringing but there was no reply. It went to voicemail. It was pointless leaving a message. Where was he? After the Eiffel Tower they had walked the whole way back to the Hotel Agincourt, holding hands, breathing in the essence of Paris, trying to embed as many memories as possible until they could see each other again. Paris had been in love today. The day before Christmas and the Invalides had been filled with photo-worthy couples, all getting ready for a special day together. She ended the call and slipped the phone back into her pocket. She had wanted Julien to be the very last thing she saw when the train pulled out. His smile, the way his dark hair was never set in the same way twice, those full, gorgeous lips that had kissed her all over...

'Ava,' Debs said. 'I know you think your mother is being overcautious but we really ought to go down now.'

Ava looked at her watch again, willing the second hand back a bit. 'One more minute?'

'Ava, I do think you're being a little unfair expecting Julien to come here,' Rhoda stated. 'His father has just got married. He was the best man. He can't really just up and leave to say goodbye to you. Didn't you say goodbye earlier? At the hotel?'

Ava nodded. 'Yes, but—'

'Well then. There we are,' Rhoda said. 'You can call him from the train. You can call him when we get back to St Pancras and you can call him when we get home.'

Debs put an arm around Ava's shoulders. 'I told Didier not to come,' she said.

'You aren't going to see each other again?' Ava asked.

'Well, I wasn't sure he would want to so I told myself I didn't want to and then...'

'Then?' Ava asked.

'He's invited me to come and stay next month.'

Ava smiled. 'I *do* like him.'

'Me too,' Debs said. 'But he knows I take my career very seriously and, at this stage in the proceedings at *Diversity*, I can't be setting all my articles in France.'

'Not until the first desk massage anyway,' Ava said.

'It's been more than a minute and if we don't go now we will be marooned here for Christmas,' Rhoda announced so the whole of the concourse could hear.

'She says that like it's a bad thing,' Debs stated.

Ava looked at her watch again and put one hand on her case. 'We should go.'

'Are you sure?' Debs asked. 'We could wait a few more minutes.'

'No... we can't afford to miss the train and it isn't like I'm never going to see him again.' She sighed. 'It might be a couple of months until I have enough money but—'

'Ava, we need to go!' Rhoda called.

Debs hugged Ava to her. 'Listen, as soon as we've both done Christmas with the family come round to mine and we'll pickle our livers with Kopparberg and Ethel's wine.'

Ava smiled. 'It's a deal.'

'I can't wait to see everyone's faces when they open the presents I got at the Christmas market,' Debs said, wheeling both her cases up the platform.

'You don't have to pretend to me, Debs,' Ava said. 'I think we both know all those "gifts" were for you.'

'They totes weren't!'

'I got myself a nice little designer number from a delightful little boutique,' Rhoda commented.

'I bought this hat,' Ava said, indicating the beanie on her head.

'You come to the very capital of European fashion, Ava and you buy a hat you could have got in Portobello market?' Rhoda shook her head.

'I bought Julien one too,' she stated sadly.

'I have to admit, Didier does look hot in a hat,' Debs said.

'I do like a man in a hat,' Rhoda agreed. 'Particularly James Spader.'

'Ooh yes,' Debs agreed.

'This is us,' Rhoda said, stopping at the open door of the train.

'Are you sure?' Ava asked, her eyes looking down the platform.

'Yes, Ava, I'm sure. Come on, let's get on board and get out of the cold.'

She didn't want to get in out of the cold. She didn't even want to get in. She had taken a liking to the cold, always having to layer up and knowing that by the end of the day her bones were going to feel like they belonged to some ancient T-Rex with arthritis. The coffee here was better. The chocolate was better. Snail butter was going to be impossible to locate in the UK, even at one of those artisan shops that seemed to only sell seeds or things that were pickled.

Rhoda stepped up onto the train. 'Ava, come on. Get on the train.'

'I can't,' she answered.

'What?' Rhoda screeched.

'Ava,' Debs said, rubbing her shoulder.

'I have to wait and say goodbye first,' Ava answered. 'Then I'll get on the train.'

'Ava, he isn't coming. It's half an hour past the time he said he would be here and the train leaves in minutes, Ava, minutes!'

'He said he would be here,' Ava repeated. 'And I trust him. He wouldn't let me down.'

'Oh, Ava, you know what the traffic is like and maybe he had to do something at the wedding like your mum said,' Debs offered.

She wanted another goodbye. She wanted to hold him again, kiss him again, let his lips be the last thing she tasted before this train took her back under the water and home.

'Get on the train, Ava,' Rhoda said again, her hand reaching for Ava's arm.

'Listen, why don't I start hauling my cases up there and that will give you a few more minutes of waiting,' Debs suggested. 'Here, Mrs Devlin, can you manage to get hold of this one.'

'I do do callisthenics you know.'

Ava stood, looking at the buzz of activity around the concourse at the end of the platform, travellers rushing like ants running towards a picnic. This was going to be her last memory of her time in Paris, looking at other happy people, searching for someone who wasn't going to come. She turned back to see Debs' last case being dragged up the step and onto the train by her mother.

'You can text him from the train,' Debs suggested. 'Or call him again. I suspect the band at the wedding are getting loud now and he can't hear his phone.'

She was going to have to give in. She was going to have to be happy with their kisses at the Eiffel Tower next to their love locks and the final farewell at Agincourt. She drew in a breath as Debs stepped up onto the train.

'I've got some pastis in my bag,' Debs said. 'I was going to give it to Auntie Reenie for Christmas but maybe we should just drink it.'

Ava stepped up onto the train behind her. 'I think we should.' She took one last look at the arched windows over the station, a little light still left in the darkening sky then moved on into the train.

'Madonna!'

Ava bristled and looked over her shoulder at a man moving into the carriage behind her. Had she heard that?

'Madonna!'

She looked to Debs. 'Did you hear that?'

'Hear what?'

'Madonna! Wait!'

'It's Julien!' Ava said. 'He's here!' She bundled into the man behind her, moving one way then the next in a bid to get past him and out of the carriage. '*Excusez-moi*! Please! Get out of the way!' She forced herself through the gap, panting and desperate to get off of the train. She ran out of the door, almost slipping down the steps until her feet finally met the concrete of the platform.

And there was Julien, sprinting from the end of the concourse towards her, coat flapping in the breeze. She ran too and within what felt like the longest seconds of her life they met, colliding in an embrace that knocked the air from her lungs. She held him tight, kissing him over and over.

'I thought you weren't coming. I thought I would have to leave Paris without you being the very last thing I saw.'

'I said I would come. I said I would be here,' he breathed, kissing her back. 'I am so sorry I am late.'

'Was it the traffic? I hate the traffic here,' she said, kissing him again.

'No,' Julien said. 'I had to go back to my apartment.'

She kissed him once more then looked at him, questioning his response.

'I had to go back to my apartment for this.'

She watched as out of his pocket he drew his passport. Her heart jumped and twisted like a pole-vaulter.

'I do not know if you want this but I am taking a chance and I have nothing...' he said, 'I have nothing but my passport, a ticket for this train and my camera. I had no time to get anything else.' He breathed. 'I suppose what I am asking is... Can I spend Christmas with you, Ava?'

She threw herself at him, holding him close and whispering in his ear. 'Oh, Monsieur Fitoussi, yes. And,' she smiled, 'just so there is nothing lost in translation. *Oui, Monsieur Fitoussi. Je suis Java.*'

THE END

EPILOGUE

Christmas Day – Rhoda Devlin's house

'Would you like some more, Julien?'

Ava tried to suppress her laughter, smothering her mouth with the glass of low-calorie, low-alcohol beer her mother had poured for her. She was heading off to the corner shop that opened all days and all hours as soon as Rhoda was sat comfortably commenting on the make-up and fashion faux pas of Christmas *Strictly*.

Poor Julien. The tofu roast Rhoda had served up was as dry as the Sahara but he was slowly munching through it probably wondering why he had left the cuisine capital of the world for this festive 'treat' in England.

'No,' Julien said a little too quickly. 'But thank you. It was delicious.'

Rhoda frowned. 'I don't know... I think there's something missing.'

Ava opened her mouth to suggest roast instead of boiled potatoes might have been it or perhaps half a plate of sage and onion stuffing, but Rhoda spoke again.

'The gravy! Oh my goodness! How could I have forgotten the gravy?!' She leapt out of her chair like she was late for her cue on the runway of London Fashion Week, heading into the kitchen.

'My throat,' Julien said, a hand going to his neck.

'I know!' Ava exclaimed. 'If the tofu doesn't get you good, then the spiky okra will finish the job. I really don't think vegetables should be furry.'

Julien smiled and slipped his hand over hers, squeezing her hand. 'Perhaps a little gravy will...'

Ava laughed. 'There won't actually *be* gravy.'

'*Non?*'

'My mother doesn't *do* gravy, even on Christmas Day,' Ava said. 'It will be a gravy substitute. My money is on some sort of watery balsamic sauce.'

Julien squeezed her hand again. 'Even with this sauce I am glad I am here for Christmas... with you.'

'Me too,' Ava replied, leaning towards him, longing to feel his lips on hers again. And there it was, his gorgeous, hot mouth on hers as Frank Sinatra warbled 'Ave Maria' from the Bluetooth speaker.

Christmas Day with Julien here was different. *She* felt different. Everything was warmer, cosier... lovelier than it had ever felt before and she was starting to get used to that feeling.

'Here we are!' Rhoda announced.

Ava broke away from Julien, looking up to see Rhoda re-entering the room, carrying a tray that was holding the biggest gravy boat she had ever seen.

'What's in the gravy boat, Mum?' Ava asked.

Rhoda looked at her as if she had just announced that Max Factor were going from liquid eyeliner to liquidation. 'What do you think is in the gravy boat, Ava?'

'Balsamic sauce?' she offered. 'It was quite tasty... well... kind of.'

'It's gravy,' Rhoda stated, putting the tray on the table, the red taper candles almost setting fire to her favourite Chanel jacket.

'Gravy?' Ava exclaimed, sitting forward in her seat. '*Real* gravy? The type Bisto make?'

'The type Waitrose sell in convenient pots if we need to be precise,' Rhoda stated.

'Not the vegetarian stuff?' Ava checked, regarding the thick brown liquid. She could smell it. That strong, comforting, beefy goodness that could probably coat your arteries in one sitting. This was a virtual alien on her mother's table. This was like Rhoda suggesting a Burger King for a quick bite instead of a multigrain bar.

'Are you a vegetarian now?' Rhoda asked her.

'No!' Ava scoffed.

'I thought not,' Rhoda said. 'In that case I can announce it is the full fat, non-vegetarian, beef version that contains more calories in one portion than I would normally eat in two days.' She let out a nervous breath before appearing to regroup. 'It's Christmas. We can "let go" a little bit at Christmas, can't we?'

Ava smiled so hard her cheeks hurt. It was such a small gesture but it meant everything. Her mum was getting it. She was really trying. Proper gravy this year. Who knew what was to come?

'Well, let's not just sit and look at it. One thing I do know about gravy is it goes cold quickly and... the tofu *was* a little dry,' Rhoda admitted. 'Gravy, Julien?'

'Please,' Julien accepted.

'Can I eat mine with a spoon?' Ava asked, picking up her spoon.

'You might want to go a little careful with your portion, Ava,' Rhoda suggested.

Ava swallowed. Controlling mother appeared to be back already.

'There's strawberry trifle for pudding,' Rhoda announced.

Ava dropped the silverware to the table and grabbed her mum, throwing her arms around her and hugging her close, the gravy boat almost toppling to the tablecloth. 'Thank you, Mum,' she breathed. 'Merry Christmas.'

'A photograph,' Julien said, picking up his camera from the spare seat next to him.

'Oh no!' Rhoda exclaimed. 'Not with me looking like this. I need to refresh my lipstick.'

'Just smile, Mum,' Ava encouraged, facing Julien and grinning with happiness. 'Smile and say "Java".'

She caught Julien's eye before he held the camera in position, and he shared a knowing look.

'Java,' he replied.

'What is this "Java" business?' Rhoda asked. 'Why are we talking about Indonesia? Are you two planning a holiday?'

Ava smiled even more then. 'Say cheese instead. After three. One... two... three... Camembert!'

Eiffel Tower – Spring

'I haven't been up here in years and I had completely forgotten how many steps there are. Goodness there are seriously totes too many,' Debs said, her hair in her face as she scrambled up the very last flight of stairs to the top of the tower.

'There are a trillion at the very least,' Didier remarked.

Ava smiled, squeezing Julien's hand in hers. 'Seeing them struggle so much is making me feel really fit.'

'You are now a master of this, even when you have eaten three or more pieces of cake.'

'I hope you have got this right, Didier. I don't know if I can walk up these stairs again at all over the next week,' Debs said.

'I have this right. My contact provides good information as always,' Didier assured. 'We now just have to wait.'

Ava moved towards the barrier and leant against it looking out at a very different Paris from the one she had left in December. Gone was the snow and the bare trees, now there were green lawns, trees in bud with blossom and the sun shining hot. Paris was now her home and next week she was starting an art course at college. She also had a part-time job at a coffee shop near her and Julien's apartment. It didn't pay as well as selling apartments but it was enough to keep her in strong coffee and

Camembert each week and who knew what was in her illustrating future?

Rhoda had been to stay and their relationship was in a good place right now. They had taken the train to the South of France and ridden horses on the beach. Quality, unpressured time was starting to plaster over the cracks. And, likewise, if her dad could drag himself away from his Tottenham season ticket she was hoping him and Myleene were going to visit her soon.

'So, where are we going to eat tonight?' Ava asked them.

Didier rolled his eyes. 'Always about the food, Ava? Seriously?'

'I thought we might go back to that very first little bistro we all ate in together,' Debs suggested.

'Ah, Brasserie Du Bec, the little bistro where these two did nothing but argue,' Didier stated.

'And we balanced wine corks on our noses,' Debs said, smiling at him.

'All you did was hiccup and talk about *coq*,' Ava reminded.

'And nothing has changed, *n'est ce pas?*' Didier said, nudging Debs.

'They are coming,' Julien stated, moving from the stairway to the fence where the others were gathered.

'Link arms,' Didier said, hooking himself up to Debs and Julien.

Ava slipped her arm through Julien's and put her other hand through the railing, fingers holding onto the fence, bracing herself.

'Step away!' Didier shouted to the two men in council overalls who had appeared from the stairs down.

'We are protesting!' Debs added.

'We will not be moved!' Ava yelled.

The men approached them, looking as much intrigued as angered.

'We are standing up for our rights as citizens of France...' Julien began.

'And holidaymakers having relations with citizens of France,' Debs added.

'And we are fighting for our right—'

'I really want to say "to party" right now,' Ava responded.

'This is serious, Madonna,' Julien reminded her. 'These men want to cut off our love locks.'

'I know but... we could just let them and then buy some more,' Ava suggested. 'No? Not the protest spirit?'

'If you do not leave us now and leave our love locks forever in this place then we will—' Didier started.

'Charge,' Debs said. She bared her teeth at the council workers.

'Charge? Like a bull?' Ava asked. 'We didn't mention charging.'

'We will stay here all day,' Didier continued. 'All day long. And tomorrow too. We will sleep here and we will dance.' He began to move his legs, his arms still linked to Julien and Debs, kicking a can-can like a Moulin Rouge performer.

'How are they not laughing?' Ava asked. 'I want to laugh.'

'All day long,' Didier called. 'Give up your cutting instruments! Go home! Let us hum the national anthem.'

The tallest council worker threw up his hands and together with his comrade they retreated to the steps that led down to the next level.

Didier raised his fist in the air. 'A victory for the people!'

Ava unlinked her arms and bent down, her fingers lifting the three locks intertwined together with their names.

'I am not sure we can come up here every time Didier's friend at the council warns us they are coming,' Julien told her.

'I know,' she answered, smiling at him. 'But, like I said, if something breaks, we can fix it.'

'And that is a life lesson, Madonna,' Julien said, putting his arms around her. 'A life lesson.'

'We need to get a love lock,' Debs said, taking Didier's arm.

'I was thinking more of handcuffs for the bedroom,' Didier answered.

Debs giggled. 'You are totes naughty.'

Ava reached up, the flat of her palm against Julien's cheek, eyes matching his. '*Je t'aime* Monsieur Fitoussi.'

He kissed her then, his fingers moving over the hair she had kept super short. '*Je t'aime*, Madonna.'

LETTER FROM MANDY

A HUGE THANK YOU for buying *One Christmas in Paris*!

Has Ava and Julien's story made you feel all Christmassy and warm inside? I really hope so! I also hope I've put you in a feel-good mood whatever the time of year you're reading this! It's always a good time to curl up with something cosy and Christmas!

With this story I really wanted to show the beauty of the city of Paris – I need to go back soon! – and create these characters I hope you can all relate to in some way. I know when I'm on a diet I feel like Ava craving everything that's full of sticky, sweet gorgeousness! Get me some Camembert and pain au chocolat!

If you enjoyed the book I would LOVE you to leave me a review – wherever you purchased it from! Reviews really do mean so much! Did you have a favourite character? Perhaps a favourite scene? Did it make you want to visit Paris... or find a sexy photographer? Let me and the rest of the world know! I love connecting with readers on Twitter, Facebook and Goodreads!

To keep right up to date with the latest news on my new releases, just sign up using the link below:

www.bookouture.com/mandy-baggot

Here's to more feel-good romantic comedies and hot heroes!

Mandy xx

🐦 @mandybaggot
❚ mandybaggotauthor
www.mandybaggot.com

ACKNOWLEDGEMENTS

A huge THANK YOU to my SUPERSTAR agent, Kate Nash. I keep her up late at night and don't let her sleep too long in the mornings either! You are my 24/7 sounding board and biggest supporter! Put up with me some more?

High fives to my gorgeous, supportive writing buddies – please check out their books – Rachel Lyndhurst, Zara Stoneley, Linn B Halton and Sue Fortin.

Thank you also to my Bagg Ladies – my beautiful bookworms who help support me on social media and beyond! Here's to 2017!

A special thank you to my lovely friend, Kate Hopkins, who will entertain my children for me if she knows I'm going to get another book out for her to read!

To all my readers, Instagram, Facebook and Twitter followers – without your fantastic support I wouldn't be on this journey. Every purchase, every review, every share and supportive comment means so much! Thank you!

Last, but by no means least, thank you to my rock, my anchor, the man who keeps me in wine and Greek treats while we pray for the next royalty payment – Mr Big. It's a crazy ride but the good kind of crazy most of the time! And much love too to my girls, Amber and Ruby, who are experts at finding fun when Mummy is head down at the computer. You are both super-awesome!

Lightning Source UK Ltd.
Milton Keynes UK
UKOW05f0702261016
286179UK00012B/311/P